REFINED AND RETURNED

Refined and Returned

Volume I

A Completed Version of *The Watsons* by Jane Austen

Eireanne Michaels

REFINED AND RETURNED

Cover Art: "Young Girl Reading" by Jean-Honoré Fragonard

Edited by Marijke Kriel

ISBN-13: 978-1-969841-02-6

First Edition: February 2025 (blog)

Second Edition: November 2025

LITERARY REALMS PRESS

Indianapolis, IN

EIREANNE MICHAELS

REFINED AND RETURNED

This book is dedicated to—

    all the people who have helped me reach my goal of publishing through their support of my writing: including but not limited to Jeonsu Byeon and Hyeongyeong Lee[1], who listened to my Austen lectures, as well as Marijke Kriel, who read my works and provided feedback.

---

[1] 변정수 and 이현경

REFINED AND RETURNED

Table of Contents

Preface xi

Prologue.. 1

Chapter Zero: Mrs Turner.. 3

Chapter One: The Watsons.. 11

BEGINNING OF EDITED FRAGMENT *11*

Chapter Two: The Edwards 19

Chapter Three: The October Assembly 27

Chapter Four: The Day After 41

Chapter Five: Unexpected Visitors 51

Chapter Six: Letters and News 57

Chapter Seven: Margaret's Return... 61

Chapter Eight: The Wickstead Party 75

END OF EDITED FRAGMENT *76*

Chapter Nine: Visit to Wickstead.. 85

Chapter Ten: Duties 95

Chapter Eleven: In Sickness and in Memory 103

Chapter Twelve: The November Assembly 113

Chapter Thirteen: Missed Calls.. 123

Chapter Fourteen: An Unwelcome Ride.. 133

Chapter Fifteen: Absent Thoughts 143

Chapter Sixteen: The Fall Out.. 153

Chapter Seventeen: Unspoken Prey.. 161

Chapter Eighteen: Penelope's Arrival.. 175

Chapter Nineteen: Ties that Bind.. 185

Chapter Twenty: A Study in Society... 191

Chapter Twenty-One: A Hunt for Decorum 205

Chapter Twenty-Two: Preparations for the Ball.. 215

Chapter Twenty-Three: The December Assembly....................................... 225

Chapter Twenty-Four: Fortune and Family.. 241

Chapter Twenty-Five: Reunions.. 249

Chapter Twenty-Six: The Wedding Dinner.. 261

Chapter Twenty-Seven: Weddings and Wistfulness.................................... 273

Chapter Twenty-Eight: A Proposal and a Predicament 283

Epilogue.. 291

Before You Go.. 295

Teaser for Refined and Returned: Volume 2.. 297

Author Bio 299

"Very few people marry their first loves."

—*Elizabeth Watson*

REFINED AND RETURNED

Preface

This story is a completed version of a fragment titled The Watsons by Jane Austen. Written on paper with watermarks from 1803 and 1804, the work was set aside by the author for reasons unknown and never finished. While many have speculated on why Austen abandoned it, the truth remains a mystery.

The original manuscript of The Watsons is preserved in two locations:

MS. MA 1034, Morgan Library & Museum, New York

MS. Eng. e. 3764, Bodleian Library, Oxford

Digitized versions can be viewed at the Morgan Library & Museum and the Bodleian Library, with further details available through *Jane Austen's Fiction Manuscripts* (https://janeausten.ac.uk).

A Memoir of Jane Austen by James Edward Austen-Leigh (1871) first published *The Watsons*, bringing the unfinished work into public knowledge. Digital editions of this work are available via Project Gutenberg and the Internet Archive. As a work first published over 150 years ago, *The Watsons* is in the public domain.

This author has chosen to complete the story by adhering to Austen's general style, allowing the characters to act within the personalities she crafted while responding to their circumstances. The original fragment, included here with slight edits and adjustments—primarily additions based on material Jane Austen removed or revised in her manuscript—has been completed in this work by Eireanne Michaels.

To preserve clarity, all modifications and additions to Austen's original fragment in this work are in italics (due to formatting issues that made brackets too bulky), allowing readers to distinguish between the fragment and the completed work. Any words that would have been italicized for emphasis within the fragment shall therefore be underlined.

Prologue

When Emma Cassandra Watson was born, she was the youngest of six children of the Reverend Mr Robert Watson and Mrs Cassandra Watson, née Willoughby, of Yorkshire. Her arrival was a surprise to her parents, who were already in their fortieth year. Her mother's health, once so robust, had become delicate after so many late confinements. Meanwhile, her father, with only one hundred and fifty pounds a year from tithes along with the interest on the couple's combined fortunes of just over four thousand five hundred pounds, struggled to stretch their income for a family of eight. In the end, it was only possible with the aid of his family and hers. Yet for all their difficulties, they cherished their children.

When Emma turned five, Mr and Mrs Edward Turner, Mr Watson's youngest half-sister and her husband, visited the Watson family with a proposal. Married for over a decade without children of their own, the Turners decided to take in one of the Watson children to raise as their heir.

With children in abundance and very little money to benefit them, Mr and Mrs Watson were eventually convinced to give up one of theirs to the cause. Reluctant though they were to part with any of their little 'blessings', the Watsons ultimately agreed, recognising the advantages the arrangement would provide for the chosen child.

The Turners stayed for a fortnight and observed the children. Since Robert was not home and Elizabeth made herself indispensable to her parents by aiding her mother in all her tasks, they were immediately disqualified. Penelope and Margaret—whom Mrs Turner had her eye on as the latter was her goddaughter and namesake—were constantly bickering and completely unruly which led their aunt to dismiss them both. Samuel was a good boy, but Mrs Turner assured her husband that "a little boy and his antics would be far too disruptive to their peace." Ultimately, it was decided that the youngest, Emma, would become the ward of the Turners.

Emma was a sweet-tempered child who remained quiet and still even when she was upset. Her unobtrusive nature was exactly what Mrs Turner was looking for in a ward.

Emma Watson was taken away from the only home she had ever known. Her mother and oldest sister had taken her aside before her departure and explained to her what was happening, but she could not understand why only she should go. She was afraid that she had done something wrong and could not comprehend why her loving mother and doting sister would discard her in such a way. While she did not kick and scream at her removal, she spent much of the trip weeping silently for her perceived abandonment.

Over time, she came to believe that her aunt and uncle loved her because her aunt told her as much. However, she soon became more attached to her uncle whose love was unstated but clearly shown. While Mrs Turner taught Emma manners and comportment, Mr Turner taught Emma about the joys of quiet reading, horse riding, and even shooting—though the latter was frowned upon by her aunt. It was with her uncle that she felt the most at ease, and so his loss—when she was but seventeen—was strongly felt.

Though her aunt spent more time complaining of the inconvenience her uncle caused with his death than she lamented his loss, Emma was sure Mrs Turner was just as devastated as herself, so she took on more of the duties to aid her aunt in finding time to mourn. However, grief is seldom permitted to linger in society, and as they set aside their black crepe, Emma could feel the shift. Mrs Turner, never one to remain idle, soon turned from sorrow to ceremony, and Emma found herself confronted with her next trial.

Chapter Zero

Mrs Turner

Emma

"I insist that you attend with me, Emma dear. How could it enter your mind that I might venture out unaccompanied now that you are in the full blossom of eighteen? Such an action would undoubtedly cast me in an unflattering light, to go on my own and leave you to the company of mere servants in my absence." She directed a stern look at Emma who could only agree with her aunt's decision.

"Oh, do not distress yourself, my dear. We shall have ample opportunity to adorn one of your old gowns—that yellow one was not dyed for mourning, was it?"

"No," she replied reluctantly, "for the maids did not think the dye would take."

"Excellent, then. I am quite sure that Lily can adjust it to your satisfaction before the assembly in two days' time."

Emma dreaded making her debut when she was barely out of mourning, and she hated the yellow dress—now wishing it had been dyed black as well. However, there was not much she could do. Her aunt had lamented that they must both miss the autumn and winter assemblies, but she insisted that they must attend in March at least, "before the weather turns and there are only private parties, we must let everyone know that we are available," was her aunt's current refrain.

Two days later, as Emma sat for the finishing touches to her hair and gown, her sense of loss deepened. She had always imagined the moment of her debut into society with her beloved uncle—a man who had embraced her as his cherished daughter—standing proudly next to her. However, it was not to be.

As she entered the foyer, her aunt came bustling out in a dress that Emma had never seen before. If Emma was not sure that her aunt was always the epitome of propriety, she would think it in a shade which was much too bright with too many flounces for her age. She was bustling everyone about, and Emma was soon distracted by other thoughts.

"And where could my cherished gold brooch have gone? Ah, there you are, Annie. Have you—Oh! Indeed, you have found it. It is about time! And Emma, where are your slippers? Surely you have not forgotten them—that would make you look the fool you know, to arrive at a dance without one's dancing shoes?" At this moment, Lily emerged from behind Emma with the slippers in her hands.

"Excellent. Now, Annie and Lily, I hope that I need not remind you," Mrs Turner addressed the two maids with a discerning gaze, "that we shall require your assistance on our return. One might surmise that the definition of mourning included an invitation for the servants to rest as if on holiday, considering the degree of indolence to which you have all succumbed."

Emma noticed the girls sharing censorious glances which she did not like. However, at that very instant, the sound of the carriage announced its arrival, thus liberating Annie and Lily. Mrs Turner and Miss Emma Watson took their seats within the carriage, departing amidst a final flurry of admonishments from the formidable widow to their longsuffering servants.

When they arrived at the rooms designated for the assembly and were announced, many of her aunt's friends and neighbours came to greet them. Though many eyed her aunt's dress with scornful expressions that made Emma uncomfortable, her aunt never once acknowledged them.

"Oh, my, Mrs Lowry," Mrs Turner exclaimed as she joined a group of local matrons. "It really has been too long. It feels an age since we have met. I hear that your eldest has finally settled on old Mr Humbug. Well, and why not? It is a good match for such a girl. She should make a wonderful mistress for his small estate, I am sure—for she is young, and he is in need of a wife and children."

Mrs Lowry's countenance bore the semblance of a smile, yet Emma was fully cognizant that her aunt's words could sound mocking when one did not understand her so well as Emma did. It was evident that Mrs Turner's intentions were amiable, accompanied by a general desire for the welfare of all. However, it proved a trial to extend congratulations to any young lady inclined to accept a suitor whose annual income fell lamentably short of even half that of her father's. The matter was made worse by his being less than a decade her father's junior.

"Ah, my dear Mrs Jeffries," Mrs Turner turned to another lady who had just joined them, "the very *oldest* companion of my heart! Pray tell, from whence did you procure that most singular headpiece? It is indeed a most peculiar article; one I am quite certain has never crossed my sight before."

Her aunt and the other ladies continued on like this for several minutes before Mrs Lowry spoke up, "Is that not Miss Emma behind you, has she already come of age to join the dancing? Yet, you must lament the difficulty in securing a suitable partner for her, without anyone to facilitate the introductions on her social debut."

Emma was shocked by Mrs Lowry's blatant disregard to propriety in mentioning the loss of her uncle in such a manner.

"Nonsense, my dear. For there are the esteemed Sir Charles and Lady Jennings-Clerke, who, I am convinced, would be exceedingly delighted to extend such a trifling courtesy to the niece of such an old friend—though he has left us all too soon," she said while procuring a handkerchief to pat at her dry eyes, "he will surely not be forgotten."

With that, she took Emma's arm in hers, and they made their way to the baronet and his lady. While Sir Charles gave his condolences once again and spoke of "the loss of such a good old chap as Mr Turner had been," his lady kept her face hidden behind her fan—and her eyes told Emma that his wife did not welcome their interruption.

However, her aunt's endeavour was a success, and Sir Charles and his lady-wife took it upon themselves to chaperone Miss Emma—making "all the introductions she could want" as he said—until her dance card was full. While it embarrassed her somewhat to have the loquacious gentleman introduce her to all and sundry—as her uncle had been a quiet and reserved man, she was pleased with her first foray into society as a young lady. She danced all but two dances and those only because Mr Egtoun had missed the beat and trampled upon her toes—causing her to sit out the last set.

Over the following year, Mrs Turner's grief over the loss of her husband seemed to fade entirely while her ward felt his absence more acutely with each passing month.

It was not her affable uncle to whom her suitors turned, but her strict aunt. It was at one particular dinner party, after the gentlemen had re-joined the ladies and dancing had commenced—though the number of young ladies far exceeded that of the available gentlemen—that Emma felt ashamed by her aunt's manner for the first time.

"It grieves me deeply that I could never persuade your late uncle to move us to a town of less obscure situation. Indeed, there are simply no gentlemen of suitable merit for you, my sweetest Emma. Mr Egtoun, being merely a younger son, can scarcely attract your attention—of that I am confident; whilst Mr Fowke, notwithstanding the respectable appearance of his estate, hails from rather dubious ancestry." She leaned in as if to whisper, but her voice was clearly heard by those around, "His parents," nodding to a couple several seats down, "acquired their fortune through the late Mr Fowke's trade business, as you may well recall." Emma's face was now aglow with embarrassment, but that did not stop her aunt.

"Now, young Mr Jennings-Clerke, who stands as the next in line for the baronetcy, would undoubtedly make a most fitting candidate; but alas, he has only recently entered Cambridge, and thoughts of matrimony are, I fear, far from his youthful mind for several years to come. Not that I mind you staying with me, my dear. In fact, I should be glad that there is no one to tempt you from my side."

Emma, now thoroughly mortified, wisely decided not to mention that the

Jennings-Clerke family had also made their fortune in trade. Later, her aunt made another remark that—though no less appropriate for their current location—caused Emma more pain than shame.

"Though your late uncle has bestowed upon me the entirety of his wealth and estates, do not fear that I would throw you off without due consideration. As long as you marry with all due regard—neither aspiring too high nor descending to levels unworthy of how we raised you—I shall assuredly attend to your welfare, my dear. In the meantime, it is only proper that you should remain in my care until such a time—for what better companion could I ask for than the child I have raised as my own?"

It seemed that Emma's future was set for her to remain at her aunt's side for many years to come—until the following spring when the militia came to town.

Emma was rather surprised when her aunt allowed the smooth-talking Captain O'Brien to pay court to her—though it soon became clear that his family was, though Irish, an old landed family of some consideration and with noble connections. Emma enjoyed his attentions for nearly a sennight before those affections were directed towards Mrs Turner herself. While Emma was a little hurt by the slight, she admitted to herself that she had not been so in love with him to take his change of affection to heart. She even felt somewhat relieved as his manner of leaning in to speak with her had often made her uncomfortable.

After several weeks, she found herself sitting across the room, practising her music while the captain continued his wooing of her aunt. While she had hoped the sound of the piano would drown out their conversation, she could not help but overhear the captain making his declarations of love.

"My dearest Mrs Turner—nay, Margaret—you must allow me to call you thus, for the cords of the pianoforte strum with the beating of my heart—its song, your name. You transform an ordinary evening into poetry. Your breath catching, the sunlight playing on your hair, and you sitting here beside me, looking up occasionally to meet my gaze—it is my idea of true happiness. When two such different people come together to paint one perfect picture—

how can anything possibly surpass this moment?"

"You, my esteemed captain, must forgive me for my inability to fully credit the earnestness of your professions. After all, I am a widow and for you—a youthful gentleman such as yourself, in the very bloom of manhood—to bestow upon me such declarations of affection—"

"It is true that I may have had the misfortune of being born after you, my heart;" he interrupted, "however, I am old enough to cherish these beautiful moments, and young enough to still believe in love. Most importantly—I am just the right age to appreciate a woman of your worth."

"Ah, Captain—I am not one of those blushing maidens, and thus ought not fall prey to the tender affections of such a youthful gentleman."

At another mention about the difference in their ages Emma wondered if a mere seven years really deserved such attention, but she had little time to consider this as her aunt continued.

"Yet, what tender beatings of my heart..." She pressed a hand lightly to her bosom, as if to steady some tremor of emotion, "Pray, how could I chastise you for possessing such fervent emotions—such exquisite sentiment? It has long been my conviction that the virtues of experience, refinement, and a genteel upbringing are scarcely appreciated in the fairer sex. It is most heartening to be acknowledged for the entirety of my being."

"Then, do not forsake me! Please accept my undying love for you and do me the greatest—most wondrous—pleasure of becoming my love—my life—my wife!"

Emma had once overheard some ladies speak of his sudden change of affection after learning that Mrs Turner held Emma's purse strings. Yet his words were spoken with such strong conviction and feeling that even she—who had once thought him mercenary—was convinced he must truly be sincere. Therefore, when Emma heard her aunt finally accept the captain, she kept her eyes averted as they embraced and did her best to smile and wish them both the greatest happiness with all her heart.

In mid-September, only a week before the militia's departure, they married, and Emma was glad for her aunt's joy. She had not been upset when her suitor turned his attentions to another; however, she was aggrieved when, only after the wedding, she learned of his plans to return to his native Ireland with his new wife. To her greater distress, she was not to be included in their relocation. She was given only a few days to pack her things, as her new uncle was expected in London by the end of the month. They would all travel to town together, and, from there, Emma would continue on with a maid to Surrey where the Watson family had settled two years after her departure.

Her aunt tried to console her by saying, "My dearest James is being very considerate of you in his reluctance to remove you so far from your already estranged family. Once we arrive in Ireland, one cannot ascertain the prospect of our return and, to take you away from them forever, would indeed be an act of cruelty most unparalleled. Furthermore, the voyage to Ireland is oft fraught with peril. Then it is imperative that we, as newlyweds, should be afforded a modicum of solitude in which to establish our humble abode. Indeed, it would be quite unjust to impose upon us the burden of your suffering whilst navigating such tumultuous circumstances." Though Emma wished for her aunt to allow her to come along and help, she quietly accepted her fate.

"Pray do not allow your mind to be troubled, dearest. I have taken the liberty of communicating with your father, who will be prepared to receive you forthwith upon your arrival. You shall find ample opportunity to familiarize yourself with your estranged siblings—though, I dare say, you may perceive their company and social graces to be somewhat inferior to those with which you are accustomed—not to mention their lack of any good education—"

She was distracted for a moment as she directed the maid in her packing before she turned back. "Nonetheless, I encourage you to offer your gentle assistance in their improvement. It shall, I have no doubt, prove a most beneficial change for your spirit."

⁓⦊⦉⁓

Emma was to return to the family that had cast her off years ago and with whom she had not had much contact with since. Her father had often written to her uncle, but it was only her mother and her eldest sister, Elizabeth, who kept up any communication with Emma. Some six or seven years ago, it was the latter who sent her the news of her mother's passing, but Emma's grief had been dulled by time and distance.

In the beginning, one or two of her siblings would add on a note to Elizabeth's letters, but she did not know much about any of them. Over the years, her guardians had informed her that the new living brought in over twice as much as the previous one, that Robert had attended Cambridge while Samuel had been sent out to apprentice, that her father had felt the loss of her mother greatly—leading to the deterioration of his spirit and health, and that Robert had become an attorney and married his associate's daughter; however, she always felt disconnected from the family of her birth, and it was not so different to hearing of the lives of strangers.

It was when they arrived in London, and Emma was—without ceremony—given only a few hours to clean up and dine with the O'Briens before being ushered back into the carriage with only the butler to see her off that the truth of her banishment began to weigh on her mind. She discovered only then that she was being sent off with no thought for her future and not a ha'penny to her name.

The inheritance that was promised to her was now under the control of Captain O'Brien as was the house she had lived in for the last fourteen years. She began to once again feel the oppressive weight of having been rejected and abandoned by her own family, and she considered that perhaps she should focus on a different kind of family for herself. In marriage, she could gain someone who would not throw her off and could create a home of her own that no one could take away from her. It was with this mindset that she began a new chapter in her life.

Chapter One

The Watsons

Tuesday, October 13th, 1801

BEGINNING OF EDITED FRAGMENT

The first winter assembly in the town of Dorking in Surrey was to be held on Tuesday, October 13th, and it was generally expected to be a very good one. A long list of county families was confidently run over as sure of attending, and sanguine hopes were entertained that the Osbornes themselves would be there.

The Edwardses' invitation to the Watsons followed, of course. The Edwardses were people of fortune, who lived in the town and kept a coach. The Watsons inhabited a village about three miles distant, were poor, and had no close carriage; and ever since there had been balls in the place, the former were accustomed to invite the latter to dress, dine, and sleep at their house on every monthly return throughout the winter.

On the present occasion, as only two of Mr Watson's children were at home, and one was always necessary as companion to himself, for he was sickly and had lost his wife, one only could profit by the kindness of their friends. Miss Emma Watson, who was very recently returned to her family from the care of an aunt who had brought her up, was to make her first public appearance in the neighbourhood, and her eldest sister, whose delight in a ball was not lessened by a ten years' enjoyment, had some merit in cheerfully undertaking to drive her and all her finery in the old chair to Dorking on the important morning.

As they splashed along the dirty lane, Miss Watson thus instructed and cautioned her inexperienced sister. "I dare say it will be a very good ball, and among so many officers you will hardly want partners. You will find Mrs Edwards's maid very willing to help you, and I would advise you to ask Mary Edwards's opinion if you are at all at a loss, for she has a very good taste. If Mr Edwards does not lose his money at cards, you will stay as late as you can wish for; if he does, he will hurry you home perhaps—but you are sure of some comfortable soup. I hope you will be in good looks. I should not be surprised if you were to be thought one of the prettiest girls in the room; there is a great deal in novelty. Perhaps Tom Musgrave may take notice of you; but I would advise you by all means not to give him any encouragement. He generally pays attention to every new girl; but he is a great flirt, and never means anything serious."

"I think I have heard you speak of him before," said Emma; "who is he?"

"A young man of very good fortune, quite independent, and remarkably agreeable—a universal favourite wherever he goes. Most of the girls hereabout are in love with him, or have been. I believe I am the only one among them that have escaped with a whole heart; and yet I was the first he paid attention to when he came into this country six years ago; and very great attention did he pay me. Some people say that he has never seemed to like any girl so well since, though he is always behaving in a particular way to one or another."

"And how came your heart to be the only cold one?" said Emma, smiling.

"There was a reason for that," replied Miss Watson, changing colour, "I have not been very well used among them, Emma. I hope you will have better luck."

"Dear sister, I beg your pardon if I have unthinkingly given you pain."

"When first we knew Tom Musgrave," continued Miss Watson, without seeming to hear her, "I was very much attached to a young man of the name of Purvis, a particular friend of Robert's, who used to be with us a great deal *and who holds the Living of Alfold*[2] *about fourteen miles off.* Everybody thought it would

---

[2] In the manuscript, it says "he has the Living of Alford about 14 miles off". Since "R" and "L" were still often exchangeable during that time and Alfold is a real place about 14 miles from Wotton (which I used for Stanton), I changed it for this story.

12

have been a match."

A sigh accompanied these words, which Emma respected in silence; but her sister after a short pause went on: "You will naturally ask why it did not take place, and why he is married to another woman, while I am still single. But you must ask her, not me—you must ask Penelope. Yes, Emma, Penelope was at the bottom of it all. She thinks everything fair for a husband. I trusted her; she set him against me, with a view of gaining him herself, and it ended in his discontinuing his visits, and soon after marrying somebody else. Penelope makes light of her conduct, but I think such treachery very bad. It has been the ruin of my happiness. I shall never love any man as I loved Purvis. I do not think Tom Musgrave should be named with him in the same day."

"You quite shock me by what you say of Penelope," said Emma. "Could a sister do such a thing? Rivalry, treachery between sisters! I shall be afraid of being acquainted with her. But I hope it was not so; appearances were against her."

"You do not know Penelope," *Miss Watson responded.* "There is nothing she would not do to get married. She would as good as tell you so herself. Do not trust her with any secrets of your own, take warning by me, do not trust her; she has her good qualities, but she has no faith, no honour, no scruples, if she can promote her own advantage. I wish with all my heart she was well married. *When once she is, she will be a very worthy character but, till then,* I declare I had rather have her well married than myself."

"Than yourself! Yes, I can suppose so. A heart wounded like yours can have little inclination for matrimony."

Miss Watson let out a long-beleaguered sigh. "Not much indeed—but you know we must marry. I could do very well single for my own part; a little company, and a pleasant ball now and then, would be enough for me, if one could be young forever; but my father cannot provide for us, and it is very bad to grow old and be poor and laughed at. I have lost Purvis; it is true; but very few people marry their first loves. I should not refuse a man because he was not Purvis. Not that I can ever quite forgive Penelope."

Emma shook her head in acquiescence.

"Penelope, however, has had her troubles," continued Miss Watson. "She was sadly disappointed in Tom Musgrave, who afterwards transferred his attentions from me to her, and whom she was very fond of; but he never means anything serious, and when he had trifled with her long enough, he began to slight her for Margaret, and poor Penelope was very wretched. And since then, she has been trying to make some match at Chichester—she won't tell us with whom; but I believe it is a rich old Dr Harding, uncle to the friend she goes to see; and she has taken a vast deal of trouble about him, and given up a great deal of time to no purpose as yet. When she went away the other day, she said it should be the last time. I suppose you did not know what her particular business was at Chichester, nor guess at the object which could take her away from Stanton just as you were coming home after so many years' absence."

"No indeed," *cried Emma*, "I had not the smallest suspicion of it. I considered her engagement to Mrs Shaw just at that time as very unfortunate for me. I had hoped to find all my sisters at home, to be able to make an immediate friend of each."

Her sister seemed to consider this for a moment. "I suspect the Doctor to have had an attack of the asthma, and that she was hurried away on that account. The Shaws are quite on her side—at least, I believe so; but she tells me nothing. She professes to keep her own counsel; she says, and truly enough, that 'Too many cooks spoil the broth.'"

"I am sorry for her anxieties," said Emma; "but I do not like her plans or her opinions. I shall be afraid of her. She must have too masculine and bold a temper. To be so bent on marriage, to pursue a man merely for the sake of situation, is a sort of thing that shocks me; I cannot understand it. Poverty is a great evil; but to a woman of education and feeling it ought not, it cannot be the greatest. I would rather be teacher at a school—and I can think of nothing worse—than marry a man I did not like."

"I would rather do anything than be teacher at a school," said her sister. "I have been at school, Emma, and know what a life they lead; you never have. I should not like marrying a disagreeable man any more than yourself; but I do not think there are many very disagreeable men; I think I could like any good-humoured man with a comfortable income. I suppose my aunt brought you up to be rather refined."

"Indeed, I do not know. My conduct must tell you how I have been brought up. I am no judge of it myself. I cannot compare my aunt's method with any other person's, because I know no other."

"But I can see in a great many things that you are very refined. I have observed it ever since you came home, and I am afraid it will not be for your happiness. Penelope will laugh at you very much."

"That will not be for my happiness, I am sure. If my opinions are wrong, I must correct them; if they are above my situation, I must endeavour to conceal them; but I doubt whether ridicule—Has Penelope much wit?"

"*Oh,* yes," *replied her sister,* "she has great spirits, and never cares what she says."

"Margaret is more gentle, I imagine?" *replied Emma after a moment with more hope than conviction.*

"Yes; especially in company. She is all gentleness and mildness when anybody is by; but she *has a good deal of spirit and* is a little fretful and perverse among ourselves." *She sighed,* "Poor creature! She is possessed with the notion of Tom Musgrave's being more seriously in love with her than he ever was with anybody else, and is always expecting him to come to the point. This is the second time within this twelvemonth that she has gone to spend a month with Robert and Jane on purpose to egg him on by her absence; but I am sure she is mistaken, and that he will no more follow her to Croydon now than he did last March. He will never marry unless he can marry somebody very great—Miss Osborne, perhaps, or something in that style."

Emma lifted an eyebrow at her sister's tale. "Your account of this Tom Musgrave, Elizabeth, gives me very little inclination for his acquaintance."

"You are afraid of him; I do not wonder at you."

"No, indeed; I dislike and despise him," *and, indeed, she was unable to hide the disgust from her voice.*

"Dislike and despise Tom Musgrave! No, that you never can. I defy you not to be delighted with him if he takes notice of you. I hope he will dance with you; and I dare say he will, unless the Osbornes come with a large party, and then he will not speak to anybody else."

"He seems to have most engaging manners!" said Emma *with clear ridicule though her sister seemed not to hear it or simply to ignore it.* "Well, we shall see how irresistible Mr Tom Musgrave and I find each other. I suppose I shall know him as soon as I enter the ball-room; he must carry some of his charm in his face."

"You will not find him in the ball-room, I can tell you; you will go early, that Mrs Edwards may get a good place by the fire, and he never comes till late; if the Osbornes are coming, he will wait in the passage and come in with them. I should like to look in upon you, Emma. If it was but a good day with *our* father, I would wrap myself up, and James should drive me over as soon as I had made tea for him; and I should be with you by the time the dancing began."

"What! Would you come late at night in this chair?"

"To be sure I would. There, I said you were very refined, and that's an instance of it."

Emma for a moment made no answer. At last, she said, "I wish, Elizabeth, you had not made a point of my going to this ball; I wish you were going instead of me. <u>Your</u> pleasure would be greater than <u>mine</u>. I am a stranger here, and know nobody but the Edwardses; my enjoyment, therefore, must be very doubtful. Yours, among all your acquaintance, would be certain. It is not too late to change. Very little apology could be requisite to the Edwardses, who must be more glad of your company than of mine, and I should most readily return to my father; and should not be at all afraid to drive this quiet old creature home. Your clothes I would undertake to find means of sending to you."

"My dearest Emma," cried Elizabeth, warmly, "do you think I would do such a thing? Not for the universe! But I shall never forget your good-nature in proposing it. You must have a sweet temper indeed! I never met with anything like it! And would you really give up the ball that I might be able to go to it? Believe me, Emma, I am not so selfish as that comes to. No; though I am nine years older than you are, I would not be the means of keeping you from being seen. You are very pretty, and it would be very hard that you should not have as fair a chance as we have all had to make your fortune. No, Emma, whoever stays at home this winter, it shan't be you. I am sure I should never have forgiven the person who kept me from a ball at nineteen."

Emma expressed her gratitude, and for a few minutes they jogged on in silence. Elizabeth first spoke: "You will take notice who Mary Edwards dances with?"

"I will remember her partners, if I can; but you know they will *all* be strangers to me."

Elizabeth considered this for a moment before correcting her direction. "Only observe whether she dances with Captain Hunter more than once. I have my fears in that quarter. Not that her father or mother like officers; but if she does, you know, it is all over with poor Sam. And I have promised to write him word who she dances with."

Curious at the sentiment, Emma observed, "Is Sam attached to Miss Edwards?"

Elizabeth was taken aback. "Did not you know?"

"How should I know it?" *she asked in a matter-of-fact tone, wondering at her sister's reaction.* "How should I know in Shropshire what is passing of that nature in Surrey? It is not likely that circumstances of such delicacy should have made any part of the scanty communication which passed between you and me for the last fourteen years."

"I wonder I never mentioned it when I wrote. Since you have been at home, I have been so busy with my poor father and our great wash that I have had no leisure to tell you anything; but, indeed, I concluded you knew it all. He has been very much in love with her these two years, and it is a great disappointment to him that he cannot always get away to our balls; but Mr Curtis won't often spare him, and just now it is a sickly time at Guildford."

Emma considered what her sister said. She had not known of her brother's interest and would not have guessed it on her own, but she made note of the information; asking, "Do you suppose Miss Edwards inclined to like him?"

Elizabeth considered her question for a moment before sighing. "I am afraid not: you know she is an only child, and will have at least ten thousand pounds."

Emma did not think this such a great sum to deny him any chance and said, "But still, she may like our brother."

"Oh, no! The *Edwardses* look much higher. Her father and mother would never consent to it. Sam is only a surgeon, you know. Sometimes I think she does like him. But Mary Edwards is rather prim and reserved; I do not always know what she would be at."

Emma did not know the two parties involved so well herself, but she knew her sister to be more familiar with the circumstances and, therefore, concluded that her brother had no hope in the matter. "Unless Sam feels on sure grounds with the lady herself, it seems a pity to me that he should be encouraged to think of her at all."

"A young man must think of somebody," said Elizabeth, "and why should not he be as lucky as Robert, who has got a good wife and six thousand pounds?"

"We must not all expect to be individually lucky," replied Emma. "The luck of one member of a family is luck to all."

"Mine is all to come, I am sure," said Elizabeth, giving another sigh to the remembrance of Purvis. "I have been unlucky enough; and I cannot say much for you, as *our* aunt married again so foolishly." *She did not notice the twinge of sadness that flashed across her youngest sister's face as she continued.* "Well, you will have a good ball, I daresay. The next turning will bring us to the turnpike: you may see the church-tower over the hedge, and the White Hart *where the assemblies are always held* is close by it. I shall long to know what you think of Tom Musgrave."

Such were the last audible sounds of Miss Watson's voice, before they passed through the turnpike-gate, and entered on the pitching of the town, the jumbling and noise of which made farther conversation most thoroughly undesirable.

Chapter Two

The Edwards

The old mare trotted heavily on, wanting no direction of the reins to take the right turning, and making only one blunder, in proposing to stop at the milliners before she drew up towards Mr Edwards's door. Mr Edwards lived in the best house in the street, and the best in the place, if Mr Tomlinson, the banker, might be indulged in calling his newly erected house at the end of the town, with a shrubbery and sweep, in the country.

Mr Edwards's house was *of a dull brick colour and* higher than most of its neighbours, with four windows on each side the door, the windows guarded by posts and chains, and the door approached by a flight of stone steps.

"Here we are," said Elizabeth, as the carriage ceased moving, "safely arrived, and by the market clock we have been only five-and-thirty minutes coming; which I think is doing pretty well, though it would be nothing for Penelope. Is not it a nice town? The Edwardses have a noble house, you see, and they live quite in style. The door will be opened by a man in livery, with a powdered head, I can tell you."

Emma *was not as excited by the thought of the liveried butler—though it increased her knowledge of the gap that existed between their upbringings. She was more concerned in the company she would be spending the next dozen or so hours with. She* had seen the Edwardses only one morning at Stanton; they were therefore all but strangers to her; and though her spirits were by no means insensible to the expected joys of the evening, she felt a little uncomfortable in the thought of all that was to precede them. Her conversation with Elizabeth, too, giving her some very unpleasant feelings with respect to her own family, had made her more open to disagreeable impressions from any other cause, and increased her sense of the awkwardness of rushing into intimacy on so slight an acquaintance. *However, they were soon ushered into their hosts' parlour and such opinions could not be made aloud.*

There was nothing in the manner of Mrs or Miss Edwards to give immediate change to these ideas. The mother, though a very friendly woman, had a reserved air, and a great deal of formal civility; and the daughter, a genteel-looking girl of twenty-two, with her hair in papers, seemed very naturally to have caught something of the style of her mother, who had brought her up. Emma was soon left to know what they could be, by Elizabeth's being obliged to hurry away; and some very languid remarks on the probable brilliancy of the ball were all that broke, at intervals, a silence of half an hour, before they were joined by the master of the house.

Mr Edwards had a much easier and more communicative air than the ladies of the family *and reminded her of Sir Charles Jennings-Clerke in his loquaciousness.* He was fresh from the street, and he came ready to tell whatever might interest. After a cordial reception of Emma, he turned to his daughter with, "Well, Mary, I bring you good news. The Osbornes will certainly be at the ball tonight." *He said this with a grin tugging at the corners of his mouth which caused his wife's face to pinch up—apparently, she did not approve of his playful banter.* "Horses for two carriages are ordered from the White Hart to be at Osborne Castle by nine." *He turned to his wife as he finished as if wanting to see her reaction to his news.*

"I am glad of it," observed Mrs Edwards *with an air of more hauteur than Emma believed the situation required,* "because their coming gives a credit to our assembly. The Osbornes being known to have been at the first ball, will dispose a great many people to attend the second. It is more than they deserve; for in fact, they add nothing to the pleasure of the evening: they come so late and go so early; but Great People have always their charm *and must always be in the vogue, just so the Little Ones will be infatuated with them.*"

Mr Edwards *seemed to find humour in his wife's pronouncements and failed at keeping it all from his expression, so he quickly* proceeded to relate every other little article of news which his morning's lounge had supplied him with, and they chatted with greater briskness, till Mrs Edwards's moment for dressing arrived, and *she broke up the party.* The young ladies were *then ushered upstairs and* carefully recommended to lose no time.

Emma was shown to a very comfortable apartment, and as soon as Mrs Edwards's civilities could leave her to herself, the happy occupation, the first bliss of a ball, began.

The girls, dressing in some measure together, grew unavoidably better acquainted. Emma found in Miss Edwards the show of good sense, a modest unpretending mind, and a great wish of obliging; and *Emma soon believed she could count Miss Edwards as her first true friend in Surrey besides her sister, Elizabeth. As she had been told, Mary, as they quickly decided they should be on a first name basis, was a very stylish girl, and she and her maid were happy and eager to aid their guest in her preparations.*

"Being an only child, I have always enjoyed when your sisters come to us for assemblies. It is like having a glimpse of what it would be like to have siblings," said Mary, smiling.

Emma did not comment on the fact that she was also unaware of such relationships, nor her next thought that such an experience could not give one a true impression of what it was like to have siblings as they would likely only see them on their best behaviour and have the benefit of seeing them off at the end of the night or the following morning.

When they returned to the parlour where Mrs Edwards was sitting, respectably attired in one of the two satin gowns which went through the winter, and a new cap from the milliner's, they entered it with much easier feelings and more natural smiles than they had taken away. Their dress was now to be examined: Mrs Edwards acknowledged herself too old-fashioned to approve of every modern extravagance, however sanctioned; and though complacently viewing her daughter's good looks, would give but a qualified admiration; and Mr Edwards, not less satisfied with Mary, paid some compliments of good-humoured gallantry to Emma at her expense.

The discussion led to more intimate remarks, and Miss Edwards gently asked Emma, *"Are you not often reckoned very like your youngest brother? For I feel I can perceive something of him in your expressions and manner."* Emma thought she could perceive a faint blush accompany the question, and there seemed something still more suspicious in the manner in which Mr Edwards took up the subject.

"You are paying Miss Emma no great compliment, I think, Mary," said he, hastily. "Mr Sam Watson is a very good sort of young man, and I dare say a very clever surgeon; but his complexion has been rather too much exposed to all weathers to make a likeness to him very flattering."

Mary apologised, in some confusion. "*I had not thought a strong likeness at all incompatible with very different degrees of beauty. There might be resemblance in countenance, and the complexion and even the features be very unlike.*"

"I know nothing of my brother's beauty," said Emma, "for I have not seen him since he was seven years old; but my father reckons us alike."

"Mr Watson!" cried Mr Edwards; "well, you astonish me. There is not the least likeness in the world; your brother's eyes are grey, yours are brown; he has a long face and a wide mouth; *and he is also very tall and long-limbed.* My dear, do you perceive the least resemblance?"

"Not the least. Miss Emma Watson puts me very much in mind of her eldest sister, and sometimes I see a look of Miss Penelope, and once or twice there has been a glance of Mr Robert, but I cannot perceive any likeness to Mr Samuel."

"I see the likeness between her and Miss Watson," replied Mr Edwards, "very strongly, but I am not sensible of the others. I do not much think she is like any of the family but Miss Watson; but I am very sure there is no resemblance between her and Sam."

This matter was settled, and they went to dinner. *It was a sumptuous meal reminiscent of the kind she used to enjoy with her aunt and uncle Turner before his passing, and the silence at the dinner table did not discomfort her as much as it might others. She had not eaten so well since she had arrived at Stanton and only thought how unfair it was that her sister, Elizabeth, should not be able to join them in enjoying such a feast.*

After they finished their meal, they removed to the family parlour for some light libations.

"Your father, Miss Emma, is one of my oldest friends," said Mr Edwards, as he helped her to wine, when they were drawn round the fire to enjoy their dessert. "We must drink to his better health. It is a great concern to me, I assure you, that he should be such an invalid. I know nobody who likes a game of cards, in a social way, better than he does, and very few people that play a fairer rubber. It is a thousand pities that he should be so deprived of the pleasure. For now, we have a quiet little Whist Club, that meets three times a week at the White Hart; and, if he could but have his health, how much he would enjoy it!"

"I dare say he would, sir; and I wish, with all my heart, he were equal to it," she replied earnestly.

"Your club would be better fitted for an invalid," said Mrs Edwards, "if you did not keep it up so late."

This was *apparently* an old grievance.

"So late, my dear! What are you talking of?" cried the husband, with sturdy pleasantry. "We are always at home before midnight. They would laugh at Osborne Castle to hear you call that late; they are but just rising from dinner at midnight."

"That is nothing to the purpose," retorted the lady, calmly. "The Osbornes are to be no rule for us. You had better meet every night, and break up two hours sooner."

So far, the subject was very often carried; but Mr and Mrs Edwards were so wise as never to pass that point; and *Emma smartly did not comment on either issue.*

Mr Edwards now turned to something else. He had lived long enough in the idleness of a town to become a little of a gossip, and having some anxiety to know more of the circumstances of his young guest than had yet reached him, he began with, "I think, Miss Emma, I remember your aunt very well, about thirty years ago; I am pretty sure I danced with her in the old rooms at Bath, the year before I married."

His eyes glazed over as if he was looking far away, "She was a very pretty girl of eighteen and quite popular among the young men. Your aunt Parker introduced her to me on the recommendation of your parents, and it may be that they hoped something would come of it," he trailed off for a moment before recollecting himself and adding, "but it is better that nothing did for I was then able to meet my dear Mary." He looked to his wife with a sheepish expression and patted her hands which were folded on her lap. She only responded with the slightest twitch of one eyebrow. So, after another moment, he smiled wanly and continued.

"She was a very fine woman then; but like other people, I suppose, she is grown somewhat older since that time. I hope she is likely to be happy in her second choice."

"I hope so; I believe so, sir," said Emma, in some agitation. *She was clearly not forthcoming enough for his taste as he continued to quiz her.*

"Mr Turner had not been dead a great while, I think?"

"About two years, sir."

"I forget what her name is now."

"O'Brien."

"Irish! Ah, I remember; and she is gone to settle in Ireland. I do wonder that you should not wish to go with her into that country, Miss Emma; but it must be a great deprivation to her, poor lady, after bringing you up like a child of her own."

"I was not so ungrateful, sir," said Emma, warmly, "as to wish to be anywhere but with her. It did not suit them; it did not suit Captain O'Brien that I should be of the party."

"Captain!" repeated Mrs Edwards. "The gentleman is in the army then?"

"Yes, ma'am. *However, he was planning to sell his commission as soon as he was able, so he may even now be a simple mister.*"

"Aye," *said Mr Edwards with humour in his voice,* "there is nothing like your officers for captivating the ladies, young or old. There is no resisting a cockade, my dear."

"I hope there is," said Mrs Edwards, gravely, with a quick glance at her daughter; and Emma had just recovered from her own perturbation in time to see a blush on Miss Edwards's cheek, and in remembering what Elizabeth had said of Captain Hunter, to wonder and waver between his influence and her brother's.

"Elderly ladies should be careful how they make a second choice," observed Mr Edwards.

"Carefulness—discretion—should not be confined to elderly ladies or to a second choice," added his wife. "They are quite as necessary to young ladies in their first."

"Rather more so, my dear," replied he; "because young ladies are likely to feel the effects of it longer. When an old lady plays the fool, it is not in the course of nature that she should suffer from it many years."

Emma drew her hand across her eyes; and Mrs Edwards, on perceiving it, changed the subject to one of less anxiety to all.

Chapter Three

The October Assembly

With nothing to do but to expect the hour of setting off, the afternoon was long to the two young ladies; and though Miss Edwards was rather discomposed at the very early hour which her mother always fixed for going, that early hour itself was watched for with some eagerness *by herself as well as the rest of the party.*

The entrance of the tea-things at seven o'clock was some relief *to Emma as the silence in the room had become nearly unbearable*; and luckily Mr and Mrs Edwards always drank a dish extraordinary and ate an additional muffin when they were going to sit up late, which lengthened the ceremony almost to the wished-for moment.

At a little before eight, the Tomlinsons' carriage was heard to go by—which was the constant signal for Mrs Edwards to order hers to the door; and in a very few minutes the party were transported from the quiet and warmth of a snug parlour to the bustle, noise, and draughts of air of the broad entrance passage of an inn.

Mrs Edwards, carefully guarding her own dress, while she attended with yet greater solicitude to the proper security of her young charges' shoulders and throats, led the way up the wide staircase, while no sound of a ball but the first scrape of one violin blessed the ears of her followers; and Miss Edwards, on hazarding the anxious inquiry of whether there were many people come yet, was told by the waiter *moving through the parlour*, as she knew she should, that "Mr Tomlinson's family were in the room."

In passing along a short gallery to the assembly-room, brilliant *in the candle-lights* before them, they were accosted by a young man in a morning-dress and boots, who was standing in the doorway of a bed-chamber, apparently on purpose to see them go by.

"Ah! Mrs Edwards, how do you do? How do you do, Miss Edwards?" he cried, with an easy air. "You are determined to be in good time, I see, as usual. The candles are but this moment lit."

"I like to get a good seat by the fire, you know, Mr Musgrave," replied Mrs Edwards *in a slightly flippant tone that showed that she took no pleasure in receiving his notice.*

"I am this moment going to dress," said he. "I am waiting for my stupid fellow. We shall have a famous ball. The Osbornes are certainly coming; you may depend upon that, for I was with Lord Osborne this morning."

Mrs Edwards merely nodded at him for the information with her pert nose in the air— though Emma could not blame her. It was rather impertinent of the gentleman to keep the ladies standing about in the passage—especially when they stood so near the door to his own rented apartments. She could not even begin to fathom the familiarity he must have assumed towards the ladies when she noticed the mocking smile he directed at Mrs Edwards who then turned and glided away from him.

The party passed on. Mrs Edwards's satin gown swept along the clean floor of the ball-room to the fireplace at the upper end, where one party only were formally seated, while three or four officers were lounging together, passing in and out from the adjoining card-room.

A very stiff meeting between these near neighbours ensued; and as soon as they were all duly placed again, Emma, in the low whisper which became the solemn scene, said to Miss Edwards, "The gentleman we passed in the passage was Mr Musgrave, then; he is reckoned remarkably agreeable, I understand?"

Miss Edwards answered hesitatingly, "Yes; he is very much liked by many people; but we are not very intimate."

Emma considered her new friend's words and the actions of the man just before. Then with a thought of how to understand his person asked, "He is rich, is not he?"

Mary looked at her a little perplexedly before replying, "He has about eight or nine hundred pounds a year, I believe." *She considered for a moment before adding,*

"He came into possession of it when he was very young *I heard*, and my father and mother think it has given him rather an unsettled turn. He is no favourite with them."

Emma took this to mean that, while Elizabeth had intimated that her sisters had a close relationship with Mr Musgrave, the Edwardses—including Mary—preferred to avoid any semblance of a connection. This encouraged Emma in her original opinion on the disagreeableness of his character, and she quit the subject entirely to look about.

The cold and empty appearance of the room and the demure air of the small cluster of females at one end of it, began soon to give way. The inspiriting sound of other carriages was heard, and continual accessions of portly chaperons and strings of smartly-dressed girls were received, with now and then a fresh gentleman straggler, who, if not enough in love to station himself near any fair creature, seemed glad to escape into the card-room.

For the next quarter hour, Emma and her companions were happy to simply observe those assembling within until the bulk of the room was nearly full and the gentlemen began to make their rounds in soliciting dance partners for the night.

Among the increasing number of military men, one now made his way to Miss Edwards with an air of impressment which decidedly said to her companion, "I am Captain Hunter;" and Emma, who could not but watch her at such a moment, saw her looking rather distressed, but by no means displeased, and heard an engagement formed for the two first dances, which made her think her brother Sam's a hopeless case.

Emma in the meanwhile was not unobserved or unadmired herself. A new face, and a very pretty one, could not be slighted. Her name was whispered from one party to another; and no sooner had the signal been given by the orchestra's striking up a favourite air, which seemed to call the young to their duty and people the centre of the room, than she found herself engaged to dance with a brother officer—*a Mr Styles*—*who was* introduced by Captain Hunter.

Emma Watson was not more than of the middle height, well made and plump, with an air of healthy vigour. Her skin was very brown, but clear, smooth, and glowing, which, with a lively eye, a sweet smile, and an open countenance, gave beauty to attract, and expression to make that beauty improve on acquaintance. Having no reason to be dissatisfied with her partner, the evening began very pleasantly to her, and her feelings perfectly coincided with the reiterated observation of others, that it was an excellent ball.

The two first dances were not quite over when the returning sound of carriages after a long interruption called general notice, and "The Osbornes are coming! The Osbornes are coming!" was repeated round the room. After some minutes of extraordinary bustle without and watchful curiosity within, the important party, preceded by the attentive master of the inn to open a door which was never shut, made their appearance. They consisted of Lady Osborne; her son, Lord Osborne; her daughter, Miss Osborne; Miss Carr, her daughter's friend; Mr Howard, formerly tutor to Lord Osborne, now clergyman of the parish in which the castle stood; Mrs Blake, a widow sister who lived with him; her son, a fine boy of ten years old; and Mr Tom Musgrave, who probably, imprisoned within his own room, had been listening in bitter impatience to the sound of the music for the last *hour*. In their progress up the room, they paused almost immediately behind Emma to receive the compliments of some acquaintance; and she heard Lady Osborne observe that they had made a point of coming early for the gratification of Mrs Blake's little boy, who was uncommonly fond of dancing.

Emma looked at them all as they passed, but chiefly and with most interest on Tom Musgrave, who was certainly a genteel, good-looking young man *for all of his faults*. Lord Osborne was a very fine young man; but there was an air of coldness, of carelessness, even of awkwardness about him, which seemed to speak him out of his element in a ball-room. He came, in fact, only because it was judged expedient for him to please the borough; he was not fond of women's company, and he never danced. *As for* Mr Howard, *standing near the former*, was an agreeable-looking man, a little more than thirty.

Of the females, Lady Osborne had by much the finest person; though nearly fifty, she was very handsome, and had all the dignity of rank.[3] *Miss Osborne and her friend Miss Carr were very fashionably dressed and wore their hair in what was like to be the newest London style. Though their clothes were very fine, Emma did not think either of them handsome and was pleased when Mary shared her opinion. The last,*

---

[3] "Lord Osborne was…" to "more than thirty" originally came after the sentence "Of the females… the dignity of rank." These were switched to allow a separation of Emma's judgement of the men and women of the party.

Mrs Blake, was clearly of a genteel background and seemed pleased with everything and everyone.

At the conclusion of the two dances, Emma found herself, she knew not how, seated amongst the Osborne set; and she was immediately struck with the fine countenance and animated gestures of the little boy, as he was standing before his mother, wondering when they should begin.

"You will not be surprised at Charles's impatience," said Mrs Blake, *whom Emma could now observe to be* a lively, pleasant-looking little woman of five or six and thirty, to a lady who was standing near her, "when you know what a partner he is to have. Miss Osborne has been so very kind as to promise to dance the two first dances with him."

"Oh, yes! We have been engaged this week," cried the boy, "and we are to dance down every couple."

On the other side of Emma, Miss Osborne, Miss Carr, and a party of young men were standing engaged in very lively consultation; and soon afterwards she saw the smartest officer of the set walking off to the orchestra to order the dance, while Miss Osborne, passing before her to her little expecting partner, hastily said: "Charles, I beg your pardon for not keeping my engagement, but I am going to dance these two dances with Colonel Beresford. I know you will excuse me, and I will certainly dance with you after tea;" and without staying for an answer, she turned again to Miss Carr, and in another minute was led by Colonel Beresford to begin the set.

If the poor little boy's face had in its happiness been interesting to Emma, it was infinitely more so under this sudden reverse; he stood the picture of disappointment, with crimsoned cheeks, quivering lips, and eyes bent on the floor. His mother, stifling her own mortification, tried to soothe him with the prospect of Miss Osborne's second promise; but, though he contrived to utter, with an effort of boyish bravery, "Oh, I do not mind it!" it was very evident, by the unceasing agitation of his features, that he minded it as much as ever.

Emma did not think or reflect; she felt and acted. "I shall be very happy to dance with you, sir, if you like it," said she, holding out her hand with the most unaffected good-humour. The boy, in one moment restored to all his first delight, looked joyfully at his *smiling* mother; and, *wanting no further solicitation before* stepping forwards with an honest and simple "Thank you, ma'am," was instantly ready to attend his new acquaintance. The thankfulness of Mrs Blake was more diffuse; with a look most expressive of unexpected pleasure and lively gratitude, she turned to her neighbour with repeated and fervent acknowledgments of "so great and condescending a kindness to *my* boy." Emma, with perfect truth, could assure her that she could not be giving greater pleasure than she felt herself; and Charles being provided with his gloves and charged to keep them on, they joined the set which was now rapidly forming, with nearly equal complacency.

It was a partnership which could not be noticed without surprise. It gained her a broad stare from Miss Osborne and Miss Carr as they passed her in the dance. "Upon my word, Charles, you are in luck," said the former, as she turned *to* him; "you have got a better partner than me;" to which the happy Charles answered "Yes!" *without understanding the hesitation in Miss Osborne's voice.*

Tom Musgrave, who was dancing with Miss Carr, gave her many inquisitive glances; and after a time, Lord Osborne himself came, and under *the* presence of talking to Charles, stood to look at his partner. Though rather distressed by such observation, Emma could not repent what she had done, so happy had it made both the boy and his mother; the latter of whom was continually making opportunities of addressing her with the warmest civility.

Her little partner, she found, though bent chiefly on dancing, was not unwilling to speak, when her questions or remarks gave him anything to say; and she learnt, by a sort of inevitable inquiry, that he had two brothers and a sister, that they and their mamma all lived with his uncle at Wickstead, that his uncle taught him Latin, that he was very fond of riding, and had a horse of his own given him by Lord Osborne; and that he had been out once already with Lord Osborne's hounds.

At the end of these dances, Emma found they were to drink tea; Miss Edwards gave her a caution to be at hand, in a manner which convinced her of Mrs Edwards's holding it very important to have them both close to her when she moved into the tea-room; and Emma was accordingly on the alert to gain her proper station. It was always the pleasure of the company to have a little bustle and crowd when they adjourned for refreshment.

The tea-room was a small room within the card-room; and in passing through the latter, where the passage was straitened by tables, Mrs Edwards and her party were for a few moments hemmed in. It happened close by Lady Osborne's casino table; Mr Howard, who belonged to it, spoke to his nephew *"Well there Charles, are you enjoying your first assembly? Not tired of dancing yet?" he inquired. Then he seemed to notice that Charles was not with Miss Osborne, but another.*

Emma, on perceiving herself the object of attention both to Lady Osborne *who had looked up at his words* and him, had just turned away her eyes in time to avoid seeming to hear her young companion delightedly whisper *in a very audible voice,* "Oh, uncle! do look at my partner; she is so pretty *is not she!*" As they were immediately in motion again, however, Charles was hurried off without being able to receive his uncle's suffrage.

On entering the tea-room, in which two long tables were prepared, Lord Osborne was to be seen quite alone at the end of one, as if retreating as far as he could from the ball, to enjoy his own thoughts and gape without restraint. Charles instantly pointed him out to Emma. "There's Lord Osborne; let you and I go and sit by him."

Emma could not quite agree to this suggestion. "No, no," said Emma, laughing, "you must sit with *my* friends."

Charles, at any rate, was very happy and, easily overruled, was contented to sit where she chose. She saw soon afterwards Lord Osborne driven away by the approach of others. She could not imagine that the companionableness of either Charles or herself would have been much to his Lordship's taste.

Charles was now free enough to hazard a few questions in his turn. "What o'clock was it?"

"Eleven."

"Eleven! and I am not at all sleepy. Mamma said I should be asleep before ten." *He looked very proud of himself for not being the least bit tired and did not notice Emma's amusement at the fact that his party only arrived shortly before the stated time.* "Do you think Miss Osborne will keep her word with me, when tea is over?"

"Oh, yes! I suppose so;" though she felt that she had no better reason to give than that Miss Osborne had not kept it before.

"When shall you come to Osborne Castle?"

"Never, probably. I am not acquainted with the family." *She thought that she also had no interest in such an acquaintance, but she kept her thoughts to herself.*

"But you may come to Wickstead and see mamma," he continued, "and she can take you to the castle. There is a monstrous curious stuffed fox there, and a badger; anybody would think they were alive. It is a pity you should not see them." *His expression was clearly torn between excitement and disappointment, and he was quiet for a while as he seemed to consider how he might show it to her. She was amused at the way his little face scrunched up while he thought and made sure to keep his plate full of delicacies as he contemplated.*

On rising from tea, there was again a scramble for the pleasure of being first out of the room, which happened to be increased by one or two of the card-parties having just broken up, and the players being disposed to move exactly the different way. Among these was Mr Howard, his sister leaning on his arm; and no sooner were they within reach of Emma, than Mrs Blake, calling her notice by a friendly touch, said, "Your goodness to Charles, my dear Miss Watson, brings all his family upon you. Give me leave to introduce my brother, Mr Howard." Emma curtsied, the gentleman bowed, made a hasty request for the honour of her hand in the two next dances, to which as hasty an affirmative was given, and they were immediately impelled in opposite directions *during which interval Charles quitted Emma's side to rejoin his mother.*

Emma was very well pleased with the circumstance; there was a quietly cheerful, gentlemanlike air in Mr Howard which suited her; and in a few minutes afterwards the value of her engagement increased, when, as she was sitting in the card-room, somewhat screened by a door, she heard Lord Osborne, who was lounging on a vacant table near her, call Tom Musgrave towards him and say, "Why do not you dance with that beautiful Emma Watson? I want you to dance with her, and I will come and stand by you."

"I was determining on it this very moment, my lord; I'll be introduced and dance with her directly."

"Aye, do; and if you find she does not want much talking to, you may introduce me by and by."

"Very well, my lord; if she is like her sisters, she will only want to be listened to. I will go this moment. I shall find her in the tea-room. That stiff old Mrs Edwards has never done tea."

Away he went, Lord Osborne after him; and Emma lost no time in hurrying from her corner exactly the other way, forgetting in her haste that she left Mrs Edwards behind.

"We had quite lost you," said Mrs Edwards, who followed her with Mary in less than five minutes. "If you prefer this room to the other, there is no reason why you should not be here; but we had better all be together."

Emma was saved the trouble of apologizing, by their being joined at the moment by Tom Musgrave, who requesting Mrs Edwards aloud to do him the honour of presenting him to Miss Emma Watson, left that good lady without any choice in the business, but that of testifying by the coldness of her manner that she did it unwillingly. The honour of dancing with her was solicited without loss of time; and Emma, however she might like to be thought a beautiful girl by lord or commoner, was so little disposed to favour Tom Musgrave himself that she had considerable satisfaction in avowing her previous engagement. He was evidently surprised and discomposed. The style of her last partner had probably led him to believe her not overpowered with applications.

"My little friend Charles Blake," he cried, "must not expect to engross you the whole evening. We can never suffer this. It is against the rules of the assembly, and I am sure it will never be patronized by our good friend here, Mrs Edwards; she is by far much too nice a judge of decorum to give her license to such a dangerous particularity—"

"I am not going to dance with Master Blake, sir!"

The gentleman, a little disconcerted, could only hope he might be fortunate another time, and seeming unwilling to leave her, though his friend Lord Osborne was waiting in the doorway for the result, as Emma with some amusement perceived, he began to make civil inquiries after her family.

"How comes it that we have not the pleasure of seeing your sisters here this evening? Our assemblies have been used to be so well treated by them that we do not know how to take this neglect."

"My eldest sister is the only one at home, and she could not leave my father."

"Miss Watson the only one at home! You astonish me! It seems but the day before yesterday that I saw them all three in this town. But I am afraid I have been a very sad neighbour of late. I hear dreadful complaints of my negligence wherever I go, and I confess it is a shameful length of time since I was at Stanton. But I shall now endeavour to make myself amends for the past."

Emma's calm courtesy in reply to all his gallantry must have struck him as very unlike the encouraging warmth and gratitude he had been used to receive from her sisters, and gave him probably the novel sensation of doubting his own influence, and of wishing for more attention than she bestowed. The dancing now recommenced; Miss Carr being impatient to call, everybody was required to stand up; and Tom Musgrave's curiosity was appeased on seeing Mr Howard come forward and claim Emma's hand.

"That will do as well for me," was Lord Osborne's remark, when his friend carried him the news, and he was continually at Howard's elbow during the two dances.

The frequency of his appearance there was the only unpleasant part of the engagement, the only objection she could make to Mr Howard. In himself, she thought him as agreeable as he looked; though chatting on the commonest topics, he had a sensible, unaffected way of expressing himself, which made them all worth hearing, and she only regretted that he had not been able to make his pupil's manners as unexceptionable as his own.

Once they got into the dance, Mr Howard began, "I believe my sister said that you are not from the area?" Emma looked confused as they parted, but she realised that Mrs Blake must have asked about the girl who offered to partner her son.

"No," she said as they came back together. "I was raised by an aunt and uncle in Shropshire until recently. I have only been in Surrey for near a fortnight."

"And how do you like your first assembly in Dorking? Did you attend many in Shropshire?" They stepped forward and back, then changed sides.

"Only a few during the last winter. My only complaint can be that I have nearly no acquaintance in the area."

"Ah, that can make finding a partner difficult. However, a handsome young lady can

never go long without attracting the attention of someone." She blushed thinking his words may hold a deeper meaning, and she was grateful for the turn that allowed her to hide her expression. "The fiddler's new, I believe. Perhaps from Reigate?" he continued.

"Is he? He has a good hand for reels." They separated and turned.

"Much better than the man we had last spring. He played every tune at the same pace—no matter how it began."

She smiled, "That does tend to tire the foot." They circled their neighbours and returned again as they moved up the line.

After some time, they parted again and moved to opposite sides of the set. Then her partner asked, "And how were your refreshments earlier? The tarts looked promising, though I have never been an enthusiast of the jellies."

"It was very refreshing. The tarts were well made, and I have heard the inn's offerings are the finest in the area." At this he nodded, and they were silent for the rest of the dance.

During the next dance, they spoke of the decorations, the size of the room, and the number of couples.

The two dances seemed very short, and she had her partner's authority for considering them so. At their conclusion, *as he returned her to her party, she saw that Miss Osborne had kept her second promise to young Charles who was beaming. Soon after,* the Osbornes and their train were all on the move.

"We are off at last," said his lordship to Tom. "How much longer do you stay in this heavenly place—till sunrise?"

"No, faith! my lord; I have had quite enough of it. I assure you; I shall not show myself here again when I have had the honour of attending Lady Osborne to her carriage. I shall retreat in as much secrecy as possible to the most remote corner of the house, where I shall order a barrel of oysters, and be famously snug."

"Let me see you soon at the castle, and bring me word how she looks by daylight."

Emma and Mrs Blake parted as old acquaintance, and Charles shook her by the hand, and wished her "good-bye" at least a dozen times. From Miss Osborne and Miss Carr, she received something like a jerking curtsey as they passed her; even Lady Osborne gave her a look of complacency, and his lordship actually came back, after the others were out of the room, to "beg her pardon," and look in the window-seat behind her for the gloves which were visibly compressed in his hand.

As Tom Musgrave was seen no more, we may suppose his plan to have succeeded, and imagine him mortifying with his barrel of oysters in dreary solitude, or gladly assisting the landlady in her bar to make fresh Negus for the happy dancers above. Emma could not help missing the party by whom she had been, though in some respects unpleasantly, distinguished; and the two *sets* which followed and concluded the ball were rather flat in comparison with the others. Mr Edwards having played with good luck; they were some of the last in the room.

"Here we are back again, I declare," said Emma, sorrowfully, as she walked into the dining-room, where the table was prepared, and the neat upper maid was lighting the candles. "My dear Miss Edwards, how soon it is at an end! I wish it could all come over again."

A great deal of kind pleasure was expressed in her having enjoyed the evening so much; and Mr Edwards was as warm as herself in the praise of the fullness, brilliancy, and spirit of the meeting, though as he had been fixed the whole time at the same table in the same room, with only one change of chairs, it might have seemed a matter scarcely perceived; but he had won four rubbers out of five, and everything went well. His daughter felt the advantage of this gratified state of mind, in the course of the remarks and retrospections which now ensued over the welcome soup.

"How came you not to dance with either of the Mr Tomlinsons, Mary?" said her mother.

"I was always engaged when they asked me."

"I thought you were to have stood up with Mr James the two last dances; Mrs Tomlinson told me he was gone to ask you, and I had heard you say two minutes before that you were not engaged."

"Yes, but there was a mistake; I had misunderstood. I did not know I was engaged. *I had forgotten that Lieutenant Carter had asked for that set*—I thought it had been for the two dances after, if we stayed so long; but Captain Hunter assured me it was for those very two, *and that he himself had already requested my last set of the evening.*"

"So, you ended with Captain Hunter, Mary, did you?" said her father. "And whom did you begin with?"

"Captain Hunter," was repeated in a very humble tone.

"Hum! That is being constant, however. But who else did you dance with *besides those two?*"

"Mr Norton and Mr Styles."

"And who are they?"

"Mr Norton is a cousin of Captain Hunter's."

"And who is Mr Styles?"

"One of his particular friends."

"All in the same regiment," added Mrs Edwards. "Mary was surrounded by red-coats all the evening. I should have been better pleased to see her dancing with some of our old neighbours, I confess."

"Yes, yes; we must not neglect our old neighbours. But if these soldiers are quicker than other people in a ball-room, what are young ladies to do?"

"I think there is no occasion for their engaging themselves so many dances beforehand, Mr Edwards."

"No, perhaps not; but I remember, my dear, when you and I did the same."

Mrs Edwards said no more, and Mary breathed again. A good deal of good-humoured pleasantry followed; and Emma went to bed in charming spirits, her head full of Osbornes, Blakes, and Howards.

REFINED AND RETURNED

Chapter Four

The Day After

Wednesday, October 14th

The next morning brought a great many visitors. It was the way of the place always to call on Mrs Edwards the morning after a ball, and this neighbourly inclination was increased in the present instance by a general spirit of curiosity on Emma's account, as everybody wanted to look again at the girl who had been admired the night before by Lord Osborne. Many were the eyes, and various the degrees of approbation with which she was examined. Some saw no fault, and some no beauty. With some her brown skin was the annihilation of every grace, and others could never be persuaded that she was half so handsome as Elizabeth Watson had been ten years ago.

Among her admirers were the Fuller, the Tomlinson, and the Arundell families along with Mr and Mrs Stanhope; however, Mrs Mary Stanhope, the visiting sister of Mr Stanhope, and her daughters sided with the Gower and Webb families in their belief that she was more plain than pretty and that her dark complexion did her no favours. Miss Edwards later pointed out to Emma that this was likely due to the fact that the former families had mostly sons while the latter families had eligible young ladies of their own to consider.

Mrs Tomlinson was friendly though not as excitable and loquacious as her husband—who rivalled Mr Edwards. The three spoke frequently of their delight in the evening as well as their pleasure—or otherwise—in the attendance of the Osborne party while Mrs Edwards looked upon them with a blank expression which Emma was sure barely hid her disgust in their manners.

Mr Fuller—a calm and quiet man unlike his in-laws—also joined in the discourse with the gentlemen, but Mrs Fuller, who was the eldest daughter of the Tomlinsons, split her attention between consoling Mrs Edwards and speaking to Emma and Mary. Her personality was more calm and genteel which, like her husband's, was a huge contrast to her parents.

Mrs Fuller was pleased to meet Emma and spoke of her elder sister, Elizabeth, as being her "personal friend".

"Indeed, we have been close since your family first came to live at Stanton," she continued.

Emma was surprised, but when she learned that her given name was Annamarie, she remembered, "Oh, indeed my sister spoke of you frequently in her letters to me—though I do not believe she ever mentioned your family name, so I did not recognise you..." she trailed off.

Mrs Fuller only smiled. "It is a shame that Elizabeth could not join you yesterday, but I know how it is. Your father must keep one daughter with him, and—had you not returned—none of the Watson girls would have attended. And what a shame that would have been. I shall be writing to my sister to inform her of your successful introduction. I am sure yours will also be glad to hear of it."

Emma was uncomfortable with her new acquaintance informing unrelated parties of her doings. "I will be speaking with Elizabeth about it later. She has asked me to remember as much as I can in order to relay it all to her when I return."

Mrs Fuller only said, "I am sure Penelope will be happy with the news as well, even though it will come second-hand. Though you had not much chance to speak with her before she left, did you?" At Emma's confused look, she continued. "Your second sister is currently staying with my younger sister Arabella—now Mrs Shaw—in Chichester."

"Oh!" Emma now understood her meaning. She had wondered at Penelope's knowing someone who lived so far from Stanton, but it made sense now. If Mrs Shaw was formerly of the area, then— "I was unaware of the connection," she finished lamely.

Mrs Fuller smiled generously, "Do not fret about it. It is such common knowledge hereabouts that I am not surprised no one thought to inform you."

Emma was grateful for her understanding and the conversation moved to other topics.

The morning passed quickly away in discussing the merits of the ball with all this succession of company; and Emma was at once astonished by finding it two o'clock, and considering that she had heard nothing of her father's chair.

After this discovery, she had walked twice to the window to examine the street, and was on the point of asking leave to ring the bell and make inquiries, when the light sound of a carriage driving up to the door *at nearly half past* set her heart at ease. She stepped again to the window, but instead of the convenient though very un-smart family equipage, perceived a neat curricle.

Mr Musgrave was shortly afterwards announced, and Mrs Edwards put on her very stiffest look at the sound. Not at all dismayed, however, by her chilling air, he paid his compliments to each of the ladies with no unbecoming ease, and continuing to address Emma, presented her a note, *and said,* "I had the honour of bringing *this note* from *your* dear sister," but to which he must observe *that* a verbal postscript from himself would be requisite.

The note, which Emma was beginning to read rather before Mrs Edwards had entreated her to use no ceremony, contained *only* a few lines from Elizabeth:

> *My Dear Emma,*
>
> *I am sorry that I have not been to pick you up, but our father, in consequence of being unusually well this morning, had the sudden resolution of attending the visitation today, and as his road lay quite wide from Dorking, it is impossible for you to come home until tomorrow morning, unless the Edwardses will send you which is hardly to be expected, or should you meet with any chance conveyance or do not mind walking so far—*

Emma had scarcely run her eye through the whole, before she found herself obliged to listen to Tom Musgrave's farther account.

"I received that note from the fair hands of Miss Watson only ten minutes ago," said he; "I met her in the village of Stanton, whither my good stars prompted me to turn my horses' heads. She was at that moment in quest of a person to employ on the errand, and I was fortunate enough to convince her that she could not find a more willing or speedy messenger than myself. Remember, I say nothing of my disinterestedness. My reward is to be the indulgence of conveying you to Stanton in my curricle. Though they are not written down, I bring your sister's orders for the same."

Emma felt distressed; she did not like the proposal—she did not wish to be on terms of intimacy with the proposer; and yet, fearful of encroaching on the Edwardses, as well as wishing to go home herself, she was at a loss how entirely to decline what he offered. Mrs Edwards continued silent, either not understanding the case, or waiting to see how the young lady's inclination lay. Emma thanked him, but professed herself very unwilling to give him so much trouble. "The trouble *is* of course *my* honour, *my* pleasure, *and my* delight—what *have* I *or my* horses to do?"

Still, she hesitated, "*I believe I* must beg leave to decline *your* assistance; *I am* rather afraid of the sort of carriage. The distance *is* not beyond a walk."

Mrs Edwards was silent no longer. She inquired into the particulars, and then said, "We shall be extremely happy, Miss Emma, if you can give us the pleasure of your company till tomorrow; but if you cannot conveniently do so, our carriage is quite at your service, and Mary will be pleased with the opportunity of seeing your sister."

This was precisely what Emma had longed for, and she accepted the offer most thankfully, acknowledging that as Elizabeth was entirely alone, it was her wish to return home to dinner. The plan was warmly opposed by their visitor, "I cannot suffer it, indeed. I must not be deprived of the happiness of escorting you. I assure you there is not a possibility of fear with my horses. You might guide them yourself. Your sisters all know how quiet they are; they have none of them the smallest scruple in trusting themselves with me, even on a race-course. Believe me," added he, lowering his voice, "you are quite safe— the danger is only mine."

Emma was not more disposed to oblige him for all this, *and she sat as silent and disapproving as Mrs Edwards.*

"And as to Mrs Edwards's carriage being used the day after a ball, it is a thing quite out of rule, I assure you—never heard of before. The old coachman will look as black as his horses—won't he Miss Edwards?"

No notice was taken. The ladies were silently firm, and the gentleman found himself obliged to submit.

"What a famous ball we had last night!" he cried, after a short pause. "How long did you keep it up after the Osbornes and I went away?"

"We had two *sets* more."

"It is making it too much of a fatigue, I think, to stay so late. I suppose your *sets were not very full ones.*"

"Yes; quite as full as ever, except the Osbornes. There seemed no vacancy anywhere; and everybody danced with uncommon spirit to the very last." Emma said this, though against her conscience.

"Indeed! perhaps I might have looked in upon you again, if I had been aware of as much, for I am rather fond of dancing than not. Miss Osborne is a charming girl, is not she?"

"I do not think her handsome," replied Emma, to whom all this was chiefly addressed.

"Perhaps she is not critically handsome, but her manners are delightful. And Fanny Carr is a most interesting little creature. You can imagine nothing more naive or piquant; and what do you think of Lord Osborne, Miss Watson?"

Emma huffed, annoyed with his conversation. "He would be handsome even though he were not a lord, and perhaps, better bred; more desirous of pleasing and showing himself pleased in a right place."

"Upon my word, you are severe upon my friend!" he exclaimed in surprise, "I assure you Lord Osborne is a very good fellow."

"I do not dispute his virtues, but I do not like his careless air."

"If it were not a breach of confidence," replied Tom, with an important look, "perhaps I might be able to win a more favourable opinion of poor Osborne."

Emma gave him no encouragement, and he was obliged to keep his friend's secret. He was also obliged to put an end to his visit, for Mrs Edwards having ordered her carriage, there was no time to be lost on Emma's side in preparing for it.

⸙

Miss Edwards accompanied her home; but, as it was dinner-hour at Stanton and Elizabeth was just sitting down to *eat, she* stayed with them only a few minutes.

"Now, my dear Emma," said Miss Watson, as soon as they were alone, "you must talk to me all the rest of the day without stopping, or I shall not be satisfied; but, first of all, Nanny shall bring in the dinner. Poor thing! You will not dine as you did yesterday, for we have nothing but some fried beef. How nice Mary Edwards looks in her new pelisse! And now tell me how you like them all, and what I am to say to Sam. I have begun my letter, Jack Stokes is to call for it tomorrow, for his uncle is going within a mile of Guildford *Friday or Saturday*."

Nanny brought in the *meal*.

"We will wait upon ourselves," continued Elizabeth, "and then we shall lose no time. And so, you would not come home with Tom Musgrave?"

"No, you had said so much against him that I could not wish either for the obligation or the intimacy which the use of his carriage must have created. I should not even have liked the appearance of it."

"You did very right; though I wonder at your forbearance, and I do not think I could have done it myself. He seemed so eager to fetch you that I could not say no, though it rather went against me to be throwing you together, so well as I knew his tricks; but I did long to see you, and it was a clever way of getting you home. Besides, it won't do to be too nice. Nobody could have thought of the Edwardses' letting you have their coach, after the horses being out so late. But what am I to say to Sam?"

"If you are guided by me, you will not encourage him to think of Miss Edwards. The father is decidedly against him, the mother shows him no favour, and I doubt his having any interest with Mary. She danced twice with Captain Hunter, and I think shows him in general as much encouragement as is consistent with her disposition and the circumstances she is placed in. She once mentioned Sam, and certainly with a little confusion; but that was perhaps merely owing to the consciousness of his liking her, which may very probably have come to her knowledge."

"Oh, dear! yes. She has heard enough of that from us all. Poor Sam! he is out of luck as well as other people. For the life of me, Emma, I cannot help feeling for those that are crossed in love. Well, now begin, and give me an account of everything as it happened."

Emma obeyed her, and Elizabeth listened with very little interruption till she heard of Mr Howard as a partner.

"Dance with Mr Howard! Good heavens! you don't say so! Why, he is quite one of the great and grand ones. Did you not find him very high?"

"His manners are of a kind to give _me_ much more ease and confidence than Tom Musgrave's."

"Well, go on. I should have been frightened out of my wits to have had anything to do with the Osbornes' set."

Emma concluded her narration.

"And so, you really did _not_ dance with Tom Musgrave at all; but you _must_ have liked him—you must have been struck with him altogether."

"I do _not_ like him, Elizabeth. I allow his person and air to be good, and that his manners to a certain point—his address rather—is pleasing, but I see nothing else to admire in him. On the contrary, he seems very vain, very conceited, absurdly anxious for distinction, and absolutely contemptible in some of the measures he takes for becoming so. There is a ridiculousness about him that entertains me, but his company gives me no other agreeable emotion."

"My dearest Emma! You are like nobody else in the world. It is well Margaret is not by. You do not offend _me_, though I hardly know how to believe you; but _do not let Margaret hear such words; she would never forgive you._"

"I wish Margaret could have heard him profess his ignorance of her being out of the country; he declared it seemed only two days since he had seen her."

"Aye, that is just like him; and yet _this_ is the man she will fancy so desperately in love with her. He is no favourite of mine, as you well know, Emma; but you must think him agreeable. Can you lay your hand on your heart, and say you do not?"

"Indeed, I can, both hands, and spread to their widest extent."

"I should like to know the man you _do_ think agreeable."

"His name is Howard."

"Howard! Dear me; I cannot think of _him_ but as playing cards with Lady Osborne, and looking proud. I must own, however, that it is a relief to me to find you can speak as you do of Tom Musgrave, _and that you are not infatuated by him._ My heart did misgive me that you would like him too well. You talked so stoutly beforehand, that I was sadly afraid your brag would be punished. I only hope it will last, and that he will not come on to pay you much attention. It is a hard thing for a woman to stand against the flattering ways of a man, when he is bent upon pleasing her."

As their quietly sociable little meal concluded, Miss Watson could not help observing how comfortably it had passed.

"It is so delightful to me," said she, "to have things going on in peace and good-humour. Nobody can tell how much I hate quarrelling. Now, though we have had nothing but fried beef, how good it has all seemed! I wish everybody were as easily satisfied as you; but poor Margaret is very snappish, and Penelope owns she had rather have quarrelling going on than nothing at all."

Mr Watson returned in the evening not the worse for the exertion of the day, and, consequently pleased with what he had done, *was* glad to talk of it over his own fireside. Emma had not foreseen any interest to herself in the occurrences of a visitation; but when she heard Mr Howard spoken of as the preacher, and as having given them an excellent sermon, she could not help listening with a quicker ear.

"I do not know when I have heard a discourse more to my mind," continued Mr Watson, "or one better delivered. He reads extremely well, with great propriety, and in a very impressive manner, and at the same time without any theatrical grimace or violence. I own I do not like much action in the pulpit; I do not like the studied air and artificial inflexions of voice which your very popular and most admired preachers generally have. A simple delivery is much better calculated to inspire devotion, and shows a much better taste. Mr Howard read like a scholar and a gentleman."

"And what had you for dinner, sir?" said his eldest daughter.

He related the dishes, and told what he had ate himself.

"Upon the whole," he added, "I have had a very comfortable day. My old friends were quite surprised to see me amongst them, and I must say that everybody paid me great attention, and seemed to feel for me as an invalid. They would make me sit near the fire; and as the partridges were pretty high, Dr Richards would have them sent away to the other end of the table, 'that they might not offend Mr Watson,' which I thought very kind of him. But what pleased me as much as anything was Mr Howard's attention. There is a pretty steep flight of steps up to the room we dine in, which do not quite agree with my gouty foot; and Mr Howard walked by me from the bottom to the top, and would make me take his arm. It struck me as very becoming in so young a man; but I am sure I had no claim to expect it, for I never saw him before in my life. By the by, he inquired after one of my daughters; but I do not know which. I suppose you know among yourselves."

Emma felt Elizabeth looking at her as their father continued to regale them with the rest of his day and his journey home. She tried to keep her face a mask of serenity, but, little did she know, that the brightness of her eyes in the candlelight and the slight upturning of her lip gave away her feelings if not her thoughts. They were both convinced that Mr Howard's attentions to their father must be due to his and his family's interactions with Emma the night before, and Emma could not be more pleased. Her gratification in knowing that he not only remembered her but that he went out of his way to seek an introduction to her father and guardian, the surest way of securing an opening to get to know her better, must be a clear sign of his reciprocating interest in her.

Emma showed every sign of paying attention to her father's story, but her mind was more agreeably engaged in thinking about what a perfect gentleman Mr Howard truly seemed to be, and how well she might like to receive his attentions. Therefore, she spent the rest of the evening, after their father retired and Elizabeth went off to finish her letter, among many pleasant thoughts of future domesticity.

Chapter Five

Unexpected Visitors

Friday, October 16th

On the third day after the ball, as Nanny, at five minutes before three, was beginning to bustle into the parlour with the tray and the knife-case *for their dinner,* she was suddenly called to the front door by the sound of as smart a rap as the end of a riding-whip could give; and though charged by Miss Watson to let nobody in, returned in half a minute with a look of awkward dismay to hold the parlour door open for Lord Osborne and Tom Musgrave. The surprise of the young ladies may be imagined. No visitors would have been welcome at such a moment, but such visitors as these—such a one as Lord Osborne at least, a nobleman and a stranger—was really distressing.

He looked a little embarrassed himself, as, on being introduced by his easy, voluble friend, he muttered something of doing himself the honour of waiting upon Mr Watson. Though Emma could not but take the compliment of the visit to herself, she was very far from enjoying it. She felt all the inconsistency of such an acquaintance with the very humble style in which they were obliged to live; and having in her aunt's family been used to many of the elegancies of life, *she could not without some mortification be* fully sensible of all that must be open to the ridicule of richer people in her present home. Of the pain of such feelings, Elizabeth knew very little. Her simple mind, or juster reason, saved her from such *humiliation;* and though shrinking under a general sense of inferiority, she felt no particular shame *and wished them away more from a sense of convenience.*

Mr Watson, as the gentlemen had already heard from Nanny, was not well enough to be down-stairs. With much concern they took their seats; Lord Osborne near Emma, and the convenient Mr Musgrave, in high spirits at his own importance, on the other side of the fireplace, with Elizabeth. He was at no loss for words; but when Lord Osborne had hoped that Emma had not caught cold at the ball, he had nothing more to say for some time, and could only gratify his eye by occasional glances at his fair neighbour. Emma was not inclined to give herself much trouble for his entertainment; and after hard labour of mind, he produced the remark of its being a very fine day, and followed it up with the question of, "Have you been walking this morning?"

"No, my lord; we thought it too dirty."

"You should wear half-boots." After another pause: "Nothing sets off a neat ankle more than a half-boot; nankeen galoshed with black looks very well. Do not you like half-boots?"

"Yes; but unless they are so stout as to injure their beauty, they are not fit for *the deep dirt of* country walking."

"Ladies should ride in dirty weather. Do you ride?" *He inquired hopefully, but his hopes were dashed with her blunt response.*

"No, my lord."

"I wonder every lady does not; a woman never looks better than on horseback."

"But every woman may not have the inclination, or the means." *Emma decided not to mention that she was a perfectly capable horsewoman provided she had a horse on which to ride, but he must surely see that their way of life could not afford her such luxuries. So she was only exasperated when he continued.*

"If they knew how much it became them, they would all have the inclination; and I fancy, Miss Watson, when once they had the inclination, the means would soon follow."

"*I am to suppose you mean a compliment of course, my lord,*" said Emma nodding her *head in pretence of a bow, "though I cannot define it." Hoping to put an end to the discussion, she added,* "Your lordship thinks we always have our own way. That is a point on which ladies and gentlemen have long disagreed; but without pretending to decide it, I may say that there are some circumstances which even women cannot control. Female economy will do a great deal my lord: but it cannot turn a small income into a large one."

Lord Osborne laughed rather awkwardly and then said, "Upon my soul, I am a bad one for compliments. Nobody can be a worse hand at it than myself. I wish I knew more of such matters." And after some minutes of silence added, "Can you not give me a lesson, Miss Emma, on the art of paying compliments? I should be very glad to learn."

A cold monosyllable and grave look from Emma repressed the growing freedom of his manner.[4]

Lord Osborne was silenced. Her manner had been neither sententious nor sarcastic; but there was a something in its mild seriousness, as well as in the words themselves and *her looks*, which made his lordship think. *He had too much sense not to take the hint*; and when he addressed her again, it was with a degree of *courteous* propriety *which he was more used to employ with his acquaintance*; totally unlike the half-awkward, half-fearless style of his former remarks *which had been modelled on the manner of his friend's way of acting and speaking*. It was a new thing with him to wish to please a woman; it was the first time that he had ever felt what was due to a woman in Emma's situation; but as he wanted neither in sense nor a good disposition, he did not feel it without effect.

"You have not been long in this country, I understand," said he, in the tone of a gentleman. "I hope you are pleased with it."

He was rewarded by a gracious answer, and a more liberal full view of her face than she had yet bestowed. Unused to exert himself, and happy in contemplating her, he then sat in silence for about five minutes longer, while Tom Musgrave was chattering to Elizabeth; till they were interrupted by Nanny's approach, who, half-opening the door and putting in her head, said, "Please, ma'am, master wants to know why he ben't to have his dinner?"

The gentlemen, who had hitherto disregarded every symptom, however positive, of the nearness of that meal, now jumped up with apologies, while Elizabeth called briskly after Nanny to "tell Betty to take up the fowls."

"I am sorry it happens so," she added, turning good-humouredly towards Musgrave, "but you know what early hours we keep."

---

[4] From 'Lord Osborne laughed' to 'freedom of his manner' was taken from the original manuscript and adjusted to fit into this completed version of the story; therefore, it is copyright in full to the author of this story.

Tom had nothing to say for himself; he knew it very well, and such honest simplicity, such shameless truth, rather bewildered him. Lord Osborne's parting compliments took some time, his inclination for speech seeming to increase with the shortness of the term for indulgence. He recommended exercise in defiance of dirt; spoke again in praise of half-boots; begged that his sister might be allowed to send Emma the name of her shoemaker; and concluded with saying, "My hounds will be hunting this country next week. I believe they will throw off at Stanton Wood on Wednesday at nine o'clock. I mention this in hopes of your being drawn out to see what's going on. *Nobody can be indifferent to the glorious sounds of a pack of fox hounds in full cry.* If the morning's tolerable, pray do us the honour of giving us your good wishes in person."

The sisters looked on each other with astonishment when their visitors had withdrawn.

"Here's an unaccountable honour!" cried Elizabeth, at last. "Who would have thought of Lord Osborne's coming to Stanton? *I wish he would give our poor father a Living, as he makes such a point of coming to see him. But, to be sure, Mr Howard will have everything of that sort he has to give.* He is very handsome; but Tom Musgrave looks all to nothing the smartest and most fashionable man of the two. I am glad he did not say anything to me; I would not have had to talk to such a great man for the world. Tom was very agreeable, was not he? But did you hear him ask where Miss Penelope and Miss Margaret were, when he first came in? It put me out of patience. I am glad Nanny had not laid the cloth, however—it would have looked so awkward; just the tray did not signify."

Emma did not reply and simply allowed Elizabeth to continue on while listening with half an ear. To say that Emma was not flattered by Lord Osborne's visit would be to assert a very unlikely thing, and describe a very odd young lady; but the gratification was by no means unalloyed: his coming was a sort of notice which might please her vanity, but did not suit her pride; and she would rather have known that he wished the visit without presuming to make it, than have seen him at Stanton.

Among other unsatisfactory feelings, it once occurred to her to wonder why Mr Howard had not taken the same privilege of coming, and accompanied his lordship; but she was willing to suppose that he had either known nothing about it, or had declined any share in a measure which carried quite as much impertinence in its form as good-breeding.

Mr Watson was very far from being delighted when he heard what had passed; a little peevish under immediate pain, and ill-disposed to be pleased *after being made to wait so long for his dinner*, he only replied, "Phoo! phoo! What occasion could there be for Lord Osborne's coming? I have lived here *twelve* years without being noticed by any of the family. It is some foolery of that idle fellow, Tom Musgrave. I cannot return the visit. I would not if I could." And when Tom Musgrave was met with again, he was commissioned with a message of excuse to Osborne Castle, on the too-sufficient plea of Mr Watson's infirm state of health.

Chapter Six

Letters and News

Friday, October 23rd

A week or ten days rolled quietly away after this visit before any new bustle arose *at Stanton Parsonage* to interrupt even for half a day the tranquil and affectionate intercourse of the two sisters, whose mutual regard was increasing with the intimate knowledge of each other which such intercourse produced. The first circumstance to break in on this security was the receipt of a letter from Croydon to announce the speedy return of Margaret, and a visit of two or three days from Mr and Mrs Robert Watson, who *would undertake* to bring her home, and wished to see their sister Emma.

It was an expectation to fill the thoughts of the sisters at Stanton, and to busy the hours of one of them at least; for as Jane had been a woman of fortune, the preparations for her entertainment were considerable; and as Elizabeth had at all times more goodwill than method in her guidance of the house, she could make no change without a bustle.

An absence of fourteen years had made all her brothers and sisters strangers to Emma, but in her expectation of Margaret there was more than the awkwardness of such an alienation; she had heard things which made her dread her *sister's* return; and the day which brought the party to Stanton seemed to her the probable conclusion of almost all that had been comfortable in the house.

The second interruption came the next day when Emma received her first letter from Aunt O'Brien—though she told no one of it. Elizabeth and Nanny were in the kitchen planning meals for Robert and Jane's visit when the post arrived. Emma was reading by the window in the front parlour when she noticed the approaching figure and decided to intercept him, sparing Nanny the trouble. She opened the door and was handed a letter addressed to herself. Surprise flickered across her face until she saw the sender's name, and, without hesitation, she slipped back upstairs with no one the wiser to her departure. The letter read:

Wednesday, October 21ˢᵗ

No. — Park Street, London

My Dearest Emma,

I must entreat your forgiveness for this belated correspondence which I shall leave with the outgoing mail post-haste, knowing full well that it should not likely reach you until after we have arrived in Bath. There we shall remain for some weeks until we must embark on the last leg of our journey to Ireland. Oh, I am so pleased with my Dear James. You can have no idea, but, when I tell you, I know you shall be delighted for me.

My husband is no longer a Captain; however, he will one day be a Lord! His uncle—the Marquess whose acquisition of another title, fortune, and estate brought us to London—has no son and heir and has made it so that his titles will devolve to his next brother's son—my James—upon his demise.

Someday, in the not-so-distant future, I—your very own aunt—shall be elevated to the title of Marchioness! Well, how soon is unknown, but his uncle is not a young man; he is nearly eighty already and in evident decline. He has elected to reside at his new estate in Buckinghamshire, entrusting the management of his Irish estates to us. We shall be living as the de facto Count and Countess—is not it grand?

I did so desire to visit you all before we quit the shores of England, but, alas, there has just been no time to spare. We could not in good conscience absent ourselves from the celebrations for his uncle's ascension, lest we should have appeared devoid of gratitude. Therefore, with the festivities now concluded, we are ready to depart London.

I do hope that you and all of my brother's family are in good health and spirits. I do not imagine I shall have time to pen another letter until I am comfortably settled in Bath, but fret not, Emma. Your dearest aunt could not be more content with the choices she has made and harbours not a single regret.

Your Loving Aunt Always,

Margaret O'Brien, future Marchioness of Thomond

After reading her letter, Emma wondered at how long it had taken to be delivered. Then she could not decide if her aunt's words were callous, or if it was simply her own dejection at being left behind that made her think so. Either way, Emma could not bring herself to inform her family of the letter or its contents—nor could she bear to face them. She spent the rest of the day confined to her room with the excuse of a headache.

The next morning, Emma was late coming downstairs for church; so, their father went ahead while Elizabeth went up to check on her, and she even offered to go out and get the local apothecary to come and see her after services; however, Emma insisted that she was healthy, and they left together. Emma was quiet through church and sat down in the parlour with a book as soon as they returned though she was unable to enjoy it.

Elizabeth soon realised, even though she was quite busy with the hustle and bustle of preparations, that Emma was extremely out of sorts. However, try as she might, she could not figure out what was bothering her sister. She tried a few more times to get Emma to confide in her; however, in the end, she could get nothing out of her younger sister but her assurances that nothing was wrong. Elizabeth decided that Emma must be worried about meeting with Margaret after everything Elizabeth had told her about their next youngest sister. Therefore, she endeavoured to speak more positively about her sister in front of Emma at dinner that day.

"I know that I have told you something of how Margaret can be, but I do not think you need to worry much about her. She is much less likely to act in such a perverse manner with someone so new to her. Even though you are our sister, you are still someone entirely unknown to either Margaret or Penelope. Therefore, I only advise that you do not speak so freely of your opinion about Mr Musgrave once our sister arrives, and I am sure that you will get on well enough. She knows how to behave when she wishes to."

Emma tried to assure her sister that she had no such fears or qualms about meeting Margaret. However, while the meeting was not the main issue on her mind, she could not say in all honesty that she was not a little scared of the coming introduction.

Elizabeth heard the uncertainty in her sister's voice and was therefore convinced that she had been correct about what ailed Emma.

REFINED AND RETURNED

Chapter Seven

Margaret's Return

Monday, October 26ᵗʰ

When Margaret's party arrived the Monday after their letter, Emma was to finally learn whether or not there was any pleasure to be had in the meeting with her Croydon family. She had tried to keep her hopes up despite her misgivings from Elizabeth's stories of them all, but she was not sure she had enough time to prepare for the introductions to come.

Robert Watson was fairer than Emma and Elizabeth showing that he was not much outdoors. He shared their shorter stature though his curves were in the form of a paunch. He was an attorney at Croydon, in a good way of business; very well satisfied with himself for the same, and for having married the only daughter of the attorney to whom he had been clerk, with a fortune of six thousand pounds. Mrs Robert was not less pleased with herself for having had that six thousand pounds, and for being now in possession of a very smart house in Croydon, where she gave genteel parties and wore fine clothes. In her person there was nothing remarkable; her manners were pert and conceited. Her figure was neither light nor pleasing, but she had a pretty enough face when she could be disposed to show a pleasant smile.

Margaret was not without beauty; she had a slight pretty figure, *was taller than Elizabeth or Emma,* and rather wanted countenance than good features; but the sharp and anxious expression of her face made her beauty in general little felt. On meeting her long-absent sister, as on every occasion of show, her manner was all affection and her voice all gentleness; continual smiles and a very slow articulation being her constant resource when determined on pleasing.

She was now so delighted to see "dear, dear Emma," that she could hardly speak a word in a minute.

"I am sure we shall be great friends," she observed with much sentiment, as they were sitting together. Emma scarcely knew how to answer such a proposition, and the manner in which it was spoken she could not attempt to equal.

Mrs Robert Watson eyed her with much familiar curiosity and triumphant compassion: the loss of the aunt's fortune was uppermost in her mind at the moment of meeting; and she could not but feel how much better it was to be the daughter of a gentleman of property in Croydon than the niece of an old woman who threw herself away on an Irish captain.

Robert was carelessly kind, as became a prosperous man and a brother; more intent on settling with the post-boy, inveighing against the exorbitant advance in posting, and pondering over a doubtful half-crown, than on welcoming a sister who was no longer likely to have any property for him to get the direction of.

"Your road through the village is infamous, Elizabeth," said he; "worse than ever it was. By Heaven! I would indict it if I lived near you. Who is surveyor now?"

Elizabeth answered him, but it was unclear whether her response was heard. There was a little niece at Croydon to be fondly inquired after by the kind-hearted Elizabeth, who regretted very much her not being of the party.

"You are very good," replied her mother, "and I assure you it went very hard with Augusta to have us come away without her. I was forced to say we were only going to church, and promise to come back for her directly. But you know it would not do to bring her without her maid, and I am as particular as ever in having her properly attended to."

"Sweet little darling!" cried Margaret. "It quite broke my heart to leave her."

"Then why was you in such a hurry to run away from her?" cried Mrs Robert. "You are a sad, shabby girl. I have been quarrelling with you all the way we came, have not I? Such a visit as this, I never heard of! You know how glad we are to have any of you with us, if it be for months together; and I am sorry," *she added* with a witty smile, "we have not been able to make Croydon agreeable this autumn."

"My dearest Jane, do not overpower me with your raillery. You know what inducements I had to bring me home. Spare me, I entreat you. I am no match for your arch sallies."

"Well, I only beg you will not set your neighbours against the place. Perhaps Emma may be tempted to go back with us and stay till Christmas, if you don't put in your word."

Emma was greatly obliged. "I assure you we have very good society at Croydon. I do not much attend the balls; they are rather too mixed; but our parties are very select and good. I had seven tables last week in my drawing-room. Are you fond of the country? How do you like Stanton?"

"Very much," replied Emma, who thought a comprehensive answer most to the purpose. She saw that her sister-in-law despised her immediately. Mrs Robert Watson was indeed wondering what sort of a home Emma could possibly have been used to in Shropshire, and setting it down as certain that the aunt could never have had six thousand pounds.

"How charming Emma is," whispered Margaret to Mrs Robert, in her most languishing tone.

Emma was quite distressed by such behaviour; and she did not like it better when she heard Margaret five minutes afterwards say to Elizabeth in a sharp, quick accent, totally unlike the first, "Have you heard from Pen since she went to Chichester? I had a letter the other day. I don't find she is likely to make anything of it. I fancy she'll come back 'Miss Penelope,' as she went."

Such, she feared, would be Margaret's common voice when the novelty of her own appearance *was* over; the tone of artificial sensibility was not recommended by the idea. The ladies were invited upstairs to prepare for dinner.

"I hope you will find things tolerably comfortable, Jane," said Elizabeth, as she opened the door of the spare bedchamber.

"My good creature," replied Jane, "use no ceremony with me, I entreat you. I am one of those who always take things as they find them. I hope I can put up with a small apartment for two or three nights without making a piece of work. I always wish to be treated quite <u>en famille</u> when I come to see you. And now I do hope you have not been getting a great dinner for us. Remember, we never eat suppers."

"I suppose," said Margaret, rather quickly to Emma, "you and I are to be together; Elizabeth always takes care to have a room to herself."

"No. Elizabeth gives me half hers."

"Oh!" in a softened voice, and rather mortified to find that she was not ill-used, "I am sorry I am not to have the pleasure of your company, especially as it makes me nervous to be much alone."

Emma was the first of the females in the parlour again; on entering it she found her brother alone.

"So, Emma," said he, "you are quite a stranger at home. It must seem odd enough for you to be here. A pretty piece of work your Aunt Turner has made of it! By Heaven! a woman should never be trusted with money. I always said she ought to have settled something on you, as soon as her husband died."

"But that would have been trusting me with money," replied Emma *surprised by the contradiction*; "and I am a woman too."

"It might have been secured to your future use, without your having any power over it now. What a blow it must have been upon you! To find yourself, instead of heiress of eight or nine thousand pounds, sent back a weight upon your family, without a sixpence. I hope the old woman will smart for it."

"Do not speak disrespectfully of her;" *she said with some feeling as the tears began to well in her eyes.* "She was very good to me, and if she has made an imprudent choice, she will suffer more from it herself than I can possibly do."

Robert, seeing the sheen in her eyes, cleared his throat in discomfort. "I do not mean to distress you, but you know everybody must think her an old fool. I thought Turner had been reckoned an extraordinarily sensible, clever man. How the devil came he to make such a will?"

"My uncle's sense is not at all impeached in my opinion by his attachment to my aunt. She had been an excellent wife to him. The most liberal and enlightened minds are always the most confiding. The event has been unfortunate; but my uncle's memory is, if possible, endeared to me by such a proof of tender respect for my aunt."

"That's odd sort of talking." *He looked honestly surprised at her passionate defence of two people who had clearly wronged her greatly.* "He might have provided decently for his widow, without leaving everything that he had to dispose of, or any part of it, at her mercy."

"My aunt may have erred," said Emma, warmly; "she has erred, but my uncle's conduct was faultless. I was <u>her own</u> niece, and he left to herself the power and the pleasure of providing for me."

"But unluckily she has left the pleasure of providing for you to your father, and without the power. That's the long and short of the business. After keeping you at a distance from your family for such a length of time as must do away all natural affection among us, and breeding you up—I suppose—in a superior style, you are returned upon their hands without a sixpence."

"You know," replied Emma, struggling with her tears, "my uncle's melancholy state of health. He was a greater invalid than my father. He could not leave home *and it fell upon my aunt to care for him. I am sure his decision was out of gratitude.*"

"I do not mean to make you cry," said Robert, rather softened, —and after a short silence, by way of changing the subject, he added: "I am just come from my father's room; he seems very indifferent. It will be a sad break up when he dies. Pity you can none of you get married! You must come to Croydon as well as the rest, and see what you can do there. I believe if Margaret had had a thousand or fifteen hundred pounds, there was a young man who would have thought of her."

Emma was glad when they were joined by the others; it was better to look at her sister-in-law's finery than listen to Robert, who had equally irritated and grieved her. Mrs Robert, exactly as smart as she had been at her own party, came in with apologies for her dress.

"I would not make you wait," said she; "so I put on the first thing I met with. I am afraid I am a sad figure." *Emma found this statement odd, considering her state of overdress and the fact that Elizabeth had been called out of their shared room to help Margaret aid their sister-in-law in dressing. The clear discrepancy between her words and behaviour told Emma all she needed to know: Mrs Robert's company was as unappealing as her husband's.*

Then Jane turned her attention to her husband. "My dear Mr W," to her husband, "you have not put any fresh powder in your hair."

"No, I do not intend it. I think there is powder enough in my hair for my wife and sisters."

"Indeed, you ought to make some alteration in your dress before dinner when you are out visiting, though you do not at home," *insisted his wife in an overly loud voice for the size of the small parlour.*

"Nonsense."

"It is very odd you should not like to do what other gentlemen do. Mr Marshall and Mr Hemmings change their dress every day of their lives before dinner. And what was the use of my putting up your last new coat, if you are never to wear it?"

"Do be satisfied with being fine yourself, and leave your husband alone."

To put an end to this altercation and soften the evident vexation of her sister-in-law, Emma—though in no spirits to make such nonsense easy—began to admire her gown. It produced immediate complacency.

"Do you like it?" said she. "I am very happy. It has been excessively admired; but sometimes I think the pattern too large. I shall wear one tomorrow that I think you will prefer to this. Have you seen the one I gave Margaret?"

Dinner came, and except when Mrs Robert looked at her husband's head, she continued gay and flippant, chiding Elizabeth for the profusion on the table, and absolutely protesting against the entrance of the roast turkey, which formed the only exception to "You see your dinner."— "I do beg and entreat that no turkey may be seen today. I am really frightened out of my wits with the number of dishes we have already. Let us have no turkey, I beseech you."

"My dear," replied Elizabeth, "the turkey is roasted, and it may just as well come in as stay in the kitchen. Besides, if it is cut, I am in hopes my father may be tempted to eat a bit, for it is rather a favourite dish."

"You may have it in, my dear; but I assure you I shan't touch it." *Or so she claimed, but Emma saw her taking a large portion for herself not ten minutes later.*

Mr Watson had not been well enough to join the party at dinner, but was prevailed on to come down and drink tea with them.

"I wish we may be able to have a game of cards tonight," said Elizabeth to Mrs Robert, after seeing her father comfortably seated in his arm-chair.

"Not on my account, my dear, I beg. You know I am no card-player. I think a snug chat infinitely better. I always say cards are very well sometimes to break a formal circle, but one never wants them among friends."

"I was thinking of its being something to amuse my father," said Elizabeth, "if it was not disagreeable to you. He says his head won't bear whist, but, perhaps if we make a round game, he may be tempted to sit down with us."

"By all means, my dear creature. I am quite at your service; only do not oblige me to choose the game, that's all. Speculation is the only round game at Croydon now, but I can play anything. When there is only one or two of you at home, you must be quite at a loss to amuse him. Why do you not get him to play at cribbage? Margaret and I have played at cribbage most nights that we have not been engaged."

Their conversation came to a halt as a sound like a distant carriage was at this moment caught. Everybody listened; it became more decided; it certainly drew nearer; *and a different sort of speculation began.*

A carriage was an unusual sound for Stanton at any time of the day, for the village was on no very public road, and contained no gentleman's family but the rector's. The wheels rapidly approached; in two minutes the general expectation was answered; they stopped beyond a doubt at the garden-gate of the parsonage. *Cries of,* "Who could it be?" *rang around the room.* It was certainly a post chaise.

Penelope was the only creature to be thought of. "She might perhaps have met with some unexpected opportunity of returning," *was someone's suggestion, but Emma was not sure who had spoken.*

A pause of suspense ensued. Steps were distinguished along the paved foot-way, which led under the windows of the house to the front door, and then within the passage. They were the steps of a man. It could not be

Penelope. It must be Samuel. The door opened, and displayed Tom Musgrave in the wrap of a traveller. He had been in London *for two days wither he travelled with the Osbornes*, and was now on his way home, and he had come half-a-mile out of his road merely to call for ten minutes at Stanton. He loved to take people by surprise with sudden visits at extraordinary seasons, and, in the present instance, had had the additional motive of being able to tell the Miss Watsons, whom he depended on finding sitting quietly employed after tea, that he was going home to an eight-o'clock dinner.

As it happened, however, he did not give more surprise than he received, when, instead of being shown into the usual little sitting-room, the door of the best parlour (a foot larger each way than the other) was thrown open, and he beheld a circle of smart people whom he could not immediately recognise arranged, with all the honours of visiting, round the fire, and Miss Watson seated at the best Pembroke table, with the best tea-things before her. He stood a few seconds in silent amazement.

Mr Watson raised an eyebrow in disapproval of the gentleman's mode of appearing wherever he chose with no notion of waiting for an invitation or even announcing his visits. However, his mood was not as it had been the last time Musgrave stopped in; so, he neither offered the man an invitation to join them nor sent him away. He simply sipped at the tea Elizabeth had just handed him and observed them all in silence. Emma was surprised at her father's calm reaction to the interruption but she also said nothing.

"Musgrave!" ejaculated Margaret, in a tender voice, *after a long moment. Hearing this, Musgrave* recollected himself, and came forward, delighted to find such a circle of friends, and blessing his good fortune for the unlooked-for indulgence. He shook hands with Robert, bowed and smiled to the ladies, and did everything very prettily; but as to any particularity of address or emotion towards Margaret, Emma, who closely observed him, perceived nothing that did not justify Elizabeth's opinion, though Margaret's modest smiles imported that she meant to take the visit to herself.

He was persuaded *by Margaret and Jane* without much difficulty to throw off his great-coat and drink tea with them. "For whether *I dine* at eight or nine," as he observed, "*is* a matter of very little consequence;" and without seeming to seek, he did not turn away from the chair close by Margaret, which she was assiduous in providing him. She had thus secured him from her sisters, but it was not immediately in her power to preserve him from her brother's claims; for as he came avowedly from London, and had left it only four hours ago, the last current report as to public news, and the general opinion of the day, must be understood before Robert could let his attention be yielded to the less national and important demands of the women. At last, however, he was at liberty to hear Margaret's soft address, as she spoke her fears of his having "had a most terrible cold, dark, dreadful journey."

"Indeed, you should not have set out so late."

"I could not be earlier," he replied. "I was detained chatting at the Bedford by a friend *of Lord Osborne's. But it matters not,* all hours are alike to me. How long have you been in the country, Miss Margaret?"

"We only came this morning; my kind brother and sister brought me home this very morning. 'Tis singular, is not it?"

"You were gone a great while, were not you? A fortnight, I suppose?"

"You may call a fortnight a great while, Mr Musgrave," said Mrs Robert, sharply; "but we think a month very little. I assure you we bring her home at the end of a month much against our will."

"A month! Have you really been gone a month? 'Tis amazing how time flies."

"You may imagine," said Margaret, in a sort of whisper, "what are my sensations in finding myself once more at Stanton; you know what a sad visitor I make. And I was so excessively impatient to see Emma; I dreaded the meeting, and at the same time longed for it. Do you not comprehend the sort of feeling?"

"Not at all," cried he, aloud: "I could never dread a meeting with Miss Emma Watson—or any of her sisters."

It was lucky that he added that finish.

"Oh! You creature!" was Margaret's reply.

"Were you speaking to me?" said Emma, who had caught her own name.

"Not absolutely," he answered; "but I was thinking of you, as many at a greater distance are probably doing at this moment. Fine open weather, Miss Emma, charming season for hunting," *he said the last with a grin and a little wink that Emma was sure Margaret had noticed by the twitch of her eyebrows and a slight dimming of her toothy smile.*

"Emma is delightful, is not she?" whispered Margaret; "I have found her more than answer my warmest hopes. Did you ever see anything more perfectly beautiful? I think even you must be a convert to a brown complexion."

He hesitated. Margaret was fair herself, and he did not particularly want to compliment her; but Miss Osborne and Miss Carr were likewise fair, and his devotion to them carried the day.

"Your sister's complexion," said he, at last, "is as fine as a dark complexion can be; but I still profess my preference of a white skin. You have seen Miss Osborne? She is my model for a truly feminine complexion, and she is very fair."

"Is she fairer than me?"

Tom made no reply. "Upon my honour, ladies," said he, giving a glance over his own person, "I am highly indebted to your condescension for admitting me in such déshabille into your drawing-room. I really did not consider how unfit I was to be here, or I hope I should have kept my distance. Lady Osborne would tell me that I were growing as careless as her son, if she saw me in this condition."

The ladies were not wanting in civil returns, and Robert Watson, stealing a view of his own head in an opposite glass, said with equal civility, "You cannot be more in déshabille than myself. We got here so late that I had not time even to put a little fresh powder in my hair."

Emma could not help entering into what she supposed her sister-in-law's feelings at the moment.

When the tea-things were removed, Tom began to talk of his carriage; but the old card-table being set out, and the fish and counters, with a tolerably clean pack, brought forward from the buffet by Miss Watson, the general voice was so urgent with him to join their party that he agreed to allow himself another quarter of an hour. Even Emma was pleased that he would stay, for she was beginning to feel that a family party might be the worst of all parties; and the others were delighted.

"What's your game?" cried he, as they stood round the table.

"Speculation, I believe," said Elizabeth. "My sister recommends it, and I fancy we all like it. I know you do, Tom."

"It is the only round game played at Croydon now," said Mrs Robert *preening that their tastes should coincide with such a gentleman who claimed friendship with the local lord*; "we never think of any other. I am glad it is a favourite with you."

"Oh, me!" said Tom. "Whatever you decide on will be a favourite with *me*. I have had some pleasant hours at Speculation in my time, but I have not been in the way of it now for a long while. Vingt-un is the game at Osborne Castle. I have played nothing but vingt-un of late. You would be astonished to hear the noise we make there—the fine old lofty drawing-room rings again. Lady Osborne sometimes declares she cannot hear herself speak. Lord Osborne enjoys it famously, and he makes the best dealer without exception that I ever beheld—such quickness and spirit—he lets nobody dream over their cards. I wish you could see him overdraw himself on both his own cards. It is worth anything in the world!"

"Dear me!" cried Margaret, "why should not we play at vingt-un? I think it is a much better game than Speculation. I cannot say I am very fond of Speculation."

Mrs Robert offered not another word in support of the game. She was quite vanquished: *even in her estimation* the fashions of Osborne Castle carried it over the fashions of Croydon.

"Do you see much of the parsonage family at the castle, Mr Musgrave?" said Emma, as they were taking their seats.

"Oh, yes; they are almost always there. Mrs Blake is a nice little good-humoured woman; she and I are sworn friends; and Howard's a very gentlemanlike, good sort of fellow! You are not forgotten, I assure you, by any of the party. I fancy you must have a little cheek-glowing now and then, Miss Emma. Were not you rather warm last Saturday about nine or ten o'clock in the evening? I will tell you how it was—I see you are dying to know. Says Howard to Lord Osborne—"

At this interesting moment he was called on by the others to regulate the game, and determine some disputable point; and his attention was so totally engaged in the business, and afterwards by the course of the game, as never to revert to what he had been saying before; and Emma, though suffering a good deal from curiosity, dared not remind him.

He proved a very useful addition to their table. Without him, it would have been a party of such very near relations as could have felt little interest, and perhaps maintained little complaisance; but his presence gave variety and secured good manners. He was, in fact, excellently qualified to shine at a round game, and few situations made him appear to greater advantage. He played with spirit, and had a great deal to say; and, though no wit himself, could sometimes make use of the wit of an absent friend, and had a lively way of retailing a common-place or saying a mere nothing, that had great effect at a card-table. The ways and good jokes of Osborne Castle were now added to his ordinary means of entertainment. He repeated the smart sayings of *Miss Osborne*, detailed the oversights of *Miss Carr*, and indulged them even with a copy of Lord Osborne's style of overdrawing himself on both cards.

The clock struck nine while he was thus agreeably occupied; and when Nanny came in with her master's basin of gruel, he had the pleasure of observing to Mr Watson that he should leave him at supper while he went home to dinner himself. The carriage was ordered to the door, and no entreaties for his staying longer could now avail; for he well knew that if he stayed he must sit down to supper in less than ten minutes, which to a man whose heart had been long fixed on calling his next meal a dinner, was quite insupportable. On finding him determined to go, Margaret began to wink and nod at Elizabeth to ask him to dinner for the following day, and Elizabeth at last not able to resist hints which her own hospitable, social temper more than half seconded, gave the invitation: "Would *you* give Robert the meeting, *we* should be very happy?"

"With the greatest pleasure;" was his first reply. In a moment afterwards, "That is, if I can possibly get here in time; but I shoot with Lord Osborne *who has brought a party of young men from London for two days*, and therefore must not engage. You will not think of me unless you see me." And so, he departed, delighted with the uncertainty in which he had left it.

Margaret, in the joy of her heart under circumstances which she chose to consider as peculiarly propitious, would willingly have made a confidante of Emma when they were alone for a short time the next morning, and had proceeded so far as to say, "The young man who was here last night, my dear Emma, and returns today, is more interesting to me than perhaps you may be aware—"; but Emma, pretending to understand nothing extraordinary in the words, made some very inapplicable reply, and jumping up, ran away from a subject which was odious to her feelings. As Margaret would not allow a doubt to be repeated of Musgrave's coming to dinner, preparations were made for his entertainment much exceeding what had been deemed necessary the day before; and taking the office of superintendence entirely from her sister, she was half the morning in the kitchen herself, directing and scolding *Betty and Nanny about their work*. After a great deal of indifferent cooking and anxious suspense, however, they were obliged to sit down without their guest. Tom Musgrave never came; and Margaret was at no pains to conceal her vexation under the disappointment, or repress the peevishness of her temper.

The peace of the party for the remainder of that day and the whole of the next, which comprised the length of Robert's and Jane's visit, was continually invaded by her fretful displeasure and querulous attacks. Elizabeth was the usual object of both. Margaret had just respect enough for her brother's and sister's opinion to behave properly by them, but Elizabeth and the maids could never do anything right; and Emma, whom she seemed no longer to think about, found the continuance of the gentle voice beyond her calculation short.

Eager to be as little among them as possible, Emma was delighted with the alternative of sitting above with her father *who was confined both days to his room*, and warmly entreated to be his constant companion each evening; and, as Elizabeth loved company of any kind too well not to prefer being below at all risks as she had rather talk of Croydon with Jane, with every interruption of Margaret's perverseness, than sit with only her father—who frequently could not endure talking at all—the affair was so settled, as soon as *Elizabeth* could be persuaded to believe it no sacrifice on her sister's part.

To Emma, the change was *a* most acceptable and delightful relief. Her father, if ill, required little more than gentleness and silence, and being a man of sense and education, was, if able to converse, a *pleasant* companion. In his chamber, Emma was at peace from the dreadful mortifications of unequal society and family discord; from the immediate endurance of hard-hearted prosperity, low-minded conceit, and wrong-headed folly, engrafted on an untoward disposition. She still suffered from them in the contemplation of their existence, in memory, and in prospect; but for the moment, she ceased to be tortured by their effects. She was at leisure; she could read and think, though her situation was hardly such as to make reflection very soothing. The evils arising from the loss of her uncle were neither trifling nor likely to lessen; and when thought had been freely indulged, in contrasting the past and the present, the employment of mind and dissipation of unpleasant ideas which only reading could produce made her thankfully turn to a book.

Chapter Eight

The Wickstead Party

Thursday, October 29th

The change in her home, society, and style of life, in consequence of the death of one friend and the imprudence of another, had indeed been striking *for Emma.*

From being the first object of hope and solicitude to an uncle who had formed her mind with the care of a parent, and of tenderness to an aunt whose amiable temper had delighted to give her every indulgence; from being the life and spirit of a house where all had been comfort and elegance, and the expected heiress of an easy independence, she was become of importance to no one—a burden on those whose affections she could not expect, an addition in a house already overstocked, surrounded by inferior minds, with little chance of domestic comfort, and as little hope of future support. It was well for her that she was naturally cheerful, for the change had been such as might have plunged weak spirits in despondence.

She was very much pressed by Robert and Jane to return with them to Croydon *on Thursday morning,* and had some difficulty in getting a refusal accepted, as they thought too highly of their own kindness and situation to suppose the offer could appear in a less advantageous light to anybody else. Elizabeth gave them her interest, though evidently against her own, in privately urging Emma to go.

"You do not know what you refuse, Emma," said she, "nor what you have to bear at home. I would advise you by all means to accept the invitation; there is always something lively going on at Croydon. You will be in company almost every day, and Robert and Jane will be very kind to you. As for me, I shall be no worse off without you than I have been used to be; but poor Margaret's disagreeable ways are new to you, and they would vex you more than you think for, if you stay at home *it would be a pity for you*."

Emma was of course uninfluenced, except to greater esteem for Elizabeth, by such representations, and the visitors departed without her.

END OF EDITED FRAGMENT[5]

Margaret made for Dorking to see Mary Edwards as soon as Robert and Jane had left them. She spent the next morning in Stanton and barely made it home before it began to rain, and Emma got to know as much of Margaret's personality as she cared to while they were trapped indoors over the next few days. Margaret was sweet one moment and peevish the next; she often took her feelings of discontent out on Elizabeth with snappish outbursts. To Emma her mannerisms changed from one moment to the next; sometimes she was all sisterly affection; sometimes she ignored her entirely; then sometimes she, like when she entered Emma and Elizabeth's room and saw some of Emma's "finery", began to flatter and cajole her to share her "good fortune".

Tuesday, November 3rd

On Sunday they plodded their way to the church with their father for service and back. Otherwise, they remained indoors. On Monday afternoon, the rain let up, but it was still much too muddy for walking; however, on Tuesday, Margaret was gone first thing to Dorking with the Misses Stokes in hopes of spying Mr Musgrave. Emma and Elizabeth had just stepped out for a walk as, though the air was crisp, it was just sunny and warm enough to encourage exercise after their seclusion.

---

[5] From this point on, all parts of the story were written, imagined, and created by this author.

They only made it to the gate when they noticed a carriage travelling their way. They waited in earnest curiosity as Elizabeth did not recognise the vehicle and horses, and they were both surprised, but not displeased, when Mr Howard, Mrs Blake, and young Charles stepped out.

Emma, who felt that their call was much more desirable than any of the previous visitors they had, greeted them warmly. She was grateful that Margaret had left them so early. When Mrs Blake and Charles noticed their dress and heard they were about to walk out, they offered to join them. While, in her heart, she wished to walk with Howard, Charles quickly offered himself as her escort, "Might I walk with you? I have been so eager to come and see you, but Mamma said we must wait; then Iggy got sick; then there was the rain keeping us at home, and—"

It was only his mother's calling him to order that stopped the stream of words, but his likeness to his mother became clear as she took over by thanking Emma for her actions at the ball and apologizing for waiting so long, "We meant to call last week once the illness had passed, but then Howard heard from Musgrave that you had guests, and so we waited—"

Between the two Blakes, Emma's attention was being entirely monopolized, and she could only just hear Howard's request to her sister.

Elizabeth was taken aback that Mr Howard should call on their family at all as she could only picture him among the Great People of the castle and was too much in awe to speak, until she felt all the gratification of his visit when he moved to her side and said, "While my sister and nephew have been eager to pay this visit to your sister, I must admit that I joined them in hopes of speaking more with your father." She knew this was one visitor who Mr Watson would be pleased to see.

Elizabeth was blushing to be in such close conference with him, and she responded quietly but in a quick voice, "I am sure my father will be glad to see you again; he spoke of the pleasure he had in meeting you at the visitation; I will just go to see if he is well enough to come down if you will follow me." Mrs Blake knew of her brother's intention and suggested they should walk nearby the house until Elizabeth returned, and Emma was left to guide them about the outside of the parsonage while her older sister had the pleasure of leading Mr Howard inside. If Mr Howard noticed her discomfort, he said nothing and only smiled at her. His expression did not ease her bewilderment, but it calmed her nerves enough for her to thank him, "for the care you showed our dear father at the visitation the other day," as she led him into the small parlour where a fire was already lit.

His smile widened, making her blush deepen as she noticed the dimples it gave him and took in his overall handsome appearance. "I must admit that, on hearing that Mr Watson—the father of the Miss Watson who was so kind as to rescue my nephew in his time of need—was attending the visitation, I became curious to meet him. When I saw that he needed assistance, how could I not repay the kindness his family had shown mine?"

In a state of awe, Elizabeth went upstairs to see her father while asking in an aside to Nanny, who had come out at the sound of the front door opening again, to bring some tea and biscuits to the parlour for their guest. She was even more surprised when she entered her father's room to see him up and dressing.

Mr Watson was much pleased to hear of his visitor and was enticed to go downstairs for the first time since Margaret's return excepting in their necessary attendance at church on Sunday. James had been coming in the back when he heard the young ladies greet their guests and, as he was on his way to see her father with a letter, informed him of their identity. He was soon ready, and James helped him to go down the stairs while Elizabeth preceded them.

Elizabeth collected the tea tray from Nanny and followed her father. Mr Howard stood to greet his host, and Mr Watson immediately took the seat across from Mr Howard. "I am sorry for the sudden invasion. I had wanted to call on you last week but waited after hearing that your oldest son was visiting." Mr Watson waved off his concerns and admitted that it had been a good decision not to call sooner as Elizabeth prepared their tea. Once she had served the men and made sure her father was comfortable being left alone, she turned to join the others outside.

As she closed the door, she heard Mr Howard inquire if he might be able to entice Mr Watson to attend the next visitation with him in January. "Of course, I would be happy to collect you in my carriage and drive you home afterwards."

She donned her outer-wear again and left the house, smiling as she thought of how lively her father was with his guest.

"I again must apologize for taking so long to call upon you after our last meeting," started Mrs Blake as Elizabeth and Howard entered the parsonage. "As Charles said, Ignatius, my youngest—who is just recently turned three—fell ill soon after the assembly, and, you know, such illness among young children spreads quickly from one to the next."

"I did not fall ill though, Miss Watson. My father always said that I was as hale and hearty a boy as ever was," said young Charles with pride.

Emma smiled at him while complimenting his heartiness. She barely managed to hold back her laughter as he puffed out his chest with pride while expounding on the truth of the matter. Emma was sad that she would have no chance to speak with Mr Howard, but she was not able to dwell on her disappointment for long. Her attention was again claimed by Charles asking, "Why did you not attend our hunt? I know you had guests last week, but Lord Osborne told me that he invited you himself a fortnight back. I was hoping that you would come to see us off as he suggested you might, but Mamma said that you must have been feeling the cold, for it was quite chilly that morning. Will you come to see us off next time?"

Emma was taken aback, she had never considered who might attend the hunt apart from Lord Osborne and Tom Musgrave, but now she remembered that Charles had informed her of his having been out with the hounds when they spoke at the assembly. "I am sorry. I had not considered that you might also be a part of the party or else I am sure I would have gone out to see you off since it was not too muddy at that time. You shall have to inform me when next you ride out."

"I will make sure to tell you, or I shall ask Mamma to write to you the next time—though I do not know when that shall be. Now that parliament is in session, Lord Osborne has set himself up at the family's house in town. Though I hope that he will return from time-to-time as he did last year."

Emma had not known that Lord Osborne would be attending parliament, though it made sense that the young viscount would have a seat in the House of Lords. She thought of her impressions of him so far and could not imagine that he would be a very effective politician between his age and his immaturity, but she did not dwell on those thoughts for long—else she might have considered how being thrust into such a position so young, not just the title but also of the responsibilities it included, might have affected his interactions and manners with those nearer his own age.

When Elizabeth returned, she joined Mrs Blake, and they all set off down a track in the nearby fields. Charles continued to speak to Emma of "how well Lord Osborne told him he had done in the hunts; how skilled he was in keeping his seat even when forced to gallop or jump; and how he was only likely to improve." Meanwhile, Mrs Blake began to speak with Elizabeth about the difference in housekeeping and other duties necessary to manage her brother's parsonage as opposed to when she had lived in rented apartments with the other sailors' wives.

Through listening in on the mother's conversation, Emma learned that Mrs Blake had only been living at the rectory since the summer and was still getting used to all the extra duties that came with the running of a parsonage, including visiting the parishioners. During a lull in his dialogue, Emma asked Charles loud enough to gain his mother's attention if he had not been at Wickstead long. "Oh yes," he said, "I have been living with Uncle Philip for nearly a year now."

On hearing the turn in the conversation, Mrs Blake turned to Emma, "Tragedy came upon us when Captain Blake was killed in battle in January last year. We had been living in apartments in Portsmouth for several years and had finally managed to purchase a small cottage near Plymouth the previous spring. However, we were not there a full year before the news came of my husband's passing during a minor naval battle in the Strait of Gibraltar." As she spoke, tears came unbidden to her eyes, but she ignored them, took a deep calming breath, and carried on.

"My brother graciously offered to take in Charles after he received the news though it was some months later as he had been on the continent with Lord Osborne. However, it was some months more before I could bring myself to part with my home. I remained there for over a year before I realised that I had been waiting for someone who would never return." She paused again, and Elizabeth patted the arm that she was holding in consolation until Mrs Blake smiled and continued. "My brother must have noticed something of my feelings in my letters and offered to help with the sale of the cottage—inviting to house us all at his own expense. He even allowed me to keep the money from the sale to add to my own small fortune. I have been so blessed and am truly grateful to have such a brother."

Emma's eyes widened at the mention of money, for it was not something to be spoken of in company, especially with such new acquaintances, but Elizabeth simply nodded, and Charles spoke of his pride in having such a "kind and gentlemanly uncle to learn from."

By this time, they had returned to the parsonage where Mr Howard was deep in conversation with Mr Watson. The two men looked up as the others joined them, but, before Mr Howard could do more than look at the clock and mention the time, Elizabeth had invited them to stay a little longer to allow Mrs Blake and Charles to warm up with some fresh tea. The men agreed and continued their discussion.

Once the tea things arrived and they were served, Mrs Blake started up where she had left off, speaking of how her brother helped them adjust to their new lives, praising him the whole time, which Mr Howard pretended not to hear. However, when his flushed countenance was noticed by Mr Watson—who suggested "the fire might be too warm for one as young and healthy" as him, his attention was clear. He directed a chagrined smile at his sister as he tried to convince his host "that he was not hot; that the temperature of the room was to be appreciated on such a day; and that he did not feel any discomfort to require the repositioning of his chair."

Mrs Blake gave a knowing smile and winked at the other ladies. "My brother is shy of hearing his own praise, but he deserves it. Being a sailor's wife, I saw and learned many things. It is not every woman who has such a person in their family who would take on a widowed relation and her four young children without even any interest in claiming some right to her small jointure." Emma blushed in mortification as Mrs Blake again mentioned money, though she and Elizabeth could both appreciate what her praise said about Mr Howard's character, and it was clear in the looks they directed towards him. Mrs Blake continued to sing the praises of her brother until his neck and ears became quite red, and Mr Watson—who had entirely ignored the other conversation—insisted that he must be overheated.

Mr Howard mentioned the hour, and they realised that their visit had far exceeded the acceptable calling time. So, he stood, leading the rest to follow his example. Mr Howard promised to send notice ahead of time when he would next attend the visitation. Mrs Blake informed Elizabeth that she would write to her and visit again to discuss parish matters if she would have her. Lastly, Charles was expressive in inviting the Watson ladies to Wickstead at their earliest convenience with the support of his guardians.

Elizabeth agreed that she would be more than happy to speak again with Mrs Blake and to host her anytime the older lady should wish it. Meanwhile, both sisters welcomed the invitation to call on the family at Wickstead whenever they might be spared by their father, and they expressed their hope that they might see more of their new friends soon. Then the guests were off.

Emma was smiling to herself in satisfaction for how the visit had gone; she was happy to see how well Mr Howard got on with her father and how well received he was in their home. She did not know much of Wickstead, but she was sure that Howard could not be so callous as to judge their parsonage wanting—being a clergyman himself. She therefore had no need to feel the shame and embarrassment on his visit that she had on the visit of Lord Osborne. Meanwhile, Elizabeth sat in bemusement until her father remarked that he felt well enough to call on his friend, Mr Edwards. Elizabeth was shocked all over again, but she duly called for James to get the chair hitched up while she ran upstairs to grab what he might need to travel out in such chilly weather.

Once their father had gone, the two girls shared their opinion of the visit. Elizabeth admitted, "After hearing Mrs Blake's account of her brother, and seeing him being so solicitous of our father, I have a new appreciation of him and can better understand your admiration." Emma took pleasure in hearing her sister praise the man she admired but, curious, pressed for more details about her conversation with Mrs Blake. Elizabeth explained that Mrs Blake had inquired about her duties towards the parishioners. Emma could not help but wonder why she had come to Elizabeth for such advice, but before she could ask more, Margaret returned.

Margaret's consternation at seeing Emma and Elizabeth so happy was clear in her expression, and Elizabeth informed Margaret of the guests that she had missed that morning. "I would not have minded some decent company, though I doubt that such guests could have meant anything to me. I have heard Musgrave mention that Howard does not always seem to like him and even persuades Lord Osborne from joining in his plans more often than not." Emma believed that this was no blemish on Howard's person but a sign of the poor character of the speaker.

"It matters not though, while we did not see Musgrave in town today as he has gone off to London again—though his man could not say when he should return—I doubt Mr Howard would have had any knowledge of it." She gave a huff of annoyance, complained that they had not saved any tea or treats for her, and then took herself upstairs and was not seen again until supper.

Emma then realised that nothing short of Tom Musgrave could arouse her sister's interest.

Nearly an hour after Mr Watson had left them, James was sent back with the chair and a note from their father saying that "he would dine with his friend who would return him in his own carriage."

As Margaret did not return downstairs and later requested her dinner be brought to her room, Elizabeth and Emma were left to discuss the morning's guests. Once they finished their meal, Emma went to the parlour with a book to read and Elizabeth went out for a while.

Elizabeth had always made sure to spend time with Emma; she was often here and there running errands for her father or dealing with the management of their home while Emma amused herself, and sometimes their father, with a book. Emma began to feel guilty for her idleness and decided she would help with more of the chores around the house as well as joining Elizabeth on her trips into the village in the future. Any company was always much appreciated by Elizabeth, and it would aid the two in deepening their friendship. However now, in her solitude, she considered all that had happened and all she had learned since her coming into Stanton. It was the first moment she had been truly alone with her thoughts, except in sleep, since Margaret's return. Emma was glad that she could make a friend out of at least one of her siblings as she had already ruled out any likelihood of building an amicable relationship with Robert, Penelope, or Margaret.

She began to consider her future. Her father's health was precarious, but he did not seem to be at death's door; he was nowhere near as frail as Uncle Turner had been in his last years. However, the others knew him better and Robert's comments that first night that they should go to Croydon should anything happen had haunted her lonely thoughts and dreams. To be reliant on the unequal society of such narrow-minded people as Robert and Jane, in the company of Margaret—who might never cease pining after Musgrave, was not to be borne. She needed to marry, but she did not wish to be like Margaret or Penelope—pining and chasing after men. However, she was sure that would not happen.

Howard's arrival today and his interest in her family could only be due to some partiality towards her as he had no contact with her family prior to their meeting. It was decided. She would encourage him—as much as was appropriate within the rules of good breeding—to pursue his course. Marriage with a good and respectable man of good education was just the thing to settle her and see to her happiness.

Chapter Nine

Visit to Wickstead

Wednesday, November 4ᵗʰ

The invitation to Wickstead arrived the following day. Elizabeth and Emma were invited to call at their earliest convenience on Friday and to stay for dinner if they wished. Though Emma was eager to make the most of such an opportunity, she did not want to appear too forward or impose upon their hosts. She quickly agreed with Elizabeth's suggestion that they arrive around ten or eleven and return home in time for dinner. Their reply was dispatched within a quarter of an hour with the young man Mr Howard had hired to deliver notes. Later that day, they received another message informing them that Mr Howard would send his carriage for them at nine and send them home again whenever they wished to depart.

While the two sisters were delighted for their upcoming plans, Margaret was not. Her attitude of goodwill towards Emma began to flag in light of her jealousy. "Why should only the two of you be invited? It's not as if they don't know that I am here as well—even if I was not here when they came yesterday. I have just as much right, and more so than Emma who is younger and has been here barely a month, to receive such an invitation."

"My dear Margaret, Emma is the only reason that such an invitation has been made. If it were not for her dancing with Charles Blake at the assembly, we would not have had the introduction to the family."

"All the more! If they wished to be intimate with our *family*, then it is only right that *all* the family should be included."

"They do not even know you. Perhaps had you been here to be introduced—"

"I do not see how that is important. It is very rude of them to only invite the two of you and leave me out; to take away all my female company and leave me alone with our ailing father," she turned to Emma now adding a sweetness to her voice which set Emma's teeth on edge, "surely you must admit to the impropriety of their neglect of me, dear Emma."

Emma did not agree, but she also did not wish to exacerbate her sister's tirade. "It is as Elizabeth said: they do not know you. But perhaps—" she was loathe to give in, even a little, to her sister's greed but suggested, "we could mention it to them on this visit; if we offer a proper introduction be made before the next meeting, I am sure they would be agreeable."

Margaret's countenance darkened when she realised she would be denied, and she nearly interrupted her sister; however, though still contrite, she was somewhat mollified by Emma's suggestion. It did not help her ill-humour though, and she spent the rest of the next two days while she was at home huffing about the injustice of it all.

Elizabeth tried to excuse Margaret's behaviour by pointing out that Musgrave had not yet returned from London; however, Emma doubted that anything short of Musgrave appearing at Stanton and bending a knee to her sister would make Margaret agreeable—an event she found highly unlikely. She could not help but feel a quiet relief that Margaret would not be joining them, and she regretted having to promise to request her sister's inclusion in future invitations. It went against both her conscience and her upbringing.

Friday, November 6th

When the carriage came on Friday, Margaret came down fully ready to join them, and Emma feared she would try to force them to bring her to Wickstead. "I see your thinking, Emma; I have no interest in going where I am not welcome, but, since you must travel through Dorking, there is no reason you cannot take me that far."

Emma held back a sigh as Elizabeth continued to speak to James and Nanny about their father's dinner and when to serve it if they had not returned by the usual dinner hour. When she was done, Emma told her of Margaret's demand. She had hoped her eldest sister would speak sense into the younger, but she was only to be disappointed. Elizabeth instead went to speak to the driver about dropping off Margaret at the Edwardses' house. Emma thought she could detect some reluctance on the part of the driver as he watched Margaret let herself into the carriage, but he tipped his hat at Elizabeth and climbed onto the box.

The ride to Dorking was an uncomfortable one for Emma, but, luckily, Mr Howard's carriage made better time than old Molly and the cart. So, it was only just over twenty minutes when they pulled up at the Edwardses' door. Once Margaret was gone, they could continue on in peace. As the carriage pulled away from Dorking, Emma exhaled, long and slow, her eyes drifting over the hills beyond the window. Elizabeth, however, showed no such relief. She sat stiffly, hands folded in her lap and brow furrowed in thought.

Emma turned to her. "Have Margaret's complaints set you on edge? You seem troubled."

Elizabeth glanced at her, distracted. "Margaret? Oh, no. I hardly heard her. I was thinking about Mrs Blake."

Emma was surprised that anyone could ignore Margaret's commotion but kept her expression smooth. "Mrs Blake?"

"She asked me in a general sense of the duties of a clergyman's wife the last time we spoke, but we did not have time to go into specifics. I expect she'll have more questions today." Elizabeth toyed with the edge of her glove. "I should know what to tell her, having followed my mother in it for so many years, but I keep wondering if I am actually qualified. There's so much I take for granted—so much I do by habit. What if she needs something more than I can offer?"

Emma turned her gaze back out the window. She could not tell her sister how much she agreed—'*Why ask Elizabeth at all? Mrs Blake is older, better educated, and a mother besides. Surely, she knows enough already. And if not,*' she felt the thought rise before she could stop it, '*would not someone more experienced in running a good household*'—someone like Emma herself—'*be the better choice?*'

But she only said, "I am sure you will think of something."

Elizabeth let out a breath, shaking her head. "I hope so. I do so wish to be useful. It's not every day that someone comes to me for such advice."

Emma hummed, offering a small, tight-lipped smile. Elizabeth was too wrapped in her own worries to notice that her sister did not quite share them. She wondered if Mrs Blake was actually sincere in her questioning—'*Or perhaps it was just a pretext for her and her brother to deepen the bond between our two families?*' With this thought, she smiled fully and was able to enjoy the view outside.

It was another hour before they reached Wickstead, and they were happy to get out and stretch their legs again. Mrs Blake, Charles, and three other children—two standing next to an older girl and one in her arms—greeted them in front of the parsonage.

"Welcome to our humble home," intoned Mrs Blake as they stepped forward. "I do hope that you have not had too long of a journey. Would you prefer to take a short walk before having tea, or shall we head on in? Ah, but before that, do let me introduce my younger children: Philip, Elizabeth, and Ignatius—whom I spoke of before. And this is Hannah, their nurse." Each of the children stepped forward with a little bow or curtsy—except the youngest who hid his head in his nurse's shawl—when their name was called. "They did so wish to greet you properly; we have all been looking forward to your visit, but now it is time for them to return to their studies—yes, Charles, you as well. If you finish then I will allow you to join us a little later. Off you go now."

Emma was surprised by the quickness of the whole event, but Elizabeth simply smiled and waved goodbye to the children. "My, what a lovely family you have, Mrs Blake."

"Yes. I am quite proud of them—though they can be scamps from time to time," she said with a loving smile. "But enough of the Mrs Blake talk—I am hoping we shall all become good friends today. Please, do call me Mary. Oh, my, your hands are cold!" She had taken Elizabeth's hand in hers to show her sincerity in the offer only to notice how chilled she had become. Emma then realised that Elizabeth must have taken off her gloves at some point in the journey—likely to avoid wearing any holes in them as they were already thread bare.

"Well, a walk is certainly out of the question. Let us head in and get you warmed up. I will have some tea ready in no time." She continued speaking amicably as she led them inside to the front parlour which was already warmed by a strong fire.

Emma looked around and noted that, while the rectory was of a respectable size and larger than her father's, the house itself bore signs of neglect. The paint on the window frames was peeling, and the roof showed uneven patches where repairs had been made with little care for appearance. She could not help but wonder—'*Could the Osbornes not have seen to such matters before bestowing the living on a friend?*' Surely a man of Mr Howard's character deserved better than a house that seemed given with indifference. Then she noticed that Mrs Blake had said nothing of her brother's absence and inquired after him.

"Oh, Philip is out today. We do not expect him to return until sometime near the supper hour—it is one of the reasons I hoped you would both be able to join me. It is one of the few days that he could leave me the use of the carriage to fetch you here and back again."

Emma worked hard to hide her disappointment, but Elizabeth's look of pity told her that she had not hidden her thoughts as well as she hoped. Happily, Mrs Blake seemed not to notice and continued on in the way she had since they arrived which gave Emma time to contemplate this turn of events. Was the invitation not an excuse to get to know her better? Perhaps Mr Howard had not known he would be called away? Or perhaps his sister's opinion meant so much to him that he wanted them to get closer?

In the end, Emma decided it would be best to use the time to strengthen her relationship with Mrs Blake—Mary, ensuring she could count on her approbation when Mr Howard came to the point. She re-joined the conversation just as the tea things were brought in, only to find that the subject had shifted entirely.

"I admit, I have been running the place much the same as our little cottage in Plymouth. Are there any particular expectations, especially with regards to hosting or how I conduct myself in the community? I would not want to offend anyone by accident."

"Indeed. You will likely be expected to host tea or small gatherings for the ladies of the parish. Though not a requirement, some clergy families invite a few parishioners for dinner on Sundays. The previous parson's wife may have done things in a certain way that the locals are used to, but every woman brings her own habits."

"What about the servants? Should they be chosen from among the parishioners?" She glanced upstairs to where the light sound of the children could be heard. "We brought young Hannah with us, and I have heard some ladies—not anyone of importance mind you—saying that I think my children too good to be nursed by such small-town folk; Hannah is the youngest of twelve and was so happy when we offered to bring her with us, but Mrs Potts—our housekeeper who brought the tea—is thinking to retire to her son's farm, and I worried about where to look for her replacement."

"Hmm..." Elizabeth considered this, "Hiring servants from the parish can be a kindness, but it depends on their qualifications—sometimes an experienced servant is needed to keep things running smoothly. You might try hiring one or two local girls but ensure you have someone reliable to oversee them."

Mrs Blake breathed a sigh. "That is good to know. I mean, it is usual to find servants locally, but the circumstances and expectations seem so different for a parson's family."

Elizabeth smiled. "Though I have lived in a parsonage all my life, I can imagine what you mean though I never thought about it before. We all have our own skills and learning, I suppose."

Elizabeth spoke in such a mature and composed manner, unlike what Emma had heard from her before, and Emma found herself a little in awe of her eldest sister for the first time. She was so captivated by the discrepancy in Elizabeth's mannerisms that she could not bring herself to do more than listen as she sipped her tea.

"What about visits to the parishioners?" continued Mrs Blake. "How often should I make them, and what sort of gifts would be appreciated?"

"Ah. That depends on the household. Some families require more frequent visits, especially if there is illness or hardship, while others prefer only an occasional call. Once a month is usually sufficient for most, but there are a few who would appreciate more, or less, regular attention. As for gifts, practical items are best—tea, sugar, or a joint of meat for larger families, or warm clothing for the elderly in winter. Small luxuries like ribbons or sweets for the children are also well received. The key is to bring something thoughtful rather than extravagant."

Mrs Blake nodded along as Elizabeth made suggestions, and smiled at the mention of children—likely thinking of her own in the same situation. "What about if there are disagreements between parishioners, am I expected to mediate, or should I leave that to my brother? There was a hubbub back in September, but I was so new to the place that Philip told me not to worry about it."

Elizabeth thoughtfully sipped her tea as she considered her response. "It depends on the nature of the dispute. My mother always said that a clergyman's wife should listen but not interfere unless absolutely necessary." She paused again before continuing, "If it's a domestic matter, it is best left alone unless advice is sought. But if it is a quarrel between parishioners that affects parish harmony, sometimes a quiet word or gentle redirection can help. I try to be diplomatic—though I admit, sometimes it is best to let my father handle it." Then she grinned ruefully, "Now, with my father being an invalid, I have taken on more of the work though James—my father's manservant—also helps. You might wish to familiarize yourself with who lives on the land and their concerns in case any problems arise in the future."

"Then I will do as you say, listening to their complaints but allowing my brother to handle matters. It is just that my brother was never sure how far I should be involved, for the widow of the previous rector chose to live nearby after her husband's death and my brother paid her a small stipend to continue her duties—though he never thought to ask what they included."

Elizabeth smiled, "I am not surprised. My father has held his living here for a dozen years, and held the previous one even longer, yet I am sure he does not know half the mistress's duties." They both laughed.

"It is just so much to take in." Then Mrs Blake turned to look at Emma. "Oh! My dear Miss Emma, I do not want you to feel you are being left out, but you must know what a lot of work it all is. You, yourself, are so new to it as well, no? It must be rather daunting—having been brought up, as I understand, in more comfortable circumstances?" she said as she refilled everyone's tea.

Emma was unable to respond as she had no idea of the duties and responsibilities that were required of her sister. After a moment's pause she simply nodded and gave a non-committal response which was apparently enough for Mrs Blake, who then continued her questioning of Elizabeth.

"If there are any particular charities the previous minister's family supported, should I continue them? Or am I expected to start my own initiatives?"

"There may be some existing charities you are expected to support, but your parishioners would have more information about which are anticipated and which are optional. My mother ran a sewing circle in Stanton on Thursdays to provide clothing for the poor, and I continued it, though I adjusted it to focus more on infant clothing and mending, as there seemed to be a greater need. If no traditions are in place, you might start with whatever you are comfortable with—whether it's visiting the poor, organizing collections, or supporting the local school."

"My goodness, you have given me much to think on, but I believe I hear the children getting up from their studies. They will be needing some exercise, and, if you are willing, you are welcome to join us on a walk. I shall promise to treat you both to some hot cocoa or cider on our return. However, I do have one last question with Christmas coming—Am I expected to organise church festivals, gatherings, or other celebrations?"

"That depends on your parish. My mother oversaw Christmas and harvest celebrations, making sure there was food for the poor and organizing a modest gathering. I find it useful to ask the older ladies of the parish what has been done before—again some churches have traditions you would not want to disrupt. But if nothing is well-established, you may have the freedom to shape it as you please."

That was all they were able to say before the children burst into the room and were almost as immediately bustled out by their mother to don their outerwear.

When they were back in the carriage and on their way home, Emma sat in contemplation for some time before finally turning to her sister.

"Elizabeth," she asked hesitantly, "do you really do all those things you spoke to Mrs Blake about?"

Elizabeth looked at her in mild surprise. "What do you mean?"

Emma frowned. "I mean, how is it you never said anything to me about it before? If it is your duty as Father's daughter, then it must be mine as well as Margaret's and Penelope's." Elizabeth only stared at her, and Emma sighed. "You could have asked me for help—you *should* have asked me for help." She shook her head, guilt creeping into her voice. "Not only have I not been helping as I should, but I did not even know you needed it. There I was, idling the days away, and you were off making clothes for children, visiting the parishioners with gifts, and handling everything alone."

Elizabeth laughed. But she saw her sister's consternation and explained, "I was not always alone as the sewing circle involves many ladies in the area." When Emma's face showed she would not accept her sister's deflection, she continued. "When you arrived, you seemed so melancholy, so out of place. I did not want to burden you further."

Emma's frown deepened. "But you could have brought it up since then."

Elizabeth sighed. "I suppose I could have, but to be honest, I simply did not think about it. I have been doing everything on my own for so long, it never occurred to me to ask for help." She offered a small, wry smile. "Penelope does offer now and then, but she is not particularly good with her hands. And with her way of speaking, she's more likely to offend the parishioners and tenants than to do any real good. As for Margaret—she can be charming when she wants to be, but she never does anything unless there's something in it for her. So, after our mother died, all the household and parish duties outside of Father's direct responsibilities naturally fell to me. I have simply become accustomed to it."

Emma considered her sister's words and was slightly mollified. But still, she set her chin determinedly.

"Well, you do not have to do everything on your own anymore," she declared. "You can expect help from me from now on. After all, I may need to learn these duties and responsibilities as well."

Chapter Ten

Duties

Saturday, November 7th

Emma did not wait to join her sister in her duties. When they had returned home on Friday, Emma had insisted they use the afternoon to start her training immediately after dinner. Margaret had not yet returned from Dorking, so they had gone to the back pantry where Elizabeth had items set aside for the poor and needy. They had spent the next few hours preparing baskets with food, blankets, and other necessities for struggling families. The task itself was not so difficult, but the pantry was rather cold, so they had not been able to work there for too long at one time.

On Saturday morning, they hitched up Molly and packed the baskets onto the old cart.

"We can use Molly and the cart to visit with most of the parishioners, but there are some we must walk to see. Some of the lanes are very ill-kept and often too narrow; we might never be able to turn the old cart around should we try them."

It was a damp, windy, and cold November, and Emma was shivering before they even reached the first of the houses.

The first stop was to and elderly widow who lived in a modest cottage not a mile from the rectory. When they arrived, Elizabeth simply knocked and announced herself before entering. Her behaviour shocked Emma so much that she stood outside for a full minute before Elizabeth returned to usher her in.

Their hostess was a tiny woman who looked several years older than their father. She was sitting in a large chair next to the fire with a knitted shawl wrapped around her shoulders and her dressing gown visible underneath. The difference in her size to that of the chair in which she sat was almost laughable, and made Emma smile.

The old woman smiled at them and said, "Do please shut the door, dears. These old bones are not what they used to be and the cold does bite."

Elizabeth smiled warmly, "Good afternoon, Mrs Brown. We have brought you a few things for the colder weather. Some bread, preserves, and a pair of stockings."

"Oh, Miss Watson, you are too kind. My old stockings are so thin, I might as well have none at all. And this jam—did Betty make it? She always does such a fine job of it."

Elizabeth chuckled, "Betty prefers to supervise jam-making rather than partake in it, but I shall pass along your compliment to Nanny." She nodded at Emma to come forward. "This is my youngest sister, Emma, recently returned to us after staying with an aunt in Shropshire. She has been very helpful to me in preparing gifts this visit."

Once the usual greetings and inquiries were made, Emma tentatively said, "Mrs Brown, if there is anything else you find yourself in need of, I should be glad to help."

The old widow smiled, "You are very good, Miss Emma. My firewood is running low—Mr Davies sent someone to chop it up for me, but carrying it in tires me so when it gets this cold. If someone could help…" she let the suggestion trail off.

"We shall send a boy from the village to help," Elizabeth said as Emma hesitated not knowing what to do, "and do not hesitate to ask when you have need. That is what we are here for."

After a little more small talk, the widow needed rest, and they continued to their next stop.

Feeling that she should give Emma some warning about their intended recipients beforehand, she informed her sister about the next family. "Mr and Mrs Porter are next. They are a young couple who have not been married above two years and their little boy has recently fallen ill." She went into more detail as they drove up to a small, slightly draughty-looking cottage.

The woman who opened the door looked not much older than Emma except for the deep, dark bags that highlighted her sunken eyes. She held an infant in her arms, and Emma could see that his face was flushed with fever as he whimpered and flailed about.

Mrs Porter was weary when she opened the door, but her look turned to one of relief when she saw Elizabeth. "Miss Watson! You are most welcome! I don' a know what to do—Harry 'as been feverish since yesterday, and, withou' the money to buy medicine, I fear the worst."

Elizabeth placed her hand gently on the child's forehead, "His fever is high, but I have seen worse—and most recover. Have you tried a cool compress?"

"I've not. I was afraid it may make him colder."

Emma, worried for the small boy, eagerly said, "We can help! If you show me where to find one, I will soak a cloth in cool water and hold it to his forehead. My governess used to do the same for me when I was ill."

Mrs Porter looked to Emma for the first time when she spoke as if she had not even noticed her. Then she shrank back with a look of distrust.

"My apologies, Mrs Porter," Elizabeth said, stepping forward. "Allow me to introduce my youngest sister—Emma—who has just returned to us from living with an aunt in Shropshire. She is eager to help and offered me her assistance in future. You can trust her the same as me." As she continued to speak in a calm, soothing voice, Mrs Porter began to relax and move forward shyly.

"I'm sorry, Miss Emma. I don' meet many new people these days."

"It is no trouble, Mrs Porter. I can understand your being wary to trust your child with a stranger; however, I only wish to help."

"Allow Emma to see what she can do with little Harry while I clean up." Mrs Porter tried to protest, but Elizabeth gently raised the child from his mother's arms and handed him to Emma who took him cautiously into her own embrace. "And *you* must rest, Mrs Porter. It won't do to have you getting sick as well. I have some broth and bread from the rectory for the both of you as well as a few more provisions to help you keep up your strength until the illness passes. Now you just come sit and get some vitals in you, then off to bed."

When they left the newly cleaned cottage two hours later, the child's fever had cooled slightly, and the newly rested Mrs Porter was wiping tears from her eyes as she saw them out. "You're too good to me, truly. I don' a know what I would've done without you."

Elizabeth left Mrs Porter with a commission to take Harry to the apothecary should the fever rise again and to bill it to the parson's account. She also promised to send someone to see about the draught.

Once they had gone a good distance from the house, Emma said, "How do you know so much about everyone? And how do you always know just what to say? I was so shocked when I saw those two—they looked so near to expiring, I almost froze on the spot."

"You forget, Emma. I have been doing this for years. Even before mother passed, I was often traveling with her to meet parishioners. When you live so long in one place, you get to know people." She turned and grinned at Emma, "And you learn who to visit to hear all the latest news. In small villages like these, there is always someone who seems to have a sense for everything going on."

Their next stop was to see Mr Haybyrne who was outside repairing a fence around his animal pen when they pulled up. He straightened to face them when he heard the carriage and covered his eyes from the glare of the midday sun.

"Good day, Mr Haybyrne. I hope your leg is troubling you less today?"

Mr Haybyrne just grunted and said, "As much as it ever does in this damp weather. But there an't much we can do about that now is there?" He looked at Emma, and Elizabeth made the introductions.

"We have brought you a stronger tonic from the apothecary that might help ease the pain," Emma said hesitatingly.

"A tonic won't fix this fence, Miss Emma," he said with a little huff, and his rough manner of speech caused her to wince.

Elizabeth was unaffected by his coolness as she answered for her sister, "Then we shall send a boy to help you mend it. There is no sense in worsening your leg over it."

He softened a little after hearing her offer. "Aye, well… if that Jones boy is willing, I'd not say no. He has a skill for this kind of work, ya know. Need to get him into a 'prenticeship o' some kind, but I'd hate to see him go."

"Then it's settled. I will ask that he come over straight after services tomorrow." They stayed to see him back inside and, with a wave, were off again.

～ 𝒸𝓮𝓸𝓮 ～

On their way back to Stanton, they stopped in to see Mrs Davies, the local blacksmith's wife. She met them outside, wiping her hands on her apron.

"Miss Watson! And you must be Miss Emma!" she said with a beaming smile to welcome them. "Have you come to see my husband? He's just finishing a fine set of horseshoes for Mr Edward's horses."

"Actually, we have come to see you," said Elizabeth with equal enthusiasm for her old friend. "How are young Jacob and little Jemima?"

The proud mother laughed. "Growing too fast! Jacob is already reaching for his father's tools, and Jemima has started her teething."

"Perhaps Jacob will grow just as large as his father and follow in his trade," Elizabeth predicted.

"Or perhaps he'll fancy himself a gentleman and read books all day like the rector!" she teased back. "Though with the way he eats us out of hearth and home, you may be right," she said more seriously.

"Whatever he chooses, he will do it well, I am sure."

They did not stay at the Davies' house long because they had some errands to run in town before returning home—including informing whoever needed to be told about the promises and plans they had made that day.

They still had to make calls on all the parishioners whose homes could only be reached on foot, but, when they returned home, Emma was chilled from the damp, cold air and exhausted from the hours of unaccustomed labour, so she fell asleep without a thought for tomorrow.

Sunday, November 8th

The next morning Emma was still fatigued when she crawled out of bed to attend the morning services with her family. As she sat in the pews, she noticed for the first time the cold draughts coming in from ill-fitted doors and windows which made her shiver through the service. But Emma had always been rather hearty, so she waved off her sister's concern.

That day they also visited many ill residents, though Emma was sure their ill-health must be due to the condition of their homes: poorly ventilated, full of stale air and smoke from hearths, and sometimes even with leaking roofs.

The latter was the case in the second house they visited. It had begun to drizzle off and on that day, and, while it was not a heavy rain, it was enough to cause some damage. They were informed that a large branch had fallen onto the house recently due to rot, and no one could come to fix it until the following day. However, the rain was just heavy enough that they decided to empty the room and close it off until it was patched. So, Emma and Elizabeth joined the family in removing the furniture and other items.

Their last visit was to a dimly lit little cottage which smelled of stale air and other scents not meant for company. The owner, Mr Jepson, was a thin, old man with a deeply furrowed brow. He was sitting by the fireplace huddled in layers of blankets, and Emma was sure he must also be wrapped in all the bed-linen he owned. Elizabeth warned her that he had a sharp tongue, but she was not prepared for his acerbic temperament.

"Good afternoon, Mr Jepson. I hope we find you in tolerable health today," she greeted him cheerily as she entered with her basket of provisions.

"Tolerable? Ha! No thanks to you or anyone else. I might as well be dead for all the good your visits do me."

Emma was startled by his hostility and glanced at Elizabeth before speaking, "I—we—brought some fresh bread and broth for you. Nanny made it herself just this morning."

He sniffed, "Ol' Mrs Pratchett's broth is it? Too thin by half, just like last time. If she thinks I'll waste my last days choking down watery soups, she's a greater fool than I thought. Still can't believe ol' Pratchett married the chit, but I'm sure that's what sent him to an early grave!"

Emma was visibly uncomfortable, shifting her weight from foot to foot, "I—I am sure it is not that bad. Nanny's cooking at the parsonage is always good."

He snorted and eyed her before responding, "'Not that bad', she says! Ha! That's the problem with you young people—thinking not bad is good enough. If I had my strength, I'd be making my own broth, and it wouldn't taste like ditch water, I can promise you that!"

Emma stepped slowly back while looking uncertainly at Elizabeth to see if they could leave now that the delivery was made. However, Elizabeth calmly ignored the old man's ravings. She had been tidying up as he spoke with Emma and continued as she said, "Next time, we will bring you something heartier, but only if you eat everything we brought you for today. There is no sense in letting good food go to waste."

"What difference does it make if I eat it? I guarantee you no one would care if I wasted away here! In this very chair! On this very day! Doubt anyone would even notice anyway." He started muttering halfway through, and Emma was not sure if she heard his last words correctly.

Elizabeth walked over to his side and took his old, gnarled hand in hers. "*I* would notice, and *I* would care," she said looking straight into his eyes.

"Hmph." He eyed her suspiciously and then repeated the sound. "I suppose you would, at that. You're just like your late mother. She never did have the good sense to leave an old man to die in peace, either."

Emma could no longer bear to listen to such offensive words and started, "Perhaps we should—"

But Elizabeth gently cut her off with, "Emma, do be a dear and warm the broth in that cauldron on the hearth? Mr Jepson prefers his food hot."

Emma, though eager to escape, did as her sister bid her while Elizabeth took great care to make their reluctant host more comfortable.

Mr Jepson continued to mutter and grumble for the rest of the visit, but Elizabeth just continued her ministrations while returning his barbed words with kindness.

"I will be back to check on you again next week, so take care of your health until then," she said as they prepared to leave.

"No use arguing with you."

"None at all," she replied with a laugh. Then they were off.

When they returned home, they only had time to clean up before they had to attend the evening services. Emma was both mentally and physically exhausted. She forewent supper and fell asleep as soon as she hit the bed.

The next day, Emma slept late. In fact, it was not until Elizabeth came to check on her for the third time just fifteen minutes before dinner that she was able to drag herself out of the room. Elizabeth encouraged her to get some rest, but Emma was sure she could still help out around the house. If nothing else, "she had to set out her gown for the assembly the next day."

By that evening, however, she was feverish with a sore throat, a runny nose, and a cough. So, Nanny prepared her some broth and powders, and sent her up to bed.

Chapter Eleven

In Sickness and in Memory

Elizabeth

Tuesday, November 10th

The next morning dawned cold, but clear; however, poor Emma was unable to rise with the others. While she was not on her deathbed, she had caught a bad cold and, after Mr Watson insisted on calling in the apothecary, was told to avoid any excessive movement. So, she was tasked to spend the next few days in bed and given willow-bark tea to soothe her throat and cough.

Downstairs, Margaret was unsympathetic to her younger sister's plight. "It serves her right," she said to Elizabeth as their father and the apothecary were upstairs with Emma. "Who told her to suddenly put on airs, playing the saint and parading her virtue—trying to show off by visiting the parishioners? She should have left it to you—*you* never fall ill from such trifling matters."

Elizabeth only sighed at her sister's tirade and continued to prepare tea for Emma without responding.

Her silence did not deter Margaret. "Well, at least now we know who'll be the one to stay behind with father. You should be pleased enough though; her getting sick means that you can take her place at the assembly. It's been quite some time since you, Mary, and I attended together. I am sure the Edwardses will be happy to have everything back to how it was before *she* came. Such a dark and prim little miss; I'm sure she will be missed by no one, certainly not Musgrave or—"

Elizabeth turned on her sister so fast that Margaret froze mid-speech, and in a harsh, no-nonsense voice said, "That. Is. Enough," enunciating each word. "I don't mind your caustic barbs and taunts towards me, but Emma has done nothing to warrant your sharp-tongued criticism, insults, or insinuations. If you cannot think of anything nice, then do not speak to me—for I have no interest in listening. Emma's interest in the parishioners and kindness in helping me with my duties—which is more than you have ever done—only show her own sweet temper and good nature."

On that note, she took up the tea tray and left the room, ignoring Margaret's huff of discontent and muttered complaints. Sometimes she simply went too far. To find fault in Emma, even now, was beyond reason. If something did not happen soon with Musgrave—one way or another—Margaret would become permanently insufferable.

As she reached the top of the stairs, the apothecary was just leaving Emma's room. She heard his conversation with her father and offered to see him out. Noticing her burden, her father offered to go down himself leaving Elizabeth to focus on her sister. She entered Emma's room after knocking lightly and hearing her sister's raspy response. Emma was lying propped up on the bed with a cold compress on her forehead. Her cheeks were aglow and glistened with sweat, and Elizabeth could not but feel for her youngest sister— especially when she thought of the cruelty that Margaret had been spouting only moments before.

Emma tried to sit up and speak but only managed a rasping cough, and Elizabeth stopped her. "My dear Emma, it pains me to see you so ill. I did try to warn you, it was all too much too soon. If you wish to continue visiting the parishioners with me after you heal, you will need to pace yourself better." She poured Emma a cup of the bitter drink and helped her to sip at it.

While Emma made a face of disgust, she dutifully drank until the tea aided in soothing her throat. "I do not understand you, Elizabeth. Such work is nothing out of the ordinary for you, and here you are whole and healthy to prove it." She coughed again, but it was less raspy than earlier. "I do not see why I should be any different. We are sisters after all."

"Sister's we may be, dear," Elizabeth said with a smile while caressing

Emma's hair, "but our lives and upbringing until now have been too dissimilar to warrant comparison."

"Well, I suppose if I do not wish to spend my life abed, I shall have to follow your guidance. I did not think it would be so tiring."

"Worry not," replied Elizabeth. "I shall stay with you and have you on the mend in no time."

"You—" Emma began to cough again, and Elizabeth helped her drink down some more tea when she calmed. "You shall do no such thing. The family cannot afford for you to be ill with me—I still cannot believe father called in the apothecary for a small cold."

Elizabeth continued stroking Emma's hair, but her eyes became distant, and she was silent for so long that Emma began to fidget.

Emma

Emma watched the change in Elizabeth's expression and felt the room still around them. Finally, when she thought she might not be able to wait any longer, Elizabeth said, "Our father was very worried for you—and for good reason. I don't know if it was ever explained—I could not bring myself to write you about the details—but Mamma—" she stopped as tears swam in her eyes and clogged her throat, and there was another pause. However, this time Emma was waiting with baited breath to hear the rest.

Eventually, Elizabeth pulled herself together and looked at Emma with haunted eyes. "Mamma was over forty when she gave birth to Sam and yourself, you know. However, she never regretted having children so late—indeed she called us all her 'blessings'." She smiled gently, and Emma returned the smile out of habit. "She was never quite healthy after those late births. She became frail and caught ill so easily."

She looked away again, but this time towards the door, "Father loved her so dearly and was always solicitous of her health. You may not believe it, but he was hardly ever ill when she was with us." She sighed, "It was nearly eight years ago—this coming January—when she was caring for one of the sick tenants who came down with consumption and went into early labour—nearly two months before her time. It was a long labour, but eventually the child was stillborn, and the mother did not long survive the babe."

Emma could only sit quietly and listen. She could see the tears in Elizabeth's eyes though her sister continued her narrative.

"Mamma came home after three days, but she did not realise that she had been infected…" Her gaze trailed off with her voice as tears streamed quietly down her cheeks. "It was good that you were not at home. I don't believe any of us quite recovered from it, though only I was left at home to see her wasting away. Penelope stayed with the Tomlinsons and, when she returned, began to argue with everything. Meanwhile, Margaret and Sam, who had been sent to the Edwardses, also changed; Margaret became the fretful creature she is now, while Sam—poor Sam—confided in me before he left to apprentice with Mr Curtis that he asked to study medicine as he hoped to never feel so helpless again. Father, though, was hit the hardest by her loss; he stopped socializing except for church matters, rarely spent time with any of us outside his room, and has hardly taken visitors since. He feels himself an invalid but fears any of us falling ill, so don't be surprised if he acts contrary to what you have become used to."

Emma was enthralled in the tale and tried to imagine the kind of person her mother was from the fragments of her distant memory and Elizabeth's story. She then found herself wondering what it might have been like if her mother had still been alive when she returned to her family. How different might it all have been?

They both sat in silence, letting their tears roll unchecked down their faces, until some noise next-door brought them back to themselves.

"Ah," using a corner of her sleeve to wipe her face, "it seems Margaret is preparing to head over to the Edwardses' house soon. But fear not, for I shall stay with you tonight."

Emma gasped in shock. She could not allow Elizabeth to forgo a night of dancing and socializing for something so trivial as a cold. "No. No, I will not allow it; do not even think of it." She began to cough and Elizabeth fretted that she had upset her. "My dear sister," she said after recovering," you must not give up your chance at amusement for me. In fact, I will not allow you to enter this room again if you should stay." She smiled slyly, though her tear-streaked face belied her humour, "This time, it is I who cannot attend, and it is you who must go and tell me of all the happenings over dinner tomorrow when you return."

They shared a look as they both remembered their conversations last month, and they laughed together before Elizabeth—after a few more minutes—ran out of arguments against it and agreed to go in Emma's place.

<hr />

Elizabeth and Margaret left for Dorking an hour later, but Emma, having dozed off, was unaware of their departure. She awoke to a light rapping at her door; Nanny came to check on her and offered to make her broth or gruel. She requested whichever was readily available, knowing she would not taste it anyway. Since her father often had gruel for supper, she expected it would be easier to make enough for two. Though she doubted she could stay awake much longer, the emptiness of her stomach had begun to trouble her.

She was startled when, fifteen minutes later, Nanny entered with a tray, followed by her father carrying a second. Nanny smiled and winked at Emma as she helped her sit up and placed the tray on her lap. Meanwhile, Mr Watson pulled out the chair beside Elizabeth's desk and sat down. Once Nanny had gone, he remarked with a chuckle, "Since we are both invalids today, it is only right that we take our gruel together."

Emma was not sure how to respond and ate in silence, occasionally glancing at her father. From time to time, she caught him watching her before quickly looking away, his expression shifting through emotions she could not begin to decipher.

Eventually, when they had both finished their meal, her father began to fidget and clear his throat. Finally, he managed to speak, "Well my dear, how are you feeling?"

Emma was taken aback by his sudden casual inquiry and she did not know how to respond. When he continued to look at her, she only managed to say, "I am well."

He exhaled a long, slow sigh of relief. "Well, that is good to hear. If you need anything, do not hesitate to ask Nanny or Betty—or even James."

With that, he reached into his pocket and pulled out several letters. "Since you have been kind enough to read to me while I have been unwell, I thought I might return the favour. These are from your Aunt Parker—you have met her before I believe—who has kept me informed of your Aunt O'Brien's latest antics. Or should we simply call her Mrs O'Brien, as it seems she no longer favours the title of aunt?"

He chuckled at his own remark, but Emma found no humour in it. Whatever Aunt O'Brien chose to call herself; she was the one who had raised Emma and cared for her when her parents had cast her aside. Though Elizabeth's earlier story had touched her deeply, she could not forget that it was her parents' decision to send her away which had kept her from her mother's final moments. Just as she had not been there when her birth mother died, the Watsons had not been there when her uncle Turner passed. They had all lived separate lives, and Emma felt it only right to stand by the family who had raised her.

Mr Watson did not see her discontent as he opened the first letter:

Thursday, October 10th

Pulteney Street No. —, Bath

My Dear Robbie,

We have just received the most disturbing news—Maggie has written to announce her recent marriage to a military man nearly a decade younger than herself. The letter, sent by regular post to Devonshire, only reached me after being forwarded by my steward. Can you believe it? She must be a fool.

We had already questioned Edward's decision to leave the house and fortune in her care without stipulation when he so clearly intended it for dear Emma. Maggie insists it was not badly done and claims I have no right to judge. But unlike her, I am not responsible for anyone's care, and Francis and I chose our possible successors together years ago the same as the Turners did, and I have not remarried and given that inheritance away to anyone else.

Maggie now plans a short stay in London before joining her new jailor in Ireland. She asks for my well-wishes, but I would rather wish her sense. And not a word of poor Emma! I hope Maggie will not force her to call this man uncle. We would rather have Emma here with us than dragged off to Ireland. As her father—though you gave up your claim long ago—we hope you will dissuade Maggie from taking Emma where her family can do little to help her should she need it.

Your exasperated sister,

Penny Parker

P.S. Aunt Dorothy wishes for me to give you her regards and tell you that she supports my wishes. Her memory is still strong though her body may not be, and she remembers Emma very fondly from her visits to Bath and Devonshire with the Turners.

Emma was surprised by her aunt's opinion of her own sister. They had always seemed to get along quite well, but Emma now wondered at how little she must have paid attention. She saw her father expecting some response and asked, "When did the letter arrive, father? And why are you only telling me about it now?"

"Oh, it came while Elizabeth was taking you off to prepare for the last assembly. I, of course, informed your Aunt Pen of your whereabouts and how it all came to be." But before Emma could say aught else, he unfolded another letter:

Saturday, October 31ˢᵗ

Pulteney Street No. —, Bath

Dear Robbie,

Well, we have seen her—we have seen them both. Maggie has only today deigned to stop in and see us—though she has been in town for a week now. She is much thinner than last summer, but her energy remains unchanged. We are relieved Emma is with you; though abandoned and penniless, she is still better off than if she remained with her aunt. Aunt Dorothy commented that she seemed more ridiculous than she was in her first season when she declared that she "would have all the men in love with her by the end of a month."

Maggie claimed she had no time to visit you—a mercy, I think. She now calls herself a Countess— "soon to be Marchioness" if she lives long enough for her husband to claim the title! Her officer—now former officer, having sold out after securing Old Turner's fortune—is the nephew of a marquess. Since he has no sons, he was granted a special remainder so the title will pass to his brother's heirs. It seems her fortune hunter is first in line, and he is whisking her off to Ireland to manage his uncle's lands while the marquis remains in England with his young wife. Amusingly enough, it seems her husband only discovered his future elevation after the marriage was registered and may now regret his haste in securing her.

Aunt Dorothy tried to explain to Maggie why she should not claim the title before it was rightfully hers, but you know that she never listens. What would the daughter and sister of a mere baronet know?

Mr O'Brien, a cocky fool, parades about Bath on his wife's funds, and, if Maggie is to be believed, his family is ever in need of financial rescue due to their love of gambling and excess. Their eventual title will likely come with a mountain of debt.

At least, thanks to old Mr Hawkins, Maggie's affairs are secure. The marriage contract ensures that her husband can only touch the interest, not the principal, so long as she lives. However, it seems her husband did not read the fine print when he signed; that he expected he would have full access to the money is plain. He openly despises her, yet he is making her pay for the entire journey—and all it entails—from London to Bath to Ireland and all his amusements out of the interest from Edward's fortune.

Aunt Dorothy is sure it was entirely Mr Hawkins's doing. I have no doubt she will try to wheedle the truth out of him when he comes down to Bath in the spring.

Well, good luck to Maggie on her voyage to the Island—for as far as we are concerned, it cannot come too soon.

Yours sincerely,

Penny P and Aunt D

Emma was silent throughout his reading, her face shifting between mortification and anger. The way Aunt Parker spoke of Aunt Margaret was too harsh for her sensibilities. The mention of Mr O'Brien's apparent hatred for his wife made Emma fear for her aunt's safety. The revelations about his family were disturbing, and she regretted that her aunt had made such a choice, leaving Emma—the person who cared for her most in the world—behind.

Staring at her father who was smiling wryly down at the paper in his hands, she became angry. They were all too cruel. How could anyone fault her aunt for seeking happiness. Emma agreed that she could have done better, but she was sure that it was the grief of loss and loneliness that caused this. Perhaps she had been worried about Emma moving on and leaving her alone?

While she was considering this, her father said, "These all came before, but I thought there might be some news in them that you were not yet aware of. As I know, you have not yet heard from your aunt?" Emma hesitated in embarrassment as she had never informed any of her family of the previous letter. However, he did not notice her hesitation and continued, "There is one more," and he took out an unopened letter, "but this one is from your Aunt O'Brien to you. And so, I will leave you to read it in peace."

He handed her the letter and, with one last smile and an awkward pat on the head, he turned and left.

The envelope was thin, just one sheet, and she opened it with mixed feelings.

Saturday, November 7th

The Paragon, No. ——, Bath

My Dear Emma,

We arrived in Bath a fortnight past and have settled ourselves most comfortably—if only you were here to share in it.

We saw your Aunt Lopie and the old crone last week, and have been in their company twice since. I must say, they were by no means gracious towards my husband or myself. Should Lopie take it upon herself to write to you, I would advise against reading her letter. She has always been a jealous, bitter creature—a consequence, I suppose, of her plainness. She envies me, I suspect, for having secured a young and handsome husband while she remains an aging widow. They were both of them rather resentful of my new title—or, more accurately, future title—though, as the present holders now assume the higher designation, it is fitting that my James, as heir, should use the secondary title, and that I, as his wife, do the same. With Lopie being only the granddaughter and niece of a baronet—and her old aunt likewise—I hold precedence, and I am assuredly entitled to it even now.

But I digress. Do give my best wishes to all, and remember me in your prayers—not that I stand in need of further fortune, but I know you, my dear, will always consider my well-being as is proper. And disregard entirely any nonsense that comes from Pulteney Street in Bath.

Your loving aunt,

Lady Margaret O'Brien, future Marchioness

Tears poured from her eyes as Emma finished reading the small missive. She immediately refolded it, placed it into a book inside her bedside drawer, and turned her back to it in hopes that she might forget its contents—and its very existence in sleep. As unfilial as it may have been, she almost wished that she should never receive another letter from her aunt.

Chapter Twelve

The November Assembly

Elizabeth

When Elizabeth and Margaret arrived at the Edwardses' house, they were greeted in the usual calm manner by the mother and daughter while Mr Edwards was ebullient in greeting the two of them and inquiring, "How are your father and Miss Emma doing? What is this I hear about illness at Stanton? I was in the village yesterday to have my horses shod and overheard Mrs Davies telling her husband that the apothecary had been called to the rectory. I do hope it is not your father. I thought to stop by, but I did not wish to be a bother and knew I would be seeing one of you soon to inquire, else I would have come on the 'morrow."

Margaret was in conversation with the ladies as soon as she sat down, so it was Elizabeth who answered, "My father is well enough—nothing but the usual complaints. It is Emma who is ill."

"Oh, my. How did one so young and healthy manage to fall ill? And at just such a time."

"Oh, it is partly my fault I am afraid."

"Your fault?" he interjected. "Come now, you cannot expect me to believe you had a hand in anyone's illness—but now do tell me."

"It was just that Emma learned of all the duties required of the mistress of the parsonage, and that I had taken on the role and work. She wished that she could help to relieve some of my burden, and I began to train her and take her with me. She is not accustomed to such busy work though, you know, and it took a toll on her health, poor thing."

As she spoke, Mr Edwards nodded along and hummed. His earlier exclamation had caught his wife's attention, and she listened to the explanation—ascertaining the full meaning; she inquired about how ill Emma was and who was with her which Elizabeth duly answered. This line of conversation continued for some time after, and it was soon time to dress.

When they were released to change for the assembly, Margaret and Mary became more vocal in their excitement—one at seeing Musgrave who was confirmed to be attending with Lord Osborne, though his family would not attend, and the other in seeing the captain. Elizabeth was more subdued as she thought about her poor sister who was unable to join them and of her disappointment. It would fall to Elizabeth to explain to Charles and Mr Howard why Emma was not there and would be unable to dance with them. Charles had been sure to request dances from both sisters before they left Wickstead the previous week, and Mrs Blake had forwarded her brother's request that they each save a dance for him as well.

Though Mary and Margaret tried to pull Elizabeth into their excitement, she simply could not feel it when she was so distracted by thoughts of her sister. It was not until Mary mentioned that the sisters might speak to their father about allowing them *all* to attend the next assembly that such happy thoughts drew her, if only briefly, out of her musings.

⁓৩৩৩৩⁓

When they arrived at the White Heart, they made their way to the back of the room by the fire. It was not long before their friends and neighbours entered and began coming over to greet them. With the cold weather setting in, people were eager for the chance to socialize and arrived earlier than the previous assembly. With so many cheerful faces and the bustle, Elizabeth found it impossible to remain withdrawn. The thought that Emma would be eager for every detail made her smile, and she soon found herself enjoying her company.

The Tomlinson boys also came over with their mother to greet the Edwardses and to claim dances with Mary before the soldiers could claim them all. While Mary informed them that the captain had already claimed the first set when they met a week ago, she promised one set to each of the brothers. Elizabeth and Margaret both shared in their attentions and they each claimed a set from one of the sisters.

When Captain Hunter made his way over, Mary and Margaret entered into conversation with him, and he claimed a second dance from Mary and one from Margaret as well before he sauntered off.

Elizabeth had purposely moved away to speak to a neighbour when the captain had approached, she may have enjoyed dancing, but she did not wish to dance with the man who had ruined her brother's chance of happiness. A quarter hour after they arrived, the room was abuzz as Lord Osborne and Tom Musgrave were announced together with the Wickstead party.

Lord Osborne entered into the room and clearly began to search for someone which was unlike his usual manner of glancing about at nothing and no one. Musgrave was standing near him and speaking though it did not seem as if his intended listener heard him. Mr Howard, Mrs Blake, and Charles were with them. They were looking about them surreptitiously while speaking with their friends and acquaintances.

Mrs Blake was the first to discover Elizabeth. They made eye contact, she smiled, and she began to lead the others over. "My dear friend," she began, "it is so good to see you. We have come early, as you see, in hopes of spending more of the evening in good company."

Elizabeth blushed, for having the party's sole attention was quite the compliment. "It's lovely to see you again so soon. May I introduce my party? You know Mrs Edwards and Miss Mary Edwards?" she gestured to each as she introduced them, and the former nodded from her chair as the latter curtsied. "And this is Margaret, my next sister after one." Margaret put on her most ingratiating smile at the group, but she looked pointedly towards Musgrave as she came up from her curtsey.

Elizabeth smiled wryly at her sister's antics then continued, "I am sorry to inform you," she looked at Charles then whose eyes had never stopped searching the room, "our sister, Emma, is not here tonight." Mrs Blake, Charles, and Lord Osborne all showed looks of disappointment though it was more prominent in the latter two—Lord Osborne being the most surprising to her and she stored that thought for later.

They all inquired after Emma's health, so she explained the situation.

Meanwhile, Margaret sidled her way over to Mr Musgrave and began to insinuate that she expected him to ask her for a set. Musgrave's hesitation was clear to any but her; however, when he noticed Lord Osborne's interest in the missing Watson sister, he agreed—assuming Osborne would wish him to find out more specific information.

Margaret was gratified and quickly accepted him for the third set. "If only you had come sooner, but how could I have known? It was not as if I could refuse James Tomlinson and Captain Hunter when they asked me for the first two sets." She secretly hoped he would be jealous, and was gratified to see his reaction, which she mistook for just such an emotion—though in truth it was surprise at hearing of the captain's interest in her.

The others ignored the two as they continued their own conversation.

"I regret to hear about your sister, Miss Elizabeth, and not just because I have lost one partner. May I assume you still have some dances available?" asked Mr Howard.

Her cheeks began to pink again at his notice; he was a man whom she could still not get used to interacting with—though she reminded herself that it was likely all for dear Emma. She nodded, "Since you and Charles here were the first to ask, I have saved the first two sets for you."

"You have saved me your first dance then?" he said with a sly smile, and her colour deepened.

"Oh, do not tease her as you would me, Philip. There now, you can just ignore him, Elizabeth." She turned back to her brother, "Do apologise for mortifying Miss Watson."

He tried to hide his smile at his sister's reprimand, but it was for naught. "I apologize if my humour has 'mortified' you. My sister has spoken of nothing but the loveliness of the Misses Watsons and especially the knowledge of the eldest since your visit."

Elizabeth's face was nearly glowing now, so he lessoned his teasing, "In all honesty, we are both very grateful for the information you shared with my sister. Should you ever wish to visit Wickstead, please do not hesitate to ask—

we would be delighted to have you, and we can both learn much from your experience."

Elizabeth was gratified by his words and felt more comfortable with his sincerity. "I would be happy to help anytime—though perhaps it would be easier to send a letter with any questions in order to save your horses."

Mr Howard smiled, "I had heard you were as thoughtful as your sister. I can see mine did not exaggerate your merits." He looked around at the musicians then, "I believe the dancing will commence soon. Will you allow me to claim your first two dances?"

Elizabeth was uncomfortable and worried about what Emma would think. Then she saw young Charles's dejected face and found her salvation. "*Actually*, I believe it is only right that the first be with young Master Blake as he *was* the first to ask me to dance."

Charles's gloom quickly turned to delight. He bounced on his feet and readily agreed. Mrs Blake smiled at them both and took Elizabeth's hand in hers to show her thanks while Mr Howard looked amused at having been passed over in favour of a ten-year-old boy. He instead turned and begged his sister to do him the honour, "So I can hold on to some of my pride."

They all laughed. Charles offered Elizabeth his arm, and they joined the dance followed by Mr Howard and Mrs Blake. They were soon joined by Margaret with James Tomlinson and Mary with Captain Hunter.

Elizabeth enjoyed her dance, but she was happy that she did not have Margaret and Penelope's taller stature as Charles, though tall for his age, was a full head shorter than herself. He told Elizabeth about the last hunt he attended with Osborne in October and how he hoped Osborne might have another soon. He also asked questions about Emma which she was happy to answer.

They went through the moves with spirit and stayed together as a group between the dances of the first and second sets as they merely switched partners.

As Elizabeth and Mr Howard danced, they had some conversation as well. "I do hope that I have not shocked you too much with my frankness, Miss Watson."

She was quiet for a few minutes, but thankfully the dance took them apart just then and it was not a problem. When they came together again, she avoided looking at him, "It's fine, Mr Howard. I am just not used to it. I also had no notion of you being so—"

"Candid? Teasing? Foolish?" He finished as they moved apart, and he was gratified to hear her chuckle after a short pause. He knew then that he had finally broken through her nervousness.

When they came together again, she agreed, but he could not tease out of her which word she would have chosen though they continued to converse through their dances.

When the dance ended, the four of them made their way to the tearoom. "I must admit, Miss Watson—when I helped your father back then, it was mainly to repay an act of kindness. However, we were interested in your family even before your sister danced with Charles." Elizabeth was taken aback and stared in disbelief. He smiled at her confusion but was kept from continuing at that moment by the crowd.

When they finally made it into the room, Lord Osborne—who had made his way in during the dancing—waved them to a table where they could all sit. Howard gave Osborne a knowing smile, but looked to Mrs Blake, "I was just telling Miss Watson of your previous interest in meeting her."

"What? Oh, yes! It is true—did I not tell you before?" Elizabeth shook her head. "Well, I had many questions as you know, and I heard about you from one of the young parishioners—Mrs Melling is from Stanton and recently moved to Wickstead after marrying Mr Melling." Elizabeth knew the young lady and nodded. "Well, she was speaking to Mrs Larkin a couple months back about 'Miss Watson'—about how you took over the duties some years back, how caring and active you are, how you tended her family when they fell ill a few years ago, and so on. I might have felt a little put out at the comparison, but I was so curious to meet you myself. I had been pushing my brother to ask Mr Musgrave—as he seems to know everyone hereabouts—for an introduction. Then your sister was so kind to Charles, and, when I learned she was one of the Misses Watson, I knew it was fate."

Elizabeth sat silently, her face flushed again as she was unused to so much praise and attention.

"So, you see Miss Watson, I have been hearing about you for some time now. If I am candid with you, it is because I feel that I have known you much longer."

Osborne had been quiet throughout, but he began to ask about the health of the whole Watson family, of her father, and finally of Emma's condition in specific—if there was anything she needed? "Should they find they wanted a more qualified diagnosis, he could call in his physician, etc."

Elizabeth was taken aback by his apparent sincerity; she began to wonder at his interest in her sister and how it could have begun. However, she assured him that Emma had only a cold and would be better in a few days' time. She thought that would be all until she received the greatest shock of her life when he asked her, "If you have a set available Miss Watson, may I request the pleasure of dancing with you?"

Her acceptance was given out of habit, and she told him her fourth and final sets were free. He requested the fourth and turned to Charles to inform him of his intention to hunt that coming Saturday.

Elizabeth's shock kept her quiet for the rest of the break which amused Mr Howard—after he overcame his own surprise. However, it bothered the others not a bit. Mrs Blake and Charles carried the rest of the conversation. The latter requesting that Elizabeth "inform Miss Emma about the hunt on Saturday if she is feeling better."

When the tea ended, Elizabeth was escorted back to Mrs Edwards who eyed her in obvious curiosity but said nothing. The party stayed nearby, and Mrs Blake apologised to Mrs Edwards for their having stolen her charge for so long. This opened a dialogue between them that pleased Mrs Edwards; she was more than happy to be noticed by one of the Osbornes' set.

Elizabeth was soon collected by Richard Tomlinson for their dances, and his flirtatious manner helped distract her from her nerves about her next partner. However, the dances were over so soon that she did not have time to notice Margaret dancing with Mr Musgrave until they met on their return.

Musgrave clearly wished to detach Margaret as he was moving towards

Lord Osborne, but he froze in shock with her sister and much of the rest of the attendees nearby when Lord Osborne stepped forward saying, "I believe the next set is mine, Miss Watson?"

The silence around them was deafening in that moment—for everyone knew that Lord Osborne *never* danced.

Elizabeth took his offered arm, even though the dance would not begin until after the break, and everyone who saw them joined those who were close enough to hear in gawking at the pair. Her own face must be beet red; she knew. Even Mrs Edwards had dropped her fan and was sitting slack-jawed—and she rarely lost her composure.

Mr Howard, in order to dispel some of the unease, came over to speak to the pair with his sister and Charles. Musgrave, with Margaret still hanging on his arm, also joined them but stayed silent. Only Osborne and the Wickstead party were able to converse normally in such a situation, and it carried on until it was time to move to the floor.

Elizabeth was stiff and silent—focussing only on the positioning of her feet—until she noticed Osborne had been speaking with her. When they came together again, she asked him to repeat his words.

He apologised for surprising her with his request, and, when she nodded, he requested that she tell him about her sister. "My sister, my lord? I have three." She was sure she knew which he meant, but she needed another moment to compose herself.

They came together again, and she saw his cheeks were pink as he informed her, "I was speaking of your youngest sister, Miss Emma. Are you confident that she will be well? Do you think she will be able to go out on Saturday?"

Elizabeth was confused, but then she remembered they had spoken of the coming hunt at tea. "I am confident that she will be well—perhaps in a day or so. I will ask her if she might attend Saturday, I know she promised Charles she would see him off on the next hunt if she could."

"Ah, that is good to hear." They separated again, and he was silent for some time. When they neared the end of the dance, he said, "Do, please, inform your sister that, should she wish to ride, my horses are available for her use anytime. They must exercise, and I will be in London much of the time—I am sure Charles would be happy to ride with her; his horse is kept in my stables as there was no space at the parsonage."

Osborne continued rambling in much the same manner until the music ended. After their set finished, he led Elizabeth back to her party. She was surprised to see that Musgrave was still with Margaret and had not danced but had simply been watching them the whole time.

Musgrave came forward to inquire about the young lord's dance, but Osborne had nothing much to say. So, Musgrave instead requested Elizabeth's final set of the evening to the chagrin of Margaret.

Elizabeth, however, refused. She felt emotionally and physically drained after dancing with Osborne and only wished to sit. This caused Musgrave to look at her oddly, but she had not the energy to interpret his expression.

Mr Howard and Mrs Blake soon stood with a sleepy Charles, and they said their goodbyes. Lord Osborne followed suit, and Mr Musgrave followed him out as always.

The rest of the night was a blur to Elizabeth, subjected to Mrs Edwards's relentless questioning at the assembly and again over white soup when they returned home.

Chapter Thirteen

Missed Calls

Elizabeth

Thursday, November 12th

The day after the assembly, Mr Musgrave had come to Stanton. Emma had been pleased that she had such a good reason not to go down and see him. He had spoken with Elizabeth and Margaret until the former had used Emma's illness as an excuse to leave the room. He had stayed with Margaret for nearly another quarter hour before the two had left together as Margaret had begged a ride to the Edwardses'.

On Thursday, they received more visitors. Margaret had been gone nearly half an hour when a carriage was heard, and Elizabeth wondered if Mr Musgrave was come again. However, it was Mr Howard and Mrs Blake who arrived at the parsonage for calling hours. Unfortunately, Emma was still too unwell to entertain guests, though she was on the mend and hopeful she would be well enough to attend the hunt that Saturday.

Mr Watson, however, joined them in their discourse. For about a quarter of an hour, the four discussed matters concerning their respective parishes. Mr Howard soon discovered that Mr Watson was just as much a repository of wisdom as his eldest daughter. While the men drifted into their own exchange, Howard kept an ear on the ladies' discussion. He found the eldest Miss Watson to be as knowledgeable as his sister had claimed—yet modest about it, too.

They spoke longer than was usual for calling hours before Mr Watson admitted he was feeling tired and had letters to write. Still deep in conversation, Mrs Blake and Elizabeth were reluctant to part just yet. As the morning was not too chilly, the remaining three decided to take a short walk before the visitors departed.

"Miss Watson, you are surely a fountain of knowledge!" Mr Howard exclaimed once they were out of the house.

His words caused her to pause and blush in bemused silence. It was Mrs Blake who noticed her discomfort and chided her brother again for embarrassing their friend.

"Please excuse me, Miss Watson. I did not mean to shock you, but I am nearly as new to all this information as my dear sister. I studied for the church, but there are far more clergymen than livings available in England. So, when I was offered a position as tutor to the young Lord Osborne, I saw no reason to refuse. You may not know, but after my pupil matriculated at Oxford, I took on other students with the former lord's recommendation. I took up the living at Wickstead less than four years ago when the previous vicar passed away. His widow—Mrs Humble—was allowed to remain in a nearby cottage and continued tending to the mistress's duties in exchange for a small stipend. Though you may not have known all the details, there are always whispers of this and that."

"I believe I heard something of it, yes," she replied.

"Then, less than a year later, when Lord Osborne left university, I joined him and his friends as a mentor for their Grand Tour. In early summer of last year, we received news of the previous Lord Osborne's death. We returned from the continent but it took several months, and we arrived in late November. That same winter, Charles came to live with me and, while I was still adjusting to all the changes, old Mrs Humble passed away in late March. I admit that I was so focussed on my own work that I never even considered learning about the duties of my future helpmeet."

Elizabeth listened in silence, but she recognised how seriously Mr Howard took his position. She smiled and said, "I understand perfectly. My mother trained me before she passed, and I have gradually taken on more of the responsibilities my father can no longer manage. Most of them have occupied my time for so long that they feel like second nature, while the rest came on so gradually that I hardly noticed. It was not until your visit the other day, when Emma's curiosity was piqued about my work in the parish, that I truly realised the extent of my duties. She wished to learn and help me, which is why she fell ill—she exerted herself too much last week and was fatigued from the strain."

"The poor dear—I do hope she recovers soon. You must be careful not to give her too much work at once when she is well again. Though, I dare say, if you have been managing everything alone for so long—pray forgive me, but how long has it been since you took charge?"

"It has been nearly eight years since my mother passed, which was five years after we moved to Stanton, so I had many acquaintances and a goodly amount of experience with aiding in the duties of the mistress." Her eyes unfocused as she thought back to the time. "It was seven years after my aunt and uncle Turner decided to adopt little Emma. I was quite sad to see her go, having assisted in her care over the years, though I had been away at school for most of her early years and had only just returned. She was such a sweet and dear thing—hardly ever crying or fussing. My mother was heartbroken over the loss, but my father convinced her that Emma would have a better future with the Turners."

"I am sure they would have felt the loss with any of their children. I know it broke my heart a little to send Charles here to study with my brother, but a loving parent must risk their own heart to secure their child's future comfort."

"I did not know you felt that way, Mary, or I would have done more to arrange visits between you last year," Mr Howard said with genuine regret.

"Oh no, Philip, you were very kind to take him in and teach him for nothing at all. One day, when you have children of your own—not just your sister's to look after—you will understand the conflicting emotions a parent suffers even at the thought of sending a child away to a better place. But I have never for a moment regretted my choice. Charles has already learned and improved so much. It was not good to keep such an impressionable boy so near the sea. Sailors, while hardworking, are a rough and sometimes crude lot."

"It is true that I was taken aback by Charles's language and mannerisms at first," said her brother. "It was clear that you taught him well, for he knew how to act properly, but he was not entirely accustomed to it."

"Yes, that is true. I tried, but what was I to do? He was a growing boy who needed to be out and busy, but I had the younger ones to see to as well. So, I left Charles to the care of others with boys of the same age, and they were not always chaperoned by the more respectable officers' wives," she said looking chagrined.

"Rather like us growing up, no? However, we turned out well enough, I think. Do you agree Miss Watson?" Mr Howard turned to her with a cheeky grin.

Miss Watson was confused and taken aback, "Like yourself? I am not sure that I quite understand."

Mrs Blake slapped her brother's arm playfully before explaining. "Our father was in the navy; it is how I met my husband. We also grew up living near port towns, though it was not quite the same. Our mother was the daughter of the late Viscount Andover, a distant cousin of our father several times removed. Also, our father reached the position of Vice Admiral before his passing, unlike my dear late husband. So, while the locations and situations were generally similar, my living with my husband was a cut below how we were raised."

"Well, I confess I know little about the navy or that way of life, but I have seen nothing in your family to suggest that your upbringing was anything but proper. I have only met Charles on a few occasions, yet his manners and speech are perfectly genteel. As for you, you are just as refined as our dear Emma—who, as you must have heard, was raised in comfort, with every advantage. She puts the rest of us to shame, though not by design. It is simply the result of having grown up without want or the necessity of labour, occupied only with the pursuits befitting a young lady of means."

"Miss Emma must be in a position to help promote you and your sisters then. Is that not so?" asked Mr Howard in a tone of pure curiosity.

"Sadly, no. Our uncle—Mr Edward Turner of Shropshire—passed away over two years ago leaving his house and fortune in the care of his wife. We all knew that he intended for Emma to be heir to all he had eventually, but our father tells us that the terms of the will did not stipulate the terms of the inheritance. He left all his earthly goods and our sister's care to his wife.

However, this last summer, the former Mrs Turner was wooed by a Captain O'Brien of the regulars."

She continued to relay the information about Emma's circumstances, ending with, "As far as I know, she has had only one letter from her aunt and that was on the day of the last assembly—though she spoke to no one of its contents."

"Did they not wish to take Miss Emma with them to Ireland?" queried Mrs Blake in astonishment. "Surely your aunt…"

"Oh, no. She is to remain with us. It seems that the captain—though I now recall hearing that he sold his commission—did not wish to take Emma with them, and our aunt was in agreement."

They were silent for several minutes, and Elizabeth began to wonder if she had said too much, but, since Emma liked Mr Howard, Elizabeth thought it best that he should know the particulars. Gossip spread quickly in small towns, and news could get twisted in the retelling.

"I am very sorry for dear Emma. It must have been a devastating blow to her, to be tossed off so easily from one to whom she had been used to mean so much," said Mrs Blake, sorry to bring up a subject so uncomfortable to her hostess.

"I agree. It was poorly done, but I wonder how your aunt might justify it—is she a relation only through marriage?" inquired Mr Howard.

"Oh, no. Mrs O'Brien is our father's youngest sister—though a half-sister. I believe that Emma was closer to our uncle Turner though. Uncle Turner would have liked a boy child, but our aunt insisted on having a girl. My parents thought they might take Penelope who was twelve—or even Margaret who was nine years old and the namesake of our aunt—but they proved to be too boisterous for our aunt's nerves. In the end, it was Emma's unobtrusive nature which pleased our aunt."

"Had your aunt and uncle been married long?" Mrs Blake inquired.

"I believe they married the year after I was born."

"I cannot imagine she found any fault in Emma based on what we have seen of her. Can there be any reason in her throwing off the child she raised as her own?" Mrs Blake wondered aloud.

"To be honest, I am sure my aunt found in Emma everything she could hope for in a daughter—I heard of her praise for Emma in the few letters my aunt wrote to my father about her growth. She is said to play both the pianoforte and the harp very well; she draws, paints, sews, and speaks both French and Italian—though she won't have much use for such skills at Stanton. From Emma's letters though, I always gathered that she was closer to our uncle. Though he could not choose a boy child, I learned through her letters that he taught her to handle the accounts, ride horses, and even to shoot. She does not speak of it now and has not since he passed, so I know not if she still remembers what she learned."

"That is interesting indeed. You must take care that Lord Osborne does not learn of this, or he will insist on her riding in the next hunt," said Mr Howard with a sly grin.

"Well, he did ask her to see them off on the hunt a few weeks back. I am not sure that such a great lord would wish to have a woman riding with them though, and I do not know the extent of Emma's skill, nor am I any judge of such things myself."

"Oh, he would not mind her riding with them," Mrs Blake responded. "His sister, Miss Osborne, often joins them on their hunt. She does not shoot, but she is as good an equestrian as any young man of the area."

"Is she? I was not aware. Though it is not surprising. If one has the means, one should learn to ride; it would be much simpler to be able to mount a horse sometimes than to wait for the carriage to be made ready, and I hear it is excellent exercise for young women."

"Yes, indeed. Once one learns to ride, it is hard to give it up. Whether it is for transportation or recreation, it is a useful skill to have. Should you ask young Charles, you will get an earful. He has quite fallen in love with Jasper, the horse that Lord Osborne gave him." Mr Howard and his sister shared a look after he said this. He looked amused while she seemed resigned to the situation.

"Well, perhaps if Emma is feeling better on Saturday, she may ride a little. Osborne asked me to inform Emma that she could ride his horses anytime she wanted, but I was not sure if he was serious or jesting."

"Did he? Now that is a surprise!" exclaimed Mr Howard. "He is very careful about who he lets ride his horses. Even Mr Musgrave is not allowed his choice and is only allowed to ride in Osborne's company. It is a great compliment he pays your sister."

"Oh, my! I had no idea. Though I don't see why—" she looked at her guests out of the corner of her eyes, "you don't think—can he possibly be serious about my sister? I mean, I cannot blame him—she is a dear, but—" she blushed at her incomprehensive chatter.

"Worry not, Miss Watson," replied Mrs Blake with a pat on the younger girl's shoulder. "I have only been living nearby for less than half a year, but I know that Osborne is not the type to show attention to young ladies without care—or even at all."

"My sister is right. Osborne has seemed more mature of late. He is trying harder to be amiable and learn to speak with more ease and clarity than in the past. I believe this is a good change in him, and it all began after his meeting Miss Emma. He will not dally with her feelings—if that is what you fear."

"Oh, it's not that—I have never heard anything to make me fear; he is not like Mr Musgrave who wishes to make all the young ladies fall for his charms, but Lord Osborne is—well, he is a Lord."

Mr Howard and Mrs Blake shared a look and laughed.

"Yes," said the latter, "So was our mother's brother, and, after his sons passed away with no heirs, so is our father's brother. However, the title sits differently with everyone."

They were silent and Elizabeth wondered if she should speak about what she knew of Emma's heart—surely, she could mention that Emma already liked someone else without giving any hint of whom it was? However, she considered her options for too long, and they soon found themselves at the parsonage again.

They went inside to warm themselves while Mr Howard's carriage was prepared, and Elizabeth was left sitting alone with him as his sister stepped away to make use of the necessary.

A comfortable silence settled between them before Elizabeth spoke. "I do hope you will visit from time to time. My father greatly enjoys your conversation—he rarely stirs from the comfort of his rooms."

Mr Howard considered this with a thoughtful expression. "I had not realised how seldom he ventures out. When I first met him at the visitation, it was by chance that I noticed him and was able to offer my aid." He hesitated, then added, "As I said at the assembly, I knew a little of your family before then."

Elizabeth tilted her head slightly. "From your sister, correct?"

"That too; but also in regards to the church." He continued, "During the service, I was seated beside Dr Richards when he mentioned Mr Watson. Upon inquiring further, I learned he was the father of the same Miss Emma Watson I had danced with at the assembly. Dr Richards also spoke highly of him, saying he is well regarded in the church, though he once declined a higher position."

Elizabeth was taken aback. "I have never heard of such a thing," she admitted.

Howard nodded. "I heard that it was before your mother's passing. Dr Richards said your father turned down the offer because it would have required moving to London, and he feared it would be the death of her."

Elizabeth regarded him thoughtfully before nodding. "Our mother's late pregnancies took a toll on her, and she was never very strong. She was always prone to illness."

"Dr Richards mentioned that the local doctors agreed—the London air would likely have hastened her decline."

Elizabeth nodded once more, absorbing the revelation.

He continued, "I wonder that he did not seek a better position after her passing."

"I believe I know," she sighed. "My father was much changed after my mother left us; he had always been a strong and handsome man, but he was suddenly pale and wan. He never recovered from her loss and did not wish to leave the last place he shared memories with her."

Mr Howard listened and nodded his understanding. "Your father's body may have grown frail, but his wits and intellect remain sharp. After our encounter that day, I felt I could learn much from him. With Stanton so near, my nephew utterly devoted to your sister, and my own sister eager to learn from you, I saw no reason our families should not grow closer. My only regret is that we did not meet sooner."

Elizabeth took in his kind words about her family and his sincerity, smiling up at him. "Your willingness to learn from a man with neither power nor influence speaks well of you, sir." She turned towards the door where she expected Mrs Blake at any moment, missing the faint blush that rose to his face at her praise of him. "Your sister is a lovely woman. I have no doubt she will make a wonderful mistress for you and your parishioners. She already has such thoughtful, well-intentioned plans—she only needed a bit of guidance in how to carry them out. Soon, she will have no need for my aid."

"I doubt that, Miss Watson."

She looked back at him, only to find him watching her with a warmth that caused her to blush deeply and turn away again.

"I believe my sister will always need a friend as steady and kind as you," he added.

Nothing more was said, for just then, Mrs Blake returned. Still trying to compose herself, Elizabeth busied herself by seeing them off to their waiting carriage.

Once they had departed, Elizabeth walked around the back of the house, hoping the cool air would steady her before she went to see Emma. She had not felt such a fluttering in her chest since she was a young girl, smitten with Mr Purvis after her brother introduced them. She thought of how warmly Emma had spoken of Mr Howard and understood all too well what it meant. The realisation struck her with horror—was she truly in danger of falling in love with the very man her youngest sister loved? She could not bear the thought of acting as Penelope had, whether by chasing after or, worse, drawing away the affections of her sister's suitor.

'You must put an end to this now, Elizabeth. Mr Howard is a good man, but you would never have thought of him at all if not for Emma—if she had not met him first and brought your family to his notice. You must see him only as you do Robert or Samuel, as a brother and nothing more.'

And so, Elizabeth resolved to master her feelings, forcing them into what she believed they ought to be.

Chapter Fourteen

An Unwelcome Ride

Omniscient

Friday, November 13th

Elizabeth had told Emma much, though not all, of the conversation she had with Mr Howard and Mrs Blake. She felt guilty in keeping anything back from her sister, but she convinced herself that her feelings could be controlled; she was also sure that Mr Howard was simply good-humoured and not at all interested in herself.

Emma had been happy to hear of the attention her family was getting from that quarter, and she seemed livelier afterwards. The next day, Emma was able to join the family in the afternoon and was clearly on the mend.

Seeing her sister was feeling well-enough to join them for dinner, Elizabeth shared, "I forgot to tell you, Lord Osborne informed me that, if you ever wish to ride, a horse could be provided for you."

Emma's reaction was a peculiar mix of emotions that flashed across her face in succession, and Elizabeth was not sure what to make of it. She only had a moment to consider it before Margaret monopolised the conversation with news of her meeting with Mr Musgrave the day before.

A light drizzle was keeping Margaret inside, so the day was not as peaceful as the past few had been. However, Margaret had been in good spirits and almost pleasant company of late due to her dancing with Mr Musgrave on Tuesday, his calling on Wednesday, and her running into him on Thursday—all with the knowledge that she would see him before the hunt on Saturday.

Later that evening, when Elizabeth and Emma were alone in their shared room, Elizabeth inquired whether Emma felt well enough to join them on the morrow. Emma replied that she must, as she had promised Charles she would at least come to see him off the next time he rode out.

Elizabeth then asked if she would take up the offer of a horse, and Emma hesitated.

"I do not mean to press you, dear Emma, as you are only just recovered," Elizabeth encouraged her, "but I remember how often you wrote of your joy in riding in our letters." She paused, watching her sister, but could not read her expression. "If nothing else, you might wear your habit—yes, I have seen it hidden among your gowns. You may as well put it to use to keep warm tomorrow, even if you choose not to ride. It will make you look much more one of the party."

Emma did not respond, but neither did she object when Elizabeth offered to lay out the garments in preparation for the next day.

Saturday, November 14th

It was a little cloudy and quite chilly the morning of the hunt, but the three Watson sisters plodded along. Elizabeth had convinced Emma to wear her habit and helped her dress. Emma was surprised to find herself anticipating the event and was not even upset when Margaret—bright and gay—took one of Emma's arms and half-dragged her along.

They arrived at the meeting spot near the tree line just as the others were arriving. Mr Musgrave came to tease the sisters about their eagerness for the hunt, but Elizabeth led Emma around him straight to where Lord Osborne, Mr Howard, Mrs Blake, and Charles stood together—ignoring both Musgrave's shocked appearance and Margaret's pleasure at being left alone with him.

They were greeted warmly and met with many inquiries about Emma's health. Once assured that she was feeling much better, an eager Charles begged her for a token of good luck for the ride. Laughing, Emma handed him her handkerchief with all the solemnity of a lady seeing her knight off to battle.

Meanwhile, Lord Osborne lingered long enough to listen and make his own inquiry into her health, to which she gave a brief, but kinder, reply than she might have if the Wickstead party had been absent. He then left them, only to return a moment later leading a lovely chestnut mare.

"I heard that you are quite the horsewoman and might be riding out with us today," he said. "May I take your choice of dress as a sign that you are feeling well enough to do so?"

Emma hesitated, embarrassed, and considered refusing, but it had been so long since she had ridden, and the expectant gazes of those around her were enough to sway her. Osborne held half an apple in his hand and offered it to her. She took it gratefully and extended it toward the mare, who accepted the treat with enthusiasm.

"This is Pippa. My sister named her Philippa some years ago, but we have only ever called her Pippa since, so it is the only name she knows. She is steady and surefooted—you should have no trouble with her, no matter how long you choose to ride today. My sister will be riding as well, so you need only tell her if and when you wish to turn back."

Emma thanked him and turned her attention to getting to know her mount. She noticed Elizabeth was wary of the horse—having never learned to ride and only having dealings with Molly who was small, old, and incredibly docile—it was not surprising. She tried to keep her distance, but Emma and Mr Howard encouraged her to pet the horse. Eventually, she gave in and made a new friend in the process.

Suddenly, Elizabeth asked, "Lord Osborne, if you do not mind me asking, why do you so often choose to hunt at Stanton?"

Lord Osborne, who had been watching Emma with a fond smile, looked at her in surprise. Mr Howard, however, was the one to ask for clarification.

Elizabeth was shocked at her own audacity, but their expressions encouraged her to continue. "It's just that I understand Holmewood to be the more popular hunting ground, and I heard that is where you staged the last hunt. It seems you rotate between Stanton Woods and Holmewood, so I was curious. I also noticed that Sir Frederick, who owns these lands," she gestured toward where he stood some distance away, "is not dressed for riding. So, I wondered—" she hesitated here.

Osborne seemed to understand. He smiled as he explained, "While Holmewood is the more famous hunting ground, I have a connection to the Evelyn family. My grandmother—my paternal grandfather's third wife—was Sir Frederick's younger sister, and he is one of my godfathers. Now that he is too old to join the hunts, I sometimes lead them in his stead when he wishes for such an event."

The connection surprised the sisters, though it was not uncommon for local landowning families to strengthen their ties through marriage.

"To be honest," he added, "my mother's maiden name was also Evelyn—though she belongs to a distant branch of the family."

Before either sister could respond, Miss Osborne approached, pausing just within earshot. "Our family is well connected not only to other noble families but also to the old Surrey families of the area—which is common enough among our set."

She gave a measured glance toward Emma before turning her attention to her brother. "Are you nearly ready? I thought to collect Miss Watson as the time is growing near."

"Of course," Lord Osborne said easily. "Try not to ride too fast for her."

Miss Osborne gave a small smile. "I shall do my best."

They were off, and, with that, the conversation turned to final preparations. Mr Howard would be going along with Charles, and Lord Osborne was to lead the party; so, the men left soon after the ladies while Mrs Blake led Elizabeth and Margaret to the lodge where they could stay warm, enjoy refreshments, and wait for the riders to return.

Miss Osborne

Miss Osborne was intensely curious about Miss Emma Watson, given her careless brother's unexpected interest. As far as she knew, it was the first time he had ever taken notice of a young lady without prompting from their own mother—or the girl's. She and her mother had already questioned Mrs Blake and her brother about the girl and her family, and neither believed her to be a suitable match. Even if she had the fortune she was rumoured to possess, it would still be a poor one. Eight, nine, or even ten thousand pounds—even at the most generous estimate—was nothing compared to Miss Osborne's own twenty thousand and impeccable pedigree, or even Miss Carr's fifty thousand from trade.

Still, Osborne was a stubborn man. His complete indifference to her old schoolfellow and her fortune—despite the young lady's three-month stay at Osborne Castle—had proven that they could not force his hand. But that did not mean they could not warn off unsuitable girls.

Miss Osborne's mother was certain that Miss Emma must be a fortune hunter, scheming to attract her brother's notice. *"Why else would an unknown young lady have requested a dance with a mere boy even after being slighted by the gentlemen at the assembly? It had to be a calculated move. She even used her dance with Charles to ingratiate herself with the Wickstead party,"* her mother had told her. Then, just the other day, she had promised Charles her first dance—no doubt to entice her brother again. Though Emma had been absent, Osborne danced with her sister—though Miss Osborne thought this odd, Mr Musgrave explained to them that her brother danced with Miss Watson to learn more of Miss Emma in the young lady's absence. It was disconcerting to say the least.

Miss Osborne intended to get the measure of Miss Emma during their ride today and determine what would be required to frighten her off. She expected it would not be difficult. If Miss Emma embarrassed herself trying to keep up with the hunt—just as Miss Carr had—she would be far easier to manage.

When the time came, they were off. She looked to her partner. "You seem to be a decent rider, Miss Emma; however, a hunt can be physically demanding. You may want to pace yourself."

Emma only smiled back—lost in the bliss of being on horseback again. "Do not worry for me, Miss Osborne. Today is not my first hunt."

They rode for some time at a leisurely pace as the hounds searched for the scent of their prey. At first, Miss Osborne only observed Emma from the corner of her eye. She did not think the girl was anything special to look at and could not figure out what about her had attracted her brother's attention. However, she noticed that Emma was often looking towards where Osborne was riding with Musgrave and Howard with an expression of admiration and something else she could not guess. She was sure Emma was hoping for more of Osborne's attentions. As she was thinking about this, Osborne looked back at them and smiled when he looked at Emma—a soft smile full of emotions, and she knew she must act.

"When I heard that one of the Misses Watson from the Stanton Parsonage would be riding with us today, I admit I was surprised. Your father must be well off to teach his children to ride." She knew that Emma had been raised by an aunt somewhere up north, but she meant to point out their difference in station.

Emma blushed a little. "As far as I know, I am the only one in my family who learned." She told a condensed version of her history. "It has been a long time since I had access to a horse."

"So, you have received some of the education of a gentlewoman? That will do well for you should you marry a *small* landowner or a merchant who wants a wife able to teach their children sums." She got no reaction as Mr Howard turned then with a smile and a nod for them, and Emma returned the gesture.

"You said it is not your first hunt, is that correct?" she asked to regain Emma's attention.

Emma glanced at her before she turned back and was silent for a moment. "My uncle, well—he was pleased when he heard how quickly I took to the horses and riding from my instructor. He began to spend more time with me outdoors, giving me extra riding lessons and such. After some time, when I proved to have a good seat and bearing, he would bring me out on hunts with him and his friends." She glanced sideways at Miss Osborne and blushed, "He—he even taught me to ride astride and to shoot."

Miss Osborne nodded at the concession, and she breathed a sigh of relief.

"So, you were very close to your uncle? Or perhaps you felt forced to humour him?"

"Oh, no. I enjoyed it very much, and it is true that I felt closer to him than even my aunt, but—" she trailed off into thought and sighed. "To be honest, I believe he truly did care about me. However, I think he would have preferred to raise a boy, but he decided to make the most of what he got."

Miss Osborne considered Emma's words and tone. She could not help but be moved by the sadness in her voice. "My father preferred to spend time with my brother and male cousins. It was only by riding out with the hunt that I could gain his attention and praise. So, I think I can understand something of how you felt." She looked away for a moment in order to compose herself. She had to remind herself that she must not give in to her sentiment, for she must protect her brother's interests.

"I have heard that your uncle passed some time ago and your aunt abandoned you to your family upon remarrying." She saw Emma's face harden and felt guilty at her words, but she knew she must persevere. "Is it true that she refused you your inheritance?" Emma began to shake, and Miss Osborne could see the tears forming in her eyes. Just a little more, and then she would beg forgiveness from God for what she had to do to protect her brother.

Just then the hounds began to bark; they had caught the scent. The horns blared and the riders took off—horses streaking through the trees. Miss Osborne prodded her mount in pursuit and was stunned to see that not only was Miss Emma a proficient equestrian but she had no trouble in keeping up with the hounds.

They rode hard for some time, but their prey managed to escape them. Eventually, they came to a hill that marked the end of the easier paths. The ladies and younger, or weaker, riders would break off here to join the waiting party at the lodge. Miss Osborne informed Emma of this as Mr Howard and Charles rode over to join them along with two more young men that Emma did not know.

Charles was eager to ask "if they had seen him riding—had seen how well he managed to keep up; if they enjoyed their ride; if they were not worried when it seemed Toliver—one of the younger lads who was returning with them—would fall off his horse; how no such thing had happened to *him*," and so on.

Charles kept up the conversation like this the entire ride back, and no one other than Miss Osborne seemed to notice Emma's lacklustre responses and veiled sadness.

Emma

They reached the lodge where the waiting party were within a quarter of an hour and were bombarded with questions from the waiting group. They all broke off, and, as the eldest Miss Watson came to claim Emma's attention, Miss Osborne left them for the company of her own friends.

After the riders had washed up and changed clothes, they all sat down to a late breakfast—which was nearly dinner for the Watson girls though they said nothing of this to anyone but Mr Musgrave who commented on it first.

Over the meal, the more talkative of the hunters regaled them with dramatic tales of their morning's hunt, the news of their catch, and of who among them was the fastest, had the best seat, and so on.

Due to all the excitement, it was a long while before Miss Osborne and Miss Emma found themselves in each other's direct company again. The former decided that, with so little time to converse alone, she had best act fast.

"You may have been raised for better things, Miss Watson, but I recommend that you know your place and do not reach too high. If you fly too close to the sun, you will get burned. I suggest you give up any hopes you have of securing my brother or anyone of his sort. My mother and I will not take kindly to your imposing yourself on our family and friends, and we have the power to make sure you and your family will regret it if you do." After this, Miss Osborne could no longer bear to look at Miss Watson; for she was sure that even fortune hunters and seductresses must have feelings after all.

Emma watched Miss Osborne walk away and focussed on her breathing; she would not allow anyone to see her tears and how deeply she had been cut. However, while she was trying to bring her emotions under control, Lord Osborne and Mr Musgrave appeared next to her.

"Miss Watson, you are quite an accomplished equestrian," stated Lord Osborne as he looked at her, but he quickly realised something was wrong. Emma was staring ahead and refused to look at them; so, she did not see

Osborne's expression turn serious as he looked after his sister's retreating form.

Mr Musgrave did not show her any such regard as he said, "Indeed. I was quite amazed for I had no idea that you could ride, Miss Emma. You seem to show yourself to better advantage each time you come out into company." He grinned at her suggestively, but she only ignored him. He was undaunted and continued with, "You must know how well you and Miss Osborne looked today. I could not even keep my mind on the hunt with such beauty and grace riding alongside us."

"I do not believe you for a moment, for it was you who made the best shot today," said Lord Osborne trying to distract his friend's attention from Emma as her expression was dimming with each word spoken.

Mr Musgrave laughed and began to boast of his own skill, and they were both free to ignore him until another of the hunters called his attention away. He left them to join the speaker's group, leaving Lord Osborne standing alone with Emma.

Osborne hoped that some easy conversation might ease her mind, so he said, "You have been in the country for more than a month now. I hope you are content in your new home. While we are close to London, there are fewer diversions than in town; some women find it quite dull."

He paused to see if she would answer and had almost given up when she finally spoke up after taking a deep breath to ground herself. "I have never been to London except in a short stop on my way to Stanton, though I used to go to Bath once or twice a year with my aunt and uncle." Her voice was quiet and a little raspy, but she continued, "I quite like country living." There was a long pause again, and he considered what he might say when she spoke once more, "I wish to thank you for your offer of a horse for the hunt. I had not realised how deeply I missed riding."

She had actually glanced at him for a mere moment as she spoke of her gratitude, and he could see a plethora of emotions playing across her countenance though he could not understand them. When she did not speak again, he simply stood next to her in companionable silence, stealing glances at her from time to time until her sisters came to collect her.

REFINED AND RETURNED

Chapter Fifteen

Absent Thoughts

Emma

Saturday, November 21ˢᵗ

For the first few days after the hunt, Emma felt only a lingering fatigue, enough to keep her quieter than usual but not enough to concern anyone. But as the weather turned, so did her health. A stretch of cold rain settled over the town near the end of the week bringing with it another fever, stronger than the last. By Friday, she was confined to her room once more, too weak to protest.

On Saturday, she was feverish as well as frail from all the coughing and shivering. Though they kept the fire in her room burning strongly, it only served to dry out the air, leading to more fits. Once the apothecary had left, Emma was again given laudanum laced tea and left to rest. However, a few hours later, she awoke to find her father sitting at her bedside reading a book.

He asked after her health, receiving a general answer that she was not feeling any worse than before. After some small talk, he took out another letter. "Your Aunt Parker has written us again, so I thought you might wish to hear the latest news as there is not much else to entertain you."

Before she could stop him or say anything, he began to read.

Wednesday, November 18ᵗʰ
Pulteney Street No. —, Bath

Dear Robbie,

Well, she is gone—left to continue her journey to Ireland on Monday with only a scribbled note to us delivered on Tuesday.

I am sorry I did not write yesterday, but we were away from home most of the afternoon and evening—a rare occurrence for us at this age, I assure you. I assume she must have written a letter to Emma, so you will likely already know this—though Aunt Dorothy has her doubts. However, I feel it likely Maggie would not share with you how it came about so soon when they meant to be a month complete in Bath.

It seems that Mr O'Brien racked up a good amount of debt during his time in Shropshire and London—apparently before he realised that he did not have access to the whole of his wife's fortune—and even here in Bath for which there can be no excuse. They are now hoping to evade the collectors with a quick escape to Ireland. While it may sound crass, we do not believe we shall be seeing Maggie again.

Now, on to another matter. While I recommend that you not speak of this to Emma herself, lest she become even more disappointed in the dissipations of her aunt, I gather from some of your comments that you are unaware of Edward's true wealth when he passed. While I do not know the exact figures, based on the spending of the foolish couple, it must have been great indeed. I know that he was involved in several investments with my own late-husband's family and his wealthy trade connections which provided significant dividends. I say this to encourage you to write to the solicitor, Mr Hawkins—whose direction I will attach—and ask about the terms of Edward's will for Emma's sake if not your own.

We could not get her to tell us what will happen with the money after her passing, or what did happen to the house, but there may still be some hope there. Perhaps, if you write to the solicitor, you may learn something more of the matter.

Maggie's avoidance of the topic and her overall attitude has given me some misgivings. Aunt Dorothy reminds me to mention that Maggie was the only one of the family who attended the reading of the will; therefore, it is unclear whether the rendition of it that she passed on to all of us was the truth.

These are only my thoughts, and you may choose to heed them or not. However, I only wish the best for all of my family. Yes, all. Even Maggie, fool though she is, does not deserve the fate she has brought on herself—to be imprisoned in Ireland, unable to return due to her husband's debts—is not anything I would have wished on her. I only ever wished her some sense.

With all our love,

Penny P. and Aunt D

When she heard what Aunt Parker hinted about the will, she felt a mix of indignation and confusion. She trusted the aunt who had raised her, but had not she wondered if something was amiss before? Could Aunt O'Brien have misunderstood some of the terms and conditions?

Emma shook her head, catching her father's eye. "Well, Emma? I know your aunt asked me to keep this from you, but the choice is yours. Do you wish to question her claims?"

Emma's head was spinning, and she felt a deep vulnerability due to her illness. When she saw the small lift of his lips, she felt that she too was being made the fool. Emma replied, her voice firm. "The *Turners* are the ones who fed, clothed, and raised me, so I *owe* my aunt my trust."

Her father's expression shifted to an unreadable mask, though Emma thought she saw pain in his eyes. *'It is not my concern'*, she told herself.

'No one thinks of my distress in all this. First Mr Edwards, then Robert, then my aunt, and even father. What have I done to deserve their ridicule?' Unable to hold back, Emma felt tears well up and slide down her cheeks as the weight of it all became too much. Her father cleared his throat, standing abruptly. "Well, then. I will leave you to rest."

He turned to leave, but paused at the door to look back at her. Emma caught the brief, vulnerable moment when she saw the sheen of tears in his own eyes. It was more than she could bear.

Emma was left alone to her silent tears with her mind a jumble of fevered thoughts and was unable to sleep for some time afterwards. When she finally did, she fell into fitful dreams full of longing and loss.

Sunday, November 22nd

On Sunday, she woke to her sister laying a cool cloth on her forehead before informing her that they would all be off to church unless she wished for Elizabeth to stay with her. She was just well enough to understand and managed to shake her head, assuring her sister that she was fine being alone for a few hours while they attended services.

Her mind felt foggy, her thoughts slipping away before she could grasp them. Yet even in such a haze, she could not forget the letter from Aunt Parker the day before. When Elizabeth left her alone again, she drifted into a drowsy half-sleep, where memory and dreams blurred together.

Emma remembered her arrival at her aunt and uncle's home in Shropshire—how the servants had cared for her, how her aunt delighted in showing her off.

"Well, Miss Knight, what do you think? A pretty little thing, is she not? But of course, she would be—she is my niece, after all. All the children were a fine, handsome bunch as I am sure you can imagine. But she is so well-behaved—much more than other children of her age. Do you not agree?"

"Oh, yes, quite pretty. But is she always so quiet? I had thought children her age to be more... spirited." This was said by Miss Martha—the younger.

"Oh, her siblings had energy enough for them all. She is simply a shy, demure little creature by comparison. But I assure you, she has very pretty manners."

"Yes, yes, I see what you mean. She will be a credit to you one day," said Miss Knight who was more outspoken and confident than her sister.

"I do believe so." Her aunt smiled down at her—was it affection or merely self-satisfaction? Emma felt a twinge in her heart.

"Mrs Shoals, you may take her now. Back to the nursery, dear Emma, and mind your lessons."

Had her aunt loved her? She must have—had she not? After all, she had wanted a child, and Emma had been her choice.

Her mind leapt back to earlier that same week.

Little Emma was curled up in the corner of her closet, making herself as small as possible, tears slipping down her cheeks and onto her neck. She heard the maid enter her room, moving about, calling for her. Soon, she would be found—but she only wanted to be left alone.

The bedroom door opened. Emma knew, from the sharp, measured steps, that it was her aunt.

"Well? Where is the girl?"

"I'm sorry, my lady. I'll find 'er and bring 'er in a minute."

"Find her? Why ever should you need to find her? How far can she have gone?" Her aunt's voice rose in irritation, and Emma trembled in the darkness.

"There now," came a deeper, calmer voice, "what is all the fuss?" Uncle Turner's tone was a gentle, soothing contrast to his wife's.

"The child is missing from her room, and we have guests arriving any minute to see her."

"Now, now, my dear, I am sure she is somewhere close by and will be ready in no time. Why do not we go down and see to the rest of the preparations for your—our—guests?"

Her aunt let out a heavy sigh. "Find her and make sure she is presentable and downstairs on time—or else..." She let the words hang, her meaning clear. The door closed behind her.

Emma heard the maid renew her search, now with greater urgency. She knew she could not hide any longer. Wiping her face with her sleeve, she took a deep breath and stepped out. The maid was just outside the door, and at the sight of her, she let out a sigh—half relief, half frustration.

"You... If I ben't to 'ave you downstairs in a quarter 'our, is mah hide that'll be 'urting come 'morrow. Let's get you ready, Miss. Go'n wash your face now, there's no time for more'n that."

Emma obeyed, though she barely understood what the girl meant. Her father and mother had never raised a hand to their children, let alone their servants. But it was not many weeks before she understood: whenever she displeased her aunt, it was not Emma who suffered for it—it was the servants.

'No,' said a voice in her head. *'She loved me. She said I was the only one she could count on to love her unconditionally. She needed me—is not that part of love?'*

But another voice rose up. *'Then why did she abandon you? Accept the truth. She never loved you.'*

Emma jolted upright, her breath coming fast. She looked around, but she was alone. Sweat ran down her face and body, chilling her as she shivered and pulled the blankets tighter around herself. She did not want to sleep again—but she was exhausted, and the effects of the laudanum Elizabeth had made her drink earlier still clung to her until she could not fight its pull any longer.

They sat in the parlour, dressed in black from head to toe. Emma sat beside her aunt; an arm wrapped around her shoulders in quiet comfort. A sea of people surrounded them.

She recognised some voices, but their faces blurred together.

Her uncle—her dearest, kindest Uncle Turner—was gone. She wanted to cry, but the tears would not fall. Not yet. Not until she was alone in her room, where no one would see. Her grief would only upset her aunt more.

Mrs Turner accepted the well-wishes of their friends and neighbours with practised grace. She sniffled delicately, dabbing her eyes with a lace-edged handkerchief, grieving just as a lady ought—never weeping, never wailing, only sighing prettily, the very picture of sorrow.

Someone spoke to Emma, and she answered, though she could not recall what was said. Grief consumed her. Her sense of loss was her whole world.

At last, the guests departed. That night, as Emma helped her aunt prepare for bed, Mrs Turner exhaled sharply.

"I do not wish to see anyone—especially those ungrateful servants—at such a time. How tiresome they are! Complaining about the funeral dinner, as if it were their concern. Of course, we must serve only the best dishes, several courses. Why should our guests not enjoy pheasant, duck, and trout? Your uncle's favourites, you know."

Emma knew they were not, but she did not correct her aunt. Her uncle had never liked the texture of fish and hated duck, though he ate them to humour his wife. The thought of him made her smile.

"What are you smirking about? Do not tell me you agree with them!"

Emma's smile vanished, and she shook her head quickly. Her aunt studied her long and hard before nodding in satisfaction.

"Of course, you would not. I have raised you better than to think like a servant. You know your duty to your uncle and to me."

Silence fell between them as Emma helped her aunt into her nightclothes.

Mrs Turner let out a sigh. "Oh, how inconvenient of that man to leave us at such a time. I must speak with the solicitor tomorrow—such a headache for me."

Emma froze. The casual way she spoke of her husband's death made Emma's stomach twist. She could no longer hold back.

"It is not as if he—as if Uncle Turner..." Her voice faltered. Tears welled in her eyes.

Her aunt harrumphed. "Oh, come now." She pulled Emma down beside her on the bed. "It is not like that. Of course, I am upset. He was my husband. My loss is greater than yours, my dear. But there is so much to do now, and it will all fall on my shoulders."

Her aunt's words only caused her more distress, and her tears spilled over.

"There, there, my dear." Her aunt mistook her grief for fear. "You have nothing to worry about. I will manage everything, and we shall be as well off as ever." She cupped Emma's cheek, smiling softly. "At least I have you. You shall be my solace. Together, we will persevere."

Emma still felt unsettled by her aunt's words as she went in and out of consciousness, but she assured herself it was just her aunt's way of staying strong—for both of them. She had spoken of the burdens ahead, so Emma had resolved to do all she could to help. In the days, weeks, and months that followed, she had taken on more and more of the household duties. Her aunt had entrusted her with the accounts, though she, herself, had spent more than Emma thought wise. Emma had overseen the servants, except when Mrs Turner had found fault with their work—though she had assured Emma it was only because they underestimated her youth.

'Then why did she abandon you?' The question continued to echo in Emma's mind as she finally slipped into a dreamless sleep.

Monday, November 23rd

When Emma next woke, Elizabeth was once again by her side. The room was dark except for the fire, casting flickering shadows along the walls. Emma stirred and asked what time it was, surprised when her sister told her it was nearing one o'clock in the morning.

She had slept the entire day. Elizabeth assured her she had woken long enough to take some broth earlier, though Emma had no memory of it. She asked why her sister had not yet gone to bed, and Elizabeth admitted she had been asleep but had woken when Emma began to fret. She had tossed and turned, murmuring words Elizabeth could not understand, and her fever had risen again.

Elizabeth handed her a handkerchief, and only then did Emma realise she had been crying. Concerned, her sister leaned in. "Are you all right, my dear Emma? Are you in pain? It is late, but the apothecary is aware we might have need of him at any hour. Shall I call him for you?"

Emma shook her head. She had no wish to be drugged into dreams she could not escape once again.

Elizabeth studied her carefully. "If it is not pain, what is it? Is there anything you need—anything I can do for you?"

Emma glanced down at the glass of water in her hands, then back up at her sister. Elizabeth was smiling, but there was a trace of worry in her eyes. How ill must she look? Had she said anything she should not? And yet, if she could confide in anyone, it was Elizabeth. For a moment, as she gazed at her sister, she thought she saw someone else—someone older. The face was familiar, and yet, try as she might, she could not recall who it was.

"I..." she began, but her throat was dry and hoarse. She drank more water and tried again. "I have been dreaming."

Elizabeth sat silently and nodded for her to continue.

"Father came earlier," she paused as Elizabeth's face took on a knowing look. "He had a letter... a letter from Aunt Parker in Bath." Her sister nodded again. "I do not like the way they speak about my aunt."

They were silent for a long moment before Elizabeth finally said, "May I ask what that had to do with your dreams?"

Emma pondered how to express her thoughts. Her mind was still fuzzy, and the words were not coming easily. "I dreamed of the past—of my life with the Turners."

Another silence. But this time Elizabeth waited.

"My aunt was a difficult woman at times, but she was not unkind," Emma insisted, her voice rising as she met Elizabeth's gaze. "She loved me—I know she did. She was simply overwhelmed when he passed." The words began to tumble out in her aunt's defence—urgent and unyielding.

"Aunt Turner—no, O'Brien—was a good mother to me. She taught me my lessons, my manners, my place in society. She introduced me to everyone of importance and spoke frequently of her pride in me. She trusted me to manage the household after my uncle's death, to oversee the finances. She *always* defended me when others doubted my abilities. *She* was the one who raised me, who remained with me these last *fourteen* years."

Emma's hands clenched in her lap; her voice thick with emotion. "I hate that they speak so cruelly of her! They know nothing of her—*nothing* of what she did for me. How could they? *They* were not there."

Tears blurred her vision, hot with anger and frustration. How *dare* they judge her aunt? They had not lived in her house, had not been shaped by her care. It was *Emma*—and Emma alone—who had the right to pass judgment.

Elizabeth patted Emma's back in a gesture of comfort. "I understand your feelings, but I hope you will forgive our father. Remember that he loves you; neither he nor Aunt Parker meant to hurt you. I think they are both just frustrated that they were unable to do more, especially after Uncle Turner died."

Emma continued her quiet sobs without speaking, so Elizabeth continued.

"We would have loved to see you more, but Shropshire is so far away, and you know we have neither the means nor the opportunity to travel there. Unlike the Parkers—who always made trips to visit us both here in Surrey and even when we were still in Yorkshire, Aunt and Uncle Turner never seemed to go anywhere but Bath with you. It is such a shame, really—if only they had visited more often, we all could have been closer."

Emma could not believe what she was hearing, and her shock was enough to cause her tears to cease. Now they were even trying to blame not only her aunt, but also her poor Uncle Turner, for their failure to be there for her. She gripped the blanket tightly and turned away from her sister. There was a pause, but just as Elizabeth was about to say something else, Emma cut in with a quiet but firm, "You were not there. You do not know what you are speaking of." Out of the corner of her eye she noticed Elizabeth's smile drop, but she refused to look at her.

"I want to be alone." Her no nonsense tone should be enough, but, just in case, she rolled over and pulled the covers over her head.

There was an ache, not just in her chest but in her whole body, a heaviness that made it hard to move, hard to breathe. Her throat felt tight from the unshed tears—the pressure building behind her eyes, but she would not give her sister the satisfaction of hearing her cry.

She listened to Elizabeth eventually get up and move around the room preparing for bed. She heard the whispered "goodnight" and listened as

Elizabeth's breathing slowed before she fell asleep. It only made Emma feel even more alone. '*Elizabeth can move on so quickly as if it all means nothing while I lie here in misery.*'

Elizabeth's words echoed over and over in her head, and, no matter how tightly she pulled the blankets around herself, she could not make them go away.

Chapter Sixteen

The Fall Out

Wednesday, November 25th

For the next few days, Emma remained trapped in a haze of memories, each dream bringing scattered moments from her past with no rhyme or reason. When she woke, the disjointed fragments left her disoriented, unsure of what was real and what was merely a shadow of recollection.

She could often hear Margaret's raised voice, but Wednesday was the first time she could understand what the trouble was. She woke in the morning to some commotion in the hall.

"Why should we all have to wait on her hand-and-foot just because she is ill," she complained as she brought in some gruel for Emma. "'Speak quieter, Margaret—you know poor Emma is sleeping,'" she spoke in a parody of Elizabeth's voice. "'Could not you walk softer, you might wake dear Emma.' Phoo!" Then, on seeing Emma's eyes were open, she said to her, "I doubt you are half as sick as Elizabeth would have us think, and I can promise we never got such treatment."

Emma said nothing, so Margaret just set the tray loudly on the bedside table. "Your meal is served, my lady. Will there be anything else?" Emma shook her head gently, as too much motion made her feel ill, and Margaret stormed out in a huff.

Elizabeth came in ten minutes later looking haggard from the long nights nursing Emma and the even longer days of doing the same with the addition of complaints and criticism from Margaret, "Do forgive me for sending Margaret. Betty needed me about the chickens, and I had just ladled out your meal, so I did not want it to go cold." She looked at the untouched tray on the table and sighed before sitting down and helping Emma to eat. It was the first day that Emma was getting more than bread and broth, and her strength was low.

Emma ate quietly, trying not to look at her sister who was muttering about Margaret, "Honestly, if this is what we are to suffer every time Musgrave is away in London, I might just force him to marry her myself."

Emma almost laughed at the thought of her level-headed sister dragging Mr Musgrave down the aisle to a beaming Margaret.

Elizabeth had continued to stay by Emma's side and care for her, ignoring Emma's cold demeanour and giving her space. The two sisters only spoke of general topics and made sure not to touch on anything personal, but it only made Emma feel guilty when Elizabeth was so careful with her.

Just as she finished her meal, a carriage was heard outside. Elizabeth looked out the window, "It is Mr Howard and Mrs Blake come to visit and ask about your health. I had better go down, or they will be stuck with Margaret as company," she made a face to show her feelings about that. "And father is not feeling well today either." She helped Emma get comfortable again, took the tray, and silently made her way out.

Emma was sad that she was again forced to be absent. She wondered what the Wickstead family must think of her; however, she saw their visits, even when she was ill, as something positive. After all, they had many small children at home, so their risking their health to come and ask about her showed their care and concern.

Sometime later, after the guests had left, Elizabeth entered the room holding a letter for Emma. It was from her Aunt O'Brien, and Emma gave Elizabeth a smug look as she took note of it.

However, Elizabeth only smiled, checked her temperature, replaced the cold towel, and silently left.

Emma was happy to receive the letter—did not it show that her aunt had not forsaken her? It was just the proof she needed. She looked at the outside of the envelope, rubbing her fingers along the seal, but she still did not open it.

Her fever had only just broken, and her head was still muddled—or so she told herself. So, she set it aside.

Thursday, November 26th

The next morning, the apothecary came to check on Emma's health again. "You are well on the mend, Miss Watson. If you continue to feel no ill effects, you may begin spending some time downstairs. But take care not to overexert yourself—fatigue might bring on another relapse."

As he left, Elizabeth turned back to her. "There is no hurry. Take your time and come down when you are ready. If not, I will be back in an hour or two to check on you again." Then she led the apothecary out.

Emma considered making her way downstairs, but she was not yet ready to face her family all at once. She had waited too long to read her letter, and this might be her last chance to find a quiet moment. She slowly took it out and broke the seal:

Saturday, November 21st

Dublin, Ireland

Dearest Emma,

I entreat your kind indulgence for this delay in correspondence, but the circumstances of our departure from England left me no leisure to write—though you may have heard some account of the matter from Lopie.

My dear James was suddenly so overcome with a desire to return to his native land that I had scarcely a moment to put my affairs in order. We quitted Bath late on Monday and journeyed towards Holyhead, changing our horses at every stop. On Wednesday morning, we caught the ferry to Dublin, though the crossing was interminable—the wind failed us, leaving us stranded upon that vast and endless sea with no land in sight for days. A torment without equal, and yet I bore it with all the dignity a Countess must display. I must admit, dearest, that while I would never refuse a visit from you, I shall not set foot in England again until I have gone to my heavenly rest. My constitution is simply not suited to sea travel. Your poor aunt was afflicted even before the shoreline receded from view.

We arrived late in the evening and took rooms, but I was unable to rise until this afternoon—rendering us unable to continue our journey to Cork until after the Sabbath.

James has absented himself on matters pertaining to our travels south, leaving me quite alone in this miserable place. Though I have been but a day upon this island, I declare that the inhabitants are little better than heathens. Not a proper cup of tea have I had since quitting English soil, and their manner of speech is wholly unintelligible. The King's English does not reach so far. It is most vexing!

Upon James's return, I shall endeavour to impress upon him the necessity of procuring a suitable repast for me. I am a Countess, after all—must I truly be subjected to such deprivations? It is not to be borne!

Add to this my delicate health, and you may well imagine the extent of my suffering. I most bitterly lament my folly in allowing my husband to dissuade me from bringing you with me. Had you been present, my dear, I know you would have attended to my comfort with all the tender affection of a devoted child. Your absence is a grievous loss to me.

I implore you to pray, my dear, for the restoration of my health. Until we meet again.

Your loving aunt,
Lady Margaret O'Brien, Countess of Inchiquin

Emma ran her fingers over the familiar handwriting. Once again, disappointment settled over her. Was this all her aunt had to offer? She could understand her aunt's desire to share her story, but it still hurt that not once had she asked about Emma's health, wants, or needs. There seemed to be no thought for the health of the girl she had left behind. She also looked to the closing. She worried about her aunt using the title of Countess so freely now. It was certainly inappropriate—though maybe it was acceptable since they were in Ireland and her husband was the heir presumptive—

Emma exhaled, not able to handle such thoughts right then, and she folded the letter with careful precision. There was no point dwelling on it. Her family would expect her downstairs soon.

The midday meal passed with little useful conversation beyond the expected courtesies. Their father had taken his meal upstairs, leaving only the three girls at the table. Margaret, as ever, filled the silence, first with idle complaints, then with her usual pointed remarks.

"Well," she said, lifting her teacup with an air of satisfaction, "it seems Aunt Turner has been quite *generous* with her letters. I suppose I ought to be grateful that I was spared the trouble of receiving one, though I daresay she would have found me a more fitting correspondent."

Emma did not look up. She had already decided that nothing Margaret said could touch her, but the words settled like a weight in her chest regardless.

"Oh, do stop, Margaret," Elizabeth said mildly. "You do not even know what the letter contained."

Margaret shrugged. "Something terribly important, I am sure. A great burden of wisdom she felt compelled to share." She turned back to Emma; eyes bright with curiosity. "What did she say, then? You must tell us, for we are dying to know. Are we not, Elizabeth?"

Elizabeth said nothing, but her silence made Emma think she must also be curious about the contents.

Emma set down her spoon with careful precision. "Only that she has arrived safely in Ireland, except for some sea sickness she suffered on the way."

"That was quick," Margaret remarked, unimpressed. "Though I suppose we ought not to be surprised. It was her intention all along or at least the reason she claimed for sending you back to us. And did she have anything to say to you? Has she reconsidered throwing you off and asked for you to join her in Ireland?"

Emma's fingers curled slightly in her lap. She kept her voice even. "No."

Margaret laughed, shaking her head. "Well, that is hardly a surprise, either. It is a wonder she wrote to you at all."

Elizabeth cast a sharp glance at her, but Margaret only responded with a smug "hmm" as she reached for another slice of bread.

Emma let the rest of the conversation fade into background noise. She was tired. It was always like this—Margaret needling because she enjoyed it; Elizabeth smoothing things over; and Emma sitting between them, aching in ways she could not name.

After the meal, Elizabeth asked Margaret to go check on their father while she and Emma cleared away the dishes. As Margaret huffed her way upstairs, the dining room grew quiet, save for the faint clatter of silverware on China and the ticking of the longcase clock in the next room.

"Emma," Elizabeth hesitated, then spoke softly. "I—may I ask—did she ask about you at all? About your health?"

Emma stopped. Her hands clenched into fists at her sides. She had dreaded such a question, and hearing it aloud sent a fresh sting through her chest. "It matters not," she muttered, keeping her gaze fixed on the stack of dinnerware.

Elizabeth sighed. "It matters because she should have wanted to know how you are faring."

"She did not ask after me," she said flatly while moving her burden into the kitchen for Nanny and Betty to clean.

Elizabeth hesitated, then followed. "I am sorry."

Emma let out a short breath, almost a laugh, but without any real amusement. "Why? I do not see why you should care."

Elizabeth frowned. "Of course I care—" Elizabeth stopped herself, her lips pressing together before she could finish the thought. Instead, she tried again, gentler this time. "I care because I know it must hurt."

Emma turned to her at that, a sudden sharpness in her eyes though her expression was blank. "And what does it matter to you?" Her voice was low, but something in it cut, something bitter and frayed. "You all expected it, did you not? You expected that she had completely lost interest in me and cast me off just as you all did before."

Elizabeth drew back with a startled gasp. "What? That's not—" She stopped, searching for the words, then simply said, "We never 'cast you off'. Mother and father only wanted to offer you a better chance—a better life."

Emma's jaw tightened. For a moment, she seemed about to speak, but instead, she turned and marched upstairs, leaving Elizabeth alone.

Elizabeth watched her go, her expression unreadable.

The next few days, the tension between the two sisters was so palpable that even Mr Watson began to notice. He made some inquiries among his daughters but heard nothing that helped him to understand.

Emma only pinched her lips together and said nothing, changing the topic to speak with him of the book they had been reading together until he forgot he had even asked. Meanwhile, Elizabeth would simply sigh and tell him the news of the parishioners, and all he got from Margaret was, "Emma has probably realised what a busy-body Elizabeth is and grown tired of her"; or, "Elizabeth has grown disillusioned with Emma's superior airs."

In the end, he gave up asking. However, he had hope that his house would regain its comfort—if not any peace—when he heard the three of them would be attending the hunting party together again on Saturday.

REFINED AND RETURNED

Chapter Seventeen

Unspoken Prey

Saturday, November 28ᵗʰ

On Saturday morning, Mrs Blake arrived with her brother's carriage to convey the girls to Holmwood to see off the hunting party. They had received a note informing them of the offer and giving the estimated time of arrival. So, they only needed to don their pelisses, scarves, hats, and gloves by the time the carriage wheels could be heard coming down the lane.

As they entered the carriage, Emma asked Mrs Blake, "Where are Charles and your brother?"

"Oh, Charles will ride in the hunt, you know, and Philip is with him. I dropped them off at the castle this morning to prepare their mounts. They should already be there with the Osborne party."

Emma was wary at hearing the last part. She wondered if Miss Osborne would be part of the party again and was glad that her father had forbidden her from riding with the others until they could be sure she was truly over her illness.

"And will Mr Musgrave be of the party?" asked Margaret. "Oh, it does feel like ages since I have seen him. Not since the last hunt at Stanton—for he has been spending much of his time in town with the Osbornes." She said the last in a tone that showed her irritation. It was enough to bring Emma out of her worries and feel embarrassed for her sister's poor behaviour.

While Mrs Blake answered graciously, Elizabeth seemed to pick up on

Emma's discomfort and began to inquire after Mrs Blake and all her family to which the other lady was happy to give them all a very detailed account which lasted the rest of the ride.

When they arrived at the starting point for the hunt, they were met by Mr Howard and Charles with Lord Osborne and Mr Musgrave as if the men were only waiting for their arrival. All the men were even more solicitous of her health than on the last meeting, even Mr Musgrave asked about her in his usual ingratiating manner of speaking.

As the others discussed preparations for the hunt and where the ladies were to wait, Charles took Emma's hand to gain her attention.

"Are you really feeling better now, Miss Emma? I wanted to visit, but Mamma and Uncle said you were too ill to receive guests."

She smiled. "I am fine now, but I am not allowed to join the hunt in case I overexert myself and fall ill again."

He nodded in understanding and launched into an account of his accomplishments over the past fortnight, eagerly sharing his hopes for a successful hunt. While he spoke, Emma glanced around at the gathering crowd, a flicker of unease settling over her.

A quiet voice at her ear startled her. "My sister has remained in London with my mother this time."

She turned to find Lord Osborne standing beside her. She had not noticed his approach, and her lingering wariness made her slow to process his words. "I... I was only looking at the horses," she stammered.

Had he somehow known she was dreading a meeting with his sister? No, it must have been a coincidence. He likely assumed Emma would want to greet her, given that they had ridden out together last time.

Relief settled over her. If Miss Osborne was not there, she would not have to face her today. Though she had barely recalled the young woman's warning while she was ill, the sight of the hunting grounds and the flurry of activity brought their conversation to her mind.

Still, Lord Osborne's watchful gaze unsettled her, and she quickly turned her attention back to Charles, who had missed the entire exchange in his enthusiasm for the hunt.

A burst of laughter cut through the morning air—Margaret's—bright and unmistakable. Emma turned instinctively toward the sound and saw Margaret engaged in lively conversation with Mr Musgrave. Their exchange carried a teasing rhythm, with Margaret's smiles growing ever more pleased, and Musgrave's usual affability on full display though he kept glancing between Emma and Lord Osborne.

Elizabeth turned to Mrs Blake. "Have things been going well with the tenants?" she asked with genuine interest.

Mrs Blake smiled warmly. "Better than expected, I think. There was some concern over the sudden change in the weather, but we have managed."

Mr Howard, who had been listening, nodded in agreement. "Your father's advice has been invaluable. I have implemented some of the methods he suggested for farming the glebe lands, and I do think it is making a difference."

Before their conversation could continue further, a rush of carriages signalled the arrival of other onlookers and participants. Today, the hunt was hosted by Lord Osborne, and Osborne Castle would be their base. Without Lady Osborne or Miss Osborne present, Mrs Blake took on the role of hostess. "Well, ladies, let us set off to the house. We need to make sure Osborne Castle is ready for its guests."

With that, they said their goodbyes and climbed into the carriage.

The carriage rattled up the long, sweeping drive of Osborne Castle, while its silhouette loomed over them from between the trees that opened onto the top of the rise. The Watson sisters could not help but stare out the windows in quiet awe. The castle, bathed in the morning light, was a testament to wealth and an ancient lineage, its stone façade stern yet elegant.

Margaret let out a low whistle. "It would be difficult not to feel like the queen of England in as grand a home as this."

Mrs Blake only smiled as the carriage came to a stop before the imposing entrance. A footman stepped forward to assist the ladies, and as soon as their feet touched the ground, Mrs Blake took charge.

"Come along," she said gently. "There is no time to linger outside. We must see to the preparations before the others arrive."

The great doors opened, revealing a well-appointed entrance hall which was covered in polished marble and rich tapestries, the autumnal light from the high windows lending the space a warm glow.

The staff was already at work, but at the sight of Mrs Blake, several footmen and maids stepped forward, awaiting instructions.

"Have the parlours been prepared as was discussed?" she asked, receiving an affirmative. "See that the fires are stoked and that the opposite windows are opened slightly to keep it from getting too stuffy. The guests should be arriving shortly, so make sure the tea service is ready and, after a quarter hour, bring it out with the refreshments."

The servants bowed and dispersed at once to carry out her orders. Margaret, watching the exchange with a smirk, leaned toward Emma and Elizabeth and muttered, "She certainly knows how to run a house, does not she? You would think she owned the place."

Mrs Blake turned at that, raising a single brow showing that she overheard Margaret's crass comment. "I have often assisted Lady Osborne and Miss Osborne when they entertain. In their absence, I was given express permission to act as hostess for the morning." Her tone was calm, but there was an unmistakable edge to it which caused Margaret to flinch. "Besides, it is hardly unusual for guests to take on such duties when needed. I daresay you have had to do much the same when your elder sister was not available, Miss Margaret."

Margaret put on one of her placating smiles and apologised, "Oh, I did not mean to offend you. I was just thinking how comfortable you seemed directing such a large household. I could not show half as much poise and expertise in such a situation myself."

Mrs Blake allowed the apology but was not fooled. Elizabeth, always quick to smooth things over, stepped forward with a small, apologetic smile. "We are grateful for your hospitality, Mrs Blake. I am sure it is no small task to manage such a large household, even for a morning."

Emma, meanwhile, remained silent, her cheeks burning with mortification at Margaret's careless words.

Mrs Blake nodded and turned back to observe the staff until she was satisfied that the preparations were in order. Then she turned back to the sisters. "Come, let me show you the main rooms before we settle in the parlour. It would be a shame to visit Osborne Castle and not see at least some of its splendour."

With that, she led them through the grand public rooms on the lower floor. The Watson sisters took in the soaring ceilings, the richly embroidered draperies, and the gilded mirrors that reflected the light from the great chandeliers.

"I suppose it is all very nice," Margaret conceded as they passed through a sitting room with exquisitely carved furniture. "Though it is a shame they do not host more gatherings to allow others to enjoy their finery."

Elizabeth cast a sharp look at Margaret, prompting Mrs Blake to turn to her with a compassionate, understanding smile before gently changing the subject. "Let us return to the parlour before the first guests arrive."

By the time they returned, the room had been set with tea and an elegant arrangement of refreshments. Mrs Blake took a seat with effortless grace, gesturing for the others to do the same before she served them. There was little left to do now but wait for the arrival of the other ladies and gentlemen who would spend the morning in conversation until the hunters returned.

⁂

The arrival of the guests at Osborne Castle brought with it a flurry of polite greetings, hushed whispers of admiration for the grandeur of the estate, and the quiet rustling of fine fabrics as the ladies settled into the parlour.

Mr and Mrs Edwards arrived first, accompanied by their daughter, Mary. Margaret's face lit up at the sight of her, and Mary wasted no time in joining her good friend while Mr and Mrs Edwards joined Mrs Blake and Miss Watson.

"I am so excited for the hunt today," Mary said as she settled beside Margaret. "Did you have a chance to see Captain—I mean—" she paused, glancing at her mother, "the gentlemen readying themselves?"

Margaret, eager to boast, lifted her chin with satisfaction. "Oh, certainly! We were among the first to arrive, thanks to Mrs Blake providing her brother's carriage for us. I saw the good captain, but I must say, he pales in comparison to Mr Musgrave."

Mary looked put out. "How can you say so? Captain Hunter is a full head taller than Mr Musgrave! And I have heard he is the finest shot in the regiment. I daresay he shall make the most impressive catch today."

Margaret laughed. "He may be taller, but Musgrave is by far the most handsome. And the best shot in town." Seeing her friend's discontent, she added, "Still, I have no doubt our gentlemen will soon find their moment to impress us."

Elizabeth, who had been listening in silence, cast a glance at Emma. Though the sisters were still not speaking freely, Elizabeth could not help but notice how Emma kept her gaze lowered, her expression betraying her embarrassment with Margaret's conversation. Margaret, naturally, took no notice and continued chatting with Mary, their conversation soon shifting to the latest fashions seen in town.

More guests arrived as the morning wore on. Mr and Mrs Tomlinson entered with their daughter and son-in-law, Mr and Mrs Fuller—the latter sat with Mrs Blake and Elizabeth while the others moved on to join their friends after greeting their hostess.

Close behind them were Mr and Mrs Gower with four of their daughters, and soon after, the Stanhopes and Webbs made their entrance, along with Mr and Mrs Arundell as well as others who were unknown to Emma. As the room filled, the gentlemen gradually gravitated toward one another, forming their own group in the corner, where a card game was soon underway.

Meanwhile, the ladies formed up near Mrs Blake who, ever the capable hostess, manoeuvred seamlessly among the guests, ensuring that tea was served, seats were taken, all were entertained, and no one was left unattended. She exchanged pleasantries with Mrs Edwards and Mrs Stanhope, listened patiently to Mrs Gower's latest complaints about her daughter's stubbornness, and directed the servants to bring in more refreshments when necessary.

At the same time, the younger ladies congregated near the windows in hopes of being the first to spot the return of the hunting party. Sophia and Georgiana Stanhope, along with the Gower sisters, speculated on the outcome of the hunt.

"Do you think James Tomlinson will distinguish himself today?" Miss Stanhope mused. "He is always boasting of his skill with a rifle."

Miss Georgiana said, "I think Richard Tomlinson is just as determined to prove himself. But I daresay they will be no match for Lord Osborne and Mr Musgrave. They always carry the finest game."

Miss Stanhope sighed wistfully. "If only we could have attended the hunt as well. It must be so thrilling to ride alongside the gentlemen and watch them shoot!"

The eldest of the Misses Gower interjected with a sly smile. "My dear Sophia, I suspect you are more interested in the gentlemen themselves than in their sport."

A chorus of laughter rippled through the group.

As time passed, the guests continued their amusements—some enjoying their tea and biscuits, others indulging in idle gossip, and a few taking up embroidery or small handicrafts they had brought with them. The gentlemen remained engrossed in their card game, occasionally calling for more refreshments. Mrs Blake ensured that the gathering remained lively, but she could not help but glance toward the windows every so often, anticipating the return of her son and her brother.

Emma spent much of the morning in quiet observation and remained near Elizabeth, though they spoke little. Elizabeth mostly spoke with Mrs Fuller and the other matrons. Occasionally, Miss Edwards attempted to draw Emma into her conversation with Margaret, but the latter insisted on holding the centre of attention.

The hours stretched on, marked by the steady hum of conversation and the occasional outburst of laughter. As midday approached, the anticipation in the room grew, for soon the hunters would return, and with them, the real excitement of the day would begin.

***

The triumphant party returned to Osborne Castle in high spirits, their horses, in contrast, looking faded as they approached the grand entrance. The air was filled with the chatter of men boasting of their prowess, the baying of hounds, and the occasional teasing remark exchanged among them. Leading the way was Lord Osborne himself, his riding coat flecked with dirt from the morning's exertions, his expression one of smug satisfaction. A fine stag was secured to one of the lead horses, along with a brace of hares and several game birds whose bright plumage was a stark contrast against the muddied hides of the horses.

Colonel Beresford, ever composed, inclined his head toward Captain Hunter as he murmured, "A good chase, though I had expected more from Musgrave."

Captain Hunter, wiping his brow with his sleeve, let out a hearty laugh. "Musgrave may talk well, but in the field, he is rather too cautious. A hunting man must have boldness, and that, my dear Colonel, is where we excel."

Mr Norton and Mr Styles, both sporting the proud air of men who had not been outdone, quickly agreed. "Indeed," Norton said, "though I wager no one can match Lord Osborne's fine shot today."

Lord Osborne flicked a speck of mud from his glove not interested in the chatter around him but feeling he must say something. "We had a good hunt today, gentlemen. Now let us enjoy our repast in good company," he said lightly, his gaze scanning the company assembling in front of the castle to welcome their return.

The Tomlinson brothers, Richard and James, rode slightly apart, each bearing the marks of a successful morning. Richard, the elder, bore the confident grin of a man certain of his own skill, while James, younger and still eager to prove himself, sat straighter in his saddle as if to command attention.

A ripple of movement went through the spectators as the men dismounted, handing off their mounts to waiting grooms. Mr Toliver, looking pale and sheepish, clung to his horse's reins a moment longer than necessary, prompting a knowing chuckle from Charles, who had also ridden out the full hunt. However, he stopped when Mr Howard put a hand on his shoulder and gave a warning squeeze—reminding him to behave himself.

The two groups met by the front entrance, and the hunters were praised for their prowess as they all began to trickle indoors for a late breakfast.

It was not long before the guests moved into the dining hall, the gentlemen offering their arms to lead the ladies to their seats. Lord Osborne, as host, naturally escorted Mrs Blake, their placement at opposite ends of the long table.

Mr Musgrave moved towards Miss Watson with a smug expression, but Mr Howard reached Elizabeth first just as Charles, intent on escorting Emma, ran up to her side. With the eldest and youngest Watson sisters claimed, Musgrave turned to the room at large—only to see that most of the young ladies were already paired with other gentlemen, forcing him to settle for Margaret—whose hopeful glances had not gone unnoticed—or Mary. He hesitated briefly, beginning to turn toward Miss Edwards, only to find her deftly avoiding his reach as Captain Hunter stepped in with an easy smile. Thus resigned, he offered his arm to Margaret, who took it with an air of satisfaction.

The seating was informal, though many of the older couples gathered at Lord Osborne's end of the table, while the militia and their chosen partners sat midway, and the rest took their places near Mrs Blake. The hum of voices filled the hall as servants began setting the dishes before them.

The meal commenced with spirited conversation. Some of the men, still caught up in the excitement of the hunt, debated who had shown the greatest skill that morning. Mr Norton declared with great assurance that Captain Hunter had made the cleanest shot, while Mr Richard Tomlinson countered that precision meant nothing without the thrill of the chase. Mr Gower, eager to participate, remarked about how unfortunate it was that Lady Osborne and Miss Osborne had been unable to attend during a lull in conversation which made his voice carry to the whole table.

"A shame indeed," Lord Osborne, to whom the comment had been directed, replied smoothly. "But you know how it is—London is full of diversions, and they had many engagements to attend."

Mrs Blake, glancing to ensure the conversation had moved on, leaned slightly toward Elizabeth and Emma—who were both seated to one side of her across from their partners. In a low voice, meant only for their ears, she murmured, "The truth is, they wanted no part in this affair. Too many tradesmen, too many lesser families under their roof—it did not suit Lady Osborne's sensibilities, and she would not allow Miss Osborne to attend." She let out a soft sigh, a flicker of disapproval in her expression. "But Lord Osborne was determined to host for the neighbourhood. So, he asked for my help, and here we are."

Elizabeth exchanged a glance with Emma, both absorbing the

confirmation of what they had each secretly suspected. The meal carried on, with laughter and conversation swirling around them, but the quiet revelation lingered between them, unspoken yet understood.

After the breakfast, which was served late enough to take the place of dinner—the gentlemen and ladies separated. The ladies moved to the East parlour—which was larger and had been opened to the connecting room where card tables were set up for later. Mrs Blake steered the ladies through various discussions while the men enjoyed their brandy and cigars in another room.

When the men re-joined the ladies, it was time for the customary performances. A few young ladies played and sang with varying degrees of success, and then Emma took her turn, her voice clear and her playing controlled, earning enthusiastic applause from most, though a few envious murmurs were exchanged among certain young ladies.

"How very accomplished Miss Watson is," murmured Miss Stanhope to her sister.

"Yes," Miss Georgiana replied with a smile that did not quite reach her eyes. "And how very pleased with herself she must be."

Elizabeth went up to Emma afterwards with Mr Howard, Mrs Blake, Charles, and Lord Osborne not far behind. "That was lovely, Emma dear. It is a shame that we have no pianoforte for you to practise on at home."

"That was marvellous! I have never heard anything so well-played, Miss Emma." Charles was gazing at her with admiration. "Even Miss Osborne and that stuffy Miss Carr could not play half so well."

While both his mother and uncle agreed with his praise of her skills, they scolded him for his remarks and manners, but he only said sulkily, "Well it's true."

He might have been scolded again, if it were not for Lord Osborne's interjection. "Charles is correct in his approbation of your skills. You would be much celebrated in London—both your playing and singing were superb. My sister plays well enough, but she has not the vocal range you exhibited."

Emma could not help but to appreciate his praise of her, but she could only lament that such commendation came from him and not Mr Howard.

As Emma was the last to perform, talk of dancing began, and the furniture was rearranged to allow for several couples to stand up while others who did not wish to participate could sit around the edge of the room or moved to the card tables in the connected parlour.

Charles, ever eager, asked Emma for the first dance just as Lord Osborne did the same. Noticing this, Mr Howard leaned in to whisper something to Charles. And, with only a brief hesitation, Charles changed his request, "I will take the second dance, if you do not mind."

Emma was discontent with the arrangement. She could have accepted Charles's offer without insulting Lord Osborne, but now she would have to take Osborne's hand or reject them both—effectively barring herself from dancing with Mr Howard should he have the chance to ask her.

Emma barely had time to accept the exchange before Lord Osborne claimed her hand, leaving her momentarily stunned before she forced herself to remain composed. She convinced herself that Howard had merely done what was expected—what was proper. Surely, it was nothing more than deference to his patron, but resentment simmered beneath her surface calm.

As they took their place, she was aware that most eyes in the room were upon them. Not only had Lord Osborne danced with her sister at the previous assembly, but now he was dancing with her at his own hunting party. She was sure that some of the matrons were hoping that he would ask their daughters as well and were probably wondering at the attention he was giving the Watson sisters.

Margaret, meanwhile, fluttered about Musgrave, lavishing him with compliments on his hunting success, though it was questionable whether he had truly been the best of the day. In the end, he felt that asking her for the first dance was his best chance at appeasing her while giving himself an escape from her once the dance was finished.

The rest of the couples took their places as the music began. Mr Howard had taken Miss Watson as his partner while Mary Edwards was paired with Captain Hunter. Meanwhile, Sophia and Georgiana Stanhope paired with the Tomlinson brothers and the Gower sisters were standing up with other militia officers.

Though many of the couples around them were enjoying themselves with smiles, laughter, and some conversation, Emma was too busy stewing in her discontent, and Lord Osborne, always sensitive to her moods, could not think what to say. So, the two danced in relative silence.

When the dance concluded, Emma curtsied stiffly and was swiftly approached by some of the young ladies wearing ingratiating smiles.

"Miss Watson, we have scarcely had the chance to speak before this evening, but I greatly admired your performance earlier," Miss Gower cooed.

Before Emma could respond, the lady's sisters joined them with the Stanhope girls in tow, their manners equally warm, though no less calculating.

"You must promise to call on us soon. We do so hope to become friends."

Emma, recognising the sudden shift in attention as the consequence of her dance with Lord Osborne, could not help but feel both irritated and amused.

Soon, some of the officers joined the ladies in their praise of her, and she received many offers to dance. Annoyed with their intentions to ingratiate themselves with her in order to get closer to the Osbornes—whom she wanted nothing to do with, she chose to dance only with Charles before sitting out the rest of the afternoon—claiming fatigue due to her recent illness.

Frustrated that the situation had kept her from dancing with Mr Howard, she placed the blame squarely on Lord Osborne. Meanwhile, the young ladies who were not dancing, along with the matrons, speculated about the Watsons' connection to the local lord. They had never heard of any closeness between the families and wondered at his sudden attentions.

Soon enough, though not as soon as Emma would have liked, their festivities wound to a close, and as the guests made their preparations to leave, it became clear that the Watsons had no easy means of returning home. The Howards would have needed to go far out of their way, and so Lord Osborne, with what he clearly viewed as gallantry, offered his own carriage.

Emma lingered a moment before departing, joining Mr Howard and Mrs Blake as they conversed with Elizabeth.

"You both must come to Wickstead next week," Mrs Blake insisted. "The children will be delighted to see you now that you are better. Just send word, and we shall send the carriage."

Emma thanked her, grateful for the invitation. As she turned, however, she found Lord Osborne standing beside her once more.

"You never congratulated me on my success today," he remarked, glancing toward Margaret, who was still showering Mr Musgrave with praise.

Emma barely concealed her exasperation. "I had not thought you required my congratulations, my lord."

He smiled at that, though whether at her words or at her evident irritation, she could not tell. "I do not require them, but I would be happy to receive them."

She congratulated him, and he seemed to accept even her begrudging compliments with a semblance of good humour.

At last, the carriage was ready. Lord Osborne handed them in, and the Watson sisters were on their way.

Margaret chattered excitedly about the evening, convinced that Mr Musgrave's attentions had been particularly marked. Elizabeth, as ever, was composed and mild in her responses. Emma, however, said nothing, merely staring out into the darkness, thinking of the evening's events and, most of all, of how little time she had gotten to spend with Mr Howard.

Chapter Eighteen

Penelope's Arrival

Friday, December 4th

The next few days after the hunt, Emma returned to helping Elizabeth in her visits to the parishioners which offered her a chance to mend her relationship with her sister. She had realised how isolated and lonely she had become during the hunting party, and her guilt for the way she treated her only real friend in Surrey could no longer be overlooked by her. Elizabeth was pleased to accept Emma's apology; however, she insisted that Emma would be limited to only visiting the parishioners closest to Stanton rectory. Emma agreed, and the days passed with ease. Emma even joined Elizabeth's sewing circle for the first time that Thursday where she learned of her sister's enviable skills with a needle and thread.

On Friday, the Watson sisters were invited to Wickstead. As Mr Musgrave was still in the local area, Margaret took advantage of the use of the carriage to be dropped off in Dorking once more while Elizabeth and Emma spent the day in the pleasant company of Mr Howard and the Blakes. Emma was thrilled to finally have a chance to get closer with the family but also envious of how easily Elizabeth was able to communicate with the others. At least now, when the three of them began to speak of their duties and meetings with parishioners, she was able to understand what they were dealing with. However, she found herself with little to contribute, aware that her own experiences had not prepared her for such in depth conversations.

Before they left, Charles reminded the sisters that there would be another hunt at Stanton Woods the following Saturday and asked that they attend. Since Mr Watson had been feeling their many absences of late, they agreed as long as they received their father's permission.

Charles took the chance to solicit dances from Emma and Elizabeth in case there was to be any dancing this time. Following his nephew's lead, Mr Howard requested a dance with each of the sisters as well, adding, "If there is no dancing at the gathering this time, we will just have to claim your first two sets at the next assembly," with a wink.

Elizabeth was saddened by this comment "I am afraid I will have to disappoint you as our father always needs one of us to stay home with him, and I cannot ask it of Emma nor would Margaret be willing to forgo the chance to dance."

"Whatever can your father need you for?" asked Mrs Blake.

"Our father insists on having one of us stay with him, so that he is not left alone the entire night, especially as we also spend a good deal of the day in preparation."

Their listeners became thoughtful, but they let the matter rest for the time being. Mr Howard rode with them on their return, "in order to greet their father," and they were off.

<hr/>

As they reached the lane where the parsonage stood, they were surprised when the coachmen had to pull the carriage aside to allow another to exit. In the time it took to reach the house, they all speculated on who it could have been as they did not recognise the carriage.

On their arrival, they were even more surprised to see their father downstairs with an unexpected relation.

"Well, there you are. It is about time the two of you returned; I expected you to be here to greet Dr Harding and me. In the meantime, you have just missed him, but I shall be able to introduce you all later." Noticing the man who had just walked in behind her sisters, she stared at him without saying anything.

Elizabeth smiled through her blush. She was used to her sister's antics, but Mr Howard's presence gave her behaviour a different sort of impression. "Welcome home, Penelope. Mr Howard, if you would allow me, this is my next oldest sister, Penelope, who has been away visiting a friend in Chichester. Penelope, this is the Reverend Mr Howard of Wickstead."

Penelope's eyes went wide as she realised just who their visitor was, and she said nothing else—only observing the situation.

"It is good to meet you, Miss Penelope. I see that I arrived at a bad time. I just wanted to give my greetings to Mr Watson and formally invite you all to attend the hunt at Stanton Wood tomorrow. My sister would be happy to come and collect any who wish to attend."

"We are glad for your offer, and I am sure some—if not all—of my daughters will be happy to take you up on it." Mr Watson was pleased with the attention and care Mr Howard and his sister showed their family.

With a nod and a bow, Mr Howard made his farewells and returned to his waiting carriage.

Once they saw off their guest, Elizabeth and Emma returned to the small parlour.

"So, how is our little sister getting on?"

Emma was taken aback at the lack of greeting from Penelope. However, she hid her disapproval. "I am well. It is good to see you again after so long, Penelope."

"Is it? I would not think you would be so happy to see any of us considering the situation that brought you here."

Emma flinched inwardly, but she kept her face passive. However, something about Penelope's expression made her feel like this sister could see through her calm mien. "Still, while the circumstances may not be ideal, it is nice to be able to spend time together with my family."

"Hmmm…" was all the response she received.

"Well, Penelope, what is this about Dr Harding?" asked Elizabeth in clear curiosity.

"Yes, well, I have come with some very important news of which I was just informing father, but, first, I am curious how you have all become so close with one of the Osbornes' set. Was it not you, Elizabeth, who once spoke of

Mr Howard as a 'proud looking gentleman' who was 'too high' for us?"

Elizabeth blushed deeply, "That—that was very wrong of me. I mean—it was before we got to know him."

"And how exactly did that come about?"

Elizabeth looked to Emma, but her sister was looking at Penelope with a coolness that made Elizabeth decide to answer for her. She explained the whole of their acquaintance with the Wickstead party. Penelope listened with attention, though her eyebrows slowly inched upwards during the whole of the tale until she looked quite incredulous.

"Well, dear me. It seems you have been a very busy girl, Miss Emma. Had I known how interesting things here would be with you around, I might not have gone to Chichester just when I did."

They were silent until Elizabeth once more asked about Penelope's news.

"Yes, yes. Dr Harding is here and you shall meet him when he joins us for dinner." She paused to look at Elizabeth, "I have already informed Nanny, but we may be eating a little later than usual to give her and Betty time to prepare properly. Dr Harding himself has just gone to procure a room at the White Hart, for he obviously cannot stay here, and, once he has cleaned himself up from his journey, he shall return."

"I am curious at your traveling here with Dr Harding. Did Mrs Shaw join you? It would be quite inappropriate to come such a distance otherwise," Elizabeth said. Though she thought she understood the reason, she decided not to make assumptions.

Penelope let out a small laugh, "Even you must know that it is acceptable for an engaged couple to travel together with a maid."

"So, you are engaged?"

"Indeed. We have come to receive father's blessing—though it is not really needed. However, Dr Harding is rather old-fashioned and wished for it anyway."

Emma considered her sister, realising how little she knew about her. Penelope had left soon after Emma's arrival, while she was still recovering from her journey and losses. In truth, they had spent no more than an hour or two together. However, she found that she did not like Penelope's way of speaking. To her, Penelope's attitude and behaviour were no better than Margaret's.

Suddenly, as if she was conjured by the thought, Margaret entered the room followed by Mr Musgrave. Both of them froze at the sight of Penelope.

"Why, Miss Penelope. It is good to see you home again. It has been some time since you were with us, and you are just in time, for I bring news of our next hunt," greeted Mr Musgrave with his usual manner.

Penelope only raised an eyebrow and stared at him as she said, "Indeed. However, you are too late as Mr Howard was just here to inform us and offer the use of his carriage."

Emma did not think it right for her sister to inform Mr Musgrave of such; however, Penelope's disillusionment with Mr Musgrave was one thing that Emma could appreciate about her, especially as she saw how discomposed it made Mr Musgrave who had expected more interest in himself.

"La!" interjected Margaret, "You are so cold, Pen! You should be more considerate towards guests," she used her defence of Mr Musgrave as a chance to sidle closer to him. "Musgrave was so kind as to offer me a ride home after hearing how I was forgotten by my sisters, and here you all are without a care for my well-being—not very sisterly if you ask me."

Emma was shocked at the accusation, but Elizabeth replied simply, "You never asked us to pick you up on our way, and we would not have known where to find you without direction."

Margaret blushed at being called out, but Mr Musgrave spoke up first. "What brings you back to Stanton with such auspicious timing?"

She snorted, "My timing is what it is. I have come to receive my father's blessing and request the reading of the banns." The two of them stood there in shock, unable to process what she was saying, which caused her to smirk.

Margaret was the first to react, having more information on the matter than Mr Musgrave. "So, you actually managed to catch that old fool you were chasing? Or did you find someone else to take you?" she asked incredulously.

"Did I not inform you in my letter of our growing attachment?"

"I just assumed it was your wishful thinking?"

Penelope arched a brow. "Unlike some people," she gave Margaret a pointed look, briefly glancing at Mr Musgrave for emphasis, "I do not indulge in delusions of grandeur, nor claim a connection with those who show me no interest."

Margaret reddened, but Mr Musgrave was now aware of some of the details and, being a lover of gossip himself, could not help but intervene. "Miss Penelope, you surprise me greatly! For I had no notion of your being courted let alone engaged to—who did you say he was again?"

Penelope gave him a sharp look. "I have been gone a full two months; during which time, I became engaged to Dr Harding of Chichester."

"I am all amazement! And who is this Dr Harping?" At her glare, he corrected himself, "Harding, did you say? Is he in the same profession as your good father?" he motioned towards Mr Watson who had been silently watching the whole display with clear irritation since the latter had entered.

"No, indeed. Dr Harding is a physician."

"A physician? Then he is in the same profession as your brother, Sam?"

"He is involved in the medical profession, yes. However, he is focussed on research rather than being a practitioner."

"Research? What sort of research?"

Before she could answer, Margaret began to titter. "As if Pen knows anything about the medical field. I doubt she has any idea what her *fiancé's* profession entails."

Penelope stared at Margaret until the latter became clearly uncomfortable before she sighed and said, "Dr Harding's research is focussed mainly on hygiene and disease transmission, questioning traditional medical beliefs like miasma theory. He is not a surgeon, but he works alongside them, contributing through study rather than direct practise."

They were all surprised, but Mr Musgrave's expression soon turned smug. "Ah, so he is a scholar rather than a man of real practise. I daresay his patients—should he have any—must find great comfort in being studied rather than treated."

Penelope looked at him gravely, and even Emma took offense on her yet unseen, soon-to-be brother-in-law's behalf and said, "Research is what allows medicine to advance. Without it, we would still be treating wounds with boiling oil and believing the king's touch could cure disease."

Penelope lifted an eyebrow at Emma's defence and nodded her appreciation when their eyes met.

Mr Musgrave gave a light chuckle, holding up his hands as if in surrender. "Oh, I would never dispute the value of clever men in libraries! But one hears of all sorts of new-fangled theories these days. You must take care, Miss Penelope, not to get caught up in such madness—lest you find yourself prescribed nothing but sunshine and good humour to cure all that ails you."

Margaret was the only one who laughed at his jest while the rest stared at him with varying degrees of distaste. Elizabeth could understand where he was coming from, but she could not understand his callous speech about a man whom none of them had met—especially when he would soon be part of their family.

With the growing tension in the room, Mr Musgrave soon made his farewells and left them. He had planned to spend more time with Miss Emma Watson on his friend's behalf, but he realised that he had outstayed his welcome.

With his departure, Margaret became livid and reproached her family for "treating dear Musgrave so harshly." After which she made her way upstairs, slamming her door behind her.

Her departure was followed by silence before they all decided to prepare for their meal and the guest it would be bringing.

⁓◦❡◦⁓

The sisters, including Margaret—whose moods were always ephemeral, were the first downstairs to await Dr Harding.

"Well, Penelope," began Elizabeth, "now that you have caught him, will you not tell us something of your courtship and our future brother?"

"Humph! Who cares about how she managed to persuade some silly old loon to marry *her*?" complained Margaret.

Penelope chuckled, "Jealousy has never suited you, Margaret."

"And why should I be jealous of some old Dr Harding?" Margaret said in the same sharp, quick way that she often spoke with Elizabeth. "What has a nobody Dr Harding have to offer?"

"A small estate on the outskirts of Chichester and a modest fortune, all of which shall belong to your sister—God willing she outlives him," said Mr Watson as he entered the room and sat down with a huff from the exertion of all his recent exercise.

Elizabeth and Margaret sat slack-jawed in shock as their father's words hit them. Emma was equally shocked, but she hid her surprise under a well-educated façade of calm. Meanwhile, Penelope sat smugly in her seat taking in their reactions.

Margaret was even more indignant at the suggestion of Penelope's future wealth. "Well—well, what can that have to do with us? Why should we care? After all, it's not even guaranteed that she will inherit his fortune. I mean, just look at Emma who—"

Her father cleared his throat loudly, "Margaret Arabella Watson! That is enough from you."

Margaret was indignant, but remained silent.

"I see you are just as foolish as always Margaret; no doubt still convincing yourself that Mr Musgrave will marry you: silly, irrational creature that you are."

Their father cleared his throat again, but that and a look were all the warning he needed to give Penelope.

She nodded and continued, "The fortune and estate shall not fully be under my control until Dr Harding's passing; however, I shall be the mistress of his estate in the meantime. Not to mention two hundred and fifty pounds of annual pin money from what he has settled on me while he lives." She gave them a moment for that to sink in, and Margaret's face was a study as she first went pale in shock and then reddened in indignation.

"Should our father's health fail; I will be just as capable as Robert and Jane at looking after my unmarried sisters—if not more so."

Margaret's expression and colour showed that her feelings had not softened, but she seemed to have no good comeback. Just then, they heard the sound of the carriage coming up the drive and prepared to greet their guest.

Chapter Nineteen

Ties that Bind

Penelope went out alone to fetch her fiancé as James was on hand to direct the coachman.

When she re-entered with her Dr Harding, the sisters were very surprised as he was not at all what they had been expecting. They had imagined him to be an old man about their father's age, but he looked to be no more than forty. However, his complexion was wan—likely due to his research keeping him indoors.

Dr Harding greeted them all cordially as he was introduced, then took a seat on the settee beside Penelope—their arms still entwined.

"It is a pleasure to finally meet you all. My dear Penny has told me so much about her family. What lovely daughters you have, Mr Watson—I find myself quite taken aback to be surrounded by such beauty," he said.

Margaret's jaw had dropped at his entrance. Though she managed to close it long enough to return his brief introduction, the expression that replaced it was one of open derision though it softened thanks to his compliment which she likely saw as directed at herself.

Elizabeth, however, greeted him with warmth and sincerity. "It is a pleasure to meet you at last. We have heard much about you from Penelope, though she never did get a chance to tell us of your courtship."

Emma schooled her features, trying not to let her discomfort show at her sister's forthrightness toward a man they had only just met.

"Is that so?" Dr Harding turned to Penelope with a smile. "While I am not sure how interesting the tale would be to others, I would not mind hearing my dear Penny's version of events."

"It is curious," added Margaret with a look that showed her malicious intent, "that someone in such a field of study as yours would take an interest in Penelope who can understand nothing of your work."

Dr Harding looked at her with clear confusion. "I am not sure what you mean by that. Your sister is very knowledgeable about recent medical advancements. It was our many discussions on such themes that led to my deep regard for her."

While his audience wanted to be amused at the thought of Penelope having any such knowledge, his serious manner of speech did not allow any but his instigator to show it.

"While you may not have cared, I was always interested to hear about what Sam was learning down in Guildford. Did you never wonder what we always wrote about and spoke of on his visits?" She paused for a moment but continued when it was clear they had not. "When I met Dr Harding, he gave me the chance to learn of theoretical medicine while Sam was focussed on the practical application of it."

"And what need have you for such information?" sniped Margaret. "It's not as if you could ever put it to any practical use."

"I may not have the ability to become a practitioner as such work is limited to men, but it does not mean that I cannot learn about it."

Margaret, in all her animosity, was the only one of the family who managed to say anything as they were all shocked into silence by the revelations that there might be more to Penelope than any of them had previously assumed.

"As to how we met, you already know that we were introduced by the Shaws—Dr Harding being the maternal uncle of Mr Shaw. Then, through an introduction at one of their dinner parties, I was able to meet and gain his attention. Our affection grew from there, and I am pleased to be marrying my dear Septimus."

"La!" the exclamation suddenly burst from Margaret, "Septimus?" she said with derision.

Penelope sighed at her sister's crude manner.

Dr Harding did not seem to mind, or at least he did not show any sign of noticing the barb. He simply explained, "My given name is John Septimus, as I was my parents' seventh child—though two of my elder siblings died in infancy."

Even Margaret could not laugh at that and was grudgingly silent.

Just then, Nanny came in to inform them that the dinner was ready, and they all made their way to the dining room.

Once they were all seated and served, Mr Watson—who had managed to compose himself—asked, "How are the Shaws doing? It has been some time since Mrs Shaw has returned to see her parents, has it not?"

"You forget that they visited the Tomlinsons when they came to collect Penelope and take her to Chichester two months ago," said Elizabeth.

Penelope nodded, "The Shaws will be here for our wedding on the 20th—after the third reading of the banns, and they plan to stay until after Christmas."

"They are a lovely young couple. Not only did the Shaws introduce Penelope and myself, but it was John who informed me that I had best take notice of her before some handsome, young buck came in and swooped her away." He completely missed the fact that his audience's expressions showed disbelief of such a thing happening as he paused to take another bite. After chewing, he spoke into the silence, "When I thought about all we had in common and the benefits of our mutual discussions, I knew I must act: we began our courtship the following day."

Mr Watson spoke up. "And what exactly was it about my second daughter that drew your attention?" His question was full of honest and simple curiosity.

"Ah. Well—at first, I just saw her as a friend of my nephew's wife. In fact, I had not thought of marriage until they suggested it. However, Penelope is an intelligent woman and a quick learner. She already knew much of the basic principles of medicine from her brother Samuel, and our discourse began from there. Since then, she has aided my research by providing insight from her brother's experience to support my theories. In fact, I am quite eager to finally meet him at our wedding. While my next younger brother is also in the profession, his information has not been half as valuable as your son's." He then looked back at Penelope and lifted her hand to his lips—staring into her eyes as he said, "All in all, I must agree with John. Penelope truly is my perfect helpmeet and has already contributed to both my research and my happiness."

Mr Watson smiled at the clear adoration in the man's gaze and admitted, "I did not know that Penelope had such an interest. However, I am pleased that she could be of help to a man such as yourself, and I am glad to hear that you both truly respect and care for one another."

Dr Harding's smile showed that he took their father at his word, and the conversation turned to talk of the wedding.

Dr Harding remained in the area until Monday when he returned to Chichester. He would be back in town the following Monday in order to attend the assembly next Tuesday with his fiancée and would stay until after the wedding. Due to the family connection, the Tomlinson's had invited him to stay in their home at that time.

While he was with them, Emma decided he was a very silly man. Though intelligent, he had little common sense. In her view, this had two advantages: first, he tolerated Penelope's bluntness without recognising her judgmental nature; and second, he remained oblivious to Margaret's snide remarks and thus never took offense.

Unlike her sisters, Elizabeth found him to be a very nice person and congratulated Penelope on her conquest of such a good man. While she found most of his conversations incomprehensible, knowing nothing of medical science herself, she was in awe of him.

Over the following week, Penelope was out of the house almost as often as Margaret. While she was more helpful to Elizabeth inside the home, her tactless nature made her useless with the parishioners. As a result, like Margaret, she spent much of her free time visiting friends in Stanton and Dorking.

When she was home, however, she and Margaret were constantly bickering. Elizabeth had mentioned they did not get along, but her words had not done justice to the reality. When they were not outright fighting, they were making snide remarks.

Whatever kindness Margaret had once shown Emma had long since worn off, while Penelope regarded her in a way that made her feel as if she were an unsightly tear in a favourite dress. It stirred all her old feelings of being surrounded by inferior minds, and any hope Emma had held for domestic peace in the near future was quickly fading. She was looking forward to Penelope's wedding, if only because it would remove at least one source of conflict from the house.

Their father stayed in his room most days even when they dined, so it was only the sisters sitting at meals. The only good thing about his reclusive nature was that Emma could get away for a few hours every day in order to read to him and keep him company. She had completely forgotten her previous cruelty towards her father in light of the distress she experienced in dealing with her sisters.

Penelope had a habit of observing Emma and making judgmental remarks. One day, Emma was slow to pick up her utensils, still unaccustomed to the simpler table setting. Penelope noticed immediately. "Why do you hesitate, Emma? Is the food not to your taste?" Emma quickly replied that she had merely been wool-gathering, but Margaret snickered at her discomfort, while Elizabeth continued eating, seemingly oblivious to the tension between her sisters.

At other times, Penelope would comment, "Is that the dress you mean to wear today? Do you not think it too extravagant for a morning at home?" or, "So it is true, what Margaret said—you spend most of your days reading and being idle."

Emma had once told Elizabeth, *"If my opinions are wrong, I must correct them. If they are above my situation, I must endeavour to conceal them."* But with Penelope's antagonism and Margaret's growing indifference—tinged with resentment— she found herself concealing more than just her opinions.

Meanwhile, Mr Musgrave visited twice that week, only adding to the tension between the sisters. Whether to annoy Margaret or to soothe his own ego by rekindling Penelope's appreciation, he spent most of his time either sidling up to her or making insinuating remarks about Lord Osborne to Emma which earned them Penelope's curious gaze. She could only hope he would return to London after the hunting party on Saturday—for even Margaret's complaints about his absence would be preferable to his continued presence if he persisted in such behaviour.

Chapter Twenty

A Study in Society

Emma

Saturday, December 12th

When the day of the hunt finally arrived, Emma could not even remember the cause of her disquiet at the previous one. Since she was perfectly healthy, her father and the apothecary both agreed that there should be no problem with her riding out. She was very much looking forward to being on a horse again especially as it would give her a chance to get away from her bickering sisters as none of them could ride, and, with no Miss Osborne, she could enjoy the company of Mr Howard and Charles.

When Emma came downstairs that morning in her riding habit, Penelope gave her a once over. For a moment, Emma tensed up assuming that her sister was going to say something, but Penelope only turned her head back towards Elizabeth and continued her conversation.

Since the hunt was taking place at Stanton Wood, Lady Evelyn would be their hostess for the day. This meant that Mrs Blake and the Watson sisters would be able to remain with the participants until the sound of the horn announced the start of the hunt.

As soon as they arrived, Mr Howard and Charles walked over with their steeds and Pippa in tow. Soon after, Emma was mounted and ready to ride. She was delighted at the opportunity to spend time with Mr Howard, knowing he always remained at the back of the hunt with Charles and never participated in the main action. So, she need not worry about slowing him down or losing him midway.

However, as they rode toward the woods and the hunting party, her elation began to fade. Against the backdrop of horses, she caught sight of the bright colours of ladies' riding habits. Mr Howard was leading her toward them. Only then did Emma realise she would not be the only woman present.

Mr Howard asked the well-dressed ladies if he might have the honour of making introductions, and the ladies agreed. He presented Miss Emma Watson to the Ladies Emma and Eleanor Bulkeley, along with their younger brother, the Honourable George Bulkeley—the children of the Earl and Countess of Anglesey. The Hon. George Bulkeley, only a few years older than Charles Blake, would be riding with the younger boys which included William and George Evelyn. The Evelyns were distant cousins, and since Sir Frederick had no heirs or next of kin, his estate would one day pass to them.

Next, she was introduced to Lady Bennet, wife of Sir Caesar Bennet, and the Honourable Miss Grimston—daughters of the Viscount Grimston; the Honourable Misses Harriet, Arabella, and Georgiana—the daughters of Viscount Cranley; and the Misses Elizabeth, Maria, and Emma de Bouverie, granddaughters of the Earl of Radnor through a younger son. While the Bulkeley ladies greeted her with open, welcoming smiles, the Bouverie girls were far less gracious. They looked at her as though there were an unpleasant odour emanating from her.

The horns sounded soon after the introductions were made, and the party set off. Relief flooded through Emma as she noticed that Mr Howard and the young men remained close to her group. That, at least, was comforting. But just as she was beginning to relax, Lady Emma suddenly remarked, "It is nice to be able to put a face to the name."

Emma turned to her, puzzled. Lady Emma continued, "We have heard something of you from Miss Osborne, though she did not mention we might meet you here."

Emma's stomach tightened. "She spoke of me?" She managed to keep her expression composed, but her thoughts raced. *She warned me not to ingratiate myself with their party. Has she made accusations? Is this what she meant by ruining my family?*

"She said she rode with a Miss Watson who was a talented horsewoman, able to keep up with the hunt with ease—"

"—even riding side-saddle, you had no trouble," finished Lady Eleanor, who had drawn up beside her with a smile.

Emma hesitated, surprised that Miss Osborne had spoken of her so favourably. At last, she admitted modestly, "I have always enjoyed riding."

Miss Bouverie made a small noise of disbelief. "Indeed?" she said, eyeing Emma's mount. "I am surprised you can afford such diversions. Did not Mr Howard inform us that you are nothing more than the child of a simple country vicar?"

Emma kept her expression serene, as though she had not noticed the slight. "I am sure you also have family among the clergy, as it is a perfectly respectable profession for younger sons."

Miss Bouverie's lips pursed. "And who exactly are your relations, Miss Watson?"

Before Emma could answer, Lady Emma turned to Miss Bouverie with an arched brow. "Miss Watson is a welcome part of our company today, Elizabeth. I should think you would understand that common courtesy ought to be observed."

Mr Howard, oblivious to the exchange, was preoccupied with thwarting the boys' repeated attempts to escape whenever his back was turned, corralling them back toward their group.

She hoped for a chance to converse with him, but the boys had their own plans—namely, slipping away at every opportunity. Emma watched them all through the hunt, half amused and half resigned. It was not the morning she had anticipated.

While she had made some new acquaintances and potential friends, Mr Howard had been wholly distracted. Nevertheless, she held her own against the elder Misses Bouverie and the eldest Miss Onslow, who were openly antagonistic toward her. It helped that she had the support of Lady Emma, Lady Eleanor, and Miss Grimston—and that the younger ladies followed their lead.

Omniscient

While Emma was off with a hunt, her sisters travelled on with Mrs Blake to the Stanton hunting lodge where conversation, companionship, and confections awaited. The main room at Stanton Lodge hummed with quiet conversation. At first, the four ladies sat together to drink tea and speak with each other, but as the lodge began to fill, they rose to mingle with their neighbours.

Margaret, wearing her best day dress, had taken it upon herself to wander alone through the gathering, alighting on conversation after conversation with all the grace of a peacock forcing its way into a flock of swans.

"Sir Frederick and Lady Evelyn, it was so good of you to extend your invitation to include us again. It was too kind. Though our father could not be here, he sends you his warm regards," she spoke with slow articulation, determined to be pleasing.

"I must say, Lady Evelyn, I absolutely adore your gown! Such a daring shade of yellow—it matches your hair quite well," Margaret said with a bright smile.

Lady Evelyn, whose complexion was rather sallow, stiffened as she was unsure if the comment could be considered a compliment. "How kind of you," she replied, her voice clipped.

Undeterred, Margaret turned to Lady Bridget Bouverie, who had just joined the conversation. "And Lady Bridget, correct? I believe I saw your son preparing to join the hunt this morning. His conversation with Miss Fuller was most interesting."

Lady Bridget blinked. "Interesting?" she echoed.

Margaret tilted her head with a knowing smile. "Well, yes, you see, she is so very lively, and he is rather studious—it is quite the contrast? And yet, I could not help but think—is not his grandfather an earl while her grandfather was only the son of a tradesman?"

Lady Bridget's expression remained composed, but there was a flicker of consideration in her gaze. "I do not see that it should be a problem. My son is very popular among the young ladies, as he ought to be, but he also knows his duty to his family." She paused, her eyes sharpening slightly. "I must admit, I am curious as to why a country parson's daughter feels compelled to bring this to my attention?"

Margaret's smile widened; her tone full of practised humility. "Oh, well, it is precisely because I am a country parson's daughter that I know my place. I felt it only proper to inform you, as I know my duty to those above me."

A brief silence stretched between them before Lady Bridget's expression softened into a small, approving smile. "How very conscientious of you, Miss Watson," she murmured, inclining her head ever so slightly in appreciation.

Meanwhile, Lady Evelyn stood and listened, her lips pressed into a thin line. She had married into a title when she became the wife of a baronet, so she did not much appreciate Margaret's insinuations and meddling nature.

"Miss Margaret," Lady Evelyn said with a polite smile. "I hope you enjoy the rest of your morning." She spoke in a manner meant to encourage the young lady to remove herself from their presence.

Margaret beamed and wandered off again to her next victim without even realizing how she had been ejected from the conversation.

⁓ೕ⃝ೖ⁓

While Margaret busied herself with flattery and offense in equal measure, Mrs Blake led Elizabeth and Penelope to meet some of the other guests. She first introduced them to a group that included some they already knew: Mr and Mrs Tomlinson, their daughter Mrs Richard Fuller and her husband, and the latter's brother James along with his wife and eldest neice—the very Miss Fuller whom Margaret was at that time gossiping about. They were standing with two other couples who were unknown to the ladies.

After greetings were made, Mr Tomlinson introduced the others as Mr and Mrs Charles Vernon of Sussex, who were currently guests of the Tomlinson family, and Mr and Mrs Robert Smith of Cheam.

"We have just been speaking of our estates and the joys of country living," said Mr Tomlinson jovially, and the group settled into polite discourse with easy familiarity.

"Have you been to Leatherhead, Miss Watson?" Mrs Vernon inquired pleasantly, turning to Elizabeth. "It is rather quieter than Dorking or Tunbridge Wells which is near my parents' estate, but there is a certain charm to it, I think."

Elizabeth smiled. "Only in passing, I am afraid. I believe my father may have attended a meeting of the clergy there, but it is not a place I know well."

"Oh! You must visit in spring," Mrs Smith interjected. "The downs near Box Hill are lovely when the hawthorn is in bloom. It quite transforms the landscape."

Mr Smith gave a small chuckle. "My wife may live near the city now, but she has always enjoyed the countryside. Since we moved some years back, she has insisted on planning outings to Box Hill and other such scenic locations every chance she gets."

"And do you disagree with her preference, sir?" Elizabeth asked in honest curiosity.

"He does not," Mrs Smith said, smiling at her husband. "He is just as enamoured with nature and appreciates Mr Tomlinson's living nearby—giving us every excuse to visit the area regularly."

They all laughed together as Mr Smith heartily agreed and thumped the other man on the back to support his claims.

"I believe a man who knows London well would argue that nothing in the countryside compares to a good view of the Thames on a fine morning," said Mr Smith with a sly smile.

"Yes. That is a lovely sight to behold when it can be had, but London air often prevents such an occurrence," replied Mr Richard Fuller who received a loud chorus of agreement from their party.

"And so, here we are. Living quite comfortably outside of London," replied Mr James Fuller.

"I believe that it is a blessing to have an estate and not be bound to London. It is an excellent place to earn one's living, but the country is a better place to enjoy it," said Mr Tomlinson.

They all chuckled at that.

Mr Vernon, who had been listening with an amused expression, said, "I am sure there are many in the city who would rather deal with tenant rents than balance ledgers."

"A mistake, I assure you," Mr William Fuller, who had just joined them with his wife, interjected. "Tenants are every bit as troublesome as clients, only with the additional burden of expecting their landlord to be endlessly generous."

Mr Tomlinson laughed at their insight. "You both must have heard such from your grandfather. Perhaps that is why he was such a successful businessman—he understood both sides of the equation."

"We must allow him his fondness for London." Mr Vernon reasoned, "I suspect Mr William fears that if he spends too much time admiring the countryside, his wife will convince him to purchase an estate."

"I should not have to convince him at all. A man of means ought to think of his heirs, and what better inheritance than land?" replied Mrs William Fuller with a smile.

"Then I suppose the country must prepare itself for another landowner," said Mr Vernon, grinning. "I suspect Mrs William Fuller will not rest until her husband is master of an estate."

The others laughed at the exchange, and Elizabeth, though quieter, found herself at ease in the company. The conversation drifted to the affairs of the neighbourhood—local gatherings, changes among the gentry, and even a discussion on class systems.

"Oh yes. The nobles may pretend that our class lines are neatly drawn, but in truth, money ties men together faster than a family name ever could." Mr Tomlinson looked at those gathered around him. "Look at Vernon, here; from a long line of landed gentry whose late uncle was an earl and whose cousin married a baron, but you would never know that he boasts such lofty connections by the company he's keeping now: first- and second generation landowners all."

The others were surprised by the fact, but Mr Vernon—always a good-natured and jovial man—simply shrugged and said, "Ah, but Mrs Vernon," he looked to his wife, "is the daughter of a baronet who condescended to marry this mere tradesman."

Mrs Vernon smiled at her husband, "It is not uncommon, I believe, for many tradesmen to be able to trace their roots back to titles and nobility. After all, it is often the only way that the sons of younger branches can make their own fortunes."

"It is true," said Mr Smith. "My father-in-law was the youngest son of a landed gentleman with no more than three thousand pounds to his name. Through first racing horses then breeding them, he was able to turn that into one hundred thousand pounds. He made enough of a fortune that my wife's sister married the heir to an earldom. Though my dear Caroline settled for a mere Mister," he finished with a laugh as his wife teased that she had since considered her choice quite rash.

While it may have seemed to some that they were bragging about their connections, Mrs Blake and the Watson sisters understood it was all just good-natured raillery.

Mrs Blake was thoughtful for a moment before speaking. "And yet, it *is* remarkable how well everyone gets on, considering our different origins. One hears so often of money dividing families rather than uniting them."

"It is true. Marriages and fortunes can make or break relationships." Mrs Smith then considered. "Perhaps it depends upon whether money was the object or merely the means."

"Let us not forget the nature of the people themselves." Mr James Fuller added thoughtfully, "There are men whose success turns them proud, just as there are those born to comfort who cannot abide a change in fortune. But I have always found that respect and familiarity matter far more than birth or wealth."

"Spoken like a man whose family has known both," said Mr Tomlinson in a manner that showed his dislike for such serious conversation outside of business.

"I suppose that is the true difference—not whether one was born to something, but how one embraces it," mused Penelope who, until then, had only been observing. "Do you think it was easier for your families, since you built your fortunes rather than inheriting them?"

Mr Tomlinson shrugged. "Easier, perhaps, in the sense that we knew how much we stood to gain—or lose. But in other ways, it's never easy. One does not move in society without noticing where one is placed, or how others regard it."

"And yet, despite it all, you are close," said Elizabeth to end the topic. She had caught on to Mr Tomlinson's growing dislike for the subject.

Then, in a curious but measured tone, Penelope said, "I cannot help but wonder—how is it that you all came to be so well acquainted? You speak as if you have always known one another, yet your families are from different backgrounds, though your fortunes, if I understand correctly, were made in a similar way."

Mr Richard Fuller lived in Dorking and knew the sisters well through his wife and sister-in-law's friendship with them; therefore, he was used to Penelope's inquisitive nature and took it upon himself to respond. "Our grandfather was of the Fuller family of Tandridge. He went into banking, made his fortune, and purchased our family estate—which you already know." She nodded. "Mr Tomlinson worked for our grandfather and was taken on as his apprentice when he showed a high aptitude for the business."

Mr Tomlinson took over. "He was a great man, too. Since his sons showed no interest, he decided to leave the running of the bank to his two best students," he glanced over at Mr Vernon with a grin as he finished.

The latter continued happily. "My father was a younger son who went into the law. After inheriting the family estate on the death of my uncle, *my* older brother—as the heir, was allowed to remain idle. However, I received only a thousand pounds and was left to find a profession. Eventually, I chose to try my hand at banking because it matched my skills—which is how our families first became acquainted."

Penelope considered this, "So it was business that first connected you, but friendship that kept you close."

"Precisely. Business made us allies, but trust made us friends. And when you trust someone, you do not let go of them so easily," replied Mr Tomlinson warmly.

"Nor do you mind when your families begin to merge together," added Mr James Fuller with a wink for Richard and his wife.

"Or when those friendships turn into lifelong entanglements," added Mr Smith wryly.

They all laughed at his façade of discontent.

Emma

The young ladies returned before the hunting party. The men had been led on a merry chase, catching several small game before the women decided they were tired and should return. Charles and his friends wished to remain with the hunt, but Mr Howard deemed they had enjoyed enough excitement for one morning.

Upon arriving at the lodge, the ladies lingered outside, taking a leisurely walk about the grounds to stretch their legs before re-joining the others. The younger Bouverie and Onslow girls had started to respect Emma for her riding skills, so she was able to converse with them more easily. By the time they finally went indoors a quarter of an hour later, they had just enough time to change out of their riding habits and into their day dresses before the hunters returned triumphant. Soon after, they were all ushered into the dining room for breakfast. Given the presence of noble and titled families, the seating arrangement would be more formal.

All the single ladies came together in one group while Lady Bennet joined her husband, and Miss Grimston went to find her fiancé—the Hon. Mr Arthur Onslow. Their group included the Bulkeley, Onslow, Bouverie, and Watson sisters as well as Mrs Blake, Miss Lock, Miss Fuller, and Miss Philips. She felt both tense and excited when she saw Mr Howard approaching and barely registered Lord Osborne, Mr Musgrave, and all the other young men from the hunt, along with one older gentleman, walking with him.

Lord Osborne was wearing a grim expression as he made his way toward the ladies. Sir Frederick had directed him to invite Lady Emma as his partner, as Osborne was the highest-ranked among the young gentlemen—though he could only think that she was not the Emma he wished to escort.

Mr Howard went to his sister with the older gentleman, "Dear sister, allow me to introduce Viscount Grimston. He has kindly agreed to be your partner." He said with a teasing smile. Mrs Blake was a little taken aback, but she curtsied and formally greeted the much older gentleman.

After exchanging pleasantries, they were off to join the rest of the older couples.

Emma had paid so much attention to Mrs Blake and Mr Howard's interaction with Lord Grimston, that she barely heard as Lord Osborne introduced all the young men. The group included Viscount Bulkeley; Lord Dunboyne—son of Viscount Grimston; the Hon. George Bulkeley; the Hon. Misters Thomas and Edward Onslow; Mr Charles Bouverie; Mr Musgrave; Mr Dennison, M.P.; the Reverend Mr Howard; Mr Frederick Locke; Misters Richard and James Tomlinson; Mr Edward Bird; and Mr Charles Philips.

Lord Osborne looked dejectedly at Miss Emma for a moment before he asked Lady Emma for her hand, but the object of his interest did not even notice as she was intent on watching Mr Howard out of the corner of her eye. Each of the titled gentlemen paired with their counterpart in station among the ladies.

Viscount Bulkeley offered his arm to Lady Eleanor while Lord Dunboyne did the same for Miss Onslow—her younger sisters being claimed by their other brothers, Thomas and Edward. Miss Bouverie seemed as disappointed as her brother when he took her arm—leaving Miss Maria to Musgrave (which gained an audible gasp from Margaret) and Miss Emma—who was not yet out in society—to George Bulkeley—who, though of higher rank, was only fourteen.

Mr Dennison had offered his escort to Miss Locke, and Emma's heart sank when she saw Miss Fuller at that same moment taking Howard's proffered arm with a coy smile.

Elizabeth noticed it too, and told Emma to cheer up. However, as Mr Locke took Miss Philips, Mr Richard Tomlinson came to claim her own hand—leading her away from her younger sisters.

After that, Mr James Tomlinson came to claim Penelope. "While I appreciate being amongst such exalted company, I am glad I was able to claim a partner I can speak freely with," he leaned in to say as she took his offered arm.

Penelope chuckled, and Emma was a little jealous of her sister—for when Mr Bird walked up to Margaret, Mr Philips came to collect herself. It made Emma uncomfortable to realise that, while it would not have been the case in the past, she was now the lowest ranking lady at the party. She lost another chance to speak with Mr Howard and must spend the whole breakfast next to someone completely unknown to her until that moment.

Emma went through all the motions of eating by habit. Charles Philips was amiable enough company, but Emma scarcely paid him any mind. Her thoughts remained fixed on Mr Howard; her mood soured by disappointment. Mr Philips, however, was undeterred, filling the silence with cheerful chatter until suddenly, a particular name caught her ear.

She started and looked up from her food, "Do forgive me, but could you repeat that?"

"Yes?" he looked confused, apparently not having noticed her lack of interest in his conversation. "Oh, you mean about my aunt?"

"Yes. I think I must have misheard."

The confusion and wonder on her face caused him to smile widely, "No, it's true. My aunt Mrs D'Arblay—better known as Frances Burney—is here today. It's thanks to her and her connections that we got an invitation."

Emma stared at him, uncertain. It seemed an odd thing to announce so casually. He was around her own age—still full young for a man—and had not yet learned discretion. Surely, if such a distinguished author were in attendance, she would have been properly introduced or at least acknowledged by their hosts? Or was it something commonly known to those in the area? She glanced around, seeking confirmation from the expressions of others, but Philips mistook her intent.

"Oh, if you're looking for her, she's right over there." He pointed to an older lady, around the same age as Lady Osborne, sitting with an older gentleman down the table. She was wearing a monstrosity of a hat, which Emma noted at the same time her partner voiced it. That almost caused her to laugh out loud, so she quickly covered her mouth.

"Shall I introduce you when we remove to the parlour?"

Emma's breath caught. It was one thing to dine at the same table and another to meet the woman herself. Of course, she was not sure if the lady would appreciate the introduction. Yet the idea of meeting her was thrilling.

"If it would not be an imposition…" she began hesitantly.

"Not at all! She would be delighted, I'm sure."

Chapter Twenty-One

A Hunt for Decorum

Penelope

When the meal ended, Penelope allowed Mr James Tomlinson to lead her back to his sister, Mrs Richard Fuller, and her husband. Soon, they were joined by his parents, Mr Dennison, Mr and Mrs Morgan, and the Hon. Mr Bouverie.

The gentlemen had been discussing politics at dinner, and they decided to continue their discourse about the ongoing war with France with a larger audience. Mr Dennison and Mr Bouverie, both experienced Members of Parliament, took it upon themselves to explain to Mr Tomlinson and Mr Fuller their views.

Mr Dennison confidently asserted, "The best course for improving our soldiers' health is ensuring ample fresh air and proper exposure to the elements. Miasma, after all, is the worst cause of illness in the ranks."

Penelope, who had been listening with rapt attention, shifted, causing Mrs Tomlinson to glance at her warily. Mr James Tomlinson and Mrs Richard Fuller, more accustomed to Penelope's sharp mind, watched with amusement.

Penelope's brow furrowed slightly. "Pardon me, sir, but recent medical research, particularly that of Dr Harding, suggests otherwise. Disease does not spread simply through foul air but through physical transmission—contaminated hands, unclean instruments, and proximity to infected persons."

Mr Bouverie hesitated for only a fraction of a second before giving her a placating smile. "Miss Penelope, you are well-read, I see; however, that sounds like a fancy put into your head by an overzealous physician. Soldiers have been dying in wars for centuries. Are we to believe a bit of hand-washing would have kept them in good health?"

Mr James Tomlinson crossed his arms with a smile playing at his lips. "If physicians such as Dr Harding are proving these theories, why should they not be considered?"

Mr Morgan huffed. "And how do you suggest we implement these ideas? Are we to provide fresh basins and soap for every common soldier? It is entirely impractical."

Mr Tomlinson, ever the diplomat, nodded thoughtfully. "It's true that change comes slowly, but should we not consider new methods if they may improve lives?"

Penelope did not waver. "The question, Mr Morgan, is not what is convenient, but what is right. Is it not our duty to protect the men who fight for our country? If simple cleanliness can prevent needless suffering, why should we deny it?"

Mr Dennison—still a banker at heart—pursed his lips. "It is an expensive endeavour, Miss Penelope. The government must balance necessity with feasibility."

Mr James Tomlinson gave a small smile. "Surely, Mr Dennison, no expense is too great if it means saving the lives of those brave men who defend us from the French scourge?"

Mr Richard Fuller nodded in agreement. He had read up on the research of Dr Harding after the man's last visit. "Dr Harding's work suggests that simple changes—boiling instruments and washing hands—could reduce deaths significantly. Why reject an idea before considering its merit?"

Mr Morgan muttered something about the absurdity of coddling soldiers. Penelope, still composed, tilted her head slightly. "If you had an injury, sir, would you prefer your surgeon's hands to be clean or caked in the filth of his last patient?"

The question hung in the air. Mr Morgan cleared his throat and glanced around as if looking for an escape, while Mr Bouverie's smirk faltered. The Fullers and Tomlinsons exchanged satisfied glances.

Mr Dennison was the first to give in, "Well, I suppose there is some sense in cleanliness."

Penelope merely smiled. "I am pleased you think so, sir."

Mr Dennison chuckled. "You argue well, Miss Penelope. Perhaps we should all be grateful you are not in the House of Commons—our debates would be much longer, I suspect."

"Perhaps," she replied smoothly, "but then, imagine how much we could advance if women were allowed a say in government."

Mrs Tomlinson gave an audible intake of breath, and Mrs Fuller barely contained her laughter behind her fan. Mr Dennison, rather at a loss for words, managed only a polite nod before shifting the subject.

Penelope, satisfied, stood back as if she had merely made a casual observation on the weather until Elizabeth came to fetch her away.

Margaret

After breakfast, Mr Edward Bird escorted Margaret towards a small cluster of his friends that included the Locke siblings, Miss Fuller, and Miss Philips.

Miss Locke was just then overheard saying, "Oh, Mr Musgrave's a most interesting fellow. His manner of flattery has taken him quite far in life."

They all looked over at Mr Musgrave on the other side of the room as he was sidling up to all the nobles and their children, and a chorus of titters and chuckles greeted their newest arrivals.

Margaret, not noticing Miss Locke's sarcastic tone, interjected. "Oh, yes. He is so accomplished and so well regarded. Why, he has long been a great friend to the Osbornes and my own family as well. Indeed, I daresay there is no one who knows him so well as I do."

Miss Philips, a placid girl with a faintly bemused expression, exchanged a glance with her brother who had just joined them after leaving Miss Emma with his aunt. "There you are, Charles. Miss Margaret was just telling us about the closeness with Mr Musgrave."

He grinned back at her, but Margaret missed it.

"Indeed," Margaret exclaimed, disregarding their clear ridicule of her assertions. "He is often at the parsonage when he is not at the castle or in London." This was true, but it also ignored the fact that he was almost always in one of the latter two locations. "Such an amiable gentleman is sure to go far, why, I would not be surprised if he were to win a position in parliament during the next election. And it is only natural that *I* should concern myself with his future prospects, given our intimacy," she added, lifting her chin with quiet pride.

"In what regard do you speak of intimacy, Miss Margaret?" Mr Locke inquired, his brow lifting, and the others looked no less curious for all that there was clear contempt in their gazes that Margaret either missed or chose to ignore.

Margaret smirked coquettishly, then responded, "Need I explain myself? After all, in order to be truly successful, a man must have a good wife to support him. A gentleman of Musgrave's standing would obviously seek such a one whose understanding and interests align with his own ambitions. Surely he could not be content with anyone less worthy."

Mr Bird let out a soft chuckle. "Indeed, I was under the impression his ambitions were quite... well-known. But I did not realise he had found a lady with the fortune to meet them?"

A ripple of amusement passed through the small group.

Margaret finally noticed their scornful tone and flushed deeply. Then she laughed loudly enough for most of the room to hear her. "You must all simply be jealous of him. After all, people from such paltry estates and insignificant families could never hope to attain his level of success—or anything approaching it."

Before any of them had time to react, Mrs Blake came to claim Margaret's attention. She greeted everyone before turning to Margaret and asking if the younger girl might take a walk about the room with her.

Margaret was pleased to have one of the Osbornes' set show her preferential treatment at such a time and accepted without recognizing the older woman's true motive—to separate her from her current course of destruction without doing any more damage.

They said their farewells, and Mrs Blake used their walk to steer Margaret towards her waiting sisters.

Emma

True to his word, after the meal, Charles made his way to his aunt, leaving Emma momentarily alone. She took the opportunity to compose herself, smoothing her skirt and steadying her breath. A meeting like this required a measure of decorum, despite the excitement bubbling beneath her exterior.

"Aunt, may I present Miss Emma Watson?" Mr Philips said cheerfully. "She's most eager to make your acquaintance."

Emma curtsied, schooling her features into careful politeness while Mr Philips, seeing some of his friends took his leave of both ladies.

Mrs D'Arblay turned a sharp, assessing gaze on Emma, then smiled kindly. "Miss Watson, a pleasure."

Emma swallowed. "The pleasure is mine, madam." She hesitated, unsure how to proceed without seeming too forward. "I—" She faltered, then found her voice. "I have had the honour of reading *Evelina* more than once. Your wit and understanding of society are unequalled."

Mrs D'Arblay's smile deepened. "Ah, a reader of novels. A rare and oft-maligned breed."

Emma felt her cheeks warm. "I am aware that some consider novel-reading frivolous, but I have always thought a well-told story both instructive and illuminating."

Mrs D'Arblay gave a knowing nod. "You have the right of it. A young lady who reads with discernment will never be at a loss in conversation."

Emma held in a sigh, feeling as though she had passed some unspoken test. "I would not impose upon your time, madam, but I must say how much I admire your work."

The much older woman regarded her thoughtfully, then said, "That is never an imposition. In fact, it is rather gratifying." She paused before continuing with a grin, "However, Miss Watson, you praise my understanding of society, yet you compose yourself as if this conversation is of no particular consequence to you. I wonder—are you truly so calm, or are you merely determined to appear so?"

Emma hesitated, but then replied, "I was taught that it is unseemly to display too much enthusiasm, but, if I have given the impression that this moment is of no consequence, then I must correct it. I could not have imagined a greater honour."

Mrs D'Arblay found it amusing and a little telling—seeing in Emma both sincerity and the weight of the expectations placed upon her. So, she softened her tone, realizing Emma was trying to balance her excitement with propriety.

It was then that Emma overheard a familiar voice nearby. It was Penelope who was clearly engaged in an argument with some of the older gentlemen. Emma winced. She could not discern the words, but the tone alone was enough to tighten her posture, and Mrs D'Arblay seemed to notice it, too. Soon after, another burst of sound drew her attention in the opposite direction: Margaret's uncontrolled laughter rang out. She was standing with a group of people who were staring at her, some in derision and some in disgust.

Mrs D'Arblay arched her brow and turned to Emma with an amused, though measured, expression.

"Well," she murmured, "at least you seem to have mastered restraint in both volume and expression. Some are not so fortunate."

Emma froze, a flush creeping up her neck. The remark was not judgemental, merely an observation, yet it landed with an almost unbearable weight. The idea that her family's conduct was so conspicuous as to warrant comment—especially from someone she admired—was mortifying.

She forced a tight smile. "Yes, some do struggle with such things."

Mrs D'Arblay continued, "Their poor relations must find it rather trying."

Before Emma could formulate a response, Elizabeth materialised at her side, her voice low but urgent. "I think it best we collect our sisters and depart before things turn more… memorable."

Mrs D'Arblay's eyebrows rose at the realisation of Emma's relationship with the other young ladies, and she gave her a sympathetic smile. "Ah. Well, my dear—we all have relations who embarrass us. Do not take it to heart."

Emma, still burning with mortification, could only curtsy in farewell; it seemed discretion was, indeed, the better part of valour.

Elizabeth

Once they reached the other girls, Elizabeth informed them that Mr Howard had gone to call the carriage for them; however, Margaret insisted that she would not leave.

"I still have not had a chance to speak with Musgrave; therefore, I cannot possibly leave yet. But if you wish to go ahead you may, and I will simply have Musgrave or the Tomlinson's return me to Stanton."

However, Elizabeth was insistent, and Penelope, aiming to help but failing, said, "Come Margaret, let us go before you make more of a fool of yourself. We could all hear your uncontrolled laughter from across the room."

The conversation itself may not have been a problem had they been outside, but if they began to bicker here, there would be no way of keeping the altercation quiet. So, Elizabeth quickly intervened, catching Margaret and Penelope each by the arm. "Not here. Outside. Now."

She guided them toward the foyer, with Mrs Blake and a flushing Emma in tow. Once they were out of the room—and, hopefully, out of earshot—she stopped, took a breath, and resignedly asked, "Margaret, do you even realise what you are doing? You are embarrassing yourself—and all of us, too. What were you even speaking of in there?"

Margaret folded her arms. "I do not know what you mean. I was simply mingling and making connections."

"Making connections or enemies?" Penelope offered dryly. "We could all see the looks of derision you were getting from your party."

"You saw nothing of the sort!" Margaret snapped back.

Elizabeth exhaled sharply. "Whatever you wish to call it, you were being inappropriate. I heard what you were insinuating about your relationship with Mr Musgrave. If you continue like this, he may assume you wish to trap him, and only you will suffer the consequences. And you," she turned to Penelope, "what were you doing? Arguing with such influential gentlemen."

Penelope was surprised. "Excuse me? I was just correcting their outdated ideas on medicine."

"And who are you to do such? Does being engaged to a physician make you one too? You were openly criticising a member of parliament—for Heaven's sake." Elizabeth sighed again. "What were you thinking? What if your actions today get back to our father?"

Penelope rolled her eyes. "I was thinking that if he is going to misrepresent the medical issues our country's heroes are facing, someone ought to correct him."

Margaret had caught on to Penelope's faux pas now, and snidely egged her on, "By telling him outright that he was wrong?"

"Well, he *was* wrong."

Elizabeth groaned, rubbing her temple. "Margaret, Penelope—you cannot go on like this. This is not our home, these are not our close friends, and you are making our family look foolish to people we cannot afford to anger. Do you even realise that it is thanks to Viscount Grimston that our father even has the living here? While he cannot take it away, he can choose to throw us all out immediately when our father is called to God."

Margaret huffed. "I don't see what harm I have done. I was only speaking with those nobody children of lesser families."

Mrs Blake, feeling sorry for Elizabeth, chose that moment to interject, stepping forward with an easy, practised smile. "I believe I hear the carriage now. Perhaps a change of scenery is in order. Shall we make a short trip into town before we return you home?"

Elizabeth caught her meaning instantly. She seized the opportunity, nodding her thanks as Mrs Blake smoothly steered Margaret toward the entrance to don her pelisse and other outerwear.

As they moved away, Penelope lingered behind, in confusion. "I still do not see that I did anything wrong."

Emma sighed and took her arm to join them. "Perhaps nothing. But it is not always about what is right or wrong. In these circles, it is about how you are perceived."

Penelope simply harumphed, and they all donned their outerwear, returned to the carriage, and were off as Mr Howard agreed to make their farewells to the hosts, citing that the Miss Watsons needed to return to their father.

While Elizabeth was completely used to her sisters' behaviour, Penelope and Margaret were wearing down Emma's patience. She was ashamed to meet with anyone from the Stanton-Dorking area after the scenes at the lodge, and she was not sure she wanted to go into public with them again—even for the assembly on Tuesday. Emma continued to stew over these thoughts even after they arrived at the parsonage.

REFINED AND RETURNED

Chapter Twenty-Two

Preparations for the Ball

Emma

In the days after they returned from the hunt, Elizabeth talked almost exclusively about the coming assembly.

When they had returned to Stanton, Mrs Blake had come in to greet their father, but it had soon become clear she had had another purpose. She had planned to convince him to allow all four sisters to attend the next assembly by finding out the reason he always kept one at home. Apparently, ever since Emma and Elizabeth's last visit to Wickstead, Mr Howard and Mrs Blake had been considering what they might do to help.

Mr Watson had claimed that he did not like being alone in the house for so long, but Penelope had pointed out that James and Nanny were always present. Embarrassed at being so directly contradicted, Mr Watson had finally admitted, "At first, I did not intend to keep my daughters at home. I simply meant for Molly and the old chair to be returned to the parsonage in case they were required. However, once all three girls entered society, the chair could no longer fit James, who had been the one to drive them to Dorking and bring it back. So, we all simply became accustomed to one of the girls staying at home." He had blushed as he finished, but they had all understood the true cause of the arrangement.

It was such a simple matter, and Emma had been surprised that none of her sisters had ever questioned their father about it. However, the fact was that the four of them could not all fit in the small chaise together. If they all wished to attend, they would need to devise another means of travelling to the Edwardses' house—that is, "if Mr and Mrs Edwards were even willing to host them all."

In the end, it had been Penelope who solved their dilemma. "I think you have all forgotten that Dr Harding will be returning to town on Monday. Since he will be staying with the Tomlinsons, he should be able to ride with them. That means he can always send his carriage to fetch us and bring us home."

They had wondered whether he would agree, but Penelope had assured them there was no difficulty, for "his carriage would soon be hers."

Though not everyone had been entirely comfortable with her reasoning, the idea had merit, and all were satisfied—except one.

Margaret had declared that she would rather stay with the Edwardses and ride with Mary, but when she had insisted that Elizabeth take her by cart, she had been refused. To pre-empt the inevitable outburst, Mr Watson had offered to have James take her instead, should she insist. This had been acceptable to her, though she had still looked somewhat displeased—Emma had suspected she was simply vexed at being thwarted in her attempt to spoil her sister's enjoyment.

Since Elizabeth and Emma had been happy to accept Penelope's offer— and since Margaret's absence meant they would not have to displace Dr Harding from his own equipage—the matter had been settled.

The gathering had ended with Emma and Elizabeth showing Mrs Blake out and the lady had reminded them—by request of her menfolk— "Philip and Charles each requested a dance from you both, and, since neither Lady Osborne nor Miss Osborne are expected to return, we shall be on time for the opening sets." It had soon been settled that Emma would dance the first with Charles and the second with Mr Howard, and Elizabeth the opposite.

Sunday, December 13ᵗʰ

While Emma wanted to dance the first with Mr Howard, she had felt that Mrs Blake expected her to put Charles first. Emma consoled herself with the fact that she would once again be able to dance and converse with the man she had pinned her hopes on.

Elizabeth was the most excited and kept repeating with a sheen of tears in her eyes, "All four of us, together at last. If only mother could have been here to see it."

By Sunday, even Emma was looking forward to it. After church, she went upstairs to her room, determined to at least make some preparations of her own. She laid out her gowns on the bed, smoothing the fabric with careful hands as she considered her options.

She was still deciding when Elizabeth appeared in the doorway. "Oh, are you choosing your gown for the assembly?" Elizabeth stepped inside, glancing over the selection. "Shall I help! You always look so well put together, but sometimes it is good to have a second opinion."

Emma smiled and, drawn in by Elizabeth's enthusiasm, saw her chance to repair the friendship between them which had been unstable since she was ill some weeks before. "All right, then. What do you think?"

Elizabeth studied the dresses thoughtfully, tapping a finger against her lips. "Hmm. You need something that suits your colouring. Your brown hair has warm tones, and your complexion—" She tilted her head, appraising Emma's skin in the light. "You have still got your summer tan, so something that complements that. Nothing too pale, either."

She hummed over the gowns and sifted through the options, finally plucking up a darker purple gown. "This one! Violet suits you—it brings out the warmth in your skin and makes your eyes richer."

Emma held it up against herself, tilting her head to consider. "You think so?"

"I do," Elizabeth said firmly. "You are going to look lovely."

Emma smiled, setting the dress aside as she decided it was a good choice. Then, glancing back at the bed, she inquired. "What about you? What are you wearing?"

"Oh, the usual," Elizabeth said breezily.

Emma raised an eyebrow. "The usual?"

"Well, I only have two gowns fit for assemblies, and one is too light for this weather, so I will wear the same one I always do."

Emma frowned. "How long have you been wearing the same dress?"

Elizabeth laughed. "Oh, for a few years now. But it has never been a problem! We always took turns staying home, so I only ever went to one or two assemblies each winter. No one noticed if I wore the same thing, especially since I altered it each time—though I do not have enough time to make many modifications for this coming assembly as I had not believed I would be attending."

Emma was speechless for a moment. "Elizabeth," she said at last, "you cannot wear the same threadbare dress while your sisters go in style. Margaret will likely wear the dress Jane gave her, and I heard Penelope has newer gowns as well."

Elizabeth waved a hand. "This is just more proof of your refinement and good upbringing. It really does not matter what I wear—I am simply happy to have the chance to attend with you. It is just one evening."

"It does matter." Emma turned to her wardrobe again, rifling through her things. "You are more excited about this than anyone. And I—I *am* excited too. This will be my first time attending an assembly with my sisters." She pulled out a gown and turned back to Elizabeth, holding it up. "So let me do this—let me give you a dress."

Elizabeth hesitated, clearly torn. "Emma—"

Emma interrupted her refusal. "No arguments." She took Elizabeth's hand and pressed the fabric into it. "Now, let us find the perfect match for your colouring."

Elizabeth ran her fingers over the material, her resistance weakening. "It really is not necessary," she said softly. "But if it means that much to you."

"It does."

Elizabeth smiled, looked again at the material, and then held the gown up against herself. "But now we must make sure it is the right one! What do you think?"

Emma studied her thoughtfully. With Elizabeth's chestnut brown hair and hazel eyes, she needed something warm, something soft. "I think you would look best in a rich burgundy. Something deep but warm—," and she once more searched around before holding another gown up to her sister. "Yes," she said approvingly, "With the right ornaments, you will be stunning in this one."

Elizabeth smiled. A sheen of tears formed in her eyes and the sunlight made them sparkle. "Thank you, Emma. You really are a dear, sweet girl."

They chose some ribbons to match, silver for Emma and pink for Elizabeth. Then they worked together to hem and fit the dress for Tuesday.

Monday, December 14th

Penelope stood before her bed, three gowns spread out before her, each one a different shade and style. She tapped her fingers against her lips, trying to decide. The blue was elegant, the rose-coloured one soft and flattering, but the deep green had a richness to it that made her feel particularly distinguished.

Margaret, having slipped into the room unnoticed, hovered behind her, eyeing the dresses with open longing. "I wish I had choices like this," she muttered, reaching out to run a hand over the fabric. "Why do you get so many nice, new things, and I get nothing? It's so unfair."

Penelope sighed, already weary of the conversation. "They are not new, Margaret. They are Mrs Shaw's castoffs, reworked to fit me before she passed them on. She wanted me to have something nice to wear when I get married."

Margaret scoffed. "I don't care if they are hand-me-downs. They are still better than *anything* I have. It's not fair. I should have nice things too."

"Then go complain to Father, not me," Penelope said flatly. "Now, get out so I can choose."

Margaret huffed but did not argue. Instead, she stormed off and made her way to Elizabeth and Emma's shared room. She pushed the door open without knocking and found Emma and Elizabeth speaking together; their gowns spread neatly across the beds to let the wrinkles out. Her eyes instantly landed on Emma's dress.

"Of course," Margaret said, voice dripping with bitterness. "Of course, you have something lovely to wear. You and Penelope always have the best things and never share. You are both so selfish. I should have nice things too. In fact, I do not see why father gives you pin money when you have so much already: it had best be given to the one who needs it. And why should not I have a new dress if you do not need anything?"

Emma sighed, bracing herself for what was to come.

But Margaret was no longer paying her heed. Her gaze had landed on Elizabeth's bed, and the sight of the gown there made her freeze. Her eyes went wide, and then she shrieked, rushing forward to snatch it up. "This— Where did you get this? You never had anything this nice. This was you, was it not?" She rounded on Emma, clutching the dress in her hands.

Emma lifted her chin. "Yes. I gave it to Elizabeth because she had nothing to wear."

Margaret's expression twisted with scorn. "Oh, so you only share with Elizabeth? You care nothing for the rest of us? What are we then? Are we not your sisters too? I cannot believe you would do this after all I have done for you!"

Elizabeth, calm and composed, tried to soothe her. "Margaret, you also have nice things, and you know that you are built differently from Emma and myself. Even if she gave you a dress, it would not fit you without a highly skilled seamstress—and we cannot afford that. It would be cruel for Emma to give you something you could never wear."

"I don't *care!*" Margaret shouted. "It is still selfish of her to hoard everything. She has money, does she not? Why should not she spend it on us? Or at least give up her pin money so that I can buy something nice too? She's never given *me* anything!"

The raised voices had drawn Penelope to the doorway. She stepped inside; arms crossed. "Margaret, you are being irrational. Elizabeth is right—the dress would never fit you, and Emma's pin money is her own." She exhaled sharply. "But if you are going to carry on like this—fine. I will give you one of my dresses. I have enough, and once I am married, I will be able to purchase more."

Margaret turned to her sulkily. "Yours are just castoffs."

Penelope shrugged. "Yes, but they are still better than what you have, are they not? They also will not need more than some slight pinning up since we have the same build."

Margaret hesitated only a moment before giving a sharp nod. "Fine. But I get to choose which one."

Penelope rolled her eyes. "As long as it is not the dark green that I have chosen for myself, I do not care."

Satisfied, Margaret finally smiled, her jealousy momentarily appeased. She ran back to Penelope's room—nearly knocking her aside on the way—to make her selection, leaving Emma standing stiffly beside Elizabeth.

Penelope's gaze flicked to Emma, unreadable. Emma felt a prickle of discomfort under that look. Was she being judged? Did Penelope blame her for this whole mess? The feeling sat uneasily in her stomach, though she could not quite justify it. It was not her fault—Margaret was the unreasonable one. But still, Penelope's eyes held something she could not decipher, and it left her wondering if she ought to do something more—if only to shake off the weight of that silent scrutiny.

After Penelope left them, Emma sat on the edge of the bed, carefully laying out a few pieces of jewellery on the quilt as Elizabeth looked on.

"I really do not think you need worry about Margaret," Elizabeth said gently. "You have surely noticed by now that is just how she is."

Emma sighed, smoothing her fingers over the garnet brooch she had placed before her. "I know, but I still feel uncomfortable. Maybe I could offer to loan you all something for the evening, something to match your dresses."

Elizabeth glanced at the jewellery. "Oh, Emma, that is very generous, but it is not necessary. And perhaps it is too much for you."

"No, really, it is fine," Emma insisted. "I just hope we can all look wonderful and enjoy the night together. It should be a good memory for all of us."

Before Elizabeth could respond, Margaret came sweeping into the room, a dress draped over her arm. "What is this? Are you giving Elizabeth something else that you are not offering us?" she demanded, her eyes narrowing at the open jewellery box.

Emma shook her head. "No, of course not. Since Penelope was kind enough to give you a dress, I thought I could loan you all some jewellery for the evening. Just a loan, though, since most of these were gifts to me. But this way we can all look our best."

Margaret's eyes gleamed with interest as she ran over to look at the display.

Elizabeth fetched Penelope, and Emma opened the jewellery box wider and began to lay out pieces she was willing to share. While the sisters examined options that might match their gowns, Margaret edged closer to the still open case—her fingers dancing over its contents before she started sifting through it.

"Oh, what have you got here?" she mused aloud, disregarding Emma's slight frown at her forwardness.

Emma quickly picked up a coral beaded necklace with matching earrings and held them out. "I think this would go beautifully with your dress. See how well it matches those blue ribbons?"

Margaret barely spared the coral set a glance before wrinkling her nose. "Those cheap corals? Anyone can get those. I probably even have some somewhere."

Before Emma could respond, Margaret's fingers closed around another piece—a delicate aquamarine pendant with a matching bracelet. She held them up to the light, her expression changing. "Oh, what is this? This looks very lovely—and expensive. I will look wonderful in this. You should give this one to me."

Emma hesitated. "Margaret, those were a gift from my uncle Turner. They have a lot of sentimental value. I do not feel comfortable—"

Margaret let out a loud sigh. "Oh, for heaven's sake, Emma! You are so stingy. It is not as if I am keeping them. I will give them back after the assembly. You would not even notice if they were missing for one night."

Emma bit her lip, glancing at Elizabeth and Penelope, who were watching but seemed unwilling to intervene. Margaret was already fastening the bracelet around her wrist, admiring the way it caught the light.

"All right," Emma relented, her voice quiet. "But please be very careful with them. They are very expensive, and I will not be able to replace them if anything happens."

Margaret waved a hand dismissively. "Oh, honestly, you are such a worrier. It is just jewellery." She turned to the mirror, preening. "Now, let us see how marvellous I look!"

Emma was starting to think this was a very bad idea and regretted that she had not given it more thought before speaking.

Chapter Twenty-Three

The December Assembly

Omniscient

Tuesday, December 15th

On Monday, Dr Harding had arrived at Stanton in the early afternoon and dined with the family. At that time, they had told him of what they had discussed with Mrs Blake for their travel to the assembly. He had informed them that both he and his carriage were at their service whenever they had need, and everyone had been pleased that the issue was so easily resolved.

On the evening of the assembly, as planned, Dr Harding arrived at the parsonage promptly at six. Margaret had already left for the Edwardses' house after dinner, so Emma, Elizabeth, and Penelope shared a light supper with him before setting off at half past seven. The roads to Stanton were as poor as Robert had said, but the careful pace allowed them to arrive at the White Hart soon after the assembly doors opened.

Dr Harding handed each of them down from the carriage, and they stepped inside, finding the rooms still empty of all but a few of the militia. The clatter of their carriage, however, was enough to draw Mr Musgrave—fully dressed and ready, for the first time in their memory, before the dancing had even begun—out from his rooms at the inn. It was clear he had taken special care this evening, expecting Lord Osborne's punctual arrival—unimpeded by his mother and sister's usual delays.

Catching sight of the Watson sisters, Mr Musgrave strode toward them with his usual enthusiasm—only to come to an abrupt halt. His mouth opened, then closed again, his expression frozen in astonishment.

They enjoyed his surprise with varying levels of amusement until he gathered himself and greeted them with a broad smile. "What a compliment to have three of the Watson beauties here today! How fine you all look. Wherever did you get such gowns and adornments?"

They did not deign to respond to the impertinence of his question, so he continued.

"And where is your fourth?" he asked cheerfully, glancing around. "Is Margaret staying home this evening?"

"Oh no," Elizabeth replied. "She went to the Edwardses' house and will be arriving with them soon enough, I imagine."

Musgrave barely acknowledged this as he was staring at the older gentleman next to Penelope.

Penelope sighed at his manner. "Mr Musgrave, allow me to introduce my fiancé, Dr Harding." Then she looked at him pointedly and said, "You may have read the announcement in the latest edition—we are to be married this Sunday. You are welcome to attend, of course."

Musgrave's eyes widened in surprise. "Goodness! I had no idea it would be so soon. I had not heard a word of it. Do allow me to congratulate you both," he said with a smirk though he offered his hand to Dr Harding. "I would be happy to attend, assuming nothing draws me back to London."

Penelope rolled her eyes and muttered. "That is exactly the sort of response I expected."

If Musgrave noticed her sarcasm, he chose to ignore it. Unbothered, he turned his attention back to Elizabeth and Emma. "I would love to solicit a dance from each of you lovely ladies. Might I have the honour?"

He asked Elizabeth for her first dance and Emma for her second, only to find that both had already promised those sets elsewhere. Taken aback, he quickly requested Elizabeth's third and Emma's fourth. Emma, though reluctant, begrudgingly agreed, which Musgrave noted with a smirk, confident she would come around eventually.

Before he could turn to Penelope, the arrival of the Tomlinsons interrupted them. Mr and Mrs Tomlinson entered alongside their sons, Richard and James, accompanied by Mr and Mrs Richard Fuller. As the group exchanged pleasantries in the foyer, the doors opened once more to admit the Edwardses and Margaret.

Margaret immediately sidled up to Musgrave as the Tomlinsons' party moved into the hall, tapping him lightly on the arm with her fan while giggling. He complimented her on her appearance just as he had the other sisters. Then Musgrave suddenly turned to her sister, "Ah, Miss Penelope, I nearly forgot—I was interrupted by the arrival of our good neighbours. Might I solicit from you your first dance?"

Penelope raised a brow. "As I have already mentioned, I am here with my fiancé. It is only right and proper that he should have my first."

"Ah, yes, of course, of course," Musgrave said hastily, clearly not having expected the doctor would dance. "Then might I claim your second?" Penelope nodded reluctantly.

Only then did Musgrave realise he had put himself in a rather unfortunate position as Margaret tapped his arm again, drawing his attention. Musgrave turned to her, fully realising what he had done in announcing that his first dance was unclaimed.

Then he saw Miss Edwards behind her and was about to move forward when Mary noticed his intentions; her eyes widened, and she hastily drew her mother and father ahead of the others and into the main room.

He sighed and reluctantly asked, "Miss Margaret, would you do me the honour of dancing the first set with me?"

Margaret lit up with excitement, though a slight pout crossed her lips as she flicked open her fan. "Why, Mr Musgrave, I should be delighted! Though I must say, it is rather vexing to be asked last."

Musgrave, sensing her mild displeasure, forced a laugh and made a small bow. "Last, perhaps, but certainly not least."

Margaret giggled, clearly mollified, and finally turned to look back at her party who had left her behind.

Musgrave stepped back, looking slightly put out as the Tomlinsons,

Fullers, Watsons, and Dr Harding all followed the Edwardses' lead to find a good place near the fire.

The entrance of the Watson sisters did not go unnoticed. As they stepped into the assembly room, a hush of admiration followed in their wake. Their gowns, previously modest and worn, had been replaced with elegant, well-tailored dresses, their jewellery catching the candlelight in delicate flashes. They were transformed, and the shift did not go unremarked.

Several of the militia officers, lounging near the far end of the room, glanced up in interest, momentarily taken aback by the sight of such well-dressed young ladies they had not previously considered. While no one immediately approached, a quiet murmur ran through the crowd, speculations forming about their apparent rise in fortune.

Usually, Mr Edwards would have made his way directly to the card room, but on this occasion, he had remained with his wife as had Mr Tomlinson. As the Watsons reached their party, Mr Edwards looked up with an expression of pleasant surprise.

"My word, we were all curious when you informed us that only Miss Margaret would be coming today, but we had no idea we would have the honour of seeing you all together. You are all looking remarkably lovely this evening. Here to break some hearts, are you?"

Emma's eldest sisters laughed as she cringed inwardly in response to his words. However, they all exchanged warm greetings with Mrs Edwards, who took a moment to survey their appearances. "While my husband's manner may be excessive, his praise is not undeserved. You are all looking very fine tonight."

They thanked her. Then Elizabeth, caught between pleasure and shyness, responded, "Thank you. Though I owe any improvements in my appearance to dear Emma. She insisted I take one of her dresses when she saw the poor state of my old gown. And is not it lovely? It is the nicest dress I have ever worn. She even lent us all some of her jewellery." She looked up; her eyes bright with emotion. "I feel overwhelmed by her kindness. It has been so long since I have received so much attention."

Emma smiled, happily accepting the praise that followed her sister's speech. "It was nothing," she assured them. But as she took in the admiration around her, a familiar feeling settled over her—this was how things were meant to be. This was the world she had once belonged to, the life she had once lived. To be well-dressed, well-regarded, to receive genuine warmth from those around her—it felt right.

Then Mr Edwards spoke again, this time with a wistful gleam in his eye.

"Oh, to have seen your father's face when all his girls came down in such fine looks—I wish I had been there. You all have such a touch of your mother's beauty about you, and never has it been clearer than now, with you all gathered together."

A small silence followed, the weight of the moment settling over them, before he cleared his throat, regaining his equilibrium. "Well, come now. Such fine ladies should not be left standing about. This old man will take himself off to the card room and leave you all to your dancing."

With that, he departed alongside Mr Tomlinson, pausing only to glance back and extend an invitation for Dr Harding to join them should he tire of "all this youthful energy."

Before long, familiar faces emerged from among the guests. Mr and Mrs Philips were the first to approach with Miss Philips in tow. "Ah, the Misses Watson. How do you all fare tonight? We were all quite worried after your sudden departure on Saturday," Mrs Philips said, her true intentions unclear.

Before they could respond though, Mr and Mrs Vernon arrived, beaming with recognition and approval. "My, how lovely you all look tonight," Mr Vernon remarked warmly. "Seeing you in all your finery, I daresay you will have all your dances claimed in no time."

When Mrs Vernon added her praise to her husbands, even Miss Philips felt obliged to compliment them in some manner by saying, "You are certainly looking much finer than at our last meeting."

Penelope, ever reserved, simply nodded in acknowledgment, but Margaret preened at all the attention.

"Well, of course, I should always be dressed in such finery," she declared, fiddling with the aquamarine bracelet. "A lady's true worth is best seen when

she is properly adorned. Perhaps now, at last, someone will recognise mine."
She glanced meaningfully toward the foyer where Musgrave had last been seen.
"It is only natural that I should attract the notice of a gentleman who can
always provide me with such finery," she added with a self-satisfied smile.

Hearing Margaret's claims and noticing the smirk that crossed Miss
Philips's face, Emma felt embarrassed on her family's behalf. Yet the warmth
of their neighbours' words settled over her like a soft embrace, setting the tone
for the evening ahead. While it was not perfect, it was acceptable—and
Elizabeth, at least, was unlikely to cause her embarrassment. She had to focus
on that small comfort.

The Watson sisters had arrived, and the night had only just begun.

Suddenly, the room around them grew silent. A ripple of surprise passed
through the crowd as heads turned toward the entrance, where Lord Osborne
stepped into the hall, flanked by Mr Musgrave, Mr Howard, Mrs Blake, and
young Charles.

The stillness spoke for itself. Lord Osborne was not a man given to
attending these gatherings—at least, not in such a timely fashion. When he did
appear, it was usually well after the evening was underway, accompanied by his
mother and sister. For him to arrive before the dancing had even begun was an
event in itself. The expressions of those assembled ranged from astonishment
to eager curiosity, as if none quite believed what they were seeing.

Lord Osborne, Mr Howard, Mrs Blake, Charles, and Musgrave
approached the gathering that included the Watson sisters. As they neared,
Osborne's gaze locked onto Emma, his expression shifting from polite
detachment to unmistakable admiration. Even as he addressed the party, his
eyes lingered on her, only tearing away when absolutely necessary to
acknowledge the rest.

He cordially greeted Mrs Tomlinson and Mrs Edwards, asking about their
husbands in turn and surprising them both with the unexpected warmth of his
manners. Then he moved on to Mr and Mrs Richard Fuller, giving them an
equal shock before greeting the Watson girls.

Emma was astonished by his sudden change in behaviour. This was nothing like how she remembered him from their first assembly. Had he learned a measure of decorum since their last encounter?

Meanwhile, Howard, ever composed, followed suit, offering greetings with an ease that contrasted with Osborne's intensity and allowing the astonished audience a chance to collect themselves. As they greeted the assembled group, both men realised they did not know the gentleman with the Watson ladies, and Osborne, to Emma's surprise, requested an introduction from her eldest sister.

Turning to Elizabeth, he said, "Miss Watson, I believe I saw your younger sisters at our hunts; however, I did not have the honour of making their formal acquaintance. May I take this moment to request a proper introduction to them, as well as to your escort?"

Elizabeth, now more used to interacting with the young viscount, replied, "Of course, Lord Osborne. Allow me to present my younger sisters, Penelope and Margaret. And may I also present Dr Harding, who is soon to be my brother-in-law, as he and my sister Penelope are recently engaged. They will be married this coming Sunday at Stanton Church. You may have read about it in the papers."

Osborne blinked. "Indeed, I did read about a wedding. I had not realised it was a relation of yours."

Mrs Blake and Mr Howard smiled warmly. "We are pleased to finally meet you, Dr Harding," Mrs Blake said. "We have heard much about you this past week."

Dr Harding inclined his head. "I am honoured by the introduction. As good friends of Penelope's sisters, please consider yourselves most welcome at the wedding." Then, with a nod to Mrs Tomlinson, he added, "Mr and Mrs Tomlinson have most graciously offered to host a dinner on Saturday for family and friends, as well as the wedding breakfast on Sunday, given that the parsonage does not have the means to accommodate all the guests. We would be delighted if you would attend."

Lord Osborne hesitated only briefly before turning to Mrs Tomlinson. "If it is agreeable to you, madam?"

Mrs Tomlinson, clearly caught off guard, stared at him for a moment before recovering enough to nod. "Of course, my lord. We would be honoured."

Osborne smiled. "Then I shall be pleased to accept your generous invitation for both events. Expect to see me there. Parliament is closed for the winter session, so I shall be remaining in the country."

The surrounding party reacted with varying degrees of astonishment. Dr Harding, oblivious to the shock rippling through the group, merely nodded in satisfaction. However, Penelope simply stood there—eyes wide, while Margaret and Elizabeth were gaping open-mouthed. Even Emma was taken aback by his sudden declaration. The idea of Lord Osborne attending not just the dinner but also the wedding itself left them momentarily speechless.

Then Osborne turned to Emma, offering her a smile—one not of self-importance but of eager approval, almost like a boy awaiting praise.

Emma felt her initial impression of his newfound decorum waver. Had Mr Howard truly influenced him, or was this merely an elaborate performance for her benefit? Her heart dipped at the thought. Had he only wished to impress her? The uncertainty left her unsettled.

Before she could dwell on it further, Osborne spoke again. "Miss Emma, might I hope for your next available set?"

The silence around them was palpable. Everyone in the vicinity who had heard their conversation froze mid-sentence, turning to stare in shock. Mouths agape, they struggled to comprehend what was transpiring. All waited with bated breath for Emma's response. She herself was taken aback by the weight of so many eyes pressing upon her. Before she could gather herself enough to speak, Osborne continued.

"I have already heard of your first two partners from Charles. However, if you still have any available sets, I would be glad to be added to the list."

Emma hesitated. She did not wish to dance with Lord Osborne. Yet, she knew how many eyes were upon them. A refusal would be akin to social disaster, an insult too great to recover from easily, especially when he had just condescended to agree to attend her sister's wedding festivities. She did not want to imagine the commotion that might erupt from that quarter. And if she refused him only to accept Mr Musgrave for the fourth, it would be an even greater scandal. Her after-tea dances were shaping up to be utterly miserable, but at least she had the comfort of Mr Howard for the second, and the promise of tea with him to sustain her.

She forced a polite smile. "My third and fifth sets are still available, my lord."

"Then I shall take the third with great pleasure," Osborne replied, his face lighting up with something like triumph.

Emma inclined her head in acquiescence, even as she braced herself for what was to come.

Margaret and Mary Edwards were approached by Captain Hunter and some of the militia men, and they moved off to the side to speak with them. Captain Hunter, who had noticed Osborne's attention to the Watson girls, decided to quiz Margaret and Mary about what was happening there, and both of them, still in shock about what they had just witnessed, explained the entire situation to him. After which, Captain Hunter requested Margaret's next available set, which was the second set while the other militia men began requesting sets from Miss Edwards.

Mary Edwards again gave away her second set to Mr Norton, and then her third to Lieutenant Carter, and her fourth to Mr Styles. Captain Hunter again claimed her last set, and, once her dance card was full, he showed a sly smile, as if everything was going according to his plan. Then he looked over at Margaret with a bit of a confused expression before his smile returned. He then encouraged his fellow militia men to ask for her dances as well. Following his lead, Mr Norton asked for Margaret's third, Lieutenant Carter requested her fourth, and Mr Styles took her last available dance, should they stay so long.

While everyone was waiting for the rest of the guests to arrive and for the music to begin, Emma's group continued conversing together. As they all spoke, they gradually started to adjust to Lord Osborne's presence and began to relax in his company. Some friends and neighbours approached to greet the local lord but often moved on quickly, casting surprised glances at how comfortably he had integrated into his current company. Despite his usual aloofness, Lord Osborne seemed at ease, his attention frequently returning to Emma. Mr Howard, ever observant, noted this with a small, knowing smile but said nothing.

Emma, for her part, attempted to act naturally, though she could not ignore the quiet awe surrounding them. She wondered if Lord Osborne was truly changing or if this unusual sociability was simply a performance. Either way, she found herself unwillingly drawn into the unexpected ease of their conversation.

Richard and James Tomlinson had briefly left to greet some friends. Initially hesitant to approach while Lord Osborne remained with their party, they soon realised he was not leaving and stopped wavering. Upon their return to the group, they quickly learned of Lord Osborne's surprising closeness with the Watson family. They heard that Mr Howard had asked for Penelope's second dance while Lord Osborne had claimed a set from both Elizabeth—the fourth—and Penelope—the fifth. Richard then claimed the remaining dances from the two eldest while James asked for Emma's last set. With that, all of the Watson sisters' dances were spoken for before the first note had even been played.

Just as Emma agreed to dance the last with James Tomlinson, the musicians struck up the first notes, causing everyone to turn toward the dance floor. Charles, who had been speaking animatedly with Dr Harding about his research, excitedly praising his theories while also declaring that he had no interest in cleanliness himself, turned at the sound of the music. Grinning, he bowed to Emma and offered his hand. "My lady, if you would do me the honour?"

Emma laughed, took his hand, and allowed him to lead her onto the dance floor. They were followed by Elizabeth and Mr Howard, Penelope and Dr Harding, Margaret and Musgrave, and Mary Edwards with Captain Hunter.

Emma led the way with Charles, who happily exclaimed, "This will be the best assembly ever as I shall dance with the prettiest girls here tonight!" which made all of his party laugh as they took to the floor.

Emma enjoyed her dance with Charles. They had a little conversation talking about the last hunt they attended and his excitement about the wedding on Sunday.

"It will be my first time attending a wedding," he said, "and I am looking forward to being one of the guests. I do hope you will dance with me at the dinner, if there is dancing," he added with a confused look, and he gained her promise for the first dance.

Meanwhile, Elizabeth and Mr Howard discussed issues in the parish, with Mr Howard mentioning some trouble with his tenants. He frequently cast Elizabeth admiring glances as she easily proposed possible solutions to his concerns.

Margaret received flattery from Musgrave, who complimented her looks and inquired about her jewellery. She lied saying, "Oh, this old thing? It was a gift from Emma as a token of appreciation for everything I have done for her." Then she playfully touched the pendant in such a way as to show off the matching bracelet before moving her hand down coquettishly to entice his gaze towards her décolletage. "I initially refused the extravagant present, but Emma urged me to keep it. She insisted it matched my eyes and ribbons so perfectly". Musgrave, intrigued, assessed the jewellery, wondering if Emma had more to offer than he had previously believed.

Penelope and Dr Harding had an amusing exchange about how shocked everyone was at Lord Osborne's simple acceptance of an invitation to their wedding. Dr Harding, seeing no reason for the fuss, remained indifferent, which amused Penelope, causing her to laugh—something her sisters had not heard her do in quite some time.

Elizabeth, happy for her next sister, showed a softer expression. Mr Howard, observing Elizabeth's quiet affection and devotion to her family, could not help but admire her all the more.

During the break between dances, the young ladies remained together while the gentlemen, including an eager Charles, went off to fetch drinks. Charles was particularly enthusiastic about "acting in the role of a proper gentleman".

For the second dance, as partners were exchanged, Dr Harding informed Penelope that he would join Mr Tomlinson and Mr Edwards in their card game, to "leave the young ladies to their enjoyment". Mary Edwards moved on to dance with Mr Norton, Captain Hunter partnered with Margaret, Elizabeth and Emma exchanged partners, and Musgrave took Penelope's hand.

Musgrave, as ever, could not resist teasing Penelope. He quizzed her about her choice of Dr Harding, implying he had always thought she would prefer someone livelier, such as himself. Penelope, weary of his antics, sighed and dismissed the notion. "I like a man who is reliable, and you could never be that," she told him bluntly, which momentarily unsettled him. However, he quickly recovered and, rather than dwelling on the slight, returned to his usual chatter, shifting the conversation to the other couples in attendance. With a knowing smile, he asked what she thought of Lord Osborne's apparent interest in Emma. She simply shrugged and listened quietly as he regaled her with all he knew of the matter.

Meanwhile, Emma finally got her dance with Mr Howard. Their conversation was polite and casual, with Mr Howard asking about her training at the parsonage. Emma explained that she was learning a great deal from Elizabeth though she was not allowed to exert herself as much as before. As they spoke, Emma noticed that Mr Howard's smile grew noticeably warmer. She assumed his affectionate expression was directed at her and was pleased to have his approval.

Elizabeth, now partnered with Charles, enjoyed his enthusiastic storytelling. He animatedly recounted his latest hunting adventures, and Elizabeth listened with genuine amusement, finding his cheerful nature endearing.

Before they knew it, it was time for tea. Margaret and Miss Edwards were led by Captain Hunter and Mr Norton back to Mrs Edwards, so they could all take tea together. Meanwhile, the other three sisters and their partners made their way into the tearoom in search of Lord Osborne and Mrs Blake. Having danced the first set together before sitting out the second, they had already secured a table for their group.

As they moved towards the back of the tearoom, they soon discovered the two had managed to save a large table for them. They were ushered over, and Emma was a little surprised when Mr Howard directed her towards Lord Osborne's end of the table. She found herself seated with Lord Osborne on one side and Mr Howard on the other. On the opposite side of Mr Howard sat Elizabeth, and the rest of their party arranged themselves suitably. They discussed how enjoyable the dancing had been so far, as well as their joy in socialising.

Lord Osborne hinted to Emma of his excitement in finally getting a chance to dance at the assembly with her as he had come to admire her skill on the dancefloor.

Coming from anyone else, this might have flattered her, but she still could not like his overbearing attentions towards her—especially in front of Mr Howard—though the latter's agreement that she was "a remarkably good dancer" did help appease her.

Due to the number of guests, they did not sit too long over tea but enjoyed their discussions while they were there. Then they moved off to return to the main room and find their party in order to prepare for the next set.

On the way out, Emma found herself walking next to Mrs Blake after getting separated from the rest of the group.

Mrs Blake linked arms with her and smiled. "Oh, goodness, it seems we have been lost in this crowd, but luckily I found you. How about we make our way back to the fire together?"

While they were walking, they came up behind Mr Howard, who had ended up walking together with Miss Watson and Charles. Mrs Blake leaned in; her voice warm. "Oh, how nice it is that we have all become so close. Your family feels just like our own, and your sister's wedding is going to be such an exciting event. We are grateful for the invitation to celebrate with you all." Her eyes began to water, "Oh, forgive me!"

She paused, dabbing at her eyes. Emma glanced at her with concern. "Are you well? Shall I call for someone?"

Mrs Blake gave a small laugh, waving her hand. "It's just that weddings are always so emotional for me. And well—" she looked ahead towards her brother, then turned back to Emma with a knowing wink. "You know what they say, one wedding tends to bring on another."

Emma's heart lifted at the words, a warmth spreading through her. She flushed—not from embarrassment, but from excitement and appreciation for the thought that Mrs Blake must be hinting at Mr Howard's interest in her. Even after re-joining their party, the thought lingered, filling her with quiet happiness. Not even her dances with Lord Osborne and Mr Musgrave could dim her joy.

Soon, as the musicians struck up the music for the next set, Lord Osborne held out his hand to Emma. He was surprised by the bright smile on her face. Emma, still lingering in the happiness caused by Mrs Blake's comment, did not notice the way his expression softened at the sight of her joy. They moved to the dance floor, followed by Mr Howard with Penelope, Mr Musgrave with Elizabeth, Mr Norton with Margaret, and Lieutenant Carter with Miss Edwards. Charles, leading his mother onto the floor, walked beside them, both he and Mrs Blake smiling happily as they joined the group.

As the dancing began, so did the small conversations that naturally accompanied it. Mr Musgrave was quizzing Elizabeth about her opinion of her new brother-in-law, but he could not coax a single criticism from her. She spoke of him warmly, calling him "a kind and wonderful man whose appreciation for her sister had earned her affection—and would always keep it, so long as he treated Penelope well".

Musgrave had no reply to that. He was always taken aback by Elizabeth's pure honesty.

Meanwhile, Mr Howard and Penelope discussed the upcoming wedding. He inquired about the preparations and whether she was excited for the match. Penelope, with little expression, simply replied, "Well, you know, practical things must be considered. There is a lot to manage. It was very kind of the Tomlinsons to offer to host and for Lord Osborne to agree to come. It should be a wonderful evening, and I will be glad to have you all there." Mr Howard, amused by how unfazed she was by his teasing manner, smiled and continued his quizzing of her.

Lord Osborne, on the other hand, struggled to maintain a conversation with Emma. He tried various topics—her health, whether she had enjoyed the hunt, even a playful remark about what she planned to wear to the wedding and whether she worried about outshining the bride with her beauty. Yet

Emma responded with brief, unreadable replies. Though their exchanges faltered, it did not deter him from admiring her all the same.

At the end of the two dances, the gentlemen once again stepped away to fetch drinks for the ladies, leaving the women to discuss their partners. They spoke of how well their companions danced and how pleasant the conversations had been—though, of course, any true lack of appreciation would have been impolite to voice. When the men returned, they chatted in good company until the next set began.

For the fourth set, Elizabeth was paired with Lord Osborne, and she blushed as she graciously accepted his hand. Penelope was led to the floor by Richard Tomlinson, while Emma found herself partnered with Mr Musgrave. Her expression, however, left no doubt as to her dim opinion of the match.

Lord Osborne found it much easier to converse with Elizabeth, as her responses naturally invited further discussion. Though he was not particularly skilled at conversation himself, she made it effortless, happily talking enough for them both.

Meanwhile, Richard Tomlinson questioned Penelope about "how the Watson family had become so close with Lord Osborne and his party".

She only shrugged, admitting she had no idea, having spent the past two months in Chichester. Instead, their conversation turned to her upcoming wedding and the amusing connections it would create. "How do you think my sister will react when she realises that once you marry Dr Harding, you won't only be her best friend but also her aunt by marriage?" he asked, and they both chuckled at the thought.

Mr Musgrave, on the other hand, made every effort to engage Emma in conversation, even going so far as to remark, "You know, Lord Osborne speaks of you quite often. Even in London, he never showed such interest in a lady as he has in you." But Emma either ignored him or redirected the conversation, leaving him increasingly disgruntled at his failure to charm her as easily as he had some of her sisters. Still, he persisted. When their two dances were over, Emma was exceedingly relieved to be away from him.

As the fifth set began, Richard Tomlinson led Elizabeth Watson to the floor. Unlike the others, she had been present throughout the growing closeness between the Watson family and the Osborne party, and Richard—

being interested in the goings-on about town—was delighted to coax the full account from her.

Meanwhile, Lord Osborne danced with Penelope. Neither was particularly inclined toward conversation, but during their second dance, he finally thought to ask about her wedding plans and whether she intended to take a trip afterward.

Penelope informed him that, "Dr Harding has many appointments through the end of the year, but we plan to visit Bath and take the waters after the New Year."

She then surprised him by changing the subject to ask after his interest in Emma, to which he was not sure how to respond except to say, "I admire your youngest sister greatly and hope only to be in her company from time to time." Penelope accepted this and they continued in amiable silence.

Emma, in the meantime, was dancing with James Tomlinson. Unlike some of her previous partners, he did not pry into her connection with Lord Osborne or her past life. Instead, he kept the conversation light and pleasant asking "how she was enjoying life at Stanton and if she had yet visited Box Hill". Hearing that she had not, he recommended that she visit it in the spring. She found him to be a most agreeable dance partner as his affable and charming nature made their time together truly enjoyable.

As the evening drew to a close, Dr Harding returned from the game room with Mr Tomlinson and Mr Edwards in tow—all of them well satisfied with the night's events.

Even Margaret had nothing to complain about, though, she still chose to return with the Edwardses. Before leaving, she remarked, "The Edwardses have graciously offered to send me home the day after tomorrow in their carriage sometime before supper as Mary and I wish to spend tomorrow in Dorking. Therefore, do not expect me home any sooner." After which she departed, leaving Penelope rolling her eyes and Elizabeth sighing at her manner.

Dr Harding then escorted the three young ladies to his carriage, ensuring their safe return home. It had been a truly pleasant evening, and as they settled in for the ride, there was an undeniable sense of satisfaction among them all.

Chapter Twenty-Four

Fortune and Family

Emma

Wednesday, December 16th

The day after the assembly, Elizabeth, Penelope, and Emma Watson truly delved into the wedding preparations. The morning began with an unexpected surprise—Mr Watson, to their astonishment, came down to have breakfast with them. He was not often present at their morning meals, so this alone was noteworthy. But what followed left the sisters in even greater shock.

After finishing his meal, Mr Watson handed Penelope a ten-pound note. For a moment, the room was silent as Penelope and Elizabeth stared, their jaws dropping in sheer disbelief. Penelope, not often prone to sentiment, found herself overcome with emotion. She clutched the note, her voice faltering as she expressed her gratitude. The gesture spoke of a kindness from their father that neither of them had expected. A five-pound note might have been reasonable with his income, but "ten whole pounds for wedding clothes and preparations? It was beyond anything they had imagined".

Emma, meanwhile, sat quietly by, confused by their reaction. In her experience, the daughters of her friends had received anywhere from fifty to five hundred pounds for their wedding expenses. A mere ten-pound note seemed insignificant in comparison. But as she watched her sisters' astonishment and deep appreciation, she slowly understood. This was another difference between her life now and the one she had known with the Turners.

The weight of the gesture, so modest by her previous standards, was monumental to Elizabeth and Penelope. She held her tongue, recognising that to speak now would only earn her another remark about "how very refined and well-brought-up she was" compared to them.

They were glad that Margaret would not return until the next day, so she need never hear of Penelope's good fortune. Dr Harding had sent his carriage to them that morning "to help with any preparations". So, the three young ladies headed off into Dorking with the ten pounds in order to do their shopping before returning home for dinner.

They stopped by many stores, including the milliner's, haberdasher's, and even the bookshop, where Penelope used some of her money to buy little gifts for her sisters to thank them for all of their help. Then they returned home to have dinner with their father before removing to the small parlour, where they gathered together to adorn Penelope's chosen wedding gown with their purchases.

Thursday, December 17th

The next morning, the house was in a state of quiet anticipation. Penelope, still pleased from her shopping, spent the morning adding the final touches to her dress while Elizabeth busied herself with household tasks. Emma, for her part, found herself glancing toward the window more often than she cared to admit. Samuel was expected sometime before noon.

Their father, unusually talkative, had already mentioned twice that it would be good to have his son home again. After all, Sam was not just coming home for the wedding, his apprenticeship was complete. This meant he could begin looking for a position of his own—perhaps even one closer to home. He should also be able to visit more, now that he was no longer living at the beck and call of Old Mr Curtis. Even Nanny seemed more energetic as she prepared extra food in anticipation of his arrival.

At a quarter to ten, the sound of carriage wheels echoed down the lane, growing louder as they approached the house. Elizabeth was the first to react, setting aside her work and rushing to the window where Emma was sitting. "It must be Sam!" she exclaimed, a large smile breaking across her face.

Emma also peered out to watch the arrival of the carriage, feeling a mixture of excitement and curiosity. She had not seen Sam since she was a child, and her memories of him were faint—more a comforting presence than a person. But Elizabeth and her father had spoken frequently of him in the past few days, making his return feel significant.

By the time the carriage rolled to a stop, Mr Watson had pushed himself up from his chair and moved to the foyer, with Elizabeth and Emma behind him. Penelope also made her way downstairs to join the welcoming party.

The front door was soon flung open, and a tall, handsome figure stepped inside, shaking off the cold. Sam's grey eyes swept across the familiar faces before settling on his father. A slow, easy smile spread across his face as he stepped forward.

"Father," he said warmly, taking his hand in a firm grasp before pulling his father into a hug.

Mr Watson's eyes shone with pride as he thumped his youngest son on the back. "Sam, my boy, it is good to have you home. I do hope we shall be seeing more of you."

Sam agreed that would definitely be the case and informed his father he would be with them until after the New Year. "While I have grown fond of Mr Curtis in a way, he was hoping to keep me as an underpaid assistant—which I wholeheartedly refused. Therefore, I am here to be a burden on my family for the time being."

Emma was taken aback at his declaration, or at least at his manner of announcing it; however, before she could consider what it would mean for the family, he turned to Elizabeth. Emma's surprise turned to incredulity as he rushed at their eldest sister, lifted her up, and spun her around in the foyer.

"Oh, do stop that, you scamp," she scolded in a loving tone.

When he set her down again, he did the same to Penelope, who, surprisingly, laughed and hugged him back.

"I have missed you. Thank you for returning for my wedding," she said with a smile as he set her down.

"Of course! I should never forgive myself if I missed such an occasion. I cannot wait to meet your gentleman. Your letters have made him sound like a most intriguing man."

Emma almost laughed at his joke, but she soon realised he was completely serious.

Penelope informed him that Dr Harding would be joining them for dinner. "He did not wish to intrude on our reunion, but I assured him that, as soon-to-be family, he would be expected."

Sam laughed. "As is only right. You did well."

Elizabeth then moved their way and bodily led Sam over to Emma who was standing off to the side.

"Sam, I know it has been some time since you have seen little Emma, but that is no reason to overlook her in your excitement to be home. Emma"—she turned to her sister with a glowing smile— "allow me to reintroduce you to our brother."

Emma had stood back and watched the obviously loving greeting between her siblings. This brother was already nothing like Robert in either looks or temperament. He was tall and thin like their father and middle sisters, but his features were softer, more like Elizabeth's, and the laugh lines—though clearly etched on his face—immediately revealed his good nature.

She had barely any memory of her siblings, but she vaguely recalled often running after—or running about with—her slightly older brother, the closest in age to herself. She was brought out of her reverie by Elizabeth's words and, before she could move or react, Sam was in front of her, wrapping her in a tight hug.

"Emma!" he cried. After a firm embrace, he took her shoulders in his hands and held her out at arm's length. "Let me get a look at you! What a lovely little thing you are. You seem well for all you have been through. I apologise that I could not get away to greet you sooner, but Mr Curtis hardly allowed me out of his sight. It is part of the reason I have left him for good, but I plan to spend my time almost entirely in the company of my long-lost baby sister."

He was nearly as verbose as Margaret, but his words held all the love, kindness, and care that hers lacked. His face was aglow with the smile that stretched across it, and Emma found herself mirroring his expression while tears ran down her face of their own accord. Her heart was full, and she felt that something she had never known was missing had finally been restored.

"It has been too long, brother," was all she could manage, and he hugged her once more before taking her arm and allowing Elizabeth to lead them to the large parlour which had been opened just for him.

Dr Harding arrived at two o'clock that afternoon, and they all gathered in the large parlour once more. Emma's morning had been spent getting to know Sam and allowing him to reconnect with the family whom he had only been able to visit thrice a year for the last seven years; however, the conversation before dinner was dominated by a lively discussion between him and Dr Harding. The two quickly fell into an enthusiastic exchange about medical theories and research, particularly Dr Harding's current studies.

While the rest of the family had little interest in medical research itself, they found themselves unexpectedly engaged simply by the energy with which Dr Harding and Sam spoke. In fact, they were all quite surprised to see how animated and expressive Dr Harding became when discussing his work.

When the dinner hour arrived, Nanny came to collect them, her excitement evident. As soon as Sam saw her, he sprang up and lifted her into his embrace before setting her back down. Then he gave her a few gentle pats on the back as she laughingly swatted his arm, exclaiming, "I still remember when you was small enough that I could lift you—and now look at you, big as an ox and still causing mischief!" she teased. Then the entire family, still smiling, made their way into the dining room.

Over dinner, the conversation was led primarily by Penelope, Dr Harding, and Sam, who were once more engrossed in discussing medical advancements. The rest of the family listened with varying degrees of interest, though they often had to ask for clarification.

"What exactly is it you are researching, Dr Harding?" Mr Watson asked as he carved the meat. "I understand it is medical in nature, but I confess, I know very little beyond that."

Dr Harding, who had been in the middle of a lively discussion with Sam about surgical tools, turned his attention to Mr Watson. "Ah, well, my primary focus is on hygiene in medical practise—specifically, the importance of cleanliness in preventing disease."

"Cleanliness?" Elizabeth asked, glancing between him and Sam. "Surely, doctors are already clean enough."

"One would think," Dr Harding replied, "but in truth, many doctors move from patient to patient without washing their hands. Instruments, too, are reused without proper cleaning. I believe this contributes to the spread of disease."

"I do not just believe it—I am certain of it," Sam added. "We have observed patterns that suggest infections are not simply the result of miasma or humours but rather something transmitted from one person to another. Though I could never convince Old Curtis to change his methods."

"You mean, illness can spread by touch?" Emma asked.

"Yes, by touch," Dr Harding confirmed, "and also through the air. We do not yet know exactly what it is—we theorise that tiny particles, invisible to the eye, may be responsible. But what we do know is that those who take extra precautions, such as midwives who wash their hands regularly, have fewer cases of fever among their patients than those who do not."

Penelope, who had been quietly listening, nodded in agreement. "And if we can prove this, it will change everything. Soldiers, for instance, suffer terrible losses to infection after injuries. If hygiene were properly enforced in hospitals and field stations, we could save countless lives."

Mr Watson hummed in thought as he took a sip of wine. "So, you are saying all these years of doctors treating patients without so much as rinsing their hands may have been doing more harm than good?"

Dr Harding smiled wryly. "I am afraid so. Tradition is difficult to change, but if we can prove the truth of it, we may yet reform the way medicine is practised."

The conversation continued with Sam and Penelope occasionally finishing Dr Harding's sentences, expanding on his points, and debating finer details of the theory. While much of it was far removed from everyday concerns, the passion with which they spoke made it fascinating.

After dinner, they moved into the large parlour and set up a table for cards. After some discussion, they settled on *Speculation*, as it allowed for more players and lively conversation. Sam, full of energy and eager to reintroduce himself to family life, insisted on dealing the first round, though his eagerness led to a few misdeals and much laughter at his expense.

Dr Harding, who had never played before, listened carefully as Penelope explained the rules. "So, the goal is to buy and sell cards, hoping to end with the highest trump?" he asked, watching as Elizabeth took her turn.

"Exactly," Penelope confirmed. "It is all about strategy—and a little luck."

"I never have much luck," Emma admitted as she pushed a button toward the centre of the table, already doubtful of her chances.

"You have had some this evening," Sam said warmly. "You have gained a brother back, after all."

Emma glanced at him, surprised by the affection in his tone. A small smile touched her lips. "That is true."

As the game continued, the mood was warm and cheerful, and for the first time in a long while, Emma felt the comfort of being part of a family.

It was in the middle of the second round that the front door banged open, and a gust of cold air rushed into the parlour from the hall. Margaret had arrived home, and she made sure everyone knew it from the shrill sound of her voice demanding to know "why no one had been outside to greet her when she arrived."

The truth was, they had not even heard the carriage; they had been having too much fun inside. But, of course, nobody would tell her that. Instead, Sam stood and walked out to greet his sister in a similar manner to the way he had greeted Elizabeth and Penelope. However, Emma could tell that he was a little more distant from Margaret, and the look on his face was one of polite warmth rather than the unrestrained affection he had shown the others.

Margaret swept into the room alongside Sam as he returned, her sharp gaze passing over each of them before she let out an exaggerated sigh.

"I cannot believe none of you came to meet me. Am I truly so unimportant to my own family?"

Penelope, without looking up from her cards, answered in a flat tone. "It would be a waste of time to get up and greet you every single time you come home. You do not do the same for us, so why should we be expected to do it for you?"

Margaret huffed in indignation, but before she could launch into another complaint, Sam stepped in smoothly.

"Come, Margaret, no need to sulk. We have just started the second round of speculation. If you wish to join, we will simply return the cards to the deck and deal again."

Elizabeth offered her a warm smile. "Yes, it is not too late. Sit with us, and you can try to win back all of Sam's buttons."

Margaret sniffed, clearly torn between continuing her complaints and taking the offered invitation. Finally, she flounced into a chair with a muttered, "Well, if you insist."

After that, the conversation drifted naturally, and the rest of the evening passed in comfortable, if not always entirely amiable, company until Nanny came in to inform them that supper was ready.

Chapter Twenty-Five

Reunions

Emma

Friday, December 18ᵗʰ

On Friday morning, the sisters gathered in the parlour, putting the final touches on Penelope's wedding dress and finishing a few small additions to her trousseau. Using the extra fabric and ribbons they had purchased in town with Mr Watson's money, they prepared additional nightgowns and other simple garments. Sam assisted where he could—threading needles, holding fabric steady, and, most usefully, trimming the fabric with a steady, precise hand. Years of surgical training had made him exceptionally skilled with a blade, and his ability to cut clean, straight lines was an unexpected but welcome contribution to their work.

Margaret, however, was nowhere to be seen. She had taken one look at the fine materials spread across the room and demanded to know where the money had come from. Penelope, without looking up from her stitches, had simply replied, "Do you think Dr Harding would let me get married in rags?" That had been enough to send Margaret upstairs in a huff, and she did not come down again that morning.

By noon, the dress was complete, the last stitches carefully tied off, and the conversation turned toward Robert and Jane's impending arrival.

At half past one, the distant sound of wheels crunching over the frozen drive reached their ears, and the sisters all moved toward the foyer. Even

Margaret came down to greet them, though she stood apart from the others, as if punishing them for what she perceived as mistreatment.

Before the carriage had even come to a full stop, Mr Watson stepped forward to open the door, eager to spare his guests from lingering in the cold. Mrs Robert Watson was the first to enter, shivering dramatically as she pulled her cloak tighter around her.

"Oh, this is a terrible time for a wedding," she declared. "Why anyone would choose December, of all months, I cannot understand. It is so dreadfully cold!"

Jane turned first to her father-in-law, offering a polite handshake rather than any warmer greeting. Then, moving down the line of her sisters, she embraced Elizabeth, Penelope, and Emma in turn—though "embrace" was too generous a word. Her arms barely touched them, and the kisses she placed near their cheeks never quite landed. The gestures of affection were there, but the sincerity was absent—making it little more than a performance.

When she reached Sam, she hesitated for half a second, as if unsure of how to proceed. In the end, she extended her hand, her fingers cool and detached. Her gaze flickered over him, assessing and lingering for a moment longer than necessary. His trim frame and handsome features were undeniable, but she huffed, lifting her chin slightly, as though to remind herself and everyone else that her Robert was superior as he bowed over the offered hand.

Then her eyes found Margaret, standing slightly apart. Her expression softened, and she moved toward her with purpose. Margaret met her halfway, and, unlike the others she was wrapped in a full embrace. They began discussing Augusta, who was once again absent from the party, just as her husband walked in the door.

Mr Robert Watson was brushing snow from his coat with a grimace. "The roads here are just as bad as ever, and the snow has only made them worse. It took much longer to get here than usual. I am afraid we will not be able to return for Christmas or New Year's—it would really be too much trouble. So, I suppose we must make the most of this visit."

Behind him, James came in with their luggage, his breath misting in the cold air as he hauled their trunks inside.

Unlike his wife, Robert strode forward to his father, grasping his hand firmly and then placing his other hand over it in a gesture of respect. When he turned to his sisters, he greeted each with a nod—acknowledging them, but nothing more. Displays of affection had never been his strong suit.

Then he turned to Sam and extended his hand. Sam smirked, grasped it, and without hesitation, pulled his elder brother into a full embrace. Robert let out a gruff sound of protest, but he accepted it, albeit stiffly, patting Sam's back twice before pulling away and stepping back a pace. Sam grinned at him, clearly amused by his resistance. Elizabeth was smiling as well, Penelope's mouth quirked just slightly, and Emma, observing from the side, looked not confused but intrigued by the exchange, as if trying to decipher the precise workings of their family's unspoken language.

They ushered Robert and Jane into the large parlour, where tea things had already been set up, and soon after, Nanny brought in the kettle with hot tea to help warm them. They all sat around in front of the fire while Jane, seated beside Margaret, whispered in hushed tones. Judging by their expressions, their conversation was not of the sort anyone else would wish to hear.

Meanwhile, Robert had turned his attention to Penelope. "Tell me more about this groom you have chosen. You said he is a physician in research. What exactly does he do? Does he know anybody of importance? Is his research funded by anyone?"

He barely paused before continuing. "By the way, I cannot believe you have already signed—" He stopped, reconsidering. "Or have you? Have you signed the marriage settlements already?"

Mr Watson, looking entirely unbothered, answered before Penelope could. "It is all settled and done. Mr Richard Fuller oversaw the process."

Robert sighed heavily. "I cannot believe you would do this without me. As her eldest brother, it is only right that I should have a say in the matter. After all, when you pass away, I will be left responsible for all of them. I think I must be the best person, therefore, to negotiate the terms of her settlement."

"Well," Mr Watson said mildly, "since it is already done much to Penelope's benefit, there is no changing it now."

Robert exhaled sharply, leaning back in his chair. "If you do not mind, after dinner, I would like to take a look at the documents. Just to make sure everything is in order." He turned back to Penelope, his brow furrowing. "Did he settle anything on you? I cannot imagine a research physician has much to give, but perhaps there was something?"

At this, Penelope met his gaze, one eyebrow raised in challenge. "In fact, he has settled upon me two hundred and fifty pounds of pin money annually— possibly more if I require it." There was an audible gasp from Jane, who sat slack-jawed in shock. "And should I outlive him, I will inherit his small estate on the outskirts of Chichester, as well as his modest fortune." She took a sip of her tea before adding, "It will be more than enough to provide not only for myself but also for my sisters, should the need ever arise."

Margaret winced as Jane's hand, which had been holding hers in sisterly affection only moments before, tightened into a vice grip. Jane's face was tense, her complexion reddening as her gaze flitted between her sister-in-law and her husband. The jealousy in her expression was unmistakable. The sum of two hundred and fifty pounds must be echoing in her mind like an insult. From what Emma had heard, Jane had only two hundred per annum, as dictated by her settlement. That this girl—this nobody Miss Watson—should be granted more must be an offense she could scarcely endure. Emma was sure that Mrs Robert would not consider the fact that the Watson sisters' status was higher than hers had been before her marriage and that, as family, the rise in her sister-in-law's situation could only reflect well on herself.

Robert blinked. He had clearly not expected such an answer. "A modest fortune," he repeated, his voice laced with incredulity. "And what exactly does that mean? What is his income? Does he have any investments? What is the value of his estate?"

Penelope's lips curved slightly—not quite a smile, but something close to satisfaction. "His fortune includes money in the banks as well as shares in the East India Company among other investments." His eyes widened at this. "Fear not. It is all laid out clearly in the marriage documents."

Robert looked impressed for a moment before a hint of calculation overcame his expression. Emma was sure that if he could gain this soon-to-be brother-in-law as a client, it would likely open new opportunities for him. He leaned back, tapping his fingers against the arm of his chair. "Even so, it would have been prudent to consult me before signing the settlements."

Mr Watson, now clearly irritated, set his teacup down with deliberate care. "It was done properly. Mr Fuller is more than competent, and I personally saw to it."

Robert frowned but could find no immediate argument. After a long pause, he relented with a sigh. "Well, since it is already signed, there is nothing to be done about it now. But I still mean to look at the documents after dinner."

Mr Watson expected this reaction, so he only nodded. "Of course. But I do not expect you will find anything amiss."

By the time Dr Harding arrived at two o'clock, everyone had already gone up and changed for dinner, ensuring they had ample opportunity to refresh themselves before their latest guest's arrival. This time, Robert Watson had heeded his wife's advice and applied fresh powder to his wig, likely remembering the humiliation he had suffered when Mr Musgrave had unexpectedly arrived to find him looking rather dishevelled on his last visit.

Thus, when Dr Harding stepped into the parlour, he was met with a family who were already seated and waiting for him, each looking their best. He was first introduced to Robert, who eyed him up and down with careful scrutiny, attempting to ascertain precisely what sort of man stood before him. It seemed his primary concern was whether there was an opportunity to gain from the acquaintance—whether Dr Harding might become a client, or better still, introduce him to other, wealthier patrons.

Meanwhile, Mrs Robert greeted him with a carefully composed smile, managing an air of cordiality while simultaneously exuding a faint sense of disdain. It irked her greatly that this man, so unassuming in appearance and manner, might possess wealth exceeding that of her own husband. The knowledge that all of it was soon to be handed over to Penelope, of all people, only deepened her discontent. However, seeing the way Robert sought to ingratiate himself, she knew better than to let her displeasure show outright. Instead, she performed the civilities expected of her, albeit with a stiffness that suggested she did so only out of obligation.

Dr Harding, for his part, seemed either unaware of or entirely indifferent to the undercurrents of emotion within the room. With his usual mild and composed demeanour, he greeted each member of the family with the same politeness, offering a respectful bow and speaking in a manner devoid of artifice or affectation. If he noted Robert's calculating gaze or Mrs Robert Watson's barely concealed resentment, he gave no indication of it, his attention seemingly more occupied with the prospect of the evening's conversation than with the unspoken tensions that surrounded him.

After greeting the latest arrivals, Dr Harding made his way to the settee, seating himself between Penelope and Sam. He took Penelope's hand in his own with a light squeeze, pressed a chaste kiss to it, and then turned to her younger brother with interest. Almost at once, the two men fell into quiet discussion, their words a mixture of Latin terminology and references obscure to most of the room.

Robert Watson, eager to join the conversation in some manner, listened carefully before seizing an opportunity to speak. "I must admit, Dr Harding, I overheard some mention of your research and found myself rather intrigued. Am I correct in understanding that you hold certain doubts about the prevailing theories on disease?"

Penelope quirked a brow, but Elizabeth placed a warning hand on her arm. It was clear that Robert had read her letter and knew of her fiancé's research, so he was only playing the fool.

Dr Harding blinked at him, looking as though he had quite forgotten Robert's presence. "Ah," he said after a pause, "forgive me. We spoke of it at dinner last evening, so I did not realise that you would be unaware. Yes, you are quite right. My work focusses on the transmission of illness—whether it is truly carried by miasma, as is commonly believed, or if there are other factors at play."

Robert nodded, feigning more comprehension than he felt he had over the subject. "And you suspect there is more to it than foul air?"

Dr Harding inclined his head. "Indeed. I have observed, for instance, that certain illnesses seem to follow patterns inconsistent with mere atmospheric corruption. There are cases of those in close quarters falling ill while others, equally exposed to the same air, remain unaffected. This suggests that proximity and direct contact may play a greater role than previously thought."

Robert, ever mindful of practicalities, frowned slightly but said, "I suppose that makes sense for physicians themselves. After all, they are exposed to illness more than most, yet they do not sicken at the same rate."

Sam, his interest keen, nodded and added, "We believe that cleanliness, or a lack thereof, plays a large part of that. Good hygiene may go a long way to help."

Dr Harding's face brightened. "Precisely. I have been conducting studies on hospital wards and tracking infection rates among patients who are kept in particularly clean conditions compared to those in more common circumstances. The results thus far are quite promising. If, as I suspect, disease may be passed by touch or proximity, then it stands to reason that habits— how one moves through the world, how often one washes, what one touches—may determine one's risk of illness far more than one's mere presence in an infected space."

Robert considered for a moment and said, "A fair point, though it is not something I had considered in the past."

For the rest of the hour until dinner was served promptly at three, Robert continued to pay attention to what Sam and Dr Harding's discussions were about. Occasionally, he added his own input when they said something he could understand. However, he had never really concerned himself with such matters before—his own head being too full of laws and numbers for much else. Meanwhile, the others engaged in their own quiet conversations in the background.

Robert was very grateful when, at precisely three o'clock, Nanny entered the room and announced that dinner was served. With that welcome interruption, they all rose and moved into the dining room, where Robert, at last, had the opportunity to steer the conversation away from medicine.

⁓ⱷⱷⱷ⁓

After they had all taken their seats at the table, Robert began speaking of a subject more to his interest: finances.

He launched into an explanation of the vital role played by attorneys and solicitors, expounding upon the importance of their work with the air of one who considers his own profession indispensable to the smooth running of society. "The role of an attorney, indeed, is one upon which many affairs depend," he declared. "Without proper legal and financial guidance, many a gentleman would find himself quite at sea."

Dr Harding, rather than offering only a polite nod, instead offered his agreement. "Oh, yes, I know well how essential such work is. In fact, my elder brother, William, is an attorney like yourself. Just as my younger brother, Judd, has taken the same path as Sam—though he has not added nearly as much to my research as your own brother here."

At this, Robert's interest sharpened and, before Dr Harding could redirect the conversation back to medicine, he said, "Oh? And do you know much about what your brother does? His work must be of great importance."

Dr Harding inclined his head. "Yes, well, my brother is not currently practising as an attorney in the usual sense. In the last five years, he has held a position as a Gentleman of the Privy Chamber to the King. It has kept him rather occupied—though he still handles legal matters for the family and, on occasion, for his friends."

A sudden hush fell upon the table. Forks hovered mid-air, conversations ceased, and all eyes turned toward Dr Harding. Only Penelope and Mr Watson carried on as before—both continuing to eat their meals and showing no sign of surprise.

Robert sat in stunned silence while Jane gaped, her mouth opening and closing much like a fish gasping at the surface. Their minds raced to grasp the full weight of this revelation.

Finally, after a few false starts, Robert managed to blurt out the first question that formed in his mind. "And—and how did he come into such a position? It must be a most respectable appointment!"

After Robert's question, Mr Watson gave him a meaningful stare, trying to deter the conversation before it could become uncomfortable for Dr Harding.

However, Dr Harding seemed entirely unbothered and simply continued, "Oh, well, my brother was working for some years as a judge for the East India

Company when he assisted in establishing a British judicial system in India[6]. The King was most grateful for his efforts, and upon his return to England, he was granted an estate and appointed as a Gentleman of the Privy Chamber."

Another silence followed. And, once again, only Mr Watson and Penelope were unaffected.

Elizabeth, who had frozen with her fork halfway to her mouth, now set it down with deliberate care. She exhaled softly and murmured half to herself, "Well, that explains why he was not even fazed at inviting Lord Osborne to his wedding this weekend."

Sam, meanwhile, blinked, let out a quiet, "Oh, goodness," and then resumed eating, as though nothing significant had been shared.

Jane, though initially startled, quickly composed herself and exchanged a glance with Robert. "That must be a most… *rewarding* position," she remarked, her tone careful, measured, and filled with veiled curiosity.

Robert, ever ambitious, recovered swiftly, puffing up slightly as though he himself had gained significance by mere association. "A most respectable appointment indeed! Such access to the court must make for invaluable connections."

Emma, who had remained silent until now, turned to stare at Penelope. Her bafflement was plain. That *Penelope*—odd, tactless, and wholly indifferent to social niceties—had found herself engaged to a man with such connections was almost beyond belief.

Mr Watson, seeing the turn the conversation had taken, cleared his throat, a warning not to pry too deeply or let ambition turn the discussion into something uncomfortable.

However, Margaret who had just come out of her own surprised stupor took her father's warning as an invitation to speak, leaning forward, her eyes wide. "The *Privy Chamber*? You mean to say your brother has *spoken* to the King?" Her voice was breathless, half in awe, half in the delighted greed of someone who saw immediate social advantage.

Dr Harding chuckled at her reaction. "It is not such a rare event. Many

---

[6] History of Baraset House: https://www.deliciouspr.co.uk/baraset-barn-hotel-gets-set-open-doors-stratford-upon-avon/

people must speak with the king on a daily basis. Even I am summoned to speak with him from time to time. The King is never alone, you know," he added with an air of casual amusement, as if explaining something perfectly ordinary.

"Why would you—" began Robert, but the conversation was shut down when Mr Watson let his silverware clatter onto his plate.

"Enough, Robert. This is a family dinner—not an inquisition. Let the man eat."

It was only then that Dr Harding became aware of the tension around him; however, Penelope set down her own utensils gently, patted his hand, and shook her head—though her face betrayed her amusement. With such encouragement from his fiancée, he mirrored her smile and, as oblivious as ever, merely continued eating, seemingly unaware that he had just dropped a revelation of considerable weight upon the table.

After dinner, they moved to the parlour to play at speculation and vingt-et-un until it was time for Dr Harding to return to the Tomlinsons' house so that the Watsons could have their supper.

Once Dr Harding was back in his carriage and on his way, Robert turned sharply on his father. "Why did you interrupt me earlier?" he asked. "It is only right that I should wish to know more about him. After all, he is soon to be our brother-in-law, and with such lofty connections, he can easily afford to make introductions for the rest of us—introductions that could greatly improve our family's status."

"Indeed," added his wife, "Do you not care about your children so much, or are you simply trying to keep this to yourself? Is this something that only Penelope should benefit from?"

Mr Watson regarded them with an unimpressed expression. "He is not even married to Penelope yet," he said dryly. "Are you trying to scare him away before he can properly become your brother-in-law? If you hope to receive any help from him, you should do it in the proper manner. Take care to make yourself someone useful to him rather than trying to make him useful to you.

After all, if you go about it the right way and earn his friendship, I am sure he will have no problem in helping you and Sam further your careers at some point in the future. But that does not mean you should force the matter at this moment."

Robert looked at Penelope then, his expression shaded with begrudging respect. That *she*, of all his sisters, had brought home such a man was an unexpected triumph.

Penelope, however, only rolled her eyes. "Oh, do give it up, Robert. Even if my husband does become a benefactor to you at some point in the future, it will not be today, and it will not be until he is actually my husband. I completely agree with Father—the conversation was getting out of hand. Poor Septimus had barely even touched his food as he was too busy answering your questions."

Jane—voice measured but sharp—archly remarked, "One must wonder: if you are hiding such things from us, what other secrets you might be keeping? Is there anything else we should know about this Dr Harding? Or is there some other information you have chosen to withhold?"

At this, Mr Watson's expression wavered. His face twitched and paled—just for a moment—but it was enough to make his children stop and stare. Then, he took a half-step back, as though the words had struck him like a blow. He cleared his throat. "Sorry. I must be more tired than I thought. It has been an exhausting day," he said stiffly. "I believe I should return to my room and take a tray at supper if you please, Elizabeth."

With that, he excused himself before anyone could press him further, leaving his children—and his daughter-in-law—staring after him in bewilderment at his sudden change in demeanour.

Chapter Twenty-Six

The Wedding Dinner

Elizabeth

Saturday, December 19th

Mr Watson did not return downstairs that evening and only permitted James to enter. In the morning, he sent James down to inform his children that he was unwell and would take both his breakfast and supper in his room.

There was some argument over who should take their father his breakfast tray, and, for the first time, more were eager than reluctant. Both Robert and Margaret wanted the chance to interrogate their father about the previous night. However, Elizabeth, ever the peacekeeper, decided to take it up. When they protested, she simply told them, "Since I prepared it and am the only one finished eating, I will take it." Then she collected the tray and made her way to her father's room.

When Elizabeth entered, she set the tray down on the table before helping him sit up, fluffing his pillows, and arranging everything neatly. At last, she placed the tray on his lap. "Don't fret too much, you know how they are," she said in a conciliatory voice.

Mr Watson made no response but nodded.

It was only when Elizabeth handed him his tea that he spoke up. "Well, Elizabeth, are you not going to ask me about last night? Are you not curious?"

Elizabeth raised an eyebrow and replied, "It is not that I am not curious. It is simply that I know you well. Even if I want answers, I shall wait until you are ready to tell me." Her father chuckled softly, and she smiled.

"Is there anything else you need from me, Father?"

His expression turned back to one of contemplation but, when she was about to leave, he said, "Take a seat, Elizabeth."

She found a small stool nearby and pulled it over to the bed. For several minutes, he sat in thought, and she waited in silence.

Finally, he heaved out a long, loud sigh. "It is not really a secret, Elizabeth—it was never meant to be, anyway. It just never came up in discussion, and it has been so long. I did not know—and still do not know—how to begin."

His words were garbled and did not make sense, but she only nodded—encouraging him to continue.

He sighed again. "Dr Harding has informed me that many of his family will attend, and some lofty connections he has. But what about your sister?"

"We shall all be there for Penelope, and she does not seem to wish for more than that," she assured him.

After only a small acknowledgement of her words, he continued. "You know my side of the family. Other than myself, there is my sister Mrs Parker in Devonshire who—though too old to travel far—did offer the use of her house in Bath for the Hardings' wedding trip in January." He smiled wryly and continued, "Then there is Mrs O'Brien—who must be in Ireland by now; and, lastly, there are their Mordaunt cousins in Warwickshire and Turner cousins in Yorkshire. I suppose I could have written to Sir John and Sir Charles to see if they were staying in town. Sir Charles and Robert were once quite close, and he did attend Robert's nuptials..."

He trailed off and his gaze grew distant, and he never finished that thought. "There is, however, still the issue of your mother's side of the family."

At this, Elizabeth's face slowly shifted, and her expression revealed that she now grasped where the conversation was leading.

"Your mother's grandfather, Thomas Willoughby, was no mere Mister. He was made the first Baron Middleton after inheriting the estates and title from a distant relation. Then, when the male line of his eldest son ended, your uncle Henry became the next Baron Middleton—though you may not remember?"

Elizabeth shook her head, eyes wide. "I do recall spending time with our aunts, uncles, and cousins; however, I had no notion of anyone's title or status." She considered, "Perhaps—was that the reason for their moving to the larger house?"

"Ah, yes. He inherited the family estates with the title." He stopped to consider his words. "Your uncle Henry died last year in June—I informed you of his death. But the title descended to his son—your cousin Henry. However, we did not see much of them after we moved south, so I did not keep up the correspondence as I should have after your mother's death. To be honest, the distance grew so naturally, I saw no need to force the connection once she was gone." He paused—composing himself. "It was not that the family bond was weak—they did so much for us when we lived in Yorkshire. In fact, it was thanks to them that we were able to send Robert to Cambridge and you girls to seminaries. However—"

He trailed off again, and they sat in thoughtful silence for a moment.

"I understand what you mean," Elizabeth said at last. "The family bond would still be there, of course. But with such distance between us, it is only natural that communication might dwindle off."

"Exactly so. But I never truly considered what it might mean for you. Your mother's connections were strong, and they could have done more for you. Had they—Had I—" his voice filled with regret for what might have been.

Elizabeth folded her hands in her lap. "Yes, perhaps they may have done more. But perhaps not. After all, Yorkshire is a long way from Surrey. However, even if they came to London and hosted us for the season, it would not have increased our portions or made us more desirable as marriage partners. It would only have increased our hopes and given rise to greater disappointment."

Her father chuckled wryly. "Oh, Elizabeth, you will make a wonderful wife someday. We just have to wait for a man to come along who can see your worth. It is not that there is any problem with my daughters. It is simply the way the world is. And with the war going on, of course, we have a dearth of young men, which does not help. To have so many young and foolish men running around while all of the responsible ones are dying elsewhere—"

"It may be true," she interrupted to stop him from becoming distressed. "However, 'what ifs' will change nothing. So, Father, how do you wish to tell everyone? Will you tell them before the wedding?"

"I had considered it, yes…" he trailed off.

Elizabeth grinned. "I know. With Robert, Jane, and Margaret as they are, learning about such connections might cause a strong reaction."

He let out another heavy breath. "Indeed. You saw them last night when they heard about Dr Harding's family and his situation. Can you imagine if they suddenly found out they had an uncle who was a baron and a cousin who still holds the title? Not to mention the baronets—though Robert knows of Sir Charles, of course, he may not remember our connection to the Mordaunts."

"Hmm… Perhaps the best time to tell them would be after the wedding breakfast, so they won't cause a scene in front of the guests?"

"I was thinking the same. But what about Penelope and Dr Harding? They will likely leave early, and I do not know how she will take it—knowing she could have had such lofty connections on her side of the church. She may resent me for it."

Elizabeth considered, "If you wish to tell her beforehand, I can send her up with your supper. At that time, everyone will be preparing for the wedding dinner, and they won't notice her absence."

He looked uncertain, but she reassured him with a grin. "Don't worry. You know Penelope will not react too strongly. And even if her words are sharp, you must not take it to heart. It is just how she is."

He exhaled and gave her a grateful look. "It is a good plan, Elizabeth. And I am grateful for your support." He took her hand in his, his eyes glistening with tears. "It is not just this. I know I have not said anything, but I am aware of how much you have taken on since your mother passed. You have done an incredible job. The parishioners tell me every Sunday how thankful they are for everything you do for them, and I am too."

They both began to cry and then laughed at their folly. When their tears finally subsided, Mr Watson pulled two clean handkerchiefs from his bedside drawer, and they wiped their faces.

With that, he turned to his breakfast while Elizabeth read to him from his most recent tome, and together they passed a comfortable morning.

Omniscient

Elizabeth followed through with her plan. Penelope, already half-dressed with her hair up for the evening, took her father's tray just before one o'clock. When he informed Penelope about her uncle the Baron, she surprised him by admitting she already knew. "Yes. I remember. He inherited the title in 1781, while we were still living in Yorkshire."

Mr Watson was taken aback. He had not realised Penelope might remember such details from so long ago. Elizabeth, two years older, had not recalled it herself, nor, he believed, had Robert, who was four years her senior. But Penelope simply pointed out that most children would not take much interest in such matters unless it directly affected them. However, she had always been good at remembering small details.

Her nonchalant manner left him chuckling.

When Penelope left her father, she returned to her preparations. She wore a light green gown accented with dark green ribbons, completing her outfit with a gold bracelet and an emerald pendant from Dr Harding.

Elsewhere, her siblings were also preparing. Jane had insisted Margaret wear the dress she had given her, leaving Margaret torn between pleasing Jane and looking her best. Fortunately, she could still wear the much nicer dress Penelope had given her to the wedding.

Penelope, Elizabeth, Sam, and Emma planned to leave early to reach the Tomlinsons' house before guests began arriving at half past three. Anticipating delays from the previous day's snow, Dr Harding's carriage was scheduled to arrive nearly an hour earlier. This left Penelope little time, so after dressing, Elizabeth and Emma helped her with the final touches.

Elizabeth's dress was another gift from Emma. The pink gown, adorned with blush ribbons, complemented her colouring, while their mother's pearls lent her a touch of maturity. Emma wore a light blue gown with deep blue ribbons, pairing it with her aquamarine necklace—the same one she had loaned

Margaret for the last assembly.

Penelope's mouth quirked at the sight of it, Elizabeth chuckled wryly, and Emma looked mildly chagrined. They all recalled how Margaret had tried to claim it as a gift, insisting Emma had no use for it. Emma had stood her ground, with Elizabeth and Penelope backing her. Afterward, Penelope had remarked dryly, "I hope you have learned your lesson."

Just as they finished their preparations, Dr Harding's carriage pulled up. In the foyer, Sam—already waiting in his second-best suit—helped them into their pelisses, and they were off—leaving the noise of the others behind.

As the four siblings entered the Tomlinsons' house, they were greeted by the sounds of instruments tuning in the background. The Tomlinsons had hired several musicians to perform throughout the evening. The butler soon led them to the parlour where Mr and Mrs Tomlinson, Richard and James Tomlinson, Mr and Mrs Richard Fuller, and Dr Harding were sitting with five people unknown to Emma.

Dr Harding stood to greet them and offered his arm to Penelope.

Mrs Tomlinson said, "Miss Emma, I believe you have not yet met my youngest, Mrs John Shaw, and her husband."

Dr Harding then gestured to the four others and said, "And allow me to introduce you all to Mrs Heywood—my younger sister, her husband, and their eldest daughter—Miss Elizabeth Heywood."

Polite greetings were made, and they all sat down to light conversation while they waited for the arrival of the guests.

Mrs Shaw suddenly asked her friend, "But where is the rest of your family? We assumed you would all arrive together."

"Jane and Margaret needed more time to prepare," Penelope explained with a small smile. "Since we had two carriages, we thought it best to arrive earlier, especially as the others are not expected to greet the guests."

Mrs Heywood smiled warmly at her soon-to-be sister. "Septimus has spoken very highly of you, Miss Penelope. I hear you are interested in his research?"

Penelope agreed and informed the lady that it was her brother Sam who had encouraged her own interest in medicine.

Mr Heywood gave a satisfied nod. "It is good that you both have a common interest. And your father—I believe he is a member of the clergy?"

Penelope confirmed it. Mrs Heywood gave an approving smile. "A fine occupation. I imagine he is very pleased for you and your upcoming nuptials."

The conversation continued on in much the same manner until around half past three when the first sounds of an incoming carriage were heard.

The Tomlinson children took charge of entertaining while their parents, Dr Harding, and the Watson siblings greeted new arrivals. Soon, the rest of the Harding family, who were staying at the White Hart, arrived: Mr and Mrs William Harding; Mr and Mrs Joseph Harding; Judd and Thomas Harding; Mr and Mrs William Shaw—the parents of Mr John Shaw—with their daughter, Miss Meliora Shaw; and Mr and Mrs Hurst with their son, Mr Lorenz Hurst.

Next came Mr and Mrs Edwards with Miss Mary Edwards. When Sam greeted her, they were both a little awkward. She smiled politely, but her discomfort was clear. Catching on, Sam gave a small, reassuring nod—silently acknowledging he had heard about her interest in Captain Hunter. Understanding his gesture, she returned his smile before entering the house with her parents.

Sir Frederick and Lady Evelyn arrived next, followed by Lord Osborne, Mr Howard, and Mrs Blake. By four o'clock, all the guests had arrived except the remaining Watsons, so they all returned to the parlour.

Dr Harding quickly led Penelope to his family, eager for her to grow acquainted with them, while Elizabeth and Emma joined the Osborne party who were with the Evelyns. Sam, meanwhile, caught up with the Edwardses, Tomlinsons, and Fullers on local news.

As the guests conversed, they noticed their hosts frequently glancing at the window.

Mr Hurst, a large man, turned to his hostess. "Are we waiting for someone else?"

Mrs Tomlinson smiled. "The rest of the Watson family. I imagine the snowfall has slowed their journey."

The Watson siblings exchanged a glance, doubtful of such a simple explanation, though no one noticed except their closest friends.

A few grumbles from empty stomachs were quietly stifled before, at last, a carriage was heard in the drive. Mr Tomlinson, Mr Edwards, and Dr Harding went to greet the arrivals, returning moments later with Mr Watson, Mr and Mrs Robert Watson, and Miss Margaret.

Jane and Margaret both looked displeased, though as Jane entered, Robert whispered something to her. She immediately forced a smile, her expression carefully composed rather than warm, as if she was reminded of the importance of appearances.

After the introductions, Mr Tomlinson gave the signal, and the grand doors connecting the small parlour to the large parlour were opened to a lovely sight. The room was set up with a long table laden with tea, delicate sandwiches, pastries, and other such treats while the space around it was filled with comfortable chairs grouped in clusters for easy conversation.

Once the guests entered, they quickly formed into smaller groups around the room, and, soon, the conversation flowed naturally.

❧

As they ate, they mingled, forming smaller groups as common interests emerged.

One such group consisted of Mr William Harding, Mr Joseph Harding, and Mr Robert Watson. Robert, having heard much of William's accomplishments, was eager to speak with him. They were joined by Mr Fuller, Mr Richard Tomlinson, and Mr Lorenz Hurst, who discussed financial matters, including recent developments in banking and law. Before long, William and Robert broke off from the others, drawn into a more serious conversation.

"Mr Harding, I hear we share a profession, though you have risen beyond a mere attorney. I read of your work in India—implementing British law must have been a challenge."

William smiled. "Indeed. However, once we adapted British law to local customs, it all worked itself out. After all, such systems only function when rules are followed. When traditional practises clash with new laws, it creates instability."

Robert nodded. "Still, consistency must be difficult. Perhaps financial structures could help. With proper oversight, accountability improves."

William's eyes lit up. "Exactly!" Then he launched into an explanation of the system's development and broader implications.

The rest of the younger men gathered around Sam Watson, including Judd and Thomas Harding, Mr John Shaw, and James Tomlinson. They discussed new medical research. Judd and Sam, both surgeons, led the conversation, with Judd and Thomas adding insights from their brother Dr Harding's work. Mr John Shaw, as Dr Harding's nephew, also had a strong grasp of the subject. James Tomlinson, though less experienced, engaged eagerly, asking thoughtful questions that spurred further discussion.

Meanwhile, the young ladies had formed two groups. One included Elizabeth and Emma Watson, Mrs John Shaw, Mrs Richard Fuller, Miss Shaw, and Miss Heywood, who discussed the wedding plans—the clothes they would wear, the food for the wedding breakfast, and other final preparations. Miss Shaw, having grown close to Mrs Shaw and Mrs Fuller over the past two years, was especially excited. She was thrilled to have more young ladies of a similar age in the family, having grown up with only her brother and many younger cousins. Miss Heywood, recently introduced into society, was enjoying her first opportunity to travel and meet people beyond her familiar circle. She listened quietly, absorbing the lively conversation.

The second group, consisting of Margaret, Jane, and Miss Edwards, was far less agreeable. They occupied themselves with scrutinizing the other young ladies' clothing and hairstyles while speculating on the prospects of the single gentlemen. Margaret, eager to flatter Jane, subtly followed her lead, while Jane voiced her opinions freely, heedless of propriety.

"Look at these girls in their dowdy dresses," Jane remarked with a dismissive flick of her hand. "I should not be surprised that none of them own anything as fine or expensive as us—" she added in an aside to Mary. "Well, except for Lady Evelyn, of course. But how could I compare to the wife of a baronet? Honestly, next to her, I must have the best dress in this whole room."

She cast a critical glance at the other young women before adding in a whisper to Margaret, "I doubt any of them can boast having a dowry of a thousand pounds—let alone six thousand."

Margaret, eager to affirm Jane's sentiments but also wanting to defend herself, nodded and said, "Indeed. They cannot hope to compare with you, but neither can I, dear sister."

Jane patted her hand and made some comment that was meant to be conciliatory but only boasted of her own superiority.

Miss Mary Edwards only listened, nodding in agreement when spoken to but otherwise keeping her thoughts to herself. Though her own dowry exceeded Jane's, she would never mention it. Unwilling to stir up trouble, her preference to remain silent was greater than her desire to object to Jane's sharp tongue.

Across the room, the older gentlemen had settled into their own corner. Sir Frederick glanced at Lord Osborne with a raised brow. "I must admit, I am surprised to see you with us rather than among the younger men."

Lord Osborne gave a small, self-deprecating smile. "I suppose I have always felt more comfortable in the company of older gentlemen. Since ascending to the title, I have had little time for the camaraderie of my peers."

Mr Watson, curious about the young lord, cleared his throat. "If I recall correctly, your father passed nearly two years ago—while you were abroad and still quite young? That must have been a great burden."

Lord Osborne nodded, looking thoughtful. "It certainly would have been more difficult without the support of so many good men in my life. Take Sir Frederick here, for example." He smiled at the older man. "As my godfather, on the request of my late father, he took on my duties in parliament until I was ready. He also assumed the role of an uncle and mentor, guiding me through my obligations to the parish and on my estate once I returned. And, of course, Mr Howard has never left the role of my instructor."

Mr Howard chuckled at his former student's comment.

Sir Frederick nodded approvingly, a hint of pride in his expression. "It was my pleasure. A good family must support one another."

The conversation shifted to matters of government, politics, and the outcome of the most recent harvest, with predictions on how it would affect prices for the coming year.

Mr Watson had dismissed Lord Osborne as frivolous, like Musgrave, but now he saw otherwise. The young Lord was well-spoken and knowledgeable for his age, and, when he heard Sir Frederick's praise, Mr Watson felt obliged to reconsider his initial judgment.

Meanwhile, the older ladies had gathered together but engaged in multiple conversations. Lady Evelyn, ever gracious, led the discussion on Penelope's bright future.

"It seems everything has been perfectly arranged," Lady Evelyn remarked. "Such a lovely match. I do believe Penelope will do wonderfully in her new role."

Her audience agreed, each adding their own thoughts.

Mrs Tomlinson, Mrs Edwards, Mrs William Shaw, and Mrs Joseph Harding, seated closest to the Lady, followed along as the conversation naturally turned to the wedding breakfast. Occasionally, they offered their own advice to those on the other end of the circle.

Mrs Blake, Mrs Fuller, Mrs William Harding, and Mrs Heywood were absorbed in discussing their younger children. The former two, whose children were still in the nursery, listened keenly to the latter two, who had children of varying ages—some out in the world, others still in leading strings. Mrs William Harding offered gentle advice, while Mrs Heywood turned to her neighbour with a quiet inquiry.

"Mrs Edwards, do excuse me," she said, her voice low and unassuming. "My daughter was admiring your daughter's hair earlier. It is quite fascinating—and, I imagine, quite fashionable. We were wondering if we might get the directions for how to style it like that. How does your maid get her curls to sit so perfectly? It creates such a lovely effect."

Mrs Edwards, flattered by the compliment, smiled graciously. "Why, thank you, Mrs Heywood. I would be delighted to share the method with you. If you would like, perhaps after the wedding on Sunday, my maid could show you how she does it herself."

As all this was happening, Penelope and Dr Harding made their rounds, stopping at each group to express their gratitude.

At six o'clock, the butler announced dinner.

As the married couples paired off, Mr Howard moved toward Elizabeth and Emma. Emma, assuming he meant to escort her, felt a thrill of anticipation—only for Lord Osborne to reach her first. Grudgingly, she took his arm but caught Mr Howard's reassuring smile as he turned to Elizabeth instead.

Mr Richard Tomlinson, with quiet purpose, offered his arm to Miss Edwards, while Mr James approached Miss Shaw, who accepted with a pleased smile. Mr Lorenz Hurst, noticing his cousin Eliza's discomfort, stepped in at once with an extravagant bow, earning a smile and thanks from Miss Heywood.

Judd Harding approached Mrs Blake with a kind smile, and she accepted his arm with quiet amusement. Meanwhile, Thomas Harding, seeing Miss Margaret left without a partner, offered his escort. Though Margaret would never admit it, she was determined to make a favourable impression, knowing the Harding family's connections.

Dinner was lively. Though Emma endured Lord Osborne's attentions, she found some solace in having Mr Howard and Elizabeth on her other side, allowing for easy conversation.

Afterward, the young ladies were asked to perform. Emma, by far the most accomplished musician, took the spotlight—much to the silent disapproval of Margaret and Jane.

Afterwards, the hired musicians struck up livelier tunes, and the dancing began. Emma had little choice but to open the first set with Lord Osborne—who had remained by her side. Her spirits lifted when she danced the second set with Mr Howard. Dr Harding, obliging his future family, partnered with each of his fiancée's sisters in turn.

Meanwhile, the older guests gathered in small groups or retreated to the card tables. As the evening waned, a light supper was served—wine, port, and an assortment of meats and cheeses. Guests lingered over the small repast before departing, the night ending in pleasant company.

Chapter Twenty-Seven

Weddings and Wistfulness

Omniscient

The previous night, after they had returned from the Tomlinsons' house, Elizabeth and Emma had been laying out their dresses, smoothing out wrinkles in preparation for the following day, when Margaret had barged into the room, her expression expectant.

"I am here for the aquamarine set that I wore before. I overheard you telling Elizabeth that you would loan her the garnet jewellery again, since she is wearing the same dress that she wore to the assembly," Margaret had said, her tone blunt and demanding. "So, there's no reason why you cannot loan me the aquamarines to match my gown."

Emma had finished smoothing her gown with deliberate care before turning to face her sister, her eyes narrowing. "Even if I wished to after what you did last time, I cannot," she said firmly. "I have already loaned them to Penelope for the wedding since they perfectly complement the peach-coloured dress that she has chosen. It is only right that she stands out and looks her best on her wedding day."

Margaret had tried to argue, but Elizabeth, who had been observing, had cut her off saying, "Even if Emma was inclined to oblige you, she cannot. You must content yourself with another ornament."

Emma had sighed and turned to Margaret. "If you wish to borrow something, I am willing to loan you the corals that I offered last time. But the aquamarines are not an option."

Margaret's face had flushed in anger. "Then I'll go and convince Penelope to give them to me."

Emma had raised an eyebrow and said coldly, "Even if you succeed, I will simply take them back, lock them in my jewellery case, and lend you nothing at all. You may take the corals, or you may borrow something from Jane. After all, the two of you get along very well."

Margaret had huffed and stormed out of the room.

First thing Sunday morning, Margaret returned, holding out her hand. "Well?" she demanded.

Emma and Elizabeth, who were both halfway dressed, looked at each other in the mirror. Elizabeth had been helping Emma pin up her hair before she would return the favour. Emma raised an eyebrow and met Margaret's gaze through the reflection.

"Well what, Margaret? Can I help you?" she asked, her voice steady but tinged with exhaustion.

Margaret huffed impatiently. "You said you would loan me the corals. I am here to get them."

Elizabeth and Emma exchanged a glance. Elizabeth could not hide her smile, but Emma simply sighed in resignation. She stood, walked to the case, and opened it. Taking out the corals, she handed them to Margaret.

"I hope you can appreciate this, Margaret," Emma said kindly, "and that you will return them without a fight this time."

Margaret simply glared at her before turning to leave. Emma heaved out another sigh. There seemed to be no use in trying with that sister.

After Elizabeth and Emma finished their preparations, they moved to Penelope's room. Betty had been tasked with helping Penelope, ensuring she would be prepared before they must leave for church. Her hairstyle was meant to be elegant, but Betty was not so skilled. So once Penelope was in her dress, with all the ribbons and flounces in place, Elizabeth and Emma stepped in to add the finishing touches.

Betty left to help clean up downstairs since Nanny had been given the morning off. Both James and Betty would have the afternoon to themselves after services. Mr Watson had decided that, in order to include them in the celebration, he would give each of them an extra half-day off. Since they were both hired locally, they were excited to spend the day visiting their families.

As they helped Penelope prepare, a clamour erupted from Robert's room down the hall. Jane had a habit of fussing over her husband whenever there was a special event, and today was no exception. His hair always had either too little powder or too much. His coat was either wrinkled or in need of mending. There was always something. But today, Robert was fighting back, which only made the hubbub worse. The sisters wanted to laugh but could only cringe as Jane's shrill voice cut through the commotion.

Though the wedding itself would be attended only by their Stanton friends, neighbours, local parishioners, and Dr Harding's visiting family, more than sixty guests were expected at the wedding breakfast. Jane and Robert were still hoping to impress several of them, as this might be their last chance to make a lasting impression—unless, of course, they could manage to behave long enough to build deeper connections.

Hurrying to finish their preparations, the sisters agreed that as soon as Dr Harding's carriage arrived, they would be off.

When they came downstairs, Sam and Mr Watson, who were waiting to take the girls to the church, fell briefly silent. Then Sam rushed forward and took Penelope's hands. "My dear sister, how well you look. I shall have to be ready to catch Dr Harding should he faint at the sight of so much beauty."

Penelope playfully slapped his shoulder, but the smile his words brought stayed with her the rest of the day. Their father, unable to speak through his tears, simply hugged her, took her arm, and led her to the waiting carriage.

⁂

Mr Watson carried out his duties, but now and then, the tears he had been holding back escaped. He had prepared his sermon with today in mind, and every word reminded him not just of his daughter's wedding but also of his wife's absence. Though a few of the younger children giggled, the congregation as a whole pretended not to notice. Mr Watson smiled—he could not have been happier for this day, hoping his other daughters would soon follow in Penelope's footsteps while also dreading it.

Once the service concluded, he called out the banns. It was the final reading, and after the customary call for objections, the ceremony proceeded.

Before beginning, Penelope and her sisters moved to the back room for the final touches. At the first notes of the organ, the sisters left one by one—Elizabeth first, then Margaret, then Emma—making their way down the aisle.

At last, Penelope stepped forward.

Dr Harding's usually placid expression broke into a radiant smile, so uncharacteristic that even his brothers looked at him in surprise. He had always been a puzzle to them, but seeing him now, they knew—he had found exactly where he belonged.

When Penelope reached Harding's side and her sisters took their places, Mr Watson opened the prayer book and began the ceremony.

Penelope's wedding caused very different thoughts in her three single sisters.

Emma stood, watching the ceremony commence with quiet anticipation. She could not help but recall Mrs Blake's suggestion at the assembly. In just a few short months, it could be her standing at the altar with Mr Howard. *'It is a shame Mr Howard could not attend, but we shall see each other at the wedding breakfast. Perhaps, if I can escape Lord Osborne's watchful eye, he might find a moment to speak with me. And if nothing else, with Charles attending, Mr Howard will have the perfect excuse to approach me.'*

Margaret, on the other hand, could barely contain her frustration as she watched her most awkward and uncomfortable sister step so easily into a future she had yet to grasp. And Penelope was not just marrying anyone, but a man of considerable family and career standing, who worked directly under the king with his brother. How had she done it? How had she managed to convince such a man to marry her—and so quickly—after only two months in Chichester?

Margaret clenched her hands in her dress. *'I have been out in society for four years, and still, Musgrave has yet to propose. Of course, at that time, he was young and wished to travel and enjoy life with his friends before settling down. He always told me I was a lively, amiable girl and his favourite of my sisters. So why has he not made me an offer? Surely, when he sees Penelope wed—when he watches Dr Harding take her away as his wife—he will finally realise that if he does not act soon, he might lose his chance with me.'*

But a voice in the back of her mind whispered that she had best look elsewhere, as Penelope had.

Meanwhile, as Elizabeth listened to her father's speech and watched Penelope and Dr Harding exchange vows, her thoughts were far different from those of her younger sisters. While Emma and Margaret anticipated their future happiness in marriage, Elizabeth half dreaded the potential outcome of hers as her mind drifted back to the previous night.

Elizabeth

At the Tomlinsons' house, Elizabeth danced her first set with Mr Howard and her second with Dr Harding. She sat out during the third, and Mrs Blake soon approached her, saying she wished to speak in private. Concerned that something might have happened with Mr Howard's parishioners, Elizabeth quickly agreed and followed her.

Mrs Blake led her to a small, unused room, and Elizabeth was surprised to find her father sitting there, beaming at her, with a pleased-looking Mr Howard beside him. Before she could process the situation, Mrs Blake turned to her, took both of Elizabeth's hands into her own, and held them to her chest as she quietly said, "I hope that I may soon call you my sister," before leaving the room.

Mr Watson stood then, walking over to Elizabeth. "Mr Howard has something he would like to say to you. I will leave you two alone for ten minutes." He gave them both a stern look as he said, "The door will remain open."

Leaning in close, he whispered in her ear, "I told you someone would come along who would appreciate you." Then he left.

Elizabeth stood frozen, visibly flustered. She was unable to fully accept what was happening. It was not that she was opposed to the idea—she was both excited and terrified by what was coming next.

Mr Howard walked over to her, took her hand, and gently led her to a nearby settee where they sat down together.

"Miss Watson—no, Elizabeth," he began, his voice gentle yet sincere. "I hope that I may call you that in private, and soon, I hope I may call you by another name," he said, looking meaningfully at her. "Even though it has been less than two months since we first met, I have long heard your praises sung. My sister reported all she heard of you from the local

parishioners, and for some time I believed you must be the most capable young lady in the area. Now that I have met you, I realise that you are also kind, amiable, and intelligent. Your love and care for others is among your most endearing qualities."

He paused, his gaze softening. "I never considered marriage for myself; my parents' marriage was far from ideal. They fought for permission to wed, and their relationship suffered because of the discontent it caused within the family. When my father died young, my mother was left to raise us alone. My sister is now in a similar position, only with four children, and I resigned myself to raising her children in place of my own."

He took a breath before continuing, his voice filled with emotion. "But after meeting you, everything changed. Every time you came to Wickstead, and I saw you with my niece and nephews, I began to imagine you with our future children. Once I did, I could not ignore the possibility of a future with you by my side."

He hesitated, his eyes searching hers, waiting for her response. But Elizabeth, torn and confused, was unable to speak. She felt a whirlwind of emotions. On one hand, everything Mr Howard said had been perfect. He was perfect. He was the man she had never known she had needed. And yet, the thought of Emma's reaction weighed heavily on her.

Emma liked him first. Could she ever accept this? Would Emma resent her? They had only just become close, and Elizabeth could not bear to lose her sister over a man. She feared that Emma might compare her to Penelope—someone willing to sabotage her own family. And yet, when she now thought about Mr Purvis, she realised that her feelings then had been nothing like now. They were only a youthful infatuation, but with Mr Howard—it was different. It was real.

As she sat there, unable to speak, tears of confusion, regret, and inner turmoil began to trickle silently down her cheeks.

Mr Howard did not understand the inner battle Elizabeth was facing. He assumed that her tears were merely those of happiness and continued, "Though my income is small and you have no dowry, I have already made plans to improve my situation. Lord Osborne has offered to sponsor the addition of a small schoolroom and extra bedrooms to the parsonage, to accommodate boarders. These improvements will allow me to take on students and earn an additional income."

She smiled through her tears at the thought of what a good teacher he would be, and it was all the encouragement he needed.

He got down on one knee. "Elizabeth, my Elizabeth, I hope that you will make me the happiest of men by accepting my hand in marriage. Will you become my wife, my helpmeet, and the mother of my future children?"

At this, Elizabeth could no longer hold back. She burst into racking sobs. At first, Mr Howard smiled at her, thinking she was simply overcome with joy. But soon, he realised that something was terribly wrong.

Fortunately, his sister, who had been waiting in the hall, heard the cries and recognised the sounds of distress. She entered quickly and asked her brother what had happened, but he could only shake his head in confusion. He looked so lost that she told him to find Mr Watson and wait with him while she spoke with her friend.

Mrs Blake sat beside Elizabeth, held her, and patted her back, cooing softly until Elizabeth began to calm down.

"Elizabeth, please, tell me what is the matter. I want nothing but to help you. Did my brother say something to upset you? I know he has grown taller than me, but I can still use my fists to correct his manners."

Elizabeth could not help but laugh through her tears. The thought of this tiny woman punching her brother and knocking him to the floor was too much for her sensibilities right now.

"Oh, no. No, Mary. It is nothing like that. He did not say anything wrong. He said everything right. It was so perfect, but do you not see? That is the problem."

She cried harder, and Mrs Blake, still unsure, continued her ministrations. After a few moments, Elizabeth managed to calm herself with several deep breaths.

"Elizabeth, please," Mrs Blake urged gently, "tell me what is wrong. Whatever it is, we can figure it out together. What could cause you such distress?"

Elizabeth finally spoke, her voice quavering. "Of course, you do not understand. It is Emma... dear, sweet Emma, my beloved little sister. The thing is, she has been in love with Howard since they first met at the October Assembly, and she hopes—nay, believes that he likes her in return. I cannot... I cannot be like Penelope. I cannot steal the man she loves away from her. I do not want to hurt her. We have only just become close again, and I cannot betray her trust."

Mrs Blake now understood the problem. "Oh, Elizabeth. Honestly, there is nothing you can do. And there is nothing your sister can do. It is not her choice who my brother falls in love with. I understand that my brother is a good man who could entice many young ladies to fall in love with him. However, he has never shown any special attention to your sister. He *has only shown her friendship. After all, you are the one he always seeks out. You are the one he speaks to. You are the one he dances with first, at every chance."*

"Oh," said Elizabeth still in denial. "But was that not just because Charles had asked Emma first? Charles was always so eager to partner her."

Mrs Blake laughed. "Even so, if my brother had wanted to dance with Emma first, Charles would have given way. Have no doubt—he would not do anything to hinder either of you from becoming part of our family. He loves you both, and my brother knows it as well. No, Elizabeth, there is nothing that can be done. Your sister is infatuated with my brother. I understand, but it is a youthful infatuation that will someday fade. Just think, Lord Osborne has liked her the same length of time, but even he understands he cannot change her heart. If she does not care for him in return, then he has no choice but to retreat. Surely, even you have seen it. It is not as if he has hidden it from anyone."

Elizabeth cried but nodded. "But how did this happen? I never meant to engage your brother's interest in me. I was simply happy to call you friends. I do not want Emma to think that I was trying to steal him away from her or any such thing. What shall I do?"

"As I said, there is nothing that can be done. My brother's heart beats only for you. If you wish to have him, if you think that you could be happy with him, then you should say yes. Of course, I feel that my brother may have been too precipitous. Perhaps..." she trailed off as she considered her words. "Rather than agreeing to an engagement, you could simply agree to a courtship. It would give you time to come to understand that he not only loves you, but that you did nothing wrong in all of this. You did nothing to entice him or to chase him away from your sister. It will also give your sister plenty of time to come to terms with your marriage to my brother."

She paused to let the idea sink in. "What say you? Do you think you would be willing to do that? Or do you think that you could live without him and not regret your decision? If so, then you may refuse."

Elizabeth was taken aback at the suggestion. She could not imagine it—in fact, she could imagine it, but it was terrible. She knew she would regret it forever if she turned down Mr Howard, especially since, if he liked her, he was not very likely to offer for her sister now or in the future. She would be the only one suffering.

As Mrs Blake had pointed out, Emma was in the same situation as Lord Osborne: whatever their wishes, no marriage could prosper unless the affection was mutual.

While she felt guilty for even considering it, she also knew that Mrs Blake was right.

She would regret it forever if she refused him. However, maybe it was too soon for an engagement, but a courtship—a courtship might be possible.

She nodded her head, as she still could not speak, and Mrs Blake smiled at her. Elizabeth soon regained her composure, and they stood to find the men.

When Mrs Blake and Elizabeth entered the next room, they found Mr Watson and Mr Howard seated, their expressions tense with worry. Both men rose at once, but Mrs Blake, looking satisfied, reassured them with a glance. Even Elizabeth managed a small smile.

"I think, Mr Watson, they might need a few more minutes," Mrs Blake said. He hesitated, before nodding and following her out.

Mr Howard approached cautiously. "Miss Watson, I am so sorry. I still do not understand, but if you hate the idea of marrying me that much—"

Elizabeth pressed a finger to his lips. "Wait, let me explain. Shall we sit?"

He looked startled but obeyed. A heavy silence stretched between them before Elizabeth spoke again.

"I am sorry for earlier, Mr Howard. Or... may I call you Philip?"

His expression softened at her use of his name.

"The truth is, I do want to marry you. But when you proposed, I hesitated because—I would have to break a confidence to fully explain, but..." She broke off, heart pounding. "Someone very dear to me—she cares for you. She had hopes... but as your sister said, feelings cannot be forced."

She swallowed, unsure how much to reveal. "So, if you truly wish to marry me, I would be happy—honoured even—to accept. But I need time. And she may need time, too. Rather than an immediate engagement, might we begin with a courtship? I do not want to keep you waiting long, but I think it would be good—for all of us..."

Elizabeth trailed off, watching him uncertainly. Howard smiled, his confusion now cleared; though he had no idea of whom she spoke, he could understand her reasoning.

"I completely understand," he said. His voice was calm and reassuring as he smiled at her. "I would be more than happy to enter into a courtship with you, Elizabeth. Of course, I still hope that one day you will agree to be my wife. But if I cannot grant you this much, what kind of husband would I make? Just tell me when you are ready, and we will send out the

wedding invitations."

Elizabeth's heart soared at his words. Though a small part of her still worried about Emma's reaction, she could not help but smile. She trusted that, in time, Emma—intelligent and understanding—would see the situation for what it truly was. She had faith that their bond could be mended, that they could move forward with grace.

For now, she was simply grateful, knowing that Mr Howard—Philip, as he now was to her—was willing to wait.

Chapter Twenty-Eight

A Proposal and a Predicament

Elizabeth

When Elizabeth came out of her reverie, the vows had been said, the kiss exchanged, and Dr Harding and Penelope had moved into the vestry to sign the marriage register.

Soon, they emerged again—lips slightly swollen and Dr Harding looking flushed and bemused while Penelope looked like the cat who got the cream.

Elizabeth took her father's arm as they all followed the newlyweds down the aisle to the waiting carriage. As the congregation saw them off, Mr Watson let his tears fall unchecked. Elizabeth realised she, too, was crying while smiling.

He leaned towards her, his voice quiet. "Soon it will be you, Elizabeth, and I do not know what I will do without you."

Elizabeth stiffened, wanting to respond but hesitating as Emma, who was standing nearby, still knew nothing of the matter. Last night, Elizabeth had decided she would ask her father to delay the announcement—at least until she summoned the courage to tell her sister. She thought he might intend to inform the family after the wedding breakfast, but she could not be sure. Therefore, she meant to ask him as soon as possible; however, this morning she had to help Emma and Penelope, then there was the service, and finally the wedding. Now was her chance, but, before she could say anything, parishioners approached to congratulate her father and offer their well wishes for the newlyweds.

Soon after, the Watsons gathered in their own carriages and left the church to make their way to the wedding breakfast.

The house, so familiar from the night before, now felt transformed. The Tomlinsons had spared no expense, the decorations and food even more extravagant than they had been for the dinner.

Mrs John Shaw came over with a grin. "It is quite something is it not? My parents made it just as grand as our own wedding breakfasts, and we are all very happy to have Penelope as part of the family. It will be odd to call my best friend aunt, but I will get used to it," she said with a wink.

After she left, Elizabeth tried once more to pull her father aside, but once again, she was thwarted.

"Well, Watson, how do you feel?" Mr Edwards called jovially. "One of your daughters finally married—you must be thrilled! And he is quite a catch. I spoke with his brothers last night, you know? Very intelligent men. Even have connections to the king! Now you have nothing to worry about, should anything happen—God forbid! I would hate to lose my best friend—but at least you can go knowing your daughters will be taken care of. Now, Dr Harding—he is a bit odd—but I like him. I like odd people, though. What can I say?" He clapped Mr Watson on the back and pulled him away to join the other men.

Elizabeth sighed, realising she would not get another chance to speak with her father for some time.

The wedding breakfast was wonderful. The guests all enjoyed good company, fine food, and generous spirits. Laughter and conversation filled the air, creating an atmosphere of warmth and celebration.

After about an hour and a half, the newly married couple snuck away to the room provided for them to change into their travel clothes. Penelope's things had been conveyed the night before, and all that was left was for the servants to take them out and secure them to the carriage.

Once everything was ready, the Watson family gathered outside to see them off. Mr Watson was once again holding back tears—the reality of his daughter moving on was inescapable. He sniffled as he embraced Penelope.

"Oh, Penelope, you look lovely. I did not think I could be this emotional over such a thing, and yet here I am. Your mother would be so proud of you, and I know she is looking down and smiling at you. I hope you will be happy in your new life, and that you will visit us from time to time."

Dr Harding laughed and patted his new father-in-law on the back. "Do not worry about that. Dorking is not so far from Chichester. In fact, if you will have us, we will return in a few days for the New Year—after we have set up our household. If you would like us to take anything to Bath for your sister, any letters or gifts, we can collect them at that time."

Mr Watson smiled at his new son and shook his hand. "Thank you for everything. I may take you up on that offer, and you are welcome here any time."

After the newlyweds left, the family returned to the house. Elizabeth was about to take the chance to speak with her father then, but the Harding brothers approached.

"Have they left then? Do not worry, our brother will take good care of your daughter. He may be a little unusual and not always all there, but he is a good man with a good heart, and your daughter seems more than capable of dealing with his oddities."

Mr Watson laughed. "Oh, I am sure she is, for she has her own eccentricities."

The men chuckled together before they offered Mr Watson a drink, "And perhaps a game of cards?"

He agreed.

Elizabeth considered taking Emma aside to inform her instead, but she found her sister with Charles and Mr Howard—who was keeping a sharp eye on his nephew. With another deep breath, Elizabeth resolved to leave the matter for later and let Emma enjoy herself. She decided to put aside her own worries for a time as well and returned inside to socialise. She finally relaxed, but then, about an hour later, Mr Tomlinson moved to the front of the room and called for everyone's attention with her father at his side—face flushed from drinking.

Elizabeth & Emma

Mr Watson, never very strong with spirits and weakened by gout, made his way to the front of the room with Mr Tomlinson. Mr Tomlinson called for silence. As Mr Watson stood to speak, Elizabeth's heart began to race. She dreaded what he was about to say. Quickly, she looked for Emma and, finding her, started in that direction; however, the crowd was too thick for her to make it in time.

At first, Mr Watson simply thanked everyone for coming. "I am so glad we could all share this day together. Penelope may be the first of my daughters to marry, but she will not be the last." A ripple of chuckles followed.

"As a clergyman, I may be used to giving speeches, but I have never been one for long, sentimental ones. So, I will keep this brief. They say one wedding brings on another, and it seems that is true. I stand here today to announce that sometime in the next few months, we shall likely be gathering again—for the joining of my eldest daughter, Elizabeth, to the Reverend Mr Howard of Wickstead."

Elizabeth froze.

"A few days ago," her father continued, "that young man came to me to declare his love for my daughter, and, just yesterday, he asked her to agree to a courtship, which she gladly accepted. While it may not be customary to announce a courtship in such a manner, I have no doubt this will soon lead to another wedding, and my happiness knows no bounds."

'What did he just say?' Emma's mind raced as she glanced at Mr Howard, whose smile was directed entirely at Elizabeth nearby—who was staring at Emma in horror. A sick feeling twisted in her stomach as the truth sank in. *'It must be true. But how? How did this happen? How could Elizabeth betray me like this? Elizabeth, who knew better than anyone how much I admired Mr Howard.'*

While Emma was processing the information, Elizabeth was being bombarded by well-wishers—though she barely heard their murmurs of congratulations. Her shock was mirrored by Emma's—but for entirely different reasons. It was only a courtship, nothing more than an understanding between her and Mr Howard. It did not need a public announcement. She worried he would announce it when they returned home, but she had never imagined he would share it with the entire party.

However, the words were out, and there was no going back now.

Elizabeth thanked everyone around her before pressing on toward her sister, who stood motionless, her expression twisted into one of barely contained anger. To anyone else, she might have seemed impassive, but Elizabeth knew her sister too well. Ever since the time Emma fell ill, Elizabeth had been able to read her expressions. She could now see the resentment simmering beneath her calm façade.

She opened her mouth, desperate to explain. "Oh, Emma. Please, allow me to—"

"No," Emma cut her off with a raised hand. "Nothing else needs to be said. I understand everything. Congratulations."

And just like that, she turned and disappeared into the crowd.

Mr Howard approached, seemingly oblivious to the tension. "Well, that was unexpected. I hope you had a chance to speak to your friend, but if not, do not worry. That is the purpose of our courtship, after all—to give everyone time to come to terms with things."

Mrs Blake, standing beside him, knew better. She had seen the exchange and the pain it left on Elizabeth's face, even if her brother was too caught up in his own felicity to notice. With a concerned sigh, she stepped forward. "I will go find her. Do not worry and enjoy the felicitations."

Mrs Blake searched for half an hour but, despite her best efforts, she could not find Emma. Finally, she learned from Mr and Mrs Tomlinson that Emma had left early. "She said she was not feeling well and asked to borrow a carriage to go home first. We already informed Mr Watson of it."

Mrs Blake found a chance to let Elizabeth know what she heard; however, she encouraged the younger girl to enjoy the party and give her sister time alone. Their friends and neighbours were eager to offer their congratulations, remarking on how lovely a couple she and Mr Howard made, and she had no chance to consider her sister's feelings again until they left the party.

Emma

When Emma returned home, the house was quiet as Nanny would not return for another hour or two. Alone at last, her mind raced.

She went to her room first, but found the space too small for her needs. So, she returned downstairs and paced in the large parlour, seeking solace in movement to sort through the storm in her mind. '*How did this happen? When? We were always together. Except—*' she stopped mid-step. For most of November, she had been sick and had also been unable to attend the assembly. '*Elizabeth mentioned dancing with Howard, but she did not go into much detail. What really happened? What was said between them to bring about such an outcome? What else has been happening behind my back?*'

Her thoughts drifted to the two weeks she had been confined to her bed. Mr Howard and Mrs Blake had visited the house, and Elizabeth had also gone to them. Emma had no choice but to leave them entirely in Elizabeth's care. She had trusted Elizabeth to help, to talk to Howard for her, to learn about him for her. She had thought that Elizabeth would tell her everything, but now Emma wondered—had she shared the truth? She had come back to their shared room after each visit, describing the encounters in a way that reassured Emma. But now, Emma felt the heavy weight of doubt. '*Did Elizabeth lie outright or by omission? Was she simply hiding the truth from me?*' Emma could not bear the thought of another betrayal.

She thought about the weeks since her recovery, when they had both been in the company of the Wickstead party. What had she missed? She thought of all the moments when she had been distracted by Charles, by her own belief that Howard was attracted to her, and by the thought that her sister was her ally. She must have been blind to the truth. Oh, how could she have missed the signs?

Of course, Elizabeth and Howard had been much together, but Emma had been too preoccupied. She had been too busy amusing Charles, too busy conversing with Mrs Blake, and too busy watching as her sisters embarrassed her with their uncouth manners. Had they all known? Had they all been in on it? Was she the only one who was blind to Elizabeth's game?

She could hardly believe what had just happened. Elizabeth had deceived her. It was as if Emma were seeing her sister for the first time. She recalled their conversation before that first assembly, when Elizabeth had spoken of Penelope chasing away her first love—*"She thinks everything fair for a husband. I trusted her; she set him against me, with a view of gaining him herself…"*

Emma never imagined Elizabeth was capable of such behaviour, but, now, she saw the truth—she was no different from their other sisters—another liar, another schemer, another sister willing to betray her family when it suited her.

All the kindness, all the support—it was just for show. Elizabeth had used her and thrown her away, just like her parents—just like her aunt. There would be no coming back from this. They had fought before over their views of her aunt's actions, but this… this was so much worse.

Her hands clenched as the realisation settled. She could not stay here. Not in Stanton. Not in Dorking. Not surrounded by those who had abandoned her, who had made her feel so utterly alone. Lord Osborne's pursuit, Elizabeth's scheming, it all felt like a cage, and she needed to escape.

In that moment, Emma made a decision. Jane and Robert would be leaving the next morning, and she would go with them. They had extended an open invitation, offering her a place for two or three months whenever she needed it. Now was the perfect time to take them up on it. She would leave, free herself from the constant reminder of Elizabeth's treachery, and avoid witnessing Howard's courtship of her sister. Let them go on with their lives without her—she would find a way to live her own.

When Nanny arrived, Emma claimed she was not feeling well and requested a supper tray in her room, asking that Nanny bring it herself in order not to worry her father. She would have to speak to Jane and Robert as soon as they returned, but otherwise, she had no desire to see her family or to explain herself.

By the time the family returned home, Emma had already moved her belongings into Penelope's empty room. It was supposed to happen in the next few days anyway—why wait? She left her things packed and ready to go.

No one found Emma's actions strange except Elizabeth, but, when she tried to visit her sister, she was sent away.

"Why bother with her," said Margaret, "she's finally revealing her true disposition. She probably could not wait to have her own room again." Then she huffed upstairs to change out of her dress, leaving Elizabeth standing alone and defeated in the hall.

Emma

Monday, December 21ˢᵗ

The next morning, Emma rose early and went down to breakfast. Elizabeth was already downstairs and attempted to speak to her, but Emma cut her off.

"I do not want to talk about it. And I do not want to talk to you."

Unfortunately for Elizabeth, Jane and Robert joined them just then.

"Well, Emma," Jane said, "have you finished your packing? Will you be ready on time? We wish to leave as soon as possible as my husband is such a busy man, you know."

Elizabeth's head snapped up in shock, and she gaped at Emma.

Emma remained calm, looking only at her food and Jane. "I finished my packing last night and have already informed James which trunks to bring down. I only need to put on my outerwear, and I will be ready."

Jane smiled. "I am glad you have finally accepted our offer. It will do you good to stay with us. Though I hope you will not be taking too many things, only your best gowns will be needed for the society we keep."

Elizabeth spoke—her voice full of disbelief. "Stay with you? Is Emma leaving? When was this all decided?"

Jane gave a knowing smile. "Well, after all the excitement here has ended, it's no surprise she would want a change of scenery, especially with the upcoming season. Emma has asked to return with us to Croydon, and we expect her to be with us for at least two months complete."

Robert spoke up then, addressing Emma. "I assume you have informed our father?"

Emma nodded. "I just spoke to him before breakfast. Everything is settled."

"Good. We will be leaving within the next quarter hour."

As Emma finished her meal, Elizabeth followed her to the kitchen, trying once more. "Emma, please—just hear me out."

Emma immediately refused. "No, Elizabeth. I have heard enough. I heard everything you did not tell me these last two months about your time with Mr Howard—for how else could this have happened? I have no interest in hearing anything else you have to say." She exhaled sharply. "I am going to Croydon. I hope you can be happy with yourself, knowing what you did." Her bitter tone made her sister flinch, and Emma felt vindicated. "I will find my own place in this world—without you, Elizabeth."

Then she left the room without looking back.

Elizabeth stood still, watching her sister leave with her words hanging in the air. The finality in Emma's tone made her heart ache, but it was the way Emma had not even looked back that stung the most. Elizabeth felt a heavy unease settle in her chest, a gnawing discomfort that would not leave. She could not quite make sense of the feeling—was it dread or guilt? Was it foreboding, or was she simply heartbroken?

Within half an hour, the family gathered in the parlour for their goodbyes. Mr Watson embraced Emma, his voice soft, "You are always welcome back whenever you like. If Robert is too busy to bring you, we will figure something out—perhaps even Howard will offer his carriage for the purpose."

His words were meant to be reassuring, but they had the opposite effect. However, she did her best to smile and nod.

Jane, standing beside Robert, tried to smile but could not quite manage it. "Croydon is so much more exciting than Stanton, Emma. It is lively, and there is always something to do. You won't even have time to think about wanting to return *here*."

Margaret, who had been standing off to one side, could not help herself. She approached her sister as if to embrace her and said, "It's not enough for you that you have claimed the affection of everyone at Stanton, now you wish to take my place with Jane and Robert?" She crossed her arms and looked at her sister with indignation, but Emma just said her farewell. She would not miss Margaret's sharp tongue.

Sam came next, "I am sorry to see you go, little sister. After we both finally returned home, I thought we might have a chance to get to know each other better—to walk, talk," he leaned in, "or even climb a few old trees?"

A flashback of their youth came to her mind, and she smiled despite her mood. "Perhaps there will come such a time, but not today. Take care, brother."

Robert, who had been overseeing the loading of their luggage returned, checked his timepiece, and cleared his throat. "Well, it has been wonderful seeing all of you. But we really must be off." He shook his father's hand, then offered his hand to Sam before swiftly drawing it back, opting instead for a quick nod. "I shall see you another time, little brother." His attention moved back to his sisters. "Elizabeth, do take care not to make Mr Howard wait too long. You are not getting any younger—and you would not wish to become a burden."

Before anyone could rebuke him, Robert offered his arm to his wife and led her outside, followed by Emma. The morning air was cutting, so Mr Watson stayed indoors. Elizabeth, Margaret, and Sam, however, all stepped out to see the travellers off.

Robert first handed his wife into the carriage before turning to help Emma up. As Robert stepped in after and closed the door, Emma caught sight of Elizabeth standing in the doorway. Their eyes met, and Emma saw the tears running down Elizabeth's face unchecked.

'Serves her right. How can she stand there, pretending to care after what she has done?' Emma thought. But guilt gnawed at her heart. Was she really doing the right thing? But then again, she could not bear the thought of staying at Stanton, watching the man she loved court her sister. She needed space—she needed time to think. As the carriage began to move, Emma told herself that this was for the best.

Jane wasted no time. As soon as the carriage was in motion, she began eagerly enlightening Emma on all the things she could expect to do and enjoy once they reached Croydon. But it was not long before a familiar tension arose.

Robert, wanting to rest on the ride, requested silence. Jane, however, could not accept him ignoring her in such close quarters. The disagreement between them soon escalated into a low argument, and Emma sank back into her seat, a deep sense of regret settling over her.

Maybe this was not such a good idea after all.

Before You Go

Did You Enjoy This Story?

Thank you for reading *Refined & Returned: Volume I.* The Watson family's story will continue in *Refined & Returned: Volume II.*

While You Wait...

You can enjoy Part 1 of the three part prequel to this series:
The Watsons: Beginnings — Arc One: Courtship & Marriages
— Available now on:

Amazon, Draft2Digital, and associated retailers

Stay Connected:

Visit my blog **to** subscribe to the newsletter**, read chapter previews, and find Austen-related extras:**
Jane Austen's Literary Lasagna

https://jaliterarylasagna.wixsite.com/jane-austen-fandom/blog

Teaser for Refined and Returned: Volume 2

Emma's state of mind is in turmoil after another betrayal, and she decides that she can no longer remain at Stanton where she has been so ill-treated. So, she chooses instead to accept Mr and Mrs Robert Watson's offer for her to stay in Croydon to enjoy new, and hopefully more refined, society. Though she cannot expect any enjoyment from the company of her hosts, she hopes that their proximity to London will offer her the chance to meet with more like-minded and well-educated people whom she might call her intellectual peers. Then news comes with the date of her eldest sister's wedding to the very man she had put all her hopes on, and she has no choice but to attend.

Will Emma enjoy her time among Croydon society, or will she find the company as lacking as it was in the environs of Dorking? Will Emma be disappointed in her situation all over again? How will she get through the wedding as she watches all her hopes crumble around her?

Stay tuned for updates on the next instalment of *Refined and Returned*.

Author Bio

Eireanne Michaels is an introvert who is currently living in Korea among some of her rescue cats. She is one of those women who is perfectly happy to be considered a "crazy cat lady" as it both keeps people away and is simply the unavoidable truth.

She is a fan of fantasy, science fiction, and old British literature. She has been a fan of Jane Austen's novels for many, many years (possibly "since tigers were smoking" which is the Korean way to say "since dinosaurs roamed the earth").

To Eireanne, Austen's works are like good lasagna; it's full of layers that bring new delicious titbits to the surface each time they are reached. However, most people only notice the toppings and miss the real meat underneath. Jane Austen was not just a great author, she had depths that we may never fully discover. It has created a passion, or possibly obsession, in this author to uncover all of the hidden gems in her sarcastic and witty novels by slowly dissecting them and, occasionally, reimagining them.

So, for her own amusement, she has decided to take up writing JAFF in order to help her better understand the time period, the characters, and the original author. While she writes for herself, she knows that there are others who are interested in the many facets of Austen's works who might also enjoy her works, and she decided to share them here.

Thank you for reading

www.ingramcontent.com/pod-product-compliance
Lightning Source LLC
Chambersburg PA
CBHW020943260626
47169CB00006B/1788